"This man is dangerous and he's looking for you..."

"I'm coming," Faith insisted.

Something akin to admiration flashed in Eli's brown eyes before he nodded. "As you wish." He leaned inside and picked up the shotgun from where he'd placed it by the door. It would be just the two of them against a man who was highly trained and motivated by having everything to lose.

Grandmother Sarah took her hand. "Be careful. Both of you."

Faith forced a smile. "We'll be okay. Lock up behind us and don't open the door until we speak to you."

The fear in her grandmother's eyes hung heavily over Faith as the door closed. She hated the need to worry this precious woman, but the reality was Vincent had killed before. He wouldn't hesitate to take *Grossmammi*'s life if it benefited him.

He could be hiding in the woods, waiting for them to come to him.

Giving in to fear made her vulnerable to mistakes.

Faith couldn't afford a single wrong move if she wanted to live...

Mary Alford was inspired to become a writer after reading romantic suspense greats Victoria Holt and Phyllis A. Whitney. Soon, creating characters and throwing them into dangerous situations that tested their faith came naturally for Mary. In 2012 Mary entered the speed dating contest hosted by Love Inspired Suspense and later received "the call." Writing for Love Inspired Suspense has been a dream come true for Mary.

Alison Stone lives with her husband of more than twenty years and their four children in Western New York. Besides writing, Alison keeps busy volunteering at her children's schools, driving her girls to dance and watching her boys race motocross. Alison loves to hear from her readers at Alison@AlisonStone.com. For more information, please visit her website, alisonstone.com. She's also chatty on Twitter, @alison_stone. Find her on Facebook at Facebook.com/alisonstoneauthor.

USA TODAY Bestselling Author

MARY ALFORD

&

ALISON STONE

Amish Country Hideout

2 Thrilling Stories

Shielding the Amish Witness and
Seeking Amish Shelter

LOVE INSPIRED

INSPIRATIONAL ROMANCE

LOVE INSPIRED®
INSPIRATIONAL ROMANCE

ISBN-13: 978-1-335-47328-8

Amish Country Hideout

Copyright © 2022 by Harlequin Enterprises ULC

Shielding the Amish Witness
First published in 2021. This edition published in 2022.
Copyright © 2021 by Mary Eason

Seeking Amish Shelter
First published in 2021. This edition published in 2022.
Copyright © 2021 by Alison Stone

For questions and comments about the quality of this book, please contact us
at CustomerService@Harlequin.com.

Harlequin Enterprises ULC
22 Adelaide St. West, 41st Floor
Toronto, Ontario M5H 4E3, Canada
www.LoveInspired.com

Printed in U.S.A.

CONTENTS

SHIELDING THE AMISH WITNESS   7
Mary Alford

SEEKING AMISH SHELTER   233
Alison Stone

SHIELDING THE AMISH WITNESS

Mary Alford

To my granddaughter Ava,
who never ceases to amaze me.
You shine bright and make the world a better place.
Love you so much, sweetie.

This I recall to my mind,
therefore have I hope.
It is of the Lord's mercies that we are not consumed,
because his compassions fail not.
They are new every morning:
great is thy faithfulness.
—*Lamentations* 3:21–23

Chapter One

She'd put thousands of miles between herself and what happened, but she hadn't been able to erase the horrific memory of watching her friend die. It had played through her mind during every one of those miles, like a movie stuck on a never-ending loop.

All her fault. Cheryl was dead because of her.

The fear stalking her since she'd left New York showed no sign of easing as she crossed into Montana. Because she knew what Vincent was capable of. He'd proved it by killing his wife in cold blood without a single hint of remorse.

Faith had prayed that the terrible things she'd read in her late husband's note would turn out to be a cruel joke, but the rage on Vincent St. Clair's face when Cheryl confronted him with the evidence had annihilated that hope, and it confirmed he was the monster her husband wrote about. And so much more.

If you're reading this, then Vincent followed through

with his threat and killed me...don't let him get away with it, Faith.

She swiped the back of her hand across her tired eyes and focused on the road in front of her. She was barely hanging on and still couldn't wrap her head around the truth. Vincent was Blake's older brother. Both were decorated police detectives. How was it possible they'd been on the take for years?

Since she'd found the note Blake had taped to the bottom of his desk, Faith had existed in a state of shock. The first person she'd thought to call was Cheryl.

Faith jerked the car onto the shoulder of the road and screamed into the confines of its interior. Pounded her fists against the steering wheel. If she hadn't been weak—hadn't called her friend for help—Cheryl would still be alive.

The horror of watching Vincent shoot his wife at point-blank range would forever be imprinted in Faith's mind. If Vincent had been ruthless enough to kill Cheryl simply because she'd seen the evidence Faith's husband had accumulated, then what would he do to Faith if he caught her? She'd grabbed the evidence and run, started the car and flown from the garage. She'd been so certain Vincent would shoot her dead right there, but God had protected her. She'd gotten away, but she'd been looking over her shoulder ever since.

"I'm so sorry." A broken sob escaped. Her heart drummed away the seconds while she glanced around at the isolation of the countryside and shivered. Sitting still was dangerous. Thirty-eight hours ago, she'd barely escaped with her life. But it wouldn't end there. Vincent knew she had evidence that would put him away for a long time. He'd follow her to the ends of the earth to silence her.

Faith eased the car back onto the road and punched the gas. Staying alive meant quickly getting the car out of sight. Vincent was aware of the type of vehicle she drove. He'd find a way to locate her. Every second she was out in the open, her life was in jeopardy.

Her gaze landed on the cell phone in the cup holder, and a terrible truth dawned. As a detective, Vincent would know how to track her phone. He could be following her now.

Faith grabbed the phone and powered it down, praying it wasn't too late.

She topped a hill. The snow flurries that had begun almost from the moment she crossed the state line continued to strengthen. An early spring storm was approaching.

Her fingers dug into the steering wheel as she drove through the deteriorating weather. More than anything, Faith hated bringing this nightmare to her sweet Amish grandmother. If there had been any other option, she would have chosen it instead.

A set of headlights struck the rearview mirror, momentarily blinding her. Faith whipped around in her seat. She hadn't seen a soul in hours. The wide-open territory surrounding the Amish community of West Kootenai was sparsely populated. There were few travelers. Especially after dark. Especially in this weather.

Her stomach plummeted. Was it Vincent?

You'll never get away from me... Vincent's parting words had felt more like an omen.

Tension bunched between her shoulder blades while she strained to see more details on the vehicle beyond the headlights.

As far as she knew, her husband and Cheryl were the only ones who had knowledge of her Amish past in Montana.

After she moved to New York, every time she mentioned once being Amish, she'd get asked dozens of questions about why she left. In the end, it was just easier to keep that part of her life secret.

Had either Cheryl or Blake mentioned her past to Vincent?

Please, God, no.

She picked up her speed while keeping close watch in the mirror. The vehicle topped the ridge behind her, its pace normal for the conditions.

She blew out a shaky breath, nerves shot. It was probably someone who had gotten trapped in the storm like her. Her grip relaxed on the wheel. She'd been jumping at shadows since leaving New York.

The car's headlights picked up the sign nailed to a tree by the side of the road announcing the different shops found in the West Kootenai community. Almost home. Just a little bit farther.

A wealth of childhood memories rushed through Faith's mind. For more than twenty years she'd longed to come back. With no other choice available, she believed God's hand had guided her throughout every mile of this frightening journey.

The Silver Creek Bridge appeared through the swirl of snow in her headlights. So many of her early childhood memories were tied to this creek. Her grandfather had taught her how to fish here. They'd searched for gold along the banks of the stream.

A smile played across her face at the way her *grossdaddi* could make anything seem like an adventure to a young child.

Tires squealed close and the sweet memories evaporated while goose bumps flew up her arms. A massive truck was a few feet off her bumper. She'd been wrong. This wasn't an innocent traveler. Her worst fear screamed out of her nightmares and into reality.

Vincent had found her. Staying alive was going to take all her skills.

He flipped his lights on bright to intimidate. Faith buried the accelerator and pushed the car to its limits. Her tires spun on the slick road. Even though it was springtime in other parts of the world, here in Big Sky Country, winter still had the community in its grip.

Silver Creek Bridge quickly came up. She had to cross it before he trapped her there.

Her tires connected with the first wooden slat on the bridge. From far too close on her bumper, Vincent revved his engine. Before there was time to have a clear thought, the truck plowed into her full force. Her car lurched forward. Faith's head flung toward the wheel then snapped backward.

She grabbed the door for support when another blow sent the full weight of her body slamming against her wrist. She screamed as pain shot up her arm. Keeping the car on the road with one working hand was difficult, but she wanted to live.

Her grandmother's home was past the bridge down the first gravel road on the right, but she didn't dare lead Vincent there. The next turnoff was several miles beyond. She'd never make it that far. If she drove the car cross country under these conditions, would she survive? Through the swatch of visibility the headlights created, much of the countryside appeared still covered in snow, and the storm was increasing.

Faith fought hard to right the car and keep it from slamming into the guardrail. She punched the gas and tried to put distance between herself and the vehicle that was inches off her bumper once more. The truck hit her again.

Her car spun sideways. Faith screamed and did her best to control the car, but Vincent didn't let up. He planted the truck's bumper against the side of her door and shoved. She watched in horror as the truck's tires coughed up smoke as he tried to force her off the bridge.

Faith yanked the wheel hard to the left in a futile attempt to pull free of the massive truck, but it was useless. Her car's engine was no match.

She stomped the brake pedal with both feet, but the car continued to inch closer to the guardrail.

The passenger side struck the railing. Metal grinding against metal sounded horrific as the car crumpled on impact. Vincent didn't let up. The guardrail bent under the pressure of the powerful truck. Faith fought a losing battle. Trapped inside the car there was nothing she could do to prevent it. She was going into Silver Creek.

Her terrified gaze shot to the water below. The creek was close to overflowing its banks and had to be five feet deep.

The railing gave way with a terrible sound of metal snapping and bolts breaking free. Both passenger tires left the bridge. The car hung suspended in midair for the time it took Faith to pull in a fearful breath. Vincent's gleeful expression would forever be imprinted in her memory. She teetered back and forth for a second longer then plunged into the icy waters of Silver Creek.

The noise of the impact was so horrendous it had her wondering if the car would break into a hundred pieces. Her injured wrist banged the door again. She screamed and blacked out for a second.

Freezing water poured in through the bottoms of the doors.

Faith fumbled with the seat belt latch. It didn't budge. *Not like this.* She wouldn't die trapped inside this vehicle. She'd fight with everything she had to live. Expose Vincent for the criminal he was.

Water continued to rise inside the car. It groaned under the shifting pressure.

"Help me. Please," she prayed and jabbed her finger against the latch several more times. The final try released the seat belt. She'd escaped her house with just the clothes on her back and the pieces of evidence she'd tucked inside her purse that would bring down Vincent. She wouldn't lose them now.

Faith grabbed her purse and phone before they were completely submerged. She shoved the phone inside the purse and closed it before she slung the strap over her head.

It was a blessing the car had manual window cranks because the water had shorted the electrical system.

Faith rolled down the driver's window and eased through the opening. Immediately, she sank under the water's surface and tried not to panic. Her feet touched the bottom, and she righted herself. Though her head was above the water, the creek was running swiftly and standing up against the current was nearly impossible.

The cold water took her breath away. From where she stood in the middle of the creek, the bank appeared miles away.

Keeping her eyes on land, she began walking. She'd taken only a few steps when she stumbled on the rocky creek bed and went under the water.

Fighting back alarm, she steadied her feet beneath her. She wasn't a strong swimmer in the best of conditions, but she'd never make it to the shore like this. There was only one choice. She'd have to swim diagonally to reach dry ground.

One stroke at a time. Her grandfather had taught her that valuable lesson. When she was in the water, panicking was the worst possible enemy. Take each stroke and follow through. Keep your focus on your destination. She sucked in a breath, tried to calm herself and did as he'd taught her.

Where had Vincent gone? She scanned the bridge above. No truck. She hadn't heard it leave, but she'd been too focused on saving herself.

As the car begin to settle, a sharp crack came from

the woods above and close to the road. She recognized the sound immediately from the many times Blake had taken her to the gun range. Gunfire. Vincent was shooting at her. He was determined she wasn't going to leave here alive.

More shots landed all around. Barrel flashes lit up the woods. Vincent scrambled down the embankment. The shots missed her by inches. Faith ducked beneath the surface to keep from being hit. She swam underwater until she reached the opposite side of the car.

"Did you really think you could get away? From me?" Vincent mocked. "There's no way I can let you live. Cheryl's dead at your house. I used Blake's weapon to kill her. You remember—the one he taught you to shoot with. Your fingerprints are all over it. By now, my police buddies have probably found her body. I'll tell them you tried to kill me too. No one will blame me for taking you down."

Those ominous words threatened to destroy her. Vincent planned to frame her for Cheryl's death. Her murder would be considered justifiable by his fellow cops.

"Where's the evidence Blake left you?" Vincent demanded. "Give it to me and maybe I'll let you live."

There was no way she trusted him to keep his word. Once he had the evidence, he'd kill her.

Using the car as a barrier, she peeked around the edge. Vincent spotted her and opened fire. Faith ducked beneath the water. As she resurfaced, the purse slipped from her head and begun floating away. The clasp worked its way open. It wouldn't take long for everything inside to be in the creek.

Faith grabbed for it like the lifeline it was. That purse contained her only means of contacting anyone and the hard copies of all the data on the thumb drive along with Blake's note describing his and Vincent's crimes.

She'd tucked the drive into a plastic bag inside her wallet and placed it in her purse before she'd called Cheryl. At the time, she hadn't imagined a scenario such as this. God had planted the notion in her mind. If she lost those items, she had nothing.

Faith dove for the disappearing purse, but the current was too swift, and it floated out of her reach. Another round of shots peppered the water around her, forcing her to retreat. Desperate, she looked around for some means of escape, but there wasn't one. It was just her and a killer who was determined to bury her at the bottom of the creek. Along with his crimes.

Gunshots—more than one—had Eli Shetler sitting up straighter on the wagon. A short time earlier another disturbing sound had interrupted his tired thoughts. Metal crunching together followed by a loud splash. Something quite large had gone into Silver Creek. Undoubtedly, a car. But that didn't explain the gunshots. Those worried him the most.

Eli shook the reins hard. The mare picked up her pace.

The bridge over Silver Creek appeared through the snowy downpour.

Though he'd been back in West Kootenai for a little more than a month, everywhere he looked moments from his past abounded. Good times. Bad times. Those he and his wife, Miriam, had spent together reminded him of all he'd lost with her death. Silver Creek was no exception. They'd picnicked here. Taken long walks through the nearby woods to spend time together when they were courting. And he'd loved her so much. Even after two years, he couldn't believe he would never see her or the baby they'd been expecting again.

Eli stopped the horse before she entered the bridge. Part of the guardrail to the right was missing where a vehicle had plowed through it. The image in his head was unsettling.

A little way down on the opposite side, a pickup truck was parked off the gravel road. Had the driver stopped to lend assistance? While he pondered these things, a half dozen more shots ricocheted from the creek below. This was no accident. Someone was in serious trouble.

Eli grabbed the shotgun he kept for protection when working out in the wilderness and started down the slippery embankment.

"Help!" A woman screamed at the top of her lungs. Her distressed voice sent Eli scrambling the rest of the way down.

As his eyes adjusted to the darkness below the bridge, the sight in front of him was like nothing he'd seen before. A woman was in the water near a car that was sinking quickly. On the bank nearby, a shadowy figure of a man. He had a gun aimed at the woman.

"Where is it?" the man demanded. "I want what Blake gave you. All of it. Now," the man barked, and the woman jumped in reaction. "You should have stayed out of this, Faith. Shouldn't have dragged Cheryl into it. Now, you're going to die like her and your traitor husband. He betrayed blood."

Eli was terrified the man would shoot her right before his eyes. Acting on sheer instinct, he charged toward the assailant.

The man whipped around, spotted Eli, and trained his weapon at his head.

"That's far enough." The man scowled as he looked Eli over without lowering the weapon. "This doesn't concern you. I'm a police officer." He reached inside his pocket and flashed a badge too quickly for Eli to read it. "This woman is being accused of murder. I'm here to take her back with me."

"He's lying!" the female yelled, her pleading eyes latching on to Eli. Something familiar about her startled him. "He tried to kill me by forcing me off the bridge. Now he's shooting at me."

The reality of those words sank in. Why would someone from law enforcement try to kill this woman? Something about the situation wasn't as this guy claimed.

The man kept his finger poised on the trigger of the weapon. Would a law enforcement officer try to kill a man who had come to assist? Eli had overheard him threatening the woman earlier. The man might be a police officer, but he was definitely not following the law.

"Please don't leave me with him." The terror on her face wouldn't let Eli abandoned her no matter how much this man threatened.

"She's coming with me," Eli said and moved toward the woman.

"I told you to stay out of it. This is a police matter." He waded into the water and grabbed the woman's arm, yanking her along with him. "Let's go. It's a long drive back to New York."

"Stop right there." Eli raised his weapon. "Let her go." Though he was far from steady on the inside, Eli kept the shotgun trained on the man's midsection.

The officer shoved the woman away and strode toward Eli.

"Don't come any closer." Eli fired the shotgun into the air as a warning, yet the man didn't back down. He pointed the handgun at Eli and shot. If Eli hadn't ducked in time, the bullet would have struck his head. He couldn't believe stopping to lend a hand had resulted in a life-threatening situation.

Eli dove for the shooter before he could get off another round. They struggled in hand-to-hand combat while his assailant tried to get the handgun into a position to shoot again. Fighting for his life, Eli slugged the man. Watched him stumble backward before losing his footing on the slippery grass. He hit the ground hard.

Not giving his attacker time enough to right himself, Eli snatched the gun free from his grasp. Without a weapon, the man's threat was greatly diffused, yet he didn't appear ready to give up. He jumped to his feet, fists balled at his sides. With a look of pure malevolence on his face, he took a threatening step closer.

Eli cocked the handgun. "That's far enough. I don't want to shoot you, but I will."

His attacker stopped short, realizing Eli had the upper hand.

He glared long and hard before he dusted off his clothes. "This isn't over, and you're in a lot of trouble for interfering in a murder investigation."

The tingle along Eli's spine convinced him it was a lie. Given the opportunity, this man would take the weapon from him and use it on Eli and the woman standing in the creek. What kind of police officer would do such a thing?

"You need to leave." He kept the weapon leveled on the man's chest. "Now, before the sheriff arrives." Though Eli had no way of knowing if some of his *Englisch* neighbors had heard the shots and called the sheriff, it was a *gut* possibility. People around these parts looked out for each other. And he wanted this man to believe help was on the way.

"You didn't call anyone." But there was just enough doubt in his tone to make it clear he wasn't certain. "And even if you did, who do you think he'll believe. An Amish man and a woman accused of murder. Or a police detective."

Eli shook his head. "We will find out soon enough. One of my neighbors would have called in the gunshots by now. Unless you want to explain to the sheriff why you tried to kill me and ran this woman off the road, I suggest you be on your way."

The man hesitated for a long moment before he tossed the woman a venomous look. "I'll be back for you and the stuff." With that warning hanging over their heads, the man stormed past Eli and slammed his shoulder against him. Without another look their way, he stomped up the embankment and into the woods.

Reality crashed down around Eli. His knees threatened to buckle beneath his weight. He'd never been in a situation like this before. One minute he was on his way home after checking out the new piece of property he and Hunter planned to log, and the next he was interrupting a murder plot.

Near the road, the truck's engine fired, and the vehicle screamed away. The man had left...for now.

Eli snapped out of his shock and hurried to the woman who appeared to be suffering from her own form of trauma. She clutched her soaked jacket around her body and shivered. Once again, he was struck by a sense of familiarity. Did he know her? Impossible, surely.

"*Komm*, my wagon is up on the road, and I have some blankets you can use to dry off and warm up. It's best if we don't stay here any longer. I don't trust him not to come back." A loud whoosh snapped their attention to the water where the car slipped farther into its watery grave. Only the roof remained visible.

If he'd taken a different path home...

Eli suppressed a shiver.

"H-he forced me off the road. If you hadn't come along when you did, he would have killed me." Her teeth chattered from the cold, and she held her wrist against her body as if it had been injured in the incident.

"Is it true he's a police officer?" Eli asked because he had to know what he was dealing with.

She nodded. "It's true. But he's a dirty cop, and he knows I can prove it. That's why he tried to kill me.

He's a dangerous man." She glanced up toward the road as if expecting the shooter to return.

"You're safe now." But for how long? Eli went to assist her, but she shrank away. Despite his coming to her aid, she didn't fully trust him yet. After what happened, he could certainly understand.

She pushed her dark hair away from her face and searched his. "I'm sorry. It's just… I was so sure he'd kill me." She blew out a sigh. "Thank you for rescuing me."

Eli found himself swept up into the turmoil burning inside her troubled green eyes, which held fear and suspicion. He wanted to understand what had happened here tonight because there was so much more to her story.

"You are welcome. My name is Eli Shetler." He introduced himself, hoping to put her at ease.

Surprise showed on her face. "Eli? I remember you," she said in amazement. "My name is Faith… Cooper."

Faith Cooper? His neighbor was Sarah Cooper. As he continued to stare at her, something about her appearance sparked the tiniest of memories. This was Sarah's *Englisch* granddaughter.

"Your *grossmammi* is Sarah Cooper, right?" He couldn't hide his shock as he realized the woman standing before him now was the grown-up version of that little girl who used to follow around her grandfather everywhere he went. The one who tagged along behind Eli whenever she could. He remembered the time when she and her parents had left the Amish faith.

Faith smiled at his surprise. "She is."

"I remember you." And he did. The sweet little dark-haired girl she'd once been. So curious about everything. How had someone like her gotten involved with a man who was trying to kill her?

"How do you know that man?" Eli asked. "He said you were wanted for murder?"

She pulled her gaze from his. "He's lying. He killed his wife who is—was—my best friend. He did it in front of me, and now he's trying to frame me for her death."

Her chilling words were hard to believe. The desire to ask more questions was hard to resist, but they both needed to get out of here before that man returned. "Those are serious accusations. Way beyond what we can handle ourselves. We need to get the sheriff involved."

She barely let him finish. "No. No police. He's a detective. The sheriff won't believe me over Vincent, and if the tables were turned, I probably wouldn't believe me either." She stumbled over the slick path as they headed up the embankment. Eli reached out to catch her before she fell. Once more, he noticed the way she kept her left wrist tucked close to her body. "You're hurt. That could be serious." He indicated her injured wrist. "At least let me drive you to the hospital in Eagle's Nest." Though the town was some ten miles away, it was the closest clinic to the community.

She shook her head. "No, it's too risky. The best thing I can do is get out of sight as quickly as possible. He may have left for now, but he won't give up." She stopped as if she'd said too much. "And it is only a sprain."

Eli kept his doubts to himself. Once they reached the

road, Eli helped her climb onto the wagon. He glanced back at Silver Creek and tried not to think about what might have happened if he'd worked a little longer. Taken a different path home. *Gott* had been looking out for her.

Grabbing blankets from underneath some of his tools, Eli then wrapped one around her legs. The other he placed over her shoulders.

Springtime in West Kootenai was deceptive. The warmer temperatures lulled you into a false sense of hope. And then a storm like this one happened.

He climbed up beside her, yet he did not attempt to take up the reins. The questions pounding his mind needed answering, but Faith appeared to be one more bad thing away from falling apart.

So far, she hadn't said anything to settle his doubts. Faith claimed this man coming after her was a dirty cop who had killed someone. Was he involved in more illegal activities? Was she?

I'm a police officer. This woman is being accused of murder. The man's troubling words played through Eli's mind again and again. Though he didn't believe Faith was capable of murder, there was much about what happened that he didn't understand.

He thought about the trouble following him for the past two years. Losing his wife was hard enough but being accused of setting the fire that caused her death was unthinkable. He'd had firsthand experience with being accused of something you didn't do.

Eli gathered the reins from where he'd slung them in haste.

"Thank you, Eli," she said and faced him. "I'm sorry I put you in the middle of this, but I'm truly grateful you stopped. I'd be dead by now if you hadn't, and I doubt if anyone would know about it."

Those alarming words confirmed the seriousness of what happened tonight.

"You and I were friends as *kinner*, and Sarah is my neighbor. I would do whatever I could to help either of you."

She smiled at his recollection. "You used to walk me home from school sometimes. I remember you always chose pretty rocks for me." Her smile disappeared. "It's been so many years ago since I left here. At times, it feels like another lifetime."

He certainly understood that feeling. He'd been gone from West Kootenai for a long time himself. The life he left behind was not the same one he possessed now. It would never be the same.

"Your *grossmammi* isn't expecting you, is she?"

She shook her head, confirming this wasn't a friendly visit to catch up. Faith was running for her life.

Eli gave the reins a shake, and the horse responded to his skilled direction.

"Why is this man trying to harm you? Why would he try to frame you for someone's murder?"

She put up her guard. "Because of the things I found out. It's better for him if I disappear." The answer didn't settle anything in Eli's mind. Far from it.

They passed by the damaged railing. Eli had a feeling the truth was going to be far worse than anything he could imagine.

The mare clomped along the slushy road while snow continued to fall. Eli kept a close eye behind them. The truck had headed away from the community, but something told him this wasn't the last they'd seen of the man.

Most people around the town and the surrounding countryside knew each other. Had grown up living with the same neighbors for several generations. A stranger would stand out. He'd ask some of his *Englisch* neighbors if they'd seen a stranger. Eli hoped the man would realize it was better off for him to go back to where he came from.

The turnoff to his and Sarah's homesteads appeared up on the right. At one time all the property on this side of the road was deeded to the Cooper family.

When he'd first come back to West Kootenai, he'd remembered the property that once belonged to Sarah's son was sitting vacant, so he'd asked to buy some of the land and the old house. She'd been more than agreeable.

Being reunited with his family again had come at a heavy price. If it weren't for his *fraa*'s passing, he wouldn't have come back. For more than ten years, his relationship with his brothers had been strained. After losing Miriam and their unborn child to the fire, living under suspicion had gotten to be too much. He'd wanted a fresh start. Eli had reached out to his *mamm* and found the welcoming he'd longed for. But he still felt it necessary to keep some distance between himself and the family. Maybe out of a sense of guilt for his part in what happened between himself and *Bruder* Mason.

And so, he'd bought the place next to Sarah's. It was

some distance from the rest of the family and away from most of the community. He enjoyed the privacy and Sarah's calming presence.

Her modest homestead came into view. Eli guided the mare down her narrow drive and stopped in front of the house. Puffs of white smoke disappeared among the snowy night air.

He turned to Faith. Tears glistened in her eyes as she stared at the house, and he wondered when she'd been here last. He of all people understood how hard home-comings could be.

Eli hopped down and helped her from the wagon. In the distance an engine revved, and she spun at the sound.

"It could be coming from the highway. Sound travels far out here." Yet he understood exactly what she was thinking because he'd thought the same.

She relaxed. "You're probably right." Without another word, she hurried up the steps to the porch. Faith stood in front of the door for a long moment before she knocked.

Eli followed at a slower pace. He didn't have it in his heart to tell her the engine noise was much closer. After what happened at the creek, there was no way he was leaving two women alone with a killer on the loose in the community. He'd find a way to stay close. Sarah wouldn't have a problem with him bunking on the sofa.

Even though he'd been home for just over a month, he and Sarah had become *gut* friends. As a widow alone, she relied on him, and he was happy to help her out in any way he could.

A single lantern showed through the window. Sarah would be working on her quilting. The one thing she enjoyed most these days.

"Sometimes her hearing isn't so *gut*," Eli told her. "You have to knock louder."

Faith drew in a breath and knocked harder. Waited.

As he listened, the familiar labored steps of the woman who had welcomed him back to the community with open arms came toward them. The curtain near the door moved.

"Sarah, it's me, Eli. I have someone here to see you."

The curtain dropped and the door opened. A smile creased her face. Sarah's smile always made the darkness that haunted him flee.

"Eli, I'm glad you stopped by. *Komm* inside. The night is cold. I'll make some coffee to warm you up." Sarah's gaze shifted from him to the woman at his side. "And who is this?"

She stepped closer. Recognition dawned in slow surprise. "Faith." Tears quickly filled her eyes. "It is you." She swept her granddaughter into her arms and hugged her tightly. "Oh, my *boppli*. My precious *boppli*. You're finally home."

As much as Sarah was overjoyed to see her granddaughter, Eli worried that the danger following Faith would find its way into this gentle woman's life.

Chapter Two

Faith clung to her grandmother and didn't want to let her go while tears she couldn't control continued to fall. Through all the years—the miles—the fears that shadowed her every bit of the way here—she was finally home. And no matter what Vincent threw at her, she needed to believe everything was going to be okay because she was in her grandmother's loving arms.

"I can't believe I'm finally here," she said with a watery smile. Faith clasped her grandmother's hand and together they stepped inside the house followed by Eli. He closed the door softly.

Childhood memories flew through her mind. Whenever she was scared or troubled by something, she'd come here and pour out her heart to this special woman. During this past year since Blake's death, after she'd found out her grandmother was still alive, her heart had been aching to come back home.

This was the first time she'd been back since her father moved the family away when Faith was ten. For a long time after they'd left, she'd begged her mother to let her write to the grandparents, but she'd said her father wouldn't approve. Several years later, her father told her both grandparents had died. Faith had cried for weeks after hearing the heartbreaking news before finally accepting the truth. At least what she'd thought was the truth until she'd realized her father had lied to her.

After Blake passed away, Faith found herself longing to return to the simple way of life she'd been forced to leave. A few weeks before she'd discovered Blake's note, she'd found the address for the bakery in West Kootenai and had written Mrs. Stoltzfus, the owner and her grandmother's good friend. Faith had wanted to visit her grandparents' graves and perhaps stop by their old homestead. When the response came, it just about floored her. Grandmother was still alive. Her father had lied to keep her from reaching out to her grandparents through the years. Faith and her grandmother had connected through letters. She'd planned a visit to West Kootenai soon, and then... Vincent had happened.

The familiar childhood scent of wood smoke and the lavender soap her grandmother made melted the years away. She was that little girl again. Running to her grandmother to make it better.

She became aware of Eli watching their exchange. Though the tears wouldn't stop, Faith was all smiles. This was the place she'd yearned to be for so long.

"I'm so happy to see you again," she told her grandmother.

Grandmother Sarah's keen brown eyes looked deeply

into hers, seeing the things that Faith wasn't ready to talk about just yet.

How could she tell this sweet lady about the deadly crimes her husband had been involved in when Faith couldn't reconcile them with the man she'd loved?

Her grandmother noticed the way Faith cradled her injured wrist. "You're hurt."

Faith dismissed her grandmother's concern. "It's only a sprain." She'd carefully examined the injured wrist during the ride over. Once she had it wrapped and a few weeks of healing, it would be better.

The heat from the woodstove called to her. She stepped closer. It warmed her chilled skin, yet she still couldn't stop shaking every time she pictured Vincent's angry face. She'd almost died tonight. Had been minutes from it before Eli came along.

"*Komm.* Sit." Grandmother Sarah gently urged her into one of the rockers. "You are soaking wet, child. What happened? How did you run into Eli?" Her eyes widened as they traveled over Faith's damp jeans, sweater and jacket. Faith's dark hair dripped water onto the floor. After more than a day without sleep and being forced into the creek, Faith couldn't imagine how bad she must look.

"I ran off the Silver Creek Bridge," she said in answer to her grandmother's probing gaze. "My car landed in the water." It wasn't the whole truth, but she didn't know where to begin to describe the horrible things Vincent had done.

Grandmother Sarah tsked and shook her head. "You could have been killed."

"Thankfully, Eli came along in time to save me." She glanced past her grandmother to where Eli leaned against the wall near the door. His intense eyes were watchful. Broad shouldered, his presence dominated the tiny living room. The lantern on the wall near him picked up hints of gold in his brown hair that touched the collar of his dark blue shirt. A neatly trimmed matching beard confirmed Eli was married. She hadn't realized the young boy who she once had a crush had wed. She felt guilty about keeping him from his wife.

"Thanks be to *Gott*," Grandmother Sarah exclaimed and turned to Eli. "*Denki*, for helping my precious granddaughter. You're a good boy." She patted the arm of the man who was far from a boy.

Eli shrugged off the thanks. "I did what anyone else would do." He met Faith's gaze and held it. "You should tell your *grossmammi* the truth. This involves her now."

Grandmother Sarah swung toward her. "What's he talking about?"

Faith pulled in a steadying breath. Forced out the words. "I didn't accidentally run off the road tonight. I was deliberately forced off by someone I know."

"Who would do such a thing?" For people like her grandmother and Eli, the thought of such evil existing had to be hard to fathom. The peaceful lifestyle of the Amish insulated them from the ugliness that sometimes took place in the Englisch world.

At one time, Faith had been just as innocent. Never imagining anything bad could happen. But that was before Blake's death. Before she knew the truth about her husband's and Vincent's crimes.

"Someone very bad." And it was true. Vincent was a bad man with everything to lose.

"With your permission, I would like to bunk here tonight." Eli spoke to her grandmother. After what happened, knowing Eli was close would help put Faith's mind at ease. Still, he wondered what she was keeping him from.

"Won't your wife be worried about you?" The words slipped out before Faith could stop them and a desolate look entered Eli's eyes.

"My wife is dead," he said in a voice devoid of emotion.

Faith wished for the floor to swallow her. "I'm so sorry."

While they continued to watch each other across the small space, Grandmother Sarah's troubled gaze turned to Eli. "You are always welcome here. I will make up the sofa for you. It will be *gut* to have you close."

A faint smile replaced the dark expression on his face. He and Grandmother were close.

"*Denki*, Sarah. I will put the mare in the barn and be right back," he said while holding Faith's gaze. She understood he was giving them time alone for Faith to tell her grandmother about Vincent. "Lock the door up behind me to be safe."

Eli grabbed his hat and the lantern, stepped outside and closed the door. Grandmother Sarah slid the lock into place and came back to where Faith sat.

She placed her hand on Faith's shoulder and nodded. "*Gut*, you are no longer shivering." Without another word, she brought over a towel then headed for the kitchen, but Faith grabbed her hand.

"Aren't you going to ask me why someone would want to run me off the road?"

Her grandmother smiled and kissed Faith's cheek. "You will tell me the whole story when you are ready."

Just like her grandmother. Growing up, whenever something was troubling Faith and she couldn't bring herself to share it, Grandmother Sarah would always wait until she was ready to talk. She never once forced the matter.

With a pat on her shoulder, Grandmother Sarah left her alone. Familiar sounds drifted from the kitchen while Faith stared at the fire in the woodstove. She could only think of what she'd left behind in Silver Creek. Though she didn't fully understand all the information on the thumb drive, one thing became apparent—Blake and Vincent were on the payroll of one of the biggest drug dealers in New York. A man Blake had referred to as Ghost.

Her husband had included detailed accounts of drug raids that had taken place with rival dealers. He'd mentioned amounts of money that had been confiscated along with the discrepancy to what got logged in. There were names of other cops listed, along with dollar amounts they'd been paid.

But something else that she'd seen on one of the pages had scared the daylights out of her. Names of people whose cause of death had been pinned on someone else. Blake claimed Vincent had handled all the murders.

"Here you are, my *boppli*. Drink up." Grandmother

Sarah handed Faith a cup of hot chocolate like she used to make when Faith was a child.

"You remembered." Her heart melted with happiness, despite the danger still coming for her.

Grandmother Sarah beamed. "Of course, I remembered. You are my baby girl. I remember everything about you."

The guilt that had haunted her since she'd reconnected with her grandmother returned full force. She should have realized her father would do everything in his power to keep Faith away from her grandparents.

"I should have ignored *Daed*'s anger and checked on you and *Grossdaddi* sooner. I missed out on so many years of happiness with you both because of it."

Even though she'd been only ten at the time, Faith still remembered the argument between her father and *Grossdaddi*. The angry words her father had thrown at his *daed* before he packed up his family and moved them thousands of miles away.

Her grandmother patted her hand. "My *sohn* was a troubled boy. Saul hated this way of life. He always wanted more than what he could find here." She shook her head and got to her feet, then brought over gauze for wrapping Faith's injured wrist.

"How are you doing, really?" Faith asked when she noticed the way her grandmother rubbed her hands together as if to ease the pain.

"I am blessed." This was always the answer whenever Faith had asked about her health in letters. But her grandmother's gnarled hands were a reminder that she was getting older. Though Grandmother Sarah had joked about the cold making it hard to work on her quilts, Faith had no idea how bad her arthritis had become until now.

She couldn't change the past, but Faith could do everything in her power to never let down the one person who truly cared about her again.

Grandmother Sarah finished wrapping Faith's wrist and stood back to examine her work. "How does it feel?"

"Much improved. I couldn't have done it better. You were my inspiration for becoming a nurse, the way you always helped others." She squeezed her grandmother's arm.

"*Komm* with me. I have an extra dress for you to change into." She followed her grandmother into her bedroom and waited while she removed one of the dresses from the peg on the wall. "I will wait for you in the living room." She patted Faith's arm and stepped from the room.

Faith slowly removed her wet clothes and smoothed the dress into place. How many years had it been since she dressed Amish?

In the living room her grandmother spotted her and clutched her hands together. "You always did look exactly like your *mamm*."

Faith settled into the rocker beside her. Quiet settled between them. Grandmother was waited for her to open up just like when Faith was a child. She wouldn't ask a single question. She'd wait. Like she had through all these years. Waiting for Faith to come home.

Good memories filled Faith's heart and brought a lump to her throat. She remembered sitting at her grandfather's feet while he read the Bible aloud to his family on Sundays, never imagining her idyllic childhood would come to an end.

"I'm sorry. I should have realized what my father was doing. I should have tried to find out the truth sooner." Faith reached for her grandmother's hand again because holding it gave her a sense of peace.

"That is not your fault, child, and you are here now." Never a negative word. Not even for the man who had torn apart their family. This woman beside her was stronger than Faith would ever be.

Faith pulled in several cleansing breaths and struggled to control the tears that were so close. "Someone tried to kill me tonight." Saying the words aloud didn't make it any easier to accept. "No, not just someone. I know who tried to kill me. It was my brother-in-law. Blake's brother." She told her grandmother everything. "He killed Blake because he was going to turn himself in and implicate Vincent and the others." She shook her head. "And he killed his wife right in front of me. Cheryl was more than my sister-in-law—she was my friend. She came to the house because I called her. I showed her Blake's note. She couldn't believe what my husband had written." Her voice trailed off as the image of Cheryl's final seconds flashed through her mind.

While she and Cheryl tried to decide what to do with the evidence tucked in Faith's purse, Vincent forced his way into the house. He'd followed Cheryl there. When she'd confronted him with Blake's note, he'd grabbed Cheryl by the throat and pinned her against the wall. Cheryl begged her to take the note and leave, but Faith tried to get Vincent off her friend. He'd slugged her hard. And then he'd shot his wife. Panicked, Faith grabbed the note from where it had fallen, snatched her purse, and ran, barely making it to the car. She'd backed out of the garage when Vincent ran out shooting into the street behind her without caring about her neighbors. She'd floored the gas pedal and dodged the bullets flying all around her.

Faith sat up straighter at the thought of something she hadn't considered before. Vincent had told her the gun he used to kill Cheryl belonged to Faith, but how was that possible? Until Vincent barged into her home, he didn't know she even had any evidence. The last time she'd seen the weapon was when Blake locked it away in the safe he kept in his office. Her sleep-deprived brain hadn't considered Vincent might be lying until now. And if he'd lied about using her gun, then what else?

"Vincent can't afford to have the information on the thumb drive out there for someone to find. And there's always the chance if he lets me live—even if he does try to frame me for Cheryl's death—someone may believe my story. He can't let me live." She shivered at how close to killing her Vincent had come already. Minutes really, if Eli hadn't happened to come her way.

"He's a dangerous man, *Grossmammi*." The language of her childhood came back as easily as if drawing her next breath.

Disbelief replaced the tenderness on her grandmother's face. At one time, Faith couldn't imagine such an evil either.

"You must go to the sheriff, Granddaughter. He can help—"

Faith didn't let her finish. "That's not possible. Vincent is one of them. He'll know what to say to make them believe his story over mine. I can't go to the sheriff. At least not until I have the evidence back."

And to get it, she'd have to return to the creek as soon as possible. If she ever stood a chance at getting out from under Vincent's threat, there was no other choice.

Grandmother Sarah leaned closer. "What can I do to help?"

Despite her fear, Faith smiled. "Nothing. I'm sorry I brought my troubles to your door, but I didn't know where else to go. I've missed you so much. We've lost so much time."

Grandmother leaned in and hugged her tightly. "*Jah*, we have, but you must not hold on to the anger, Faith. It will tear you apart."

She'd told herself this many times. Forgiveness was as much a part of her healing as it was about letting go of her father's wrongdoings, yet no matter how hard she tried, she hadn't gotten there yet.

After Blake passed, her thoughts kept returning to her Amish life in West Kootenai. But could she stay? She'd traveled so far away from this Plain life. Gotten off track. More than anything, she wanted to change all that.

She jumped when a rap sounded from the front of the house. Grandmother Sarah patted her arm. "It's Eli." She rose and unlocked the door.

Eli stepped across the threshold. The frown on his face grabbed Faith's attention. Something had happened.

"I heard the vehicle again. It sounded close to the turnoff. It appears to be sitting still." His gaze homed in on Faith. "It could be the same truck that ran you off the bridge."

She was on her feet in an instant. "How did he find us so quickly?" Eli had stabled the horse and wagon. There would be nothing to lead Vincent to this house unless he somehow knew about her past.

Please, no.

Eli's dark eyes held hers. "If he is knowledgeable in tracking, he could quite possibly have seen the wagon tracks and followed."

The news threatened to break her. She rubbed a trembling hand across her eyes.

"Perhaps it isn't him," Eli said at her reaction. "There are many cars that travel the road by the creek. It could be someone passing through the community."

At this time of the night? Under these conditions? The likelihood of it being anyone other than Vincent was slim. She'd come all this way hoping her troubles would just disappear the moment she stepped foot on community property. Instead, she'd come close to dying. Involved her grandmother in her troubles. Had almost gotten Eli killed at the hands of a man who would stop at nothing to cover up his crimes.

"I will slip down to the road and take a look," Eli told them and headed out the door.

Faith couldn't let him go there alone while she hid in the house. "I'm coming with you."

Eli's forehead furrowed. "That's unwise. This man is dangerous, and he's looking for you. There's a chance he may not recognize me. You should stay with your grandmother."

"I'm coming," she insisted, expecting some more push back.

Something akin to admiration flashed in his brown eyes before he nodded. "As you wish."

He leaned inside and picked up the shotgun from where he'd placed it by the door. The need for the weapon reminded her again of the serious dangers Vincent presented.

It would be just the two of them against a man who was highly trained and motivated by having everything to lose.

Grandmother Sarah gathered her hand in hers. "Be careful. Both of you."

Faith forced a smile. "We'll be okay. Lock up behind us and don't open the door until we speak to you."

The fear in her grandmother's eyes hung heavily over Faith as the door closed. She hated the need to worry this precious woman, but the reality was Vincent had killed before. He wouldn't hesitate to take Grandmother's life if it benefited him.

Faith waited until the lock slid into place before she followed Eli from the porch and toward the woods that separated her grandmother's place from the road.

Newly fallen snow muted their footsteps. The only sound in the night was the noise the idling vehicle made close by. What if Vincent had left the truck running to draw them out? He could be hiding in the woods and waiting for them to come to him.

Shoving down the fear was hard but giving in to it

made her vulnerable to mistakes. She couldn't afford a single false move if she wanted to live.

The man beside her remained silent as they walked.

Faith glanced around at the snowy wonderland and remembered how much as a child she'd loved roaming these woods. Exploring every inch with her *grossdaddi*.

Eli stopped so suddenly she was caught off guard. He barred the path in front of her. In an instant, those fond memories evaporated, and the reality of her situation pumped adrenaline through her veins.

"Do you see something?" she whispered.

"Jah." He pointed through the growth. "That's the same truck from earlier."

Her heart hiccupped. Vincent was right down the road from her, and she knew what he was capable of. Just being this close to him scared the daylights out of her.

"What's he doing?" she asked. The truck had been sitting still for a while. The windows were foggy and she couldn't see inside it.

"Whatever it is, it can't be good." They exchanged a look. An uneasy feeling slipped between her shoulder blades. Was she risking their lives by being out here?

"Maybe we should go back. If he finds us here, he could try to finish what he started earlier."

The truck's interior light flashed. Vincent had opened the door, and he was getting out.

Eli grabbed her arm and tugged her behind the closest tree.

A tense breath slipped past her lips as footsteps headed into the woods in their direction. She tried to control her labored breathing. The last thing she wanted was to alert Vincent they were there.

Faith closed her eyes and prayed with all her heart as seconds ticked by. Finally, Vincent moved away, and she could breathe again. It sounded as if he was heading back to the truck. Why had he gotten out? Had he heard something and gone to investigate? She glanced back toward her grandmother's house. With the thick tree coverage, the house wasn't visible from the road.

A door was slammed shut.

"That was close," she whispered.

The truck pulled back onto the road. Its headlights flashed across the space where they hid as Vincent made a U-turn and started back toward the bridge.

Faith forced herself to leave the cover of the tree. The truck picked up speed as it headed down the road. An object was tossed from the driver's-side window into the woods just past where they stood.

"Did you see that?" she asked Eli.

He nodded. "*Jah*, I did. I'm guessing he was looking for a place to get rid of something."

Vincent sped down the road. Soon, his taillights disappeared.

Faith hurried over to the spot where he'd tossed the item. As soon as she got close enough, she recognized it and the ground seemed to be taken out from underneath her. It was her purse. Vincent had found it. Did he have the thumb drive?

She bent over, picked up the purse and opened it.

"This is yours?" Eli asked, watching her.

"Yes." The only thing in the purse was a photo she'd

saved of herself and Blake taken during happier times. She'd kept it because it reminded her of the man she'd fallen in love with. Not the person she hadn't known existed.

"It's not here." She held the empty purse in her hands. Her troubled gaze found Eli's.

"What's not in there?"

"The evidence that proves Vincent is a dirty cop and responsible for taking the life of his brother, my husband."

Eli's eyes widened. "This man is your brother-in-law? He killed your husband along with his wife?"

As hard as it was to admit her own ignorance, Eli deserved to hear the truth. Every ugly detail. "Yes. My last name is really St. Clair, but after everything that's happened, I don't want to be associated with that family." She stopped long enough to look at Eli. She couldn't imagine what he was thinking.

"Vincent and my husband were New York City detectives. He killed Blake because his brother was going to turn him in."

The shock on Eli's face was clear to see. "This is where you are living?"

She slowly nodded. "Yes. I moved to the city after I graduated from nursing school." Her fragmented thoughts returned to what occurred at the creek. She told him about what happened before he'd arrived. The frantic fall from the bridge. "Vincent started shooting as soon as I cleared the car. My purse popped open. I've no doubt my phone is gone. It's probably at the bottom of Silver Creek by now."

Faith gave a detailed account of what was on the thumb drive. "And there was a video. It showed Blake and Vincent discussing the upcoming murder of a rival dealer with a man I didn't recognize, but Blake made it a point to use his street name. Ghost." Even the name was frightening.

"Blake had obviously been compiling information to take down his brother, the rest of the dirty cops and Ghost for a long time. He left a note for me taped under his desk. He warned me not to go to any of the cops in the city for help." Faith gathered her jacket closer around her body and looked to Eli. "I don't know how widespread the corruption really is."

Terrified, she'd been convinced the conversation on the video was important, and so she'd sent a copy of it to her phone. Now, the information she'd need to bring down Vincent was missing. Without it she had nothing, and Vincent was determined to make her and the problem she represented disappear just as easily as he'd taken out Blake and Cheryl.

"I printed everything on the drive and placed it in my purse. The plastic bag containing the drive itself was hidden in my wallet." She shook her head.

"Even if there's the slightest chance Vincent doesn't have all the evidence, I have to go back to the creek. Finding those items may be my only chance to stop him from killing me."

Eli's frown deepened. "There's a good chance the documents were destroyed by the water. There could be nothing to save and this man will probably be expecting you to go back there. He'll be watching for you."

She of all people knew Vincent St. Clair's capabilities.

When she'd found the note from her husband almost a year to the day of his death, it had taken away part of her innocence. She'd always believed the police were the good guys. There to protect people. Yet Blake wrote that he and his brother had been on the take for years. Sometimes bad guys came disguised as men carrying badges.

"I know he will be." She'd need everything she could get to fight Vincent, including Eli's help. She couldn't do it on her own. Tonight had taught her that.

"He killed my husband, Eli. Vincent shot his brother and told me Blake died during a drug raid." She could still remember her reaction. The shock. The disbelief at hearing her husband was dead.

She'd been so naive. Had never imagined Vincent would be capable of doing such a despicable thing.

"My world collapsed," she said as they headed back to her grandmother's house. "I couldn't bring myself to go into Blake's office until a few weeks ago."

And then she'd learned everything she'd been told was a lie.

"I found the note by accident. Blake had taped a key there with it. The key fit a safe-deposit box in Upstate New York that contained the thumb drive."

"You had no idea your husband was involved in such crimes?" She heard the disbelief in his tone and couldn't blame him. If she were hearing this story for the first time, she'd probably have plenty of doubts too.

"I know how hard it is to imagine, but I had no idea." Blake had kept her insulated from his illegal dealings.

"Looking back, those last few days before he'd died, something was troubling him." He'd barricaded himself in the office long into the night. He'd become jumpy and constantly checked the windows. Blake wouldn't tell her what was wrong, just that it was something with the job.

"I didn't know who to trust, only that I couldn't go to any of Blake's cop friends with the information."

"That must have been terrifying." The simple acceptance in Eli's tone drew her attention to him. An old memory from childhood came to mind. She was probably only six or seven. Her mother was supposed to be waiting to pick her up after school. Faith ran outside to find she wasn't there. She'd been scared, but Eli had walked her home and held her hand the entire time.

Up ahead, her grandmother's house appeared through the trees. The same sense of returning home filled her with longings of a simpler time. Yet nothing about her return here had been simple. Far from it.

"Vincent knows I have evidence against him because he read part of Blake's note. I have to get that drive back before he finds it."

Eli glanced up at the falling snow. The early spring storm continued to grow stronger and the weather was deteriorating quickly. "We'll never see it in this weather. At first light, we'll go back and search. If it's there, we'll find it."

With hours standing between her and being able to look for the drive, Faith's thoughts churned with worst-case scenarios. Undoubtedly, with or without the drive, Vincent would follow her to the ends of the earth to put her down.

* * *

Eli guided Sarah's buggy through the woods behind her place. Though he hated leaving Sarah alone, the kindly woman had assured him she would be *oke*. Eli confirmed both doors were locked, and Sarah had her husband's shotgun within arm's reach, just in case Vincent tied the homestead to Faith.

It was too risky to take the road back to Silver Creek, but he didn't want to go in on foot in case they ran into trouble. There was a good chance Vincent would be trolling the area around the creek looking for Faith. They'd need the buggy to escape.

The woman who had consumed his thoughts most of the night sat rigidly at his side. She wore her fear like a cloak tucked tight around her body. Faith hadn't said more than a handful of words since they'd left the house.

After his own sleepless night, Eli had risen well before dawn, unable to quiet his mind enough to rest. The things Faith told him rattled around in his mind. At each little sound outside he'd checked the window because he'd seen the lengths the man coming after Faith would go to keep his secrets.

"Eli?" Her soft voice interrupted his troubled thoughts, and he turned at the sound of his name. Faith's brows scrunched together as if she'd been trying to get his attention for a while.

"I'm sorry." He shook his head. "I'm a million miles away."

She smiled and his attention was drawn to the way it transformed her entire face. Those once-serious green eyes sparkled. Worry lines eased. The inquisitive little girl from his past had grown into a beautiful woman.

Beautiful?

He hadn't considered another woman beautiful before, and it felt as if he were betraying Miriam by the mere thought.

Heat crept up his neck, and his gaze shifted to the road ahead. Miriam held his heart still, but he and Faith had grown up together.

"When I first saw you, it took me only a second to remember how we knew each other," Faith was saying. "Your grandfather and mine were such good friends. You and I kind of fell into our friendship through them."

"*Jah*, they were *gut* friends, for sure. And you always hung out with your *grossdaddi*, as I recall." He cast a sideways look her way. "Whenever he visited my grandfather, you were at his side." He smiled at the memory. She'd been just a little thing back then. Much smaller than other kids in her class. It had brought out his protective instincts at an early age, especially when the bigger kids at school tried to pick on her.

"He was my hero," she murmured with a whimsical expression on her face. The look reminded Eli of the girl who used to follow him around. Always excited about every little thing.

"I remember Amos coming to the school to walk you home many times. He was a big man but kind to everyone. Unless they messed with his granddaughter." He winked at Faith. And whenever Amos or Faith's *mamm* were unable to see her home, Eli would take her to her grandparents.

"Yes, I was his little girl. He taught me so many things. We used to have these amazing adventures. He and my grandmother were my whole world back then. I thought *Grossdaddi* Amos hung the moon." She shook her head, and the smile disappeared as if something ugly had taken its place in her memory.

Like him, she had plenty of secrets. Some best left alone.

"It was a sad day when he passed," Eli said. Especially sad when Amos's wife was the only relative at the funeral. Though everyone in the community was there to support Sarah, she missed her family terribly. Her granddaughter in particular.

Years ago, Eli remembered overhearing conversations between his grandpa and Amos. They'd talk about Amos's son, Saul. How difficult the relationship had become between father and *sohn*. Saul seemed to resent the hard work associated with the Plain life. He wanted more than to be a farmer. Something Eli didn't understand at all. He couldn't imagine living anywhere other than among the Amish people.

The Silver Creek Bridge appeared in front of them. Eli's hands tightened on the reins as they drew closer, the events from the previous evening fresh on his mind. Even from their limited vantage point, the damaged guardrail was a stark reminder of what had happened the night before. How close Faith had come to dying. The danger that faced them now.

Today, there didn't appear to be any vehicles parked along the roadside. He wondered if Vincent had found the information Faith was counting on. As much as Eli wanted to be done with such an evil man, he had no doubt that someone who had gone to such lengths as to follow Faith all this way—and run her off the road—would not give up until she was dead.

Eli pulled back on the reins and brought the mare to a stop. Faith turned to him with a worried look on her face.

"Stay here. I'm going to check up at the road." He handed her the reins. "I'll be right back."

He hopped down and started through the snowy woods. As he walked, Eli checked the ground for any sign Vincent had been there. Only animal tracks disturbed the pristine countryside. Once he made sure the truck wasn't parked near the road, he returned to Faith.

"I think it's best if we leave the buggy here. Just in case," he added when her fear level rose before his eyes. "I didn't see any sign of him near the road, and there are no fresh tire tracks." Yet the hairs on the back of his neck assured him they were far from being out of danger.

Eli tied the reins to a sturdy tree branch and held out his hand to assist Faith as she used the buggy's step to reach the ground.

With her hand in his, another memory from childhood flew from its resting place in his mind. She'd been so young. Maybe even before she'd begun her schooling. Her grandfather had come to visit his friend at their family's newly operational lumber mill. Eli, several of his brothers and their *daed* had been there. The machines used to cut the trees into lumber were massive. Faith was curious. She'd snuck away when the grown-ups were talking and had gotten a little too close to the blade.

Eli had snatched her away before she could get hurt, but she'd been terrified. Tears falling down her cheeks, she'd clung to his hand as he brought her back to her grandfather. Their lives had been interlocked for many a year.

He glanced down and found her watching him. Those huge green eyes searching his face. Eli untangled his hand and pulled himself together.

After grabbing the shotgun from behind the seat, he headed down the slippery bank to the creek below. Faith followed at a slower pace, choosing her steps with care while he tried to understand what had gotten into him since seeing her again.

After Miriam's death, he'd gotten *gut* at shoving down his feelings. Maybe it was being back in West Kootenai. Seeing Faith again. She represented part of his childhood that was simpler.

At the edge of the water, a handful of papers were scattered around the bank. What appeared to be a couple of fast-food wrappers had floated ashore and caught on the brush.

Faith hurried past him and sifted through the ones on the ground with a hope that soon faded. "It's not them," she said with a defeated sigh. "The last time I saw my purse was in the water over there." She pointed to a spot midway under the bridge. "The thumb drive was in a small plastic ziplock bag. It has a blue closure." Faith glanced around the bank where more debris had floated from the car. "We should split up. I'll start over there."

They'd cover more ground if they went in different directions. Getting in and out of the area before Vincent returned was important. The last thing he wanted was to get caught out here in the open with a killer.

Eli headed along the bank. As he walked, he kept a careful eye on his surroundings. The road was just up from there. So far, there'd been nothing to indicate Vincent was close. Eli hoped it stayed that way.

A few more pieces of paper lay on the shore covered in mud. He picked up one. It was a flyer for a restaurant in New York. Eli kept walking.

As much as he wanted to believe Faith would find what she needed, the creek was fed by runoff from the year's heavy snowfall in the mountains. He couldn't remember the last time he'd seen the creek running so high. Chances were that anything as small as a plastic bag would have washed downstream by now. They might never find it.

The faintest of sounds grabbed his attention. Eli straightened and turned. He could no longer see Faith.

Sensing something was wrong, Eli started running back to where he'd left her when he heard her scream. He couldn't get back to her fast enough.

"Where is he? I know you didn't come here by yourself." Eli immediately recognized Vincent's voice. "Well, it doesn't matter. I'll take care of him after I've finished with you." Vincent's tone dripped with smugness and Eli ran harder. "I should have known Blake wouldn't go quietly. I cut him in on a way to make more than he ever could as a detective, and this is how he repaid me."

Eli stopped when he spotted Vincent looming over Faith and ducked behind a bush. He had to save her. If he could reach Vincent before the man spotted him…

"How could you kill your own brother?" Faith lunged for Vincent, but her moment of bravery was short-lived when he pointed a gun at her. She stopped short.

"The same way I killed Cheryl," he yelled. "She always was weak. In the past, she never would have dared question me until you got her involved. Killing her was easy. My brother used to be weak too, until he married you. Then he changed. Started questioning things he shouldn't have. I didn't have a choice. I had to kill him…just like I have to kill you." The fear on Faith's face was clear. Eli slowly eased from his hiding spot. "The person I work for won't take kindly to his livelihood being exposed. He wants you dead." With his finger on the trigger, Vincent prepared to follow through with his threat. Eli moved closer while trying to disguise the sound of his footsteps.

Faith's eyes widened when she spotted Eli. "If you kill me, the evidence I have against you and your boss will go public." She was trying to give Eli time to reach them. "Everyone will know what you've done."

The weapon in Vincent's hand lowered ever so slightly. "You're lying. I have the note Blake left you. The documents. I have everything." But just enough hesitation in his voice confirmed he wasn't sure.

When he was just a few feet from Vincent, Eli raised the shotgun. Vincent whirled at the tiniest of sounds.

"You! I told you to stay out of this."

Before Eli got off a single shot, Vincent fired his

handgun. Eli hit the ground before the shot could take him out.

Vincent prepared to fire again. Eli leaped to his feet, grabbed the shotgun by the barrel, and swung. It connected with the side of Vincent's head before the man could get off another shot. The look of shock on Vincent's face was short lived. His eyes slammed shut and he dropped to the ground where he stood.

Eli's hands shook as he covered the space between himself and Faith. "Are you *oke*?" She managed a nod. "We have to go. Now. Before he wakes." Eli did a quick search of Vincent's pockets to make sure he didn't possess the evidence before he grabbed Faith's hand. Together, they started up the steep embankment, his boots slipping over the slick earth. The snow from the previous evening had turned to slush, and it was hard to gain traction.

Once they reached the buggy, Eli untied the reins, and they climbed up on the bench seat. He urged the mare back through the woods. It was too risky to take a direct path to Sarah's. They'd be leading Vincent straight to Eli's elderly neighbor. He'd have to find another way.

"I had no idea he was there until he was right on top of me." It was difficult for Eli to understand Faith's unsteady words. "He has Blake's letter and the printouts from the thumb drive."

"But he doesn't have the drive." Eli truly believed that. He glanced over his shoulder in time to see Vincent running toward them. He had the gun in his hand. In his rush to get them away from the man, Eli hadn't thought to grab Vincent's weapon.

"He's coming after us. Get down," Eli yelled. The words just cleared his lips when Vincent opened fire on them. The mare spooked and charged through the woods at a rapid pace.

Why hadn't he heard Vincent's truck before he ambushed Faith? The only answer was he'd parked it somewhere down the road and had been waiting for them to show up.

Once they were out of Vincent's line of sight, Eli headed the animal toward the shortcut he'd used as a kid. Behind them, an engine fired. Vincent was coming.

Faith held on to the bottom of the seat as Eli crossed the road onto a narrow path. "I hope you're right about the thumb drive. It could either be at the bottom of the creek or maybe it floated downstream. Either way, I have to go back."

After what happened just now, Eli didn't want her anywhere near the creek again. "It's too dangerous. I think it's time to go to the sheriff."

She barely let him finish. "I can't. Don't you understand? Vincent is willing to kill to cover up his crimes, and he's a cop." Her voice cracked with frustration and tears shone in her eyes. "He said he'd frame me for Cheryl's death. The police may be looking for me already. I can't go to the sheriff. Not without the drive."

Eli, of all people, understood how hard it was to clear your name, and he didn't want that for Faith.

"*Oke*, we won't go to the sheriff yet."

She held on to his gaze. "What if Vincent finds the drive first? It's all I have."

Eli reached for her hand. "It will be *oke*. You told

him if anything happened to you the evidence would go public. Chances are, he'll think the drive is hidden somewhere else."

A relieved smile spread across her face, sweeping him back in time while he prayed his words proved to be true. For a moment, she was that little girl again, holding his hand as they walked home. That same smile on her face whenever he'd find a pretty rock along the way because he remembered she always picked them up in the schoolyard. She'd trusted him completely back then. He hoped she would now.

Eli's attention shifted from the pretty woman at his side to the overgrown path ahead. It had been years since he'd used it. Much had changed during that time.

The snow from last night's storm had probably melted on the road from the vehicles passing over it. Would Vincent see the tracks where the buggy crossed?

Eli listened. The truck continued down the road past the turnoff. A moment of relief was short-lived when a far more disturbing thought occurred. Vincent had once been part of Faith's family. What had she told him about her past?

The thought of Vincent showing up at Eli's innocent neighbor's house terrified him.

"Does this man know you were once Amish?" Eli frowned and watched her reaction.

Faith pinched the bridge of her nose. "I don't know. Both my husband and sister-in-law knew about my past. It's possible they might have mentioned it to Vincent."

They rode in silence for the time being while Eli thought about what she'd said. The ways of the *Eng-*

lisch world were beyond his understanding, and he was glad of it.

The community shops appeared in front of them. Eli eased the buggy toward the back and into the woods there.

"Best not to take any chances," he said when Faith looked his way. "He could be anywhere around the community. I wouldn't put it past him to try to get information from the shop owners." Sarah was at the foremost in his thoughts. Was she safe? The sooner they reached her house the better he'd feel.

"How long have you lived near my grandmother?" Faith asked as if she were searching for something to take her mind off what was happening. The question surprised him. A look her way indicated she was watching him. He knew so little about her life beyond what she'd told him. Sarah hadn't mentioned her granddaughter. Did Faith know about his ugly past?

Don't go back there...

He forced himself to answer. "About a month. I lived in Libby before I moved back to West Kootenai, and now I live in your former home."

"I didn't realize you'd left the community," she said in a halting voice. "I remember your family well. You had lots of brothers, but Mason was the one you were closest to, right? You two were always together."

He flinched as if she'd struck him. She had no idea the pain her words brought forth. Not a second went by that he didn't remember the things he'd lost because of love. The guilt he carried. Because of him, his brother had walked away from their faith. If it hadn't been for him, Mason would still be Amish. If it hadn't been for him, Miriam would still be alive. And if he failed Faith now, she might end up dead just like Miriam.

Chapter Three

Growing up, she'd been a child of the light. Terrified of the darkness because it held so many secrets. Bad things she couldn't see.

Her *mamm* had always been there to comfort her. She'd done her best to make sure her daughter knew there was nothing to be afraid of, yet Faith had struggled with the fear long into adulthood, and she had no idea why.

She stared out the kitchen window as dark clouds hung low around the farm, turning the midday to twilight. Despite that she'd seen no sign of Vincent since she and Eli left the creek, letting herself relax was impossible.

Every little sound sent her jumping. Vincent was still out there somewhere. Twice he'd seen her with Eli. He must know she was hiding somewhere in the Amish community.

"What do you see out there, child?" Faith jerked at the sound of her grandmother's voice. They'd been clearing away the dishes after the midday meal, yet throughout the simple chore, Faith's attention had remained on the darkness outside.

"Nothing. I'm just…" She didn't finish. Wasn't sure what she was about to say. Instead, she squeezed her grandmother's arm and carried the plates she held in her hands to the sink.

Grandmother Sarah took them from her. "Eli will help figure this out. You can trust him. He's a *gut* man."

Faith could see how much her grandmother adored Eli, but he couldn't stop a monster from stalking her. Could anyone?

"You two have really gotten close, haven't you?" She tried not to let the dark thoughts take over. She was safe here. Vincent didn't know where she was.

Grandmother Sarah's face brightened. "*Jah*, we have. He reminds me a lot of your *daed* before…" She didn't have to finish. Faith understood. Her mother tried to protect Faith from her father's dark moods as a child. And then that summer had happened. The argument between her father and *Grossdaddi* had been terrifying for a little girl to witness. The next thing Faith knew, she and her mother were being forced to leave the only way of life they'd ever known.

After she left home and moved to New York, her parents had died in a car accident. The police who investigated the accident believed excessive speed was the cause. Had her father's anger been out of control, costing both him and his wife their lives?

Eli stepped into the kitchen, capturing Faith's attention. He wore his hat and coat. "I'm going to feed the animals in the barn," he told her grandmother and then shifted his gaze to Faith. "Will you come with me? I could use an extra hand with the chores." Though he smiled, she knew the real reason. Eli didn't want her to be out of his sight for a minute.

Grandmother Sarah squeezed her close. "Go with him, *boppli*. I have some quilting to work on. I promised Eva Klimer I'd finish the quilt before her daughter gives birth soon."

Still, Faith hated leaving her grandmother with Vincent lurking around the community. Hurting her grandmother would mean nothing to him.

"You could come with us?" Faith asked.

Her grandmother shook her head. "I will be fine, and I have work to do."

The barn wasn't that far from the house, and they wouldn't be gone for long. "Alright but come lock the door behind us." Faith double-checked the back door to make sure it was still locked.

"*Jah*, I will." Grandmother Sarah held her hand as they walked to the door together. She took down her warmest cloak from the peg by the door and wrapped it around Faith's shoulders. "Use this one. It's getting colder."

The familiar scent of her grandmother clung to the garment. Faith drew in a deep breath, found comfort in the familiar and stepped outside with Eli.

Grandmother Sarah's smile was the last thing she saw before the door closed. The lock slid into place. And the nightmare she faced hit her head-on.

"There's been no sign of him," Eli assured her as if he'd sensed the necessity.

She nodded and stepped from the porch beside him. They walked toward her grandparents' old barn.

Eli removed the board holding the doors together and opened them. So many good memories waited for her inside these four walls. It was here that she'd learned how to ride. Helped her *grossdaddi* milk the cow.

Faith waited just inside the door while Eli struck a match to the lantern and the barn was illuminated. The light caused some of her fears to flee.

The cow was stabled here along with her grandmother's old mare.

"How's she really doing?" She swung toward Eli and asked.

He'd taken the milking stool down in preparation. His expression softened. "Most days she is *gut*. The cold is hard, though. She tells me her arthritis gets worse every year. I can tell she's happy you're back."

What he said broke her heart. "I didn't know. My father told me my grandparents were dead." She shook her head with regret. "I shouldn't have believed him. He was so angry with *grossdaddi*."

Eli's jaw tightened. "That's a horrible thing to do to a *kinna*."

"It was. I will never understand why my father did the things he did," she said with a sigh. "Or why he hated this way of life so much."

Eli didn't understand either. "When did you realize your *grossmammi* was still alive?"

"Not too long ago. I contacted my grandmother's

friend, Mrs. Stoltzfus at the bakery, and found out the truth."

"I'm sorry," he said. The sympathy in his eyes almost brought her to tears. "But you are here now and your *grossmammi* is happy to have you home."

Faith turned away. Was she home? Did she dare let herself return to the place she longed for the most? She'd already brought something dreadful to this peaceful community. How many more innocent people would have to suffer because Vincent had followed her to West Kootenai?

She pulled in an unsteady breath and let that worry go for the moment. *Don't take on tomorrow's troubles before their time,* her grandmother used to say.

Though it had been years since Faith had performed farm chores, she scooped a bucket of oats and carried them to the mare her grandmother spoke about in her letters.

"How are you today, Jenny?" The mare knickered her thanks, and Faith stroked her muzzle before bringing over some water that Eli had pumped from the well earlier.

Once she'd finished, Faith continued to pet the mare while watching Eli as he milked. He'd tipped his hat back on his strong forehead, his full attention on the task at hand, and he was unaware of her.

As a little girl of ten, she'd thought Eli was the most handsome man alive, except for her grandfather. And he still was. Eli was a good man who had gone out of his way to help her when she had no one else to turn to. Spending time with him again made her wonder what her life would have been like if she'd stayed. Perhaps she and Eli would have married.

At one time, she'd thought herself blessed beyond everything to have found someone like her husband. But if Blake had been able to fool her so easily, how could she ever trust another man with her heart?

Eli looked up and found her watching him. She turned away, paid extra attention to the mare and tried to calm her chaotic pulse.

Once the milking was finished, Eli carried the pail to the door.

With a final pat for Jenny, Faith stepped out into the chilly afternoon.

"I fed the chickens and gathered the eggs earlier," Eli told her. "If you're ready, we can go back to the house."

He shut the barn back up and lifted the pail. He started for the house with Faith beside him. They'd covered only a few feet when something captured her attention and she froze. The noise of an engine disturbed the peace and quiet of the countryside. The vehicle wasn't just passing by on the nearby road. It had turned onto the path leading past her grandmother's house. It was coming their way. Even before she had a visual of the vehicle, she knew. Vincent was here.

Eli dropped the bucket of milk and grabbed Faith's arm. "We've got to get out of sight before he reaches the road out front." He tugged her along beside him to the shelter of some trees while all sorts of dreadful thoughts flew through his mind. If this was Vincent, none of them was safe here any longer.

His heart drummed a frantic rhythm as the vehicle crept along the road. No one drove that slowly deliberately.

From his hiding spot, Eli could tell the truck was Vincent's. Did he know this was Faith's grandmother's property, or was he checking all the roads around in the community for them?

The truck eased past Sarah's home and continued until it was even with the place where he and Faith were hiding.

"He's stopping," Faith murmured, her tone heavy with fear.

Eli inched away from the tree in time to see the truck stop. He couldn't tell what Vincent was doing inside, but the man was armed and extremely dangerous, and they were out in the open and vulnerable.

Seconds ticked by while Eli kept his attention on the truck. Suddenly, the driver's door opened, and Vincent jumped out. Eli ducked back behind the tree when Vincent started through the woods and onto Sarah's property. Eli guessed for someone who had killed, trespassing meant nothing.

Faith inched nearer. Alarm in her eyes. Eli slipped his arm around her waist and tugged her close.

The noise of Vincent moving through the underbrush warred with Eli's panicked breathing.

Please, Gott, help us.

Footsteps halted near their hiding spot. Labored breaths appeared to come from just a few feet away.

Vincent entered Eli's line of sight. It was only a matter of time before they were spotted.

Eli handed Faith the shotgun and pushed her out of sight. The noise grabbed Vincent's attention. Before Eli had time to pull in a breath, Vincent had his gun drawn and pointed at him.

With his pulse skyrocketing, Eli tried not to show fear though plenty ran through his body.

"This is private property, and you are not welcome here. I want you to leave. Now." He moved closer to Vincent and away from Faith.

The man didn't react to the request. He kept the weapon on Eli. "I know you. You're the one who was with her before." Vincent looked him up and down. "Where is she?"

Eli stood his ground. "She left and you have no right to be here. You're trespassing."

Vincent didn't budge. "I know she didn't leave because she has no means to. She's somewhere in this community, and you know where." The words seethed from Vincent's lips as he stepped closer. "Is this your house? I've been going house to house, but no one seems to know anything about Faith being here. I'm guessing that's because you've been hiding her." He moved toward where Faith hid.

Eli blocked his path. "There's no one here other than me and my elderly neighbor."

Vincent eyed him suspiciously. "I don't believe you. You're protecting her. She's in the house."

"I told you there's no one inside the house except for my neighbor. It's time for you to go."

Vincent lowered his gun a fraction and released an angry breath. "Look, I know you people are peaceful and don't like violence, so if you want to keep it that way, stay out of this. I'll get her and leave." He paused with a nasty look on his face. "I'd hate for something bad to happen to you because you stuck your nose where it didn't belong."

Before Eli could respond, the tiniest of sounds came from close by.

Vincent swung that direction. "What was that?" His gaze drilled into Eli, who fought to keep a blank expression.

"I don't know what you're talking about. I didn't hear anything."

Vincent started toward the tree. Eli couldn't let him get to Faith. Acting on instinct alone, he dove for the man and tackled Vincent before he reached the tree.

"Run!" Eli yelled and wrestled for control of Vincent's weapon. The man slugged him hard, sending Eli's head snapping sideways.

"Stop right there." Faith stepped from behind the tree with the shotgun pointed.

Vincent swung toward her. Momentarily distracted, Eli grabbed for his weapon and managed to pry it free from Vincent's hand.

Eli scrambled to his feet and hurried over to Faith while keeping the handgun trained on Vincent.

"On your feet," he ordered.

The man rose and raised his hands. "Alright. There's no need to get testy. I'll leave." Vincent tossed Faith a nasty look. "But this isn't over. I'll be back for you." With that parting threat, he turned on his heel and started walking to the truck.

Eli didn't lower the weapon until Vincent reached the vehicle. With a final angry glance, Vincent climbed into the truck and eased it around.

All Eli could think about was that the man who had tried to kill both of them now knew where they were staying. He didn't trust Vincent one little bit. He'd park the truck out of sight and wait. Give them a false sense of security. They had to escape before Vincent returned to finish the job. When he did, he'd take them all out, because he couldn't afford to leave any witnesses behind to tell of his deadly acts.

Chapter Four

"I can't believe that just happened." Faith's hands were shaking. She couldn't believe Vincent had been just a few feet away.

"He'll come back. We can't stay here," Eli told her.

She had no doubt. She'd been so certain Vincent would kill Eli.

Eli tucked the handgun into his jacket pocket and took the shotgun from her. "We can go to my home. It's hidden from the path that runs in front of Sarah's place. If you aren't looking for it, you wouldn't know a house was there."

His home had once been hers. So many good memories were made there. And just as many bad ones.

Together they started for the house at a fast pace. Faith climbed onto the porch steps and called out to her grandmother. "It's us. Open the door." Even with Eli close, she felt exposed. Her eyes grazed the gloomy afternoon. The truck's engine sounded close.

"I can't tell if he's sitting still or moving," Eli said.

Faith looked up at the persistent storm clouds that had turned the day cold. Though there was no sign of Vincent or the truck in her limited line of sight, she couldn't help but believe time was running out.

Eli leaned past her and knocked again while her thoughts chased over themselves.

Her grandmother's slow footsteps headed toward them. Locks slid open. Grandmother Sarah opened the door, her worried gaze jerking between them. *"Was iss letz?"* She stepped aside to let them pass. As soon as Eli crossed the threshold, he closed the door and locked it.

"He's been here." The words rushed out and Faith grabbed a breath before continuing. "The man who forced me off the bridge was here on your property just now. He threatened to search the house. If Eli hadn't stopped him, he would have. We must leave, Grandmother. It's not safe for us to stay here under the circumstances."

Her grandmother's eyes grew large as she struggled to comprehend what her Faith told her. "But this is my home." She didn't understand there was no longer an option.

Faith clasped her hands and her grandmother focused on her. "If we stay, he will come back. He could kill all of us."

Grandmother Sarah flinched at those disturbing words. A gentle woman who had never met a bad man could not understand the depth of evil in Vincent's heart.

Eli hurried over to the window and looked out. "I don't see him yet." He turned from the window. "Quickly, Sarah. Pack some of your things. You and Faith will stay at my house until it is safe to come back."

Grandmother Sarah shook her head. "But Eli, my *mann* built this home before we wed. How can I leave it?"

Faith understood the reasons why her grandmother didn't wish to go. She couldn't imagine how difficult it would be to leave the one place you'd called home since you were but a young woman.

"It won't be forever. Just until we know it's safe to return. Come with me and I'll help you gather your things." Faith clutched her hand and tugged her toward the bedroom she'd shared with her husband.

Grandmother Sarah moved as if she were in a trance. "I can't believe this is happening. Why is this man doing such things?"

Explaining Vincent's actions was impossible. "He's a bad man without a conscience."

Faith pulled the weathered suitcase that had been in the family since Grandmother Sarah was young out from under the bed. Placing it on the bed, she walked to the pegs where Sarah's dresses hung, gathered them and placed the dresses inside.

Grandmother Sarah rose and placed her arm around Faith's waist. The strength in her touch surprising. "I am so sorry you have to go through this, my *boppli*, but with Eli's help, we will all be safe again."

If only it were that simple. But without the drive, she had no proof of Vincent's crimes. And while she believed he was not telling the truth about manipulating the evidence to make her appear guilty of killing his wife, he was quite capable of swaying his fellow law enforcement agents into believing his story. Vincent was setting the trap. He'd make the claim he had no choice but to kill her.

"We should hurry. He's probably watching the house now. We can slip out the back."

Grandmother Sarah nodded. "I am ready. Let's get Eli."

Faith grabbed the suitcase, and she and her grandmother returned to the living room where Eli still stood near the window keeping careful watch. He turned as they approached.

"Is there any sign of him?" Faith set down the suitcase and stepped to the window. The storm that had threatened most of the day was releasing snow and ice on the countryside.

"*Nay*, but we should get out of here while we still can."

As Eli lifted the suitcase and started toward the back of the house, a truck eased onto her grandmother's drive.

"Oh, no."

Eli jerked toward her, his brow deep with furrows. "What's wrong?" He hurried back to her side.

She pointed out the window. "He's here." Vincent's truck headed straight for the house.

"Hurry." Eli gathered Grandmother Sarah close and headed to the back door. "Be as quiet as you can," he told them. "Head for the woods bordering our two properties."

Faith slipped out the back door with her grandmother. Eli clicked the lock on the doorknob, closed the door and followed them.

At the front of the house, the truck stopped. Seconds passed and a vehicle door slammed shut. Faith's worried gaze flew to Eli's. There wouldn't be time to reach the woods.

"The equipment building off to the right. It's been years since it's been used. We can go in through the side door. The building is in bad shape. Maybe he won't look at it too closely," Eli whispered.

The building he spoke of had been one big playground for Faith as a child. She'd climb on the tractor and pretend to drive it. When she got a little older, her grandfather let her steer while he worked. It was a defining moment for a little girl.

With her grandmother's hand tucked in hers, they crossed the yard to the building where *Grossdaddi*'s old farming equipment was still stored.

A noise came from the front of the house. It sounded as if the front door had been forced open. Had Vincent broken into the house? Faith shouldn't have been surprised Vincent hadn't thought twice about breaking into the home. The man had killed two people that she knew of.

Once Vincent reached the back of the house, he'd be able to see them through the windows. They had to get out of sight quickly.

She and Eli pushed and shoved to budge the door. It squeaked in protest as it opened, and Faith was terrified Vincent would hear.

Eli closed the door after them. An unnerving silence permeated the building. Were they sitting ducks? The only working entrance into the building was the door they'd forced open. The large double-doors that grand-father used to drive the tractor through had fallen in on themselves long ago. Someone had attempted to patch them but had given up and boarded them. There would be no escaping that way.

The tractor sat rusting to the ground. Several farm implements were in worse shape. The Amish helped those in need around the community. She had no doubt Eli would do everything he could for Grandmother, but Eli hadn't been home for long. How had her grand-mother gotten by before?

A tingle of apprehension shot between Faith's shoul-ders. She was trapped inside a nightmare that kept get-ting worse.

Faith scrambled over to where Eli stood. This side of the building faced the back of the house.

"I can't see what's going on inside the house." Eli peered through some of the gaping boards in the wall. She did the same. Nothing moved near the back win-dows. What was Vincent doing in there?

The state of the decaying building broke her heart. Several boards were loose. Snow had piled up inside. Multiple gaping holes in the roof above where the trac-tor sat covered in snow left the machine open to the elements.

"I see him." Eli's whispered words brought her atten-tion back to the house in time to see the back door fly open and slam against the wall, bouncing off it several times. The rage on Vincent's face sent Faith scrambling backward. She'd seen that look before. When he'd killed his wife. Tried to shoot her at the creek. It served as a deadly reminder of Vincent St. Clair was capable of.

He huffed out several breaths that fogged the misty air in front of him. Vincent reminded her of a rampaging bull as he stormed down the steps and looked around the property with a wild expression on his face.

For one brief second, he stared straight at the building where they hid. Faith clasped her hand over her mouth to keep from making a sound.

Vincent's attention shifted to the chicken coop. He stomped across the yard with a purposeful gate and threw open the door. Chickens squawked as he entered their domain. Several flew from the coop and landed across the yard like a small invasion.

"My chickens," Grandmother Sarah whispered. She'd told Faith all about her laying hens in her letters. She spoke of each bird as a friend.

Faith hugged her grandmother close and watched Vincent swat at chickens as he stormed from the coop huffing and puffing his anger.

The barn was the next one in his path of rage.

It was only a matter of time before he came here. "Do you think we have time to get to the woods once he enters the barn?" Faith asked Eli while keeping her focus on the man moving toward them one building at a time. It was like watching a horror show. Vincent entered the barn with complete disregard for the animals inside.

Before Eli answered, Vincent appeared in the open door again. His fury grew with each failure. He left the barn doors wide open.

"The animals." Grandmother Sarah's tender heart was focused on the creatures in the barn.

"It will be okay." But Faith wasn't sure she believed it. Vincent had everything to lose, and she stood between him and freedom. He'd do whatever was necessary to end her existence and anyone else's who got in his way.

"He disappeared around behind the barn," Eli said with a doubtful tone.

She had a feeling she knew. "He's checking the woods to see if we went that way."

"It won't take him long before he comes this way." Eli glanced around the inside. On the opposite wall, several boards had worked their way loose and were barely hanging by a few nails. Eli pointed to them. "Over there."

They headed for the boards when the sound of footsteps tromping their way froze Faith in her tracks. She claimed Eli's gaze. "He's coming."

The truth had just cleared her lips when Vincent confirmed their worst fears. "I know you're in there. Did you really think you could hide from me?" He laughed. Chills ran up her arms. "You should have stayed in New York. Kept your mouth shut. Now I have to take care of you." Vincent's frightening voice appeared right outside the door they'd entered. "You and those innocent people with you will have to die."

Grandmother Sarah clutched Faith's arm when the sound of something being moved replaced the silence.

Peering through the boards, Faith was horrified at what happened. Vincent muscled one of the old farming implements from the side of the building to the front of the door. He wanted to make sure they weren't able to escape that way. What did he have planned? The question still chased through her head when Vincent headed to the back porch and grabbed something.

"Oh, no," Eli said. He pointed to the can in Vincent's hand. "That's gas. He's going to burn the building down with us in it."

The depth of wickedness in this man's heart was beyond Eli's comprehension. He couldn't move as the scene unfolded before his eyes with deadly intent. Vincent tossed gas around the outside wall where he stood. Eli had glimpsed the barrel of a handgun holstered under his jacket.

"Where did he get that second gun?" Eli whispered in amazement. He couldn't believe Vincent had found another weapon.

"He's a cop," Faith reminded him. "He probably has several backups in the truck."

Powerless to do anything, Eli watched Vincent strike the match. The structure would go up like a tinderbox of dried Montana wood. They'd have only a matter of minutes to get out with their lives.

Eli pulled Faith and Sarah close as Vincent's silhouette moved around the building, visible through the gaping holes.

Whoosh! The sound left nothing to his imagination. The fire took life, crawling up the exterior wall on the opposite side from the loose boards. If they didn't act quickly, their exit path would soon be engulfed.

The acrid scent of smoke poured into the building.

Eli squinted through the fog and located where Vincent stood watching with a satisfied smile on his face.

"We have to go now." Eli grabbed Sarah's hand and tried not to think about the images of his sweet Miriam desperately searching for a way out of the blazing inferno.

Sarah clutched his jacket, and he wished he could spare her this anxiety, but he wasn't about to let her or anyone else die here in this building because of a bad man.

They reached the wall where the boards were the loosest. "He's still up front. With all the noise of the fire and the smoke, we should be able to get out without him seeing us. Run for the cover of the woods. Sarah, take off your cloak and wrap over your head and shoulders for protection. Don't think about what you're doing. Just go."

Sarah's frightened eyes clung to his. "It will be *oke*," he assured her. "Go, Sarah."

Hunched over, Sarah slipped through the opening and ran. Eli watched until she was safely in the woods. But the fire was intensifying. He turned to Faith. "Go. Quickly. I'll be right behind you." The flames were spreading rapidly across the decaying roof.

Faith hesitated only a second before following her grandmother's path through the opening. The blaze continued to burn red hot as it slithered down the wall toward the missing boards and the only means of escape. Once she cleared the building, Faith ran after her grandmother.

It was his turn now. Eli glanced over his shoulder. It wouldn't be long before the walls collapsed. The roof had already begun to cave in on itself.

Eli tucked the shotgun inside his jacket and started through the hole in the wall. Flames singed the hair on his hands. The heat was intense, and he held a deadly weapon in his hand. If the flames reached the shotgun shells and handgun in his pocket or in the gun tucked under his jacket, it could have deadly results.

Though it took only a couple of seconds to get through the space, with flames licking all around him, it felt like an eternity. His jacket caught fire in several places. Eli slapped at the flames with his hat while thankful that the noise of the fire's roar helped drown the sound of his movements.

He clamped the hat back on his head and headed toward the spot where he'd seen Faith and Sarah disappear. By now, the blaze made it hard to see anything. His eyes streamed from the smoke.

The roaring fire became like a living beast calling for vengeance. Gobbling up everything in its path. A chilling sight and one that had roots in Eli's past.

He'd only seen the aftermath of the fire in Libby that took his *fraa*'s life. Now he'd experienced firsthand the horror involved, and it was a struggle to hold it together when he thought about what Miriam had gone through. It somewhat comforted him to know that Miriam had died from smoke inhalation long before the fire claimed the house.

Eli shoved aside those heartbreaking memories and

ran for the woods. He kept a careful watch over his shoulder, expecting Vincent to materialize behind him.

Once Eli reached the trees, he pulled in several needed breaths and coughed the toxic smoke from his lungs.

"You're still on fire," Faith exclaimed and beat out the flames with her uninjured hand.

Eli took off the jacket and threw it on the ground. Once he'd finished stamping out the fire, he clasped Faith's wrist, humbled by her willingness to disregard her own well-being for him.

"Let me have a look." He examined the burns carefully. "They are not too serious." He scooped up a handful of snow and placed it over the burns on her hand. "I have something at my house that will help with the pain."

He'd gotten used to taking care of himself during the past two years. Living a simple life. Choosing not to draw attention. Far different from when he was younger. He'd been ambitious. Desired to do better for his wife and child. He'd wanted to be the man she'd believed him to be. When she'd died, the future—his ambitions—had turned to so many ashes.

Coming on the heels of losing Miriam, it just about destroyed him when the police had told him they had evidence the fire was set deliberately and believed he had done it. They'd searched his property countless times. Had taken him into the station. Questioned him for hours. Insisted he knew more about the fire than what he'd told them.

At the time, the pain he felt at losing his *fraa* was so

intense that he didn't much care what happened physically to him. He couldn't imagine life without Miriam. The days stretched to months. Living in the barn on his property and working as many hours as he could just to shut out the horror of losing his wife and child.

Eli swallowed deeply and realized he still held Faith's wrist in his hands. The confused look on her face assured him she'd been trying to get his attention.

He let her go and faced the terrifying scene behind them. The building was now completely engulfed and had begun to crumble.

Where was Vincent?

"We should keep moving," he said in a low voice. "This man is capable of anything. With all the smoke and flames, we'd never see him in time."

Keeping Faith and Sarah close, he headed through the dense woods at a fast pace. He prayed they would be safe at his home. Though it was some distance from Sarah's place, was it enough?

With the fire burning so intensely, not much would be left inside the structure except smoldering ashes. Would they be enough to satisfy Vincent, or would he search the entire surrounding landscape?

The snowfall hadn't stuck to the ground where the heavily populated trees kept everything including sunlight out. Heat from the fire would melt any accumulation around the outside of the building and vanish any evidence of them getting away.

Through all of his chaotic thoughts, a sound penetrated. An engine.

Eli stopped walking. "Do you hear that? He's leaving." He cocked his head and listened. The truck eased from the property. He couldn't believe it. Vincent had gone to all the trouble of setting the fire to kill them, but he wouldn't wait to be sure they were dead.

Faith stood close by his side, watching the smoke plume up through the trees. "Maybe he's afraid someone from the community will spot the fire and come to put it out."

It made sense. The Amish watched out for each other. But whether or not Vincent knew this didn't matter. Something had spooked him enough to make him fall backward. Eli believed he wouldn't go far. He'd wait for the fire to burn itself out then return to ensure they were dead.

If the wind shifted, the fire might spread to Sarah's home. Eli couldn't allow that to happen.

"I still can't believe he is willing to burn us alive to save himself," Faith said in shocked disbelief. "He has to be stopped."

Eli agreed with her, but the only way would be to find the evidence Faith's husband gathered. Which meant, one way or another, they had to go back to the creek.

"I have to stop the fire from spreading. Why don't you take your grandmother and go to my house?"

Faith searched his face before shaking her head. "It's too much for one person. Let me help you." She turned to her grandmother. "Can you make it to Eli's house alone?"

Sarah's troubled expression didn't ease any, but she nodded. "*Jah.* I can make it."

"Good. Go ahead of us and stay inside. I'll bring your suitcase later." When Sarah hesitated, Faith assured her they would be okay. "Hurry, Grandmother."

With her cloak clutched tightly around her body, Sarah turned and picked her way through the foliage toward Eli's home.

Were he and Faith walking into a trap by trying to put out the fire? Vincent could have parked the truck off somewhere and walked back.

He prayed under his breath for their safety and kept close to Faith in case trouble came.

Eli removed his singed jacket and placed it over Faith's shoulders as they reached the clearing. He couldn't explain it, but that same protective instinct he'd experienced when he and Faith were younger had resurfaced.

"Thank you," she murmured as if the gesture meant the world to her.

He'd protect her with everything he had. No matter what, he wasn't going to let Vincent hurt her again.

With Faith by his side, he stepped into the clearing while the hackles on the back of his neck alerted him to the importance of working quickly. Smoke covered the farm. Even if Vincent were right on top of them, it would be impossible to see him with all the smoke.

The wind shifted the plume away for them. Eli scanned the area near the road. "I don't see his truck." He turned to Faith. "Do you?"

She shook her head. "I don't, but I feel he's close. If that were me, I wouldn't leave."

"I'll draw some water from the well and start fighting the fire. Sarah keeps extra buckets near the back door."

While Faith retrieved the buckets, Eli headed to the well on the other side of the barn where he kept a bucket for drawing the daily water.

At this point, there would be no saving the building, and there was no phone nearby to call the fire department. It would be up to them to prevent the fire from spreading to the house. The barn and chicken coop were some distance away, and the wind had shifted off from being a threat to them.

On his way, Eli herded the chickens into the coop and shut the door.

After he'd secured the barn doors, he lowered the bucket with a splash. He quickly hauled it up and started for the blaze.

Faith met him halfway with four extra buckets.

"Carry only what you can and leave the rest," he told her. The fire burned so hot that it was hard to get close enough, but he did his best and soaked the ground near to the house.

Working together, he and Faith carried buckets of water to the smoldering site.

When Eli dumped the last one onto the soaked remains, he surveyed the scene. "The fire appears to be contained. Let's get out of here before he returns."

As he glanced at the destroyed building, he was grateful the fire hadn't spread. Though the tractor and several farming implements were ruined, the cost could have been far worse with their lives. He'd help Sarah clean up the mess once this man was no longer a threat.

Once they reached the place where they'd left Sarah's suitcase, Eli picked it up. He went over everything in his head and still couldn't believe the man's ruthlessness. He voiced his thoughts aloud.

"He stands to lose his freedom if not his life," Faith said with a sigh. "I have no doubt the man he and Blake worked for will be furious when he realizes his drug empire is being threatened." Nothing she said eased Eli's worries. "Vincent's probably waiting until dark to come back. He'll search every square inch of the place looking for proof that we're dead."

"After getting a taste of what Vincent is like, I can't imagine the level of violence the man he works for is capable of." Eli found it hard to believe someone in law enforcement would allow their convictions to be compromised in such a way. All for money.

She and Eli continued to move through the overgrowth.

"Blake told me about such men, but I had no idea he worked for one." She shook her head. "These men pump drugs into the city at an alarming rate, and they take out any competition standing in their way."

Faith kept her attention ahead of them. "At the time, I didn't have any idea what Blake was up to, but now—looking back through different eyes—there were signs. I guess at the time I didn't want to see them."

Being a trusting person had its downside. Eli couldn't imagine the betrayal she'd experienced by someone she loved.

"I should have seen the truth." She lifted her shoulders. "All the expensive gadgets Blake would come home with. The gifts he bought me. All of it was far more than we could afford on our salaries. Blake told me he'd worked overtime to pay for everything, but he never really did. In the beginning, I worked the night shift at the hospital, so I had no way of knowing when he got home at night." She grew quiet for a time.

"When did you realize he wasn't working overtime?" Eli found himself curious about her marriage to this man. She'd loved him dearly.

"A few years after we bought the house, I started working regular hours. Blake was always home before me. Usually doing something in his office. I walked in on him one time, and he appeared nervous. When I came into the room, he shut the desk drawer as if he didn't want me to see what was inside." She shook her head. "But I was so naive. I trusted Blake. Once he passed away, I found out he'd paid the house off within the first year."

Eli shot her a look. "From dirty money?"

She nodded. "Yes. After I read his note, I knew I had to get out of that house. I was literally living in a crime scene." She glanced over her shoulder. "What Vincent did back there is nothing compared to what the man he works for will do to him if he doesn't take care of the threat I pose."

Eli struggled to understand how such men existed. "We should be safe enough at my place. The house itself is hidden from view of the road by the mountain. If you didn't know it was there you would miss it." He stopped when he realized he wasn't telling her anything she didn't know. His house had once been her home.

Most people outside the community didn't realize another house past Sarah's property existed. The road leading to it was little more than a path. Eli had enough room to get his wagon in and out, but he was grateful for the seclusion.

He hoped Vincent wouldn't think to look that closely at the mountain because if he came that way, they'd be blocked by a sheer wall of stone.

He'd known Vincent was dangerous after the bridge incident, but the seriousness of the situation had been driven home to him with deadly accuracy upon their fiery attack at Sarah's.

With that much rage inside Vincent, how could Eli and Sarah stop him? Somehow, Eli had to find a way to convince Faith to speak with the sheriff. Though he understood her concerns, they'd need someone from law enforcement to help them bring down Vincent, and they couldn't do it without the information on the drive.

If they didn't find it, would Faith end up going to prison for a murder she didn't commit? Or worse... die at the hands of a man who had once been part of her family?

Chapter Five

Glimpses of the mountain jutted upward through the tall pines. They were almost to her former home. Though she couldn't see it, the familiar outcropping of rocks that hid the small farmhouse from view was there, along with an overflowing of memories. Both good and bad.

The woods she and Eli had traversed had been her and *Grossdaddi*'s playground. So many adventures had taken place here. *Grossdaddi* would explain about the different plants that grew in the forest. Many had medicinal powers.

All those years she'd lost with him and her grandmother for believing they were dead.

Forgiveness isn't for the guilty. It's for the wronged... Her grandmother's words came to mind.

For a long time, she'd resented her father for taking her from them, and it had almost destroyed her. After her parents' car accident, she'd struggled to forgive him. Maybe it was about time to let go of the past.

The rocks that concealed the homestead from anyone wandering through the woods came into view. As a child, she'd spend hours climbing them. Finding joy in the simple things. Living the Plain life to its fullest.

The past was all around her, pulling her back to that little girl she'd once been. She stopped walking. Things she hadn't thought about in years resurfaced from the place where she'd imprisoned them. No matter how hard she tried, she'd never understand why her father chose to walk away from this way of life.

Eli turned back to her with a frown on his face. "Did you hear something?"

She pulled in a shaky breath and fought against the resentment that had encased her heart for too long.

Let it go... Let God have it.

"No, nothing." She glanced over her shoulder before catching up with him.

Clearing the rocks, she watched the old homestead come into view. It was like going back in time. Little had changed through the years.

"That is a welcome sight," Eli said beside her. "I pray we will be safe here."

Grandmother Sarah must have been watching. As soon as they neared the house, she came out to them.

"Is everything *oke* at the house?" She looked between them.

Eli patted her arm. "*Jah*, everything is *oke*. The house is safe. Faith and I put out the fire. It shouldn't spread." He kept his arm around the elderly woman's shoulders as they returned to the house.

Eli placed the suitcase on the floor near the door and locked it before he closed the curtains.

"Is he gone?" Grandmother Sarah's worried eyes clamped on to Faith's.

She couldn't lie to her grandmother. "For now."

"But he will come back?"

Eli met Faith's gaze across the room. Saw her struggle to find an answer for her relative.

"We should be safe here. The house is hidden, and I will keep a careful watch. If he comes near the place, we'll know."

Sarah smiled at him. "You are right. We have you to protect us."

Faith hated putting such a burden on Eli. It wasn't fair. But she needed his help more than ever.

He patted Grandmother Sarah's arm but retained his attention on Faith. "We will be *oke*."

She smiled at the reminder of the strong young boy who'd looked after her as a child. Eli's protective instincts ran deep.

As they continued to watch each other across the space, something shifted in his eyes, and he cleared his throat and looked away. "It's cold in here. Let me get some wood from the shed and start the fire, then I'll take a look at your hand." He disappeared into the living room. Soon, a door opened and closed.

Faith glanced around her former family kitchen. Not much had changed through the years, though the place was showing signs of age. All her family's old furniture was where they'd left it. She stood near the table that her grandfather had given her mother as a wedding present and smoothed her hand across the surface. Nicks in the wood where the family had shared countless meals were still right here.

The good moments she'd shared here with her father returned. She'd almost forgotten about them. The way he made her mother laugh. And her. The times she'd walk into a room and find them hugging.

Once when she'd been about four or five and had woken to a thunderous clap outside her window. Terrified, Faith had run to her parents' room. Her dad had scooped her into his arms and held her until the storm passed.

She'd been so angry with him for leaving West Kootenai that she'd deliberately hidden the good times they'd shared.

"I miss them both," Grandmother Sarah whispered with a reminiscent look on her face.

She hugged this sweet woman. "Me too. Even though it's been years since the car accident, at times I still can't believe they're gone." She looked around the kitchen. "I loved living here so much. I'd almost forgotten how much until now."

Grandmother Sarah nodded with a sad smile on her face. "We have both lost so much. First, your grandfather, then your *daed* and *mamm*. Too much has been lost. We can't let this man take anything else from us."

"No, we can't," she said. Faith would do everything in her power to keep that from happening. She'd brought this nightmare to her grandmother, but she couldn't let Vincent hurt anyone else in her family. She wouldn't.

Eli came back inside and dumped wood on the floor.

Seconds later he appeared in the kitchen doorway. Both women turned. When Faith looked at his face, she knew something was wrong.

"He found us," Faith said in a strangled voice.

Eli's troubled eyes met hers. "I believe so. After I gathered the wood, I looked around and spotted him walking through the woods past the road. I don't think he noticed me, but if he keeps coming this way, eventually he will spot the house."

Faith pulled her grandmother close. "What do we do?"

"Help me secure the doors in case he decides to break in like he did at Sarah's place. We should close the curtains, as well. Sarah, extinguish that lantern. If he thinks no one is home, perhaps he will leave."

Faith rushed to the sink and slid the curtains shut while Eli shoved a kitchen chair underneath the doorknob to secure it. Faith helped him heave the heavy wooden bookcase in front of the living room door. If Vincent broke down the door, the bookcase would at least slow him down. After she finished closing the rest of the curtains, Faith and Eli returned to the kitchen and waited.

The silence of the fading day was soon broken when someone stepped up on the front porch. Grandmother Sarah reached for Faith's arm and held it tightly.

A shadow moved across the porch to the door. Rattled it hard enough to shake the door on its hinges. Porch boards squeaked under the weight. A shadow appeared near the drawn curtains over the sink as if Vincent was trying to look inside.

Silence stretched on for a long period. The shadow appeared near the back door. Faith's nerves strung tighter when someone yanked on the doorknob several more times.

Grandmother Sarah's fearful eyes watched the door. Everyone in the room remained quiet. No one dared move. Soon footsteps left the porch and Faith breathed out a huge sigh and prayed Vincent had believed the place was empty.

Still, the reprieve would only be temporary. Vincent would search the rest of the property—every square inch of it—until he'd found her.

Should they take this chance to escape or wait it out? The ruthless way Vincent had burned the structure to the ground knowing they were inside kept playing through Eli's head.

He had no idea how much time had passed but it seemed like forever. His mind raced about what to do next. They couldn't stay hidden inside the house like this forever.

"I'm going to check outside," he told Faith at last. "Stay here with your grandmother."

He started to leave the room, but she caught his arm. "Eli, no. It's too dangerous. He knows you."

The worry on her face was for Eli alone and so undeserved by him. While he wished to reassure her everything would be alright, he wasn't anywhere close to believing it for himself.

"Stay here with Sarah," he said and untangled her hand from his arm. "I'll be right *oke*."

Faith handed him his jacket, and Eli moved to the living room and inched the curtains apart. Nothing out of the ordinary appeared as far as he could see. But Vincent was out there somewhere.

Eli continued through the rest of the house searching windows. Where had the man gone?

He grabbed the shotgun and removed the chair from beneath the doorknob. Easing the kitchen door open, he slipped outside and listened as the quiet of the place settled around him.

Muddy footsteps covered the porch. Eli flattened himself against the wall and edged toward the side facing the barn. Right away he witnessed a chilling reminder of what happened at Sarah's. The barn door stood wide open. So far, none of the animals were loose. As much as he wanted to rush over and close it, not knowing where Vincent was hiding held him back.

Sticking close to the house, he stopped short when he glimpsed Vincent's truck through the trees. Eli jerked out of sight. Was Vincent inside the truck? While he thought about the best plan to get them out of this dangerous situation, footsteps tromped through the trees between the front of the house and the road.

Eli made sure Vincent wasn't nearby before he moved toward the closest tree. Once he reached it, he steadied his breathing and peeked around the side. A group of lodgepole pines obscured his visual, but he didn't see anyone. Had Vincent slipped past him and headed for the house?

Panic threatened to overtake him. He'd left Faith and Sarah all alone. Eli ran for the house while moving from tree to tree to stay out of sight, his breath pumping from his chest. Mind whirling with all his past failures. He'd failed Miriam. Now those who trusted him were vulnerable.

Faith's face peeked through a sliver in the curtain. She pointed at something behind him. Eli dove for the closest tree.

Crack! A gunshot pierced the silence. He'd been seconds away from dying. If Faith hadn't warned him...

"You thought you could outsmart me?" Vincent huffed breaths.

Eli edged away from the tree in time to see the deadly intent in Vincent's eyes as he prepared to fire again.

Ducking quickly, Eli narrowly avoided the next bullet that lodged near where his head had been seconds earlier. Vincent wasn't letting up, and he'd never make it back to the house like this.

Eli raised the shotgun to fire. Vincent had closed the space between them and was inches away. Eli squeezed the trigger, but Vincent knocked the shotgun barrel away with his hand. The shot flew past Vincent's shoulder as he hit Eli full speed. Both went flying backward onto the ground. Eli lost the weapon in the process.

Vincent grabbed hold of his jacket and slammed his fist into Eli's jaw. His head struck the ground. The rage on Vincent's face was all he saw. Eli shoved Vincent hard enough to get him off, then jumped to his feet and searched for the shotgun that had flown from his hand.

It had landed near one of the trees. Before he had time to grab it, Vincent was standing and aiming the weapon at Eli's head. With no other choice, Eli threw his body at the man and somehow managed to keep his feet beneath him when Vincent slugged him again and tried to get the weapon into a position to shoot.

Eli grabbed for the gun and struggled with all his might to free it while Vincent fought just as hard to kill him.

A noise nearby sounded over the battle raging between them. Vincent's head flew up and he listened. Eli took advantage and shoved hard. Vincent stumbled backward, but his attention was focused on something behind Eli.

Eli whirled in time to see Faith pull the trigger on the shotgun. The bullet seared through Vincent's shoulder. He screamed and grabbed his injured arm.

Before Faith had time to reload, Vincent took off toward the truck at a fast pace.

Stunned, Eli watched the man disappear and couldn't believe what happened.

Vincent had somehow figured out that they weren't dead and had come looking for them. Now he knew where they were hiding. He'd keep coming. And the next time the outcome might be far more deadly.

Chapter Six

"Eli!" Faith ran to his side. "Are you okay?" The side of his reddened face where Vincent had struck him had begun to swell.

"I am, but this man is not giving up." He looked straight at her. "And we are no match for him."

Faith was shaking all over and couldn't help it. She picked up Eli's black felt hat from where it had fallen and dusted it off before handing it to him. Because of her, Eli had almost lost his life. And he was right. Vincent wouldn't let up. He wasn't even trying to pretend any longer that this was about bringing her in for a crime. He was here to kill her and anyone else who might get in the way of his freedom.

She clasped his chin and turned him with a gentle touch to examine his injured cheek. He winced and jerked away.

"I'm so sorry," she said. "I never meant to pull you into my troubles." This wasn't what she wanted. So many people had gotten hurt because of her. First

Cheryl. Now Eli and her grandmother. All because of Vincent's and Blake's crimes.

Eli reached for her wrist and turned her hand up so that he looked at the red burn marks. "You have nothing to be sorry for. Nothing at all. This isn't your fault."

She smiled sadly. "But it is. All of it. And you're right—it's time to speak with the sheriff. There are more lives at stake besides mine. Vincent must be stopped." She heaved a sigh. Every time she thought about Cheryl's murder, it was like a nail drove through her heart.

"We'll do it together. I will go with you. I am told the sheriff is a fair man."

The relief she felt at hearing him say this was priceless. "Thank you, Eli, but I have to try one more time to find the drive."

His expression softened. "Of course." The sincerity in his eyes had been there so many times in the past. Now it tugged her back in time. Awoke feelings that she thought she would never experience again after Blake's betrayal. "We'll take Sarah and go there together."

She shivered and the ticking clock in her head warned their time was almost up. She glanced around the homestead that had once been her family's. "I don't want Grandmother to be part of what's happening any more than she already has been. Is there someplace safe she can stay while we speak with the sheriff?"

Eli didn't hesitate. "There is. My *bruder*'s home is not far from *Mamm*'s. Aaron will help us."

The thought of bringing someone else into this dangerous situation was the last thing she wanted, but what other choice did she have?

"Okay." She slowly pulled her gaze from his. Amid so much danger and uncertainty, something unexpected was happening and she wasn't sure she could trust her instincts again. She'd believed Blake was a good man who would never hurt her.

Faith dragged in several breaths and tried to think beyond her emotions. Her sweet grandmother watched them from the window. Faith couldn't imagine how frightened she must be.

Eli let her go and stepped back, his breathing as unsteady as hers. "The wagon is still at Sarah's, but I have my buggy in the barn and my older mare. She can pull it. I'll get the buggy ready to travel. There is some salve for your burns in the kitchen cabinet. Can you and Sarah treat them?"

With all that had happened, she'd almost forgotten the burns. While they weren't serious, they might slow her down if left untreated.

"Of course," she said, moved by his concern for her after everything he'd gone through.

Eli slowly nodded. "Good. There are extra jackets by the door. One for you and one for Sarah. It's getting colder by the minute. You will need them for warmth. We won't be able to take the road. I have no doubt he'll be waiting for us to make that move. Taking the buggy through the thick trees will be difficult, but Vincent shouldn't be able to get his massive truck in to follow us."

"I'll get Grandmother Sarah, and we'll meet you in the barn soon."

As they continued to watch each other without moving, Faith pulled in an unsteady breath. Lost in his eyes, it was easy to forget the danger facing them. That time was critical.

Eli responded, then started for the barn. She couldn't take her eyes off him. This handsome man was working his way into her heart, and she wasn't ready to let him in. Could she let him in?

Faith turned toward the road. The day was fading and they wouldn't have much time to search for the drive before nightfall.

She hurried up the steps of the porch and the door opened. Grandmother Sarah had been watching for her.

"I saw that man attack Eli." The worry on her grandmother's face was crushing. "If you hadn't fired at him when you did…"

Faith came inside, closed the door and relocked it. "We are both *oke*, but we can't stay here and wait for him to come back." She hurried to the kitchen and found the salve Eli mentioned along with some gauze. She smeared the salve on the burns then waited while her grandmother wrapped it.

"Let's get your suitcase," she said once they were finished. "We're leaving as soon as Eli gets the buggy ready."

Her grandmother picked up the suitcase from where they'd left it earlier.

"Where will we go?" Grandmother asked in a worried tone as they headed toward the front of the house.

Faith handed her one of the jackets and slipped into the second one.

"Eli is taking you to his brother's place while he and I go to speak with the sheriff. You will be safe there." She hoped it proved true.

Faith explained they would be stopping along the way to look for the drive once more.

Outside, a horse snorted. Faith parted the curtains and looked out in time to see him guiding a horse and buggy to the porch.

Somewhere out there, Vincent was lurking. Licking his wounds. Regrouping. Preparing for the next attack.

She had a feeling Vincent would not let a little thing like a gunshot stand in his way.

Faith opened the door and ushered her grandmother down the steps. Eli stowed the suitcase and helped them both into the buggy.

He eased the horse behind the house. "We should be safe enough going through the woods, but we'll have to steer clear of any place where Vincent may be able to ambush us, though."

The weather had continued to grow colder with the lengthening shadows, yet much more than the cold burrowed down into Faith's bones. A fear that wouldn't go away had her watching each passing tree as if she expected Vincent to jump out from behind one.

Faith tugged the jacket closely around her body. The gathering darkness had turned the woods to night.

"I have battery-powered lights on the buggy, but I don't think it's wise to use them. We would be giving away our location."

She was glad Eli was thinking for them. Lack of sleep was inhibiting her from keeping her thoughts together.

The fading daylight wouldn't lend itself to finding the drive, but what choice did she have? She didn't believe Vincent had it yet, but if he managed to find the drive, nothing would stop him from ending her.

Eli covered her hand with his. "If it's still there, we'll do our best to locate it."

She smiled despite the circumstances and took comfort in having him at her side. Eli would do everything in his power to help her bring Vincent to justice. She prayed it would be enough.

As they continued through the silty darkness in the woods, the only sounds were the mare's breathing and Faith's racing pulse drumming against her ears. Letting go of her fears wasn't possible until Vincent was no longer a threat.

In the distance, river sounds overtook the mare's breathing. They were close to the water.

"There it is." Eli nodded up ahead. The mare grew skittish as they neared, and Eli stopped her some distance away.

As much as Faith hated having her grandmother out in the open like this, the river was closer to Grandmother Sarah's house than it was to Aaron's place, which was halfway across the community, according to Eli.

Eli hopped down and tied off the mare while they climbed out.

"Careful. It's slippery." Faith interlocked her arm with Grandmother Sarah's, and they picked their way down the bank.

"I'll search across the creek." Eli pointed to a spot

on the opposite side. "There's a downed tree where I can get across. You and Sarah should stay where I can see you both." Though he didn't say as much, she believed he was thinking about what happened the last time they'd been here.

"We'll start here," she told him. "With the current running this strong, it could be anywhere."

Inches away, Eli held her gaze for a moment, and everything but the man before her disappeared.

She chewed her bottom lip. Why did she feel this connection to Eli? They hadn't seen each other in years. Was it the past and happier times creeping into this moment of vulnerability? Before she could pin the truth into place, Eli started for the tree that had fallen across the creek, and she let go of an unsteady breath.

Her grandmother had witnessed the moment shared between Faith and Eli. What must she be thinking?

"Let's start over there," Faith said without looking at her grandmother. She pointed to the spot where they hadn't searched yet. "The drive is in a plastic ziplock bag. Since Vincent didn't appear to know about the drive, it must have fallen out when my purse opened. Before he found the purse." She glanced around them. "I know it's a long shot, but I need it if I'm going to convince the sheriff I'm telling the truth."

Grandmother Sarah grabbed her arm when Faith would have moved away. She turned toward this sweet lady.

"It will be *oke*, child. *Gott* will not let you suffer for this man's crimes. He sees all. He will keep you safe."

Despite the circumstances, she smiled. Faith had

heard her say that same thing many times while she was growing up. Her grandmother was a woman of strong faith who put her trust in God and refused to let anything, no matter how difficult, shake that foundation.

When the trouble between Faith's father and grandfather reached a breaking point, her grandmother spent many an hour on her knees praying for God to intervene. But that hadn't happened, and everything in their lives had changed.

"*Gott* will hear, child. He answers in His own way. His own time."

Faith wished she shared that same steadfastness, but if life had taught her anything, it was that the only person she could count on was herself.

Darkness descended little by little until there was very little light left to see. There'd been no sign of the drive so far and Eli had a sinking feeling it was lost for good. Every second they were out here like this, there was a chance they would be spotted by Vincent.

He returned to the women. Faith glanced up as he approached.

"We shouldn't stay here any longer. It's too dangerous."

The disappointment on her face was hard to take.

"I know." She scanned the water where the car's roof just broke the surface. "I pray it's at the bottom of the creek. At least there it will be out of Vincent's reach."

Eli held on to Sarah's arm and helped her along the uneven path while Faith kept close. As they neared the spot where he'd left the buggy, he stopped short as a prickling of danger slithered into his stomach.

Seeing through the pitch black was difficult. As his eyes adjusted more to the deeper woods, something caught his attention. The buggy was where they'd left it, but the mare was gone.

Vincent. He'd been here and unharnessed the animal.

"Hurry!" Eli grabbed hold of Faith and Sarah and raced through the woods.

They'd taken only a handful of steps when a terrifying sound drowned out his labored breathing. Rapid gunfire.

"Stay low!" Eli yelled over the noise and didn't let go of their hands.

The road came into view. Silence permeated the woods.

While Eli tried to come up with a way to escape the man coming after them, the quiet evaporated into another round of gunfire. Bullets peppered the trees all around them. One struck Eli's right shoulder. Hot lead and pain drilled a hole through his flesh. He struggled to keep his footing.

"Eli!" Faith screamed when he dropped her hand and grabbed his shoulder.

"Keep going," he said through gritted teeth. If they stopped, they'd die in these woods.

The road opened in front of them. Vincent's truck stood parked off the shoulder.

"Over there." Faith pointed to the truck. "If the keys are in it, we can get use it to get away."

The pain in his shoulder had begun to trickle down his arm. Through his body. He was fading quickly.

Faith wrapped her arm around his waist while her

grandmother did the same, and they helped him to the truck. Behind them, Vincent stormed through the trees at a fast pace.

She opened the driver's door and looked inside. "Nothing." Had she been wrong? She remembered Blake sometimes left his keys above the visor whenever he planned to return to his vehicle soon.

"Can you stand on your own?" Eli managed a semblance of a nod but could see her doubts. "Hold on to him," she told her grandmother. As soon as Faith loosened her grip, he swayed and reached for the truck bed.

While he watched, Faith flipped down the driver's side visor. Still nothing. "The driver's fender," she exclaimed and dipped out of sight.

Seconds passed while he looked behind them expecting Vincent to appear at any moment.

"Thank You, God." Faith held up the key.

With Sarah's help, they got Eli inside the vehicle. He leaned heavily against the closed door. Sarah slipped in beside him and Faith started the vehicle.

"Oh, no," she said when Vincent emerged from the trees behind them.

Faith pressed down on the gas pedal and the truck sped away.

Eli watched the side mirror. Vincent was running after them with the gun waving wildly. "Get down, Sarah." He urged the woman out of sight. Vincent unloaded his weapon into the back of the truck.

Faith never slowed down. The truck swerved on the slick road, and she fought to control it.

Vincent ran after them, shooting until they were out of range.

Faith's attention flew to Eli. "I'm *oke*," he murmured, but the words were jumbled. He didn't even know if they were clear. "We need to get out of sight now."

"You've lost a lot of blood, Eli, but we can't afford to stop until we're away from Vincent's danger." Her sweet voice drifted his way. So full of promises. If only he deserved those promises.

"Grandmother, can you use your prayer *kapp* to put pressure on the wound for now?" Faith's worried gaze blurred before Eli's eyes and he closed them.

"Eli, stay with me." Her voice rose an octave.

"I will." He thought he said it aloud but couldn't be sure.

Sarah applied gentle pressure against his wounded arm, a reminder that there were many people who cared for him. Just as many he'd let down. His family. Mason. His *fraa*. Now Faith and Sarah. He thought he was making the right choice by heading to the creek to search for the drive, but instead, he'd almost cost them all their lives.

"I'm sorry," he murmured. "Sorry, Miriam." His wife's face drifted in his mind. Someone shook him. He opened his eyes and saw the worry etched on Faith's face. All for him. "I let you down," he mumbled.

"No, you didn't. You saved us. And I'm not going to let anything happen to you, so stay with me, Eli. Stay focused on me."

He forced his heavy eyes to remain open and held his attention on her pretty face while wondering how anyone could hurt someone like her. He'd done his best to protect her. He would always try to protect her.

"Which way to Aaron's?" A frown line appeared between her brows. He struggled to stay alert.

Eli rousted himself and looked behind them. Nothing but blackness. "He's not there."

Faith's full attention was on the road ahead. "No, that's right, he's not back there. We have the advantage because we have his vehicle." Her attention went briefly to Sarah, who continued to hold pressure against his arm, and then back to the road.

Eli sucked in a breath, winced and stared out the windshield. "Aaron lives on the other side of the community. To get there, you will need to get off this road. There's a path coming up on your left, past the community shops." He frowned and tried to hold on to his thoughts, but the blood loss was taking its toll. He could feel himself slowing down.

With Vincent still on the loose, they'd be in danger every mile of the long drive to Eagle's Nest and the sheriff's office there. He didn't want to put Sarah through that ordeal after everything she'd gone through so far. She would be safe at Aaron's home and he wouldn't have to worry about her. "It's not very well kept. I'm not sure the truck will make it through."

Faith chewed her bottom lip. "We don't have a choice."

He understood what she meant, but if the truck got stuck, they'd have a long walk ahead of them and he wasn't sure he was up to it.

"There it is." Sarah pointed to the narrow opening barely visible through overgrown trees.

Faith stopped close to the entrance and stared at it with doubts. "We don't have a choice," she repeated to herself and eased the truck into the space.

Potholes formed from recent weather slung the truck all around. Eli slammed against the door and grabbed his shoulder.

Faith slowed to a crawl and glanced his way. "I'm sorry. I'll try not to do that again."

She steered the truck through a series of holes big enough to break a buggy wheel. Eli gripped the bottom of the seat and did his best to keep from being sick. His pulse pounded through his veins and down his wounded shoulder. It hummed a rhythm that seemed to chime, *a long way to go before the nightmare ends*. A long way before they were safe.

Chapter Seven

The truck lurched along the rough road. Faith gripped the wheel with both hands but it was a battle even at the slow speed.

"How much farther?" she asked and glanced over to where Eli had slumped against the door. "Eli!" She braked the vehicle and shook him.

His eyes popped open. He said something she couldn't understand.

Putting the truck in Park, Faith grabbed the gauze she'd stuffed in her jacket and found an old T-shirt. She hopped out and went around to Eli's door. Her grandmother's white prayer *kapp* was now bloodred, but by putting pressure on the wound she had slowed down the blood loss.

"Try to relax, Eli. Help me get his jacket off," she said to her grandmother. With the older woman's assistance, they eased the jacket from Eli's shoulders. He winced from even the smallest of movements.

"I'm sorry—I know it hurts." As a nurse at one of

the busiest hospitals in New York, Faith had seen many gunshot victims, but she'd never witnessed a shooting until she'd watched Cheryl die at the hands of her husband. And now Eli had been shot by this ruthless man.

Once the jacket had been removed, Faith unbuttoned his shirt and moved it away from the wound so she could get a good look at what she was dealing with.

Her fingers felt around the back side of Eli's shoulder until she found a wound where the bullet had exited.

She used part of the gauze to wipe blood away while Eli clamped his lips together. The glazed look in his eyes was one she'd witnessed many times.

All her fault. The truth repeated through her mind, an unwelcome thought.

Faith secured the wound as best she could. With her grandmother's help, she eased his shirt back into place. "That should stop the bleeding for now. We need to keep moving."

Eli reached for her hand before she moved away, saw the bloodstains there. His eyes latched on to hers. She wished things could be different.

"Rest now," she said, then tugged her hand free and stepped back. Pulling in a shaky breath, she closed the door and circled the back of the truck. Her mind went over all the conversations she'd had with Eli, replaying everything that happened between them. He'd been her protector since she was a little girl. Had always been part of her life. Through the years, she'd thought a lot about her life here. Her grandparents. Eli.

Foolish… Her life was in shambles. She was the target of a man who would stop at nothing to silence her. She had to stay focused.

She got behind the wheel without looking Eli's way, put the truck into Drive and eased down the path.

As she fought to keep the truck from bottoming out in places, the missing drive kept popping into her thoughts. If Vincent discovered it, her only play was gone. He would want to tie up all loose ends, which meant he'd have her grandmother and Eli killed along with her. The sooner they had the chance to speak with the sheriff, the better. She just hoped he would believe her.

"If you take the next turnoff coming up, my *bruder*'s home will be down that way." Eli's thread of a voice interrupted her troubled thoughts, and she glanced his way. His eyes were closed. Complexion pale.

The road he spoke of appeared, and Faith turned onto it. After they'd traveled some distance along the relatively smooth path, Grandmother Sarah pointed to another turnoff coming up. "That one runs in front of Aaron's home."

Faith smiled her way while casting a worried look to what appeared to be an unconscious Eli.

"He will be *oke*. Eli is a strong man."

But he hadn't been shot before. She chose not to share that with her grandmother.

With her attention on the road ahead, she couldn't get to Aaron's house quickly enough. Though they'd escaped Vincent tonight, this was far from over. Leaving the truck at Aaron's house wasn't a good idea.

"That's Aaron's home."

Faith's attention went to the house on the left. It was typical of so many other Amish homes. White clapboard siding. A wooden fence separated the property from the road. The house set some distance away.

She didn't remember much about Aaron from their childhoods, but her grandmother had told her Aaron's wife, Irene, had passed away a few years back. He'd recently remarried.

As she slowed enough to turn onto the drive, Eli woke with the rocking movement. He glanced around with confusion in his eyes.

"We're at your brother's house," Faith told him.

As they neared the house, a man stepped out onto the porch holding a lantern high. He clamped his black hat down over dark hair. His resemblance to Eli was clear.

Faith stopped the truck and opened the door. After climbing out, she went around to help Eli from the vehicle. As soon as Aaron saw his injured brother, he hurried down the steps.

"Eli, what has happened?" The concern etched on Aaron's face was clear in the lantern's glow.

Eli did his best to explain.

"Let's get you inside." Aaron grabbed his brother around the waist and helped him inside while Faith and Grandmother Sarah followed.

Once they reached the door, Faith glanced back at the road they'd just traveled. Darkness covered the community. The countryside appeared peaceful, but nothing could be further from the truth. As a cop, Vincent would have a way of using the truck's GPS to find the missing vehicle. He'd be tracking them, but with Eli injured there was no way he could have walked the entire distance to Aaron's house.

Still, they'd have to move the truck quickly and as far away from Aaron's house as possible. Before Vincent found them. Because somewhere out there he waited, plotting his next desperate move.

Eli's shoulder felt much better after Faith's gentle care, but his mind wouldn't let him relax. Even though they were safe for now, and Aaron's wife, Victoria, was a former trained CIA agent, he couldn't get Vincent out of his head. The man appeared unstoppable.

Victoria brought over a cup of *kaffe* to take the chill away.

"Denki." Eli smiled at his sister-in-law. He'd liked her from the moment they met.

Victoria nodded, but he could see there was something troubling her. "I can ride to the phone shanty and reach out to one of my former colleagues." She looked him in the eye. "They will be able to help."

"That may be our next move, but first we try to reach the sheriff."

Aaron spoke highly of Sheriff Collins. Eli believed they could trust the law enforcement officer.

Victoria nodded. "Anything I can do to help." She hesitated and he dreaded what she was about to say. "I hate to be the bearer of more bad news, but if this man has gone to such extremes to find you, then he won't let a little thing like not having a vehicle stop him from continuing to search for you." She glanced from Eli to

Faith. "There's a good chance he may be able to tap into the truck's GPS system. If he does, he'll track it here."

The idea horrified Eli.

"She's right," Faith said with a nod. "We have to move it. I'll take the truck off somewhere and leave it. Someplace far from here so he can't trace it back to you and Aaron."

"I can come with you," Victoria offered, and Aaron clasped his wife's hand.

"Do you forget you are having a baby?" The gentle smile on his *bruder*'s face was all for his wife. "I'll go with Faith."

Aaron's *sohn*, Caleb, rose. "*Daed*, let me." Young Caleb would be starting his *rumspringa* soon enough.

He headed for the shotgun near the door, but Eli stopped him. "I will go with Faith."

Faith rejected the idea immediately. "You're not strong enough. You've been shot, Eli."

He got to his feet and tried not to wobble. "I am fine. If its *oke* with you, *bruder*, I'll take the buggy and follow Faith. That way, we can ride back together."

Aaron readily agreed. "But you should let me come with you for added protection."

Eli appreciated his *bruder*'s desire to help, but he couldn't accept the offer. He shook his head. "*Nay*. Stay here with your family and Sarah."

Aaron agreed. "Alright. Stay here where it's warm. I'll get the buggy ready." He patted Eli's arm and grabbed his coat. With Caleb at his side, Aaron removed the lantern from the peg near the door and headed out into the night.

"Are you sure it is wise for you and Faith to go alone?" Sarah asked Eli.

She was worried, with good reason, and he struggled to reassure her. "The fewer people involved, the better. I'll take Aaron's weapon for added protection. Faith can use my shotgun. We'll be safe enough."

Yet Sarah's worry didn't ease, and Victoria placed her arm around the older woman. "They will be alright."

When he'd come home, Aaron had told him about the nightmare Victoria had gone through when she arrived in West Kootenai. The former CIA agent had been hunted by men who wanted to silence her, much like Vincent did Faith.

The buggy approached the house. Eli eased into his torn jacket and tugged on his hat.

"Take *Daed*'s gun with you, *Onkel* Eli." Caleb handed him the shotgun and a box of shells. Eli smiled at his nephew. He'd gotten to know Caleb while the young man had begun learning the logging part of the family business. He was smart and caught on quickly. The family furniture and logging business would be in *gut* hands when Caleb took over one day.

"*Denki*, Caleb." With Faith at his side, they stepped from the warmth of the house into the cold night.

Aaron headed up the steps. "There's no sign of anyone on the road, but if he's still on foot, it will be hard to know where he's at until it's too late."

"We will be careful, *bruder*," Eli assured him.

"The best place to leave the truck is on the opposite side of the community away from Silver Creek," Aaron told Faith. "It is a less-traveled path."

"Thank you. For everything." She faced Eli. "Are you ready?"

"Jah." He headed down the steps. With Faith's help, he made it up to the bench seat. Eli placed the shotgun at his feet so it would be close enough to reach at a second's notice. "Let me lead the way," he told her and glanced up at the clearing skies. "There should be enough light from the stars to see where we're going. Keep off your headlights. We don't want to draw attention to ourselves."

She started toward the truck. Once it was running, Eli guided Aaron's gelding to the drive while Faith crept along behind him.

Eli's shoulder ached with each jostle of the buggy. He wasn't anywhere close to being 100 percent and hoped there wouldn't be another run-in with Vincent.

At the end of the drive, he turned left onto the road. With Faith close behind him, they inched their way toward the edge of the community. It was slow going that seemed to take forever to reach the place Aaron suggested.

A small logging trail came into view. Eli pulled the buggy off the road and indicated Faith should take the truck farther down the trail.

She turned onto the trail and he followed. Once she'd traveled far enough to be out of sight from the main road, Faith drove off into the woods and got out. With a final glance at the truck, she hurried to the buggy and climbed up beside him.

The gelding responded easily to his command to turn around the buggy. Eli headed back toward the street.

Being out in the open had his nerves on edge. With his heart in his throat, Eli pulled onto the road.

"How's your shoulder?" Faith asked when she noticed the way he favored it.

Eli sought to reassure her although the wound hurt terribly. "Better, thanks to you."

She rubbed her hands across her arms. "Not thanks to me. This is all my fault."

He wouldn't let her take on blame for something she couldn't have foreseen. "*Nay.* You are just as much a victim as Cheryl. She can no longer speak for herself. You must tell her story. Must make sure this man is held accountable for what he did to her and to your husband. The others."

She searched his face before she slowly smiled. It lifted some of the weariness around her eyes. Her smile made everything they'd gone through worth the cost. Faith was *gut* person who'd gotten involved with someone who wasn't.

As they continued along the road, a car crested the hill in front of them still some distance away. Eli sat up straighter and tried to see the vehicle beyond the headlights but couldn't. Still, at this time of the evening on a road rarely traveled by *Englischers*, this wasn't some strange coincidence.

Faith grabbed his arm. The headlights would pick up the buggy soon enough. While Eli didn't understand the *Englischers'* technology, the tension tying his gut into knots seemed to warn that they were in big trouble. "We have to get off the road before he picks us up in the headlights."

And that wouldn't take long. Their only option was to head off into the woods near the road.

Eli clicked his tongue and directed the horse from the road. The animal balked, then climbed the embankment with ease.

There was barely enough time to get off the street before the car passed. Eli strained to see the driver, but the cabin was unusually dark.

"Whoa." Eli stopped the horse and turned to Faith. "Were you able to see who was driving?"

She shook her head. "No, it was too dark inside."

Eli handed her the reins and hopped from the buggy. "I'm going to walk down a little way to see if it turns onto the road where we left the truck. If so, then I'd say there's no doubt that it's Vincent."

Faith got down beside him and tied the reins to a nearby tree. "I'm going with you."

"That's unwise." He stepped closer. "You know what this man is capable of."

"I do. That's why I'm coming with you."

Her concern for him was touching. She was a caring woman who hadn't deserved any of what was happening to her.

Eli retrieved his shotgun and handed it to Faith, then loaded Aaron's and shoved the extra shells into his coat pocket.

"We stay in the trees," he told her while his racing heart sent him jumping at every little noise.

Faith glued herself to his side as they started through the woods.

The road where the truck was parked came into view. There was no sign of the car. Had the driver kept going?

Eli breathed out a sigh. "I don't see the car." He looked toward Faith. Instead of relief, the expression on her face was pure horror. Her huge eyes stared at something behind him.

He whirled around with a sinking feeling. Vincent stood a few feet away with a leer on his face and a gun in his hand.

Chapter Eight

"I knew that was you two I saw on the road," Vincent said as he closed the limited space between them without lowering his weapon. Before Faith had time to react, Vincent snatched the gun from her hand and then pointed his at her head. "Toss that weapon over to me now," he told Eli. "Before I shoot her right where she's standing."

"Don't do it, Eli," Faith warned. If Eli gave up his weapon, they'd be completely defenseless, and she was positive Vincent planned to kill them.

Vincent fired a shot above her head. "Next one won't miss."

Eli slowly tossed the gun at Vincent's feet. Faith edged closer to him and reached for his hand. He made her feel safe, and she believed after everything they'd been through—the things that happened in New York—*Gott* wouldn't let them die like this.

While keeping a close eye on them, Vincent picked up both weapons and hurled them into the underbrush.

With the gun still trained on them, Vincent moved closer. A triumphant grin played across his face. "This could have been avoided if you'd kept what Blake told you to yourself. Instead, you had to blab it to Cheryl. Now this guy and that old woman. Look what's happened because you couldn't keep your mouth shut." He waved the gun in her face and winced. Vincent appeared to be favoring his injured shoulder. Their only chance at getting through this would be finding a way to disarm Vincent.

"Let's go!" he barked and they jumped. "You're both coming with me."

Vincent pointed toward the road. "Get going!" His expression twisted into rage when they hesitated. He shoved Eli's injured arm, and Eli bit back his reaction to the pain. "Go." Faith started toward Eli, but Vincent grabbed her by the arm and hauled her along with him toward the truck.

If they got into that vehicle with Vincent, they'd be dead. He'd probably take them somewhere off the community and shoot them. Maybe into the mountains where he'd leave their bodies for the animals to dispose of. Faith couldn't let that happen. Eli was right. She had to tell Cheryl's story. To do so, she had to survive.

Vincent dragged her along beside him, then crossed the road and headed for the truck.

The closer they came to their fate, the more frantic she became. "I made copies of all the evidence Blake gathered. If I go missing, it'll be sent to someone with enough authority to bring down you and the rest of your dirty cop friends along with Ghost."

Vincent jerked her to face him. "You're bluffing. You have nothing. And my wife's body is still in your house. You fled the scene of a murder."

His eyes narrowed as he watched her. "That really doesn't look good for you. I'll tell them I was forced to kill you both in self-defense. And the old lady won't be of much help. I know where she lives. I'll make sure she's taken care of next."

Faith tried not to take the bait no matter how hard it was. Aaron and his wife would protect her grandmother.

Out of the corner of her eye, Faith noticed Eli reaching inside the bed of the truck. She had to keep Vincent talking and distracted.

"You're wrong. The evidence is on its way to the FBI as we speak, along with the recording." She held Vincent's gaze. Saw a glint of doubt and pressed on. "I told them where to find you. They'll be coming soon. If I were you, I'd get out of here while you still can."

He jerked her to within a few inches of his face. Anger radiated from his pores. "What recording?" Facing her, Vincent didn't realize that Eli, who had a bat concealed behind his back, was slowly advancing.

"The one I recorded of you at the creek confessing to killing Cheryl and Blake. You had no idea I was taping you, did you?"

He shoved the weapon against her temple. Faith stifled a scream. Eli raised the bat. She closed her eyes and prayed his attack would be in time to save her.

The bat made contact. In an instant, she was freed. Her eyes opened and she stumbled away in time to see Vincent hit the ground.

Eli dropped the bat and grabbed Vincent's weapon, then her hand. "Let's go. I didn't hit him all that hard. We won't have long before he wakes up and when he does, he'll be madder than ever."

They ran toward the main road, crossed it, and kept going.

All Faith could think of was how she'd been seconds from dying. The sensation of the cold barrel against her temple remained strong.

Once they reached the buggy, Eli retrieved their weapons and quickly untied the reins while Faith scrambled onto the seat. When Eli was beside her, he didn't waste time getting the gelding headed through the sparse woods as fast as possible under the conditions.

They traveled for a long while before either spoke.

"Are you *oke*?" Eli asked and looked her over.

She wasn't—far from it. She couldn't stop shaking.

Though she was never close to Vincent, Faith and Blake had spent holidays and other special occasions with him and Cheryl. All the while she had no idea about the monster that lurked beneath the surface. Or the secret Vincent and her husband held on to.

Something Cheryl said came to mind. At the time, Faith had wondered if it was a joke, but there'd been something in Cheryl's eyes that said different. They'd gone out for a late movie when both their husbands were working. Afterward, they'd had coffee.

She and Cheryl were finishing their drinks when Vincent called. Right away, Cheryl's demeanor changed. She joked about getting home before Vincent killed her. That troubling look on her face had haunted Faith for a long time afterward. When Faith had asked Cheryl what she meant, she'd tried to downplay it by saying they'd had an argument.

After he'd killed her friend, Faith kept remembering the times Cheryl had bruises on her arm yet excused the injuries as clumsiness.

"His wife was my best friend. We spent the holidays together. How could I not see the truth about him?"

"He is *gut* at hiding his true self. That's how he got away with the crimes he's committed for so long."

She shifted toward him. He was a good man who had suffered the loss of his wife and she'd been so focused on staying alive that she hadn't thought to ask him about his life.

There were many things she didn't know about Eli, but she wanted to.

Faith touched his arm. "I'm so sorry to hear about your wife, Eli," she said in a gentle tone. "How did she die?"

His body tensed and he didn't look at her for the longest time. "She died in a fire two years ago."

Faith had no idea the depth of pain he'd had to live with. "Eli, I'm so sorry. What was her name?"

He turned his head toward her. "Miriam. She moved here after you left West Kootenai. She has family here still. Willa, her sister, is close to your age, and her *mamm* lives here, though she has been ill for a while."

He pulled in a breath. "Miriam and I married at seventeen. We moved away to the Libby community and lived there for many years." He stopped speaking. Didn't look at her.

"Oh, Eli." She touched his hand.

His broken look reached out to her. They were kindred spirits. Both had lost so much.

"She was my everything, and she died in a fire because I wasn't there to save her."

Faith couldn't keep her surprise to herself. "I'm sure you did everything you could."

Before she even finished, he shook his head. "I wasn't there. I was working at a logging camp. Miriam needed me, but I was more concerned about making money than being there for her."

She didn't believe that for a moment. "You were doing what was necessary to provide."

His laugh held a derisive air. "That's what I told myself, but I enjoyed the extra money my *Englisch* employer paid me. The more hours I worked, the more money I made." He shook his head. "I was supposed to come home the night of the fire, but I was tired and decided to go home in the morning. So, I spent the night in one of the bunkhouses set up for workers. I was sleeping while Miriam died." He shook his head. "The fire department said the fire was set deliberately. Someone came into our house and started it."

She struggled to take it all in. "Did they catch the person?" He was silent for so long that she regretted asking. "I'm sorry. It's none of my business."

"They believed I set the fire," he said in such a soft voice that she almost didn't hear him. The hurt in his eyes was hard to take.

"But you were at the logging camp." She would never believe Eli was capable of such a thing.

"The camp wasn't that far from our home. No one there remembered seeing me during the time frame when the fire was started. The police were called in to investigate. They brought me in for questioning. Told me they were certain I was responsible for my wife's death and they planned to prove it."

A sliver of apprehension sped up her spine. Vincent threatened to frame her for Cheryl's death to destroy her credibility. She understood what it felt like to be accused of something you didn't do.

"But you didn't do anything wrong. The truth will come out." She wanted to believe that for Eli and for herself.

He stared straight ahead. "Miriam and I were going to have a child. I thought if I worked harder, I could provide better for my family. But she'd asked me to come home. Something was troubling her. She needed me, and I let her down. If only I'd listened to my *fraa* and not been so caught up in making money, Miriam may still be alive."

She had to make him understand that if he had been home the consequences of the evening might have been far different. "If you had gone home, you would be dead, as well."

He managed a tiny smile, but she could tell he didn't believe her.

Eli had lost so much. Like her, he was a troubled soul caught up in circumstances beyond his control.

She glanced down at her hand still on his. Eli had risked his life for her. Now, it was her turn to help him. No matter what it cost her, she would find out what really happened to Miriam. And then...

He'd been there in one of the best parts of her past. Would he have a place in her future?

The horse clomped through the wilderness with sure footing. Now that they'd put space between themselves and Vincent, she tried to relax, but it was hard because she knew Vincent wouldn't let a little blow to the head slow him down. He'd keep coming until she was dead, or he was in custody.

"Vincent's more afraid of the man he works for than he is of being arrested." Faith voiced her concerns aloud. "He has everything, including his life, to lose, if Ghost comes after him. And he will if Vincent doesn't handle the problem."

"We need to tell the sheriff what is happening, but with Vincent combing the community, I think it's best if we stay out of sight for a while."

Eli was right. Every minute they were out in the open they were in jeopardy. But Faith had to wonder if she would be putting her freedom at risk instead of Vincent if he actually followed through on his threat to frame her for Cheryl's death. It didn't matter. It was time to protect the ones she loved like she hadn't been able to protect Cheryl.

Eli skillfully maneuvered the buggy through the thin woods beyond the road. So far, there had been no sighting of Vincent through the gaps in foliage. Eli had been surprised he'd hit the man hard enough to knock him out. By now, he was convinced Vincent would be awake and searching for them. They couldn't slow down for a second.

"How did he get the second car?" Faith asked.

Only one explanation made sense.

"He probably stole it. Victoria was correct. He had some way of tracking the truck on his phone. I'm glad we were able to get it away from Aaron and Victoria's home, but I hope he didn't see their location before we moved it. I don't want that man near them."

The road to Aaron's homestead intersected the woods. Instead of getting on it, Eli turned the buggy right and ran parallel with the road.

"Do the rest of your brothers still live in West Kootenai?" Faith asked the question innocently enough. If only she'd realized the answer would be anything but.

While he struggled to respond, she turned toward him. Waited. Undoubtedly sensing something was off.

He did his best to answer without bringing up Mason. "Fletcher lives at our family homestead with *mamm*. Hunter has a place on the other side of the community." He stopped. Read the next question coming as if he had asked it himself.

"What about Mason? You two were always so close."

She was right. At one time, he and Mason had been close. They'd done everything together. Then, Mason, younger by a couple of years, became interested in Miriam without realizing she only had eyes for Eli.

When Mason first started talking about Miriam, Eli had wanted to tell his brother about the attraction he and Miriam shared, but Miriam had asked him to keep their courting secret until she spoke to her *daed*, so he had. Then Mason found out and became furious. Accused him of taking Miriam from him. Though Eli had tried to tell him the truth, Mason didn't want to hear it. The rift between the brothers grew. Mason left the faith before being baptized and moved away. A regret Eli carried with him to this day.

"He moved from the community many years ago."

Her brows rose. The questions were all there, yet she must have sensed he didn't want to talk about his *bruder* because she let it go.

The clearing near the family workshop came into view. Aaron and Fletcher created handcrafted furniture the family sold around the state. The sight of it was a relief. They were almost to Aaron's home.

"Your family still makes furniture?" Faith commented as they passed by the building.

"*Jah.* Aaron and Fletcher are the craftsmen of the family. Hunter and I mill the lumber we harvest from the woods on our property."

Eli kept the gelding at a steady pace as they approached the house. He expelled a sigh of relief when he spotted the plume of woodstove smoke spiraling into the night air. The flicker of lantern light behind closed curtains. Each represented safety, but until they were inside, he wouldn't relax completely.

As the horse tramped along the path between the workshop and the house, a familiar yet disturbing sound traveled through his exhausted thoughts. A vehicle was heading down the road at a high rate of speed.

A second later, Faith heard it too. "Someone's coming." Her eyes latched on to his. "We'd better get out of sight while we still have time."

Eli commanded the gelding to a faster trot. Getting

the buggy out of sight was critical. If this was Vincent, he'd seen them earlier. As a police officer, he was probably more observant than most and would likely recognize the buggy as theirs. Not many buggies would be out at this late hour. The last thing he wanted was to throw suspicion on the rest of the household if he hadn't already. His family had been through enough. They deserved better than for him to bring trouble to their doorstep, even though his *bruders* and *mamm* would tell him he was doing *Gott*'s will by helping those in need. And Faith was definitely in need.

When he reached the barn, Eli pulled up on the reins and climbed down. He didn't waste time getting the doors open while Faith drove the buggy inside.

Working together, they freed the horse, and Eli led the animal to its stall.

Outside, the wind howled around the corner of the barn, carrying Eli's worst fear. The vehicle appeared to be heading toward Aaron's home.

Eli eased to the door and cracked it. Headlights bounced through the trees. He closed it and turned, almost slamming into Faith.

"Is it him?" Her panicked expression compelled him to ease her mind, but he couldn't because he believed it was Vincent. No one from the *Englisch* world would be visiting Aaron, especially at this time of the night.

Chapter Nine

"What do we do?" After their last run-in with Vincent, Faith couldn't imagine the level of his fury at having his plans foiled once again. The vehicle was almost right on top of them.

He looked her in the eyes. "We stay here."

Through the sliver of gaps in the walls, the headlights flashed across the barn. Faith ducked away from the wall as if Vincent could see her.

The vehicle rolled to a stop. A door slammed shut. Footfalls crunched along the gravel and up the steps.

Faith stood beside Eli and watched through the slats as a dark figure stood in the shadows of the porch and pounded on the door. Though their view was limited, the outline of Vincent's truck was visible.

The front door opened. Aaron stepped out onto the porch. From the lantern's glow, Vincent's angry profile was highlighted.

Faith grabbed on to Eli's arm for support. She couldn't

make out what Vincent was saying but his stance was all threat.

He took a step closer to Aaron in recognizable intimidation. When Aaron didn't back down, Vincent shook his fist in his face.

"I'm asking you politely to leave my property," Faith heard Aaron say. Vincent appeared to hesitate.

"I'm going, but I know your brother is the one helping her... That's right. I know all about your brother and how he lives next to Faith's grandmother." Vincent's ominous laugh resounded among the silence. "If you're helping him, or her, you could get yourself into a lot of trouble. Maybe even end up dead." Vincent reached into his jacket pocket and Aaron stepped closer.

"I'm only showing you my badge, mister. I'll overlook the fact that you're taking a threatening stance with me for now, but I'm warning you. If you know where they're hiding, you'd better turn them over to me for your own good."

Aaron didn't waver. "I don't know anything about what you're talking about. You need to leave my property now."

"Fine," Vincent growled. "I'm leaving, but you should know when I come back, I will have the sheriff with me. He will force you to cooperate." With those angry words, he stormed to the truck and climbed inside. The engine fired and Vincent whipped around the vehicle and flew down the drive, spewing gravel everywhere.

And the words he'd spoken scared the daylights out of her.

"He's not telling the truth," Eli told her as if sensing the effects Vincent's lies had. "I don't believe he's ever spoken to the sheriff and he won't."

Faith turned to him. "I hope you're right, but I'm so scared, Eli."

Inches separated them. The strength she'd seen in him since childhood was still there. He would always be there for her.

"I won't let him hurt you. I promise," he whispered.

A breath slipped from her lips. Both moved. She went into his arms because it was as natural as breathing. He held her against his heart, and she was safe. All the fears that had followed her here, the ones that they both still faced, seeped from her body for just a little while.

She and Eli had history. Good history. But she also doubted. Not him—herself.

You felt the same way about Blake...

She'd believed everything Blake told her right from the beginning. He'd seemed like a true hero when she'd first met him in the ER after Blake had been shot while defending a fellow officer. She'd fallen hard, married quickly and spent ten years thinking she knew her husband.

But she'd been wrong. So wrong about Blake.

She pulled away and searched his eyes. More than anything, Faith wished she could believe what was happening between them now was more than a reaction to their desperate circumstances.

Eli didn't look away. "We should go inside. I'll feel safer there if he returns."

Her voice just wouldn't come out, so she nodded. Eli cracked the door and peeked outside before they left the confines of the barn.

Faith kept at his side as they crossed the yard to the porch.

Eli knocked several times. "It's me, Aaron." He wanted to make sure his brother knew Vincent hadn't returned.

Faith glanced around the darkness suppressing a shiver. Door locks slid open inside the house. Most who lived in this peaceful community rarely locked their doors. The fact that Aaron had chosen to spoke of how frightening Vincent's appearance here had been.

Aaron opened the door with a look of concern on his face. Eli ushered Faith inside and relocked the door.

"Are you both *oke*?" Aaron's frightened gaze shifted between them.

"We are." Eli explained what happened. "I'm sorry, *bruder*. I didn't mean to bring more troubles to your door."

"No, Eli, this is all my fault," Faith insisted. "I shouldn't have come back here."

Grandmother Sarah came over to where Faith stood beside Eli. "Nonsense, child. This was once your home. Where else would you go?"

She loved this woman so much, but her presence here in West Kootenai had endangered so many people already.

"Your *grossmammi* speaks the truth," Eli said. When she looked at him all she could think about was the tender moment they'd shared in the barn. "This man must be stopped before he kills you and anyone else he believes will stand in his way."

Vincent's threats had gone beyond just being directed at her. He intended to come after her grandmother and Eli. Now he'd threatened Aaron.

"The man who showed up on my porch tonight is capable of great violence," Aaron told her. "He will try to twist things to deceive people into believing he is a *gut*, law-abiding person."

"He's right, Faith," Victoria said. "You are doing the right thing and Sheriff Collins is an honorable man. He helped me. He will do the same for you."

Two weeks ago, when she'd found the evidence Blake left, she wasn't sure what to do with it. Faith had anguished over getting Cheryl involved. That decision had cost Cheryl her life. She couldn't afford to make any more wrong ones.

Eli understood how hard it was to let someone else in, but like him, Faith didn't have an option. He struggled to make the right decision under circumstances that were beyond his understanding. His gut told him they needed to get the sheriff involved as soon as possible, but he and Faith were both exhausted. They needed to take a breath to rest and gather their thoughts. Eli had no doubt Vincent would be trolling the community looking for them. They couldn't afford to make a mistake.

Help me, Gott. *I don't know what to do...*

"Supper is ready. Thanks to Sarah, I've mastered her friendship soup recipe." Victoria smiled at the older woman. "*Komm* and sit. We should enjoy the soup while it is still hot."

Eli glanced out the window, sure they were running out of time.

"It will be *oke* for a little while. You must eat, Eli," Victoria told him.

He waited while the family took their usual seats. Even though his *bruder* had welcomed him home, he was still getting used to being part of this loving family again.

Sarah clasped Faith's hand. Together they followed the family to the table where Faith stopped and looked back at him. There were questions in her eyes he couldn't answer. The tender moment they'd shared in the barn was unexpected, yet still burned in his thoughts.

Being close to her made him feel something he hadn't in a very long time, but he and Faith were wounded deeply. And the guilt he carried in his heart had become part of who he was just as assuredly as the heart that beat in his chest. Could he let it go? Believe himself deserving of this wonderful woman he cared so much about?

Eli claimed the seat beside Faith that Victoria indicated. A bowl of hearty friendship soup, brimming with split peas, lentils, barley, ground beef and tomatoes, was placed in front of him. The aroma reminded him of the hours that had passed since he'd eaten.

Once the table quieted, heads bowed. It was time for the silent prayer.

Eli lowered his head and closed his eyes. Though he

knew *Gott* was always there, waiting for him to return, after what happened to Miriam, he'd struggled to find his way back to the Almighty.

Instead of praying, his thoughts wandered to the meals he'd shared with Miriam. Back then, everything seemed so perfect. Though what happened between him and *Bruder* Mason cut deeply, Miriam made him happy. They'd looked forward to a future with *kinner* of their own. And then everything was taken away.

"Amen," Aaron said aloud into the quiet room. The lump in Eli's throat wouldn't go away. The past could not be changed. He'd hurt many people with his actions. Best to keep his head down and do his work. Not hope for anything more than what the Lord chose to give him.

"I will take my soup into the living room and keep watch in case Vincent shows up here." He carried the bowl from the room and resumed his earlier perch by the window.

As he dug into the soup with relish, all he could think about was getting to Eagle's Nest and speaking with the sheriff, but with Vincent out there somewhere, it was too risky for now.

"This is good." He turned at the sound of Faith's gentle voice. "I thought I would help you watch," she said.

He smiled at her consideration. *"Denki."*

"Your *mamm* always was a *gut* cook." Sarah brought her soup into the room to join them. She came over to Eli and patted his arm as if sensing the turmoil inside him.

"Things will work out in *Gott*'s timing," Sarah murmured as if she'd read his thoughts. She had a smile for him like so many times before. His old friend knew him well. She'd listened to him talk. Comforted him when he'd cried. Prayed for him when he didn't ask for it.

With his attention on the bowl in front of him, he didn't answer. Quiet conversation from the kitchen drifted their way. Growing up, he'd loved being from a big family. Meals, in particular, were a favorite. Now he was no longer sure of his place in the Shetler family.

"It's hard, isn't it?" Faith said with her attention on his face. "Coming back to a past that was good and painful."

Despite his heavy heart, he smiled. "*Jah*, it is." She too had endured hardships in her life here in West Kootenai.

"It will get better." He wondered if she meant this for herself or for him. He hoped for both.

He nodded and spooned soup once more. For the first time since he'd returned, he didn't feel like he was standing on the outside looking into the life he wanted again.

When they'd finished their meal, Faith and Sarah carried the bowls to the kitchen.

Once Faith had helped with the cleanup, she returned to the living room and slipped into one of the rockers while Eli watched the darkness outside.

Time passed in silence as his worried thoughts went over everything they'd gone through. Did they risk leaving now when they had the cover of darkness working in their favor, or wait until morning and pray Vincent had left the immediate area? Frustration settled in. He had no idea.

With the fire dying in the woodstove, Eli added more wood. Once he was satisfied with the blaze, he sat beside Faith. The quiet between them wasn't awkward, which scared him. It reminded him of the many nights he and Miriam had shared like this. Once more, the past and all its failures returned to haunt him. Some men were better off alone.

While Eli pondered the future afforded to him, the smallest of sounds pulled his attention away. A board creaked near the door as if something or someone had stepped up on it. Footsteps paced across the porch. There would be no reason for anyone to be outside at this time of the evening. Which left only one explanation—Vincent was back.

Chapter Ten

Faith jumped to her feet. Before she could say a word, Eli held his finger to his lips and grabbed her hand, urging her toward the kitchen.

Aaron came forward as they approached. Eli stopped him before he spoke and moved close enough to whisper, "Someone's on the porch."

Aaron's eyes widened. Victoria hurried to her husband's side when she spotted his troubled expression.

"That man didn't go far," Aaron told her. "Faith, you and your *grossmammi* go upstairs with Eli and Caleb. Let Victoria and I handle this man. *Sohn*, show them where to go." The young man headed toward the stairs. Faith grabbed her grandmother's hand and followed with Eli.

"In here. This is my room," Caleb whispered and opened the closest door. They followed him inside. Caleb hurried to the window and looked out below to the porch. "I do not see anyone."

Eli cracked the door so they could hear. The front door opened. Boards squeaked.

"There's no one here," Aaron's deep voice said.

"But footprints are everywhere," Victoria insisted.

Faith bit her bottom lip. Someone had been out there minutes earlier. Where had Vincent gone?

The answer came quickly.

"What are you doing here?" Aaron again. This time tension filled his voice.

"You lied to me!" Vincent said. "I saw the buggy tracks leading onto the property. Your brother was here. Where are you hiding them?"

What sounded like a scuffle could be heard. Eli started out the door, but Faith grabbed his arm. "You can't go out there."

He turned toward her. The helpless look on his face pulled at her heart. She understood the guilt because she was drowning in it. This was her fault. If Aaron or Victoria were hurt, she would never be able to forgive herself.

"That's far enough." Victoria spoke up. "One more step and I will shoot. And I should warn you, I'm a former CIA agent. I don't miss."

An uncomfortable silence stretched out far too long.

"Alright, I'll leave. But I will find them wherever they're hiding. If you want to keep your brother out of jail—or worse, alive—I suggest you tell him to turn in the woman to me."

Faith's heart slammed against her chest. Seconds ticked by. The door finally closed. Aaron and Victoria waited until Vincent was gone before they came up the stairs and entered their son's room.

"You heard what was said?" Aaron asked.

Eli looked to Faith before answering. "*Jah*, we did. Do you think he left the property?"

"I can't be sure. He's incredibly determined." Victoria looked Faith's way. "A dirty cop with plenty to hide is a dangerous man. You are a major liability to him."

Faith blew out a breath. "I know and I'm so sorry I've brought this man to your home."

Victoria smiled. "There's nothing to be sorry for. I understand what it's like to be hunted by someone who wants you dead."

Faith admired this strong woman. "You were *Englisch* before you and Aaron married," she said, and Victoria nodded. Eli had told her little about the couple with the exception of Victoria not being from the community. She'd heard what the woman said. "You were once with the CIA?"

That someone from the CIA had chosen to leave the way of life behind and join the Amish community made her wonder if perhaps it wasn't too late for her. Maybe, even after being forced to leave her family behind, she could find her place here again.

She glanced at Eli, who watched their exchange with an unreadable expression on his face. Was he remembering the tragedy he'd faced with his wife? The suspicion he'd endured from law enforcement and his own community?

"I was born Amish, but my *mamm* died when I was five and I was forced to leave the only home I ever knew.

I grew up *Englisch*. Joined the CIA and thought that was my place in life. But I never forgot my past and I spent most of my adult life trying to recapture the sense of community and the simple ways I loved so much as a child." She turned to her husband and smiled. "And then I came here and met Aaron. He helped me find my way back."

It sounded so simple, but until Vincent's threat was eliminated, she couldn't think about a future here among the Plain people she'd once called family.

"It wasn't easy for me either," Victoria said, interrupting her concerns. "I had people coming after me who wanted me dead. But with Aaron and some *gut* people, including Sheriff Collins from Eagle's Nest, I was able to free myself of the past and let go of that life. You can too. With Sheriff Collins's help, I will use my former connections to help bring down Vincent and the rest of his corrupt cops."

Faith prayed her story would have the happy ending Victoria's did. "Thank you," she said with a sigh.

"You and Sarah are part of our family now," Victoria assured her. "And your family will help you through this. So, why don't you start from the beginning and tell me everything you know about this man. Let me see what I can do to get the ball rolling in a new direction."

Even though Faith was a long way from being free of Vincent, the weight of the past few days slowly lifted. She wasn't alone. She had her grandmother and these wonderful people. And she had Eli. More than anything, she wanted to walk past this valley of death and step toward being happy again. Was it possible? Only *Gott* knew.

* * *

"She is a *gut* woman. It's a shame she's caught up in something like this," Aaron said when it was just the two of them. He added more wood to the stove before looking to Eli. "I remember little Faith from when her *mamm* and *daed* lived here."

Eli watched his *bruder* stir the fire and realized there was more coming.

"You always had a soft spot for Faith, and you've been alone for several years."

Eli couldn't let him finish. "I am only helping her because of Sarah. She is worried about her granddaughter. And as you said, Faith and I were once close." Aaron watched him without saying a word. Eli felt the need to add, "She has no one to look out for her. That's not right."

Aaron clasped Eli's shoulder. "I am not telling you how to live your life, *bruder*. I know how much you loved Miriam, but she's gone, and she wouldn't want you to mourn forever. You deserve to be happy. To be a *daed*. Have a family of your own. *Kinner* around your table."

Each word struck deep in his heart. "I am a *daed*— or I was to be. Miriam was pregnant when she died." The only person he'd told about the baby before now was Faith.

The surprise on Aaron's face turned to pity. "I'm so sorry, Eli. I didn't know."

Eli fought against the hurt that was always there. "How can I simply move on with my life when they are gone because of me."

"The fire was not your fault. You deserve happiness, Eli. It's time you believed that for yourself."

Before Eli could respond, Faith came into the room. Her distraction was a welcome one. Helping her eased his conscience a little. Maybe that was why *Gott* brought him back to West Kootenai? To help her. Sarah. He would seek ways to fulfill his Godly purpose and not expect anything more.

"Do you think he's still out there?" she asked, as if seeking his reassurance.

Eli came over to where she stood. "I doubt it, but I will have a look around outside to ease your mind. You should try to get some rest."

She ran her hand across her eyes. "Thank you, but I can't sleep knowing he's still out there. I'm coming with you."

Exposing her to another one of Vincent's attacks was something he wanted to avoid. "It would be safer for you to remain here." Eli turned to his older *bruder* for support, but she wasn't having it.

"I'll be okay, and I have to do something." She threw up her hands. "I can't sit around and wait for Vincent's next attack to happen."

Aaron grabbed his shotgun from near the door where Eli had placed it earlier. "Victoria and I will come with you. It will be safer with more people." Aaron turned to his *fraa*.

The love between Aaron and Victoria was clear in the way they looked at each other…and it gave him hope that perhaps one day he would be free of the guilt he carried on his shoulders, because he was so weary of it.

"I don't think we can risk using any lights," Eli said. The last thing they needed was something to direct Vincent to their location.

Aaron and Victoria slipped outside and waited while Faith and Eli did the same.

"Victoria and I will head toward the workshop," Aaron told them. "Be careful."

"We will." He watched Aaron and his wife start for the workshop before he faced Faith. "Stay close to me." The chill bouncing between his shoulder blades warned him they might be walking into a trap Vincent set.

With her at his side, he crossed the yard to the barn. Instead of using the main entrance, he slipped through the side door with Faith.

There were no signs Vincent had been there. Eli wasn't sure what he'd hoped for. Another run-in certainly wasn't it, but he did want this to be over for Faith.

He reached for her hand and held it. The uneasy feeling continued to grow.

"He's not been here," he said. "Perhaps he figured we kept going and he's moved on. We should go back to the house. As soon as it's light out, we'll head to phone shanty and call the sheriff. We need his help to bring down Vincent. I just hope he isn't expecting that move."

She kept her attention on his face. "Whatever happens, Eli, I want you to know how much I appreciate you risking your life for me."

He looked at her and saw things he never thought possible again. A future. A *fraa*. *Kinner*.

But how could two damaged people hope to have any of those things?

*With Gott, all things were possible…*the thought was placed in his mind as if from above.

"*Komm*, let's head back to the others." He started for the door again when a noise outside stopped him in his tracks. Someone was moving around near the back of the barn. It couldn't be Aaron and Victoria. They were searching near the workshop so far away. But if it wasn't them, then… Vincent.

Eli grabbed Faith's hand and tugged her along beside him until they were hidden in one of the empty stalls.

The door opened. Someone stepped inside the barn. Had Vincent seen them come inside?

Please, Gott, no.

It was up to him alone to keep Faith safe.

A cell phone shrilled, echoing through the cavernous space. Eli's heart almost jumped out of his chest when he realized the man stopped next to where they hid.

"Hello." Vincent's tone was laced with anger as he answered the call. Eli hoped the call would distract him and he wouldn't search the stalls.

"Yes, sir." In an instant, Vincent changed his tune. "Yes, I do know where she is, and I will take care of her soon. Don't worry, I have this under control. I will call you once it's finished."

Who was this person Vincent spoke to?

"No, there's no need to come here. As I've said, I have it under control. She's not walking out of here alive." Silence followed and Eli could just make out Vincent's astonished expression through the slats in the stall door. His brow was furrowed as he listened. "Five hours! That's not much time… No, I can handle it. And if she told anyone else about what Blake wrote, I'll take care of them, as well."

A moment of silence followed before Vincent expelled a menacing sigh and slapped the nearby shovel across the barn. The gelding whinnied along with the cow, but Vincent paid no mind. The side door slammed against the wall. Vincent stormed from the building.

Eli was too shocked to move for the longest time. He and Faith huddled in the empty stall while he prayed the man would leave the property for good, but Eli feared Vincent would search every square inch of the place.

After what felt like an eternity, they slipped from their hiding spot.

"I can't believe that just happened," she murmured, in as much shock as he was.

"Who do you think he was speaking with?"

She looked him in the eye. "My guess would be the drug dealer he works for. Ghost. And if that's the case, then this is bad. Really bad. If Ghost comes here, he'll bring an army."

Chapter Eleven

"The enclosed buggy should keep us mostly hidden from view," Eli said to ease her fears. She appreciated his efforts. But until Vincent was in jail, she couldn't let down her guard for a second because she wasn't sure how many more run-ins with him they would survive. "If we take the back way into the community, we may have a chance at using the phone without Vincent spotting us. I'll feel better once we are able to tell Sheriff Collins what's been happening."

Faith watched the woods pass by while the conversation she and Eli had overheard the night before replayed in her head. More than the five-hour deadline had passed. Vincent's employer had given him an ultimatum. Find her, or he'd take over the search. When he did, he wouldn't need Vincent any longer.

"Do you think he'll really come here?" she asked. Faith couldn't imagine how bad things would become if a ruthless drug dealer showed up in this peaceful community.

"I sure hope not." He shook his head, exhaustion

clinging to him. He'd survived a gunshot and countless attacks from a man determined to end their lives, and they were still no closer to being free of Vincent's threat. "Once we speak to the sheriff, and perhaps get Victoria involved, I'll feel better."

She smiled despite the circumstances. "I will too."

Only *Gott* knew what their outcome would be, but she had to believe He wouldn't want her or Eli to pay the price for Vincent's crimes.

The horse clomped along the path leading to the road and Faith's mind returned to the years she'd spent here in West Kootenai. The times she and Eli had been together were some of the best.

"Do you miss this way of life?" Eli asked almost as if she'd spoken her thoughts aloud.

"I guess I do. For so long, I've wanted to come back, but the thought of returning to the community without my grandparents was just too hard."

"You are home now," Eli said. "And regrets won't change anything."

Home. The word hadn't felt the same since she left West Kootenai. No matter where she lived, this would always be home.

Something changed in his eyes when he glanced her way. She bit her bottom lip and gazed into his eyes wanting so much. Eli leaned closer. She touched his face. Read the uncertainty in his eyes. Eli was nothing like Blake, and for that she was glad. The gentleness she found in this rock of a man shattered all her doubts and made her want to keep fighting. Hoping. Praying there was a chance for them.

The mare snorted and the tender moment passed.

Her hand dropped away and she struggled to recapture her composure.

Eli blew out a breath and faced forward.

Did he feel the connection between them changing? Or was he remembering the woman he'd lost? The love they shared that could never be replaced. The promise of a family gone.

Once, she and Blake had talked about starting a family, but there never seemed to be the right time. She'd wanted a baby for so long. She'd cried over the lost opportunity when Blake passed away and thought she'd spend the rest of her life grieving. Then, she'd found his note and the pain of losing him was overshadowed by the crimes he'd committed.

She was in the middle of a fight for her life. The future and its possibilities were something she didn't have the luxury of thinking about right now. If she wanted to live long enough to bring Cheryl and Blake's killer to justice, she had to keep her head on straight and not get bogged down by what-ifs.

The community shops appeared through the trees in front of them. Though darkness still clung to most of the countryside, the owners of the Amish businesses were hard at work. The café where Eli enjoyed a meal on occasion was open for service. The Grabers served the best *frühstück* around, and the Amish bakery fry pies were famous in the community.

Eli guided the mare along the slushy path. Last evening was the first night that it hadn't snowed since he'd been home. The clear skies were a welcomed relief.

He caught glimpses of several buggies along with

a few cars parked in front of the café. Many of the *Englischers* around the area came to the community to enjoy the Grabers's cooking.

The buggy slowly eased past the back of the café and the bulk-food store. One of the last shops at the end of the businesses was the bakery. The Stoltzfuses were *gut* people who had an additional bakery in Eagle's Nest. Their *dochder* and her *mann* had taken over the running of the original bakery here in West Kootenai.

"Those cinnamon rolls smell so good," Faith said with a hint of wistfulness that was hard to resist. Though it was best if they kept moving, if they pulled the buggy around back, what would it hurt to purchase a couple of fresh-baked cinnamon rolls to go?

Eli headed the buggy toward the back of the building and out of sight. Faith turned to him with raised brows.

"We will only stop for a second."

She smiled. "Thank you."

He stepped from the buggy and held out his hand. More and more, his heart was opening up to Faith. His feelings growing. They shared history and he wanted to make her happy.

Eli knocked on the back door and Sadie Zook peeked out the window, smiled and unlocked the door.

"*Gut* morning, Eli." Sadie's gaze shifted to Faith and Eli introduced her.

"We're here for two of your cinnamon rolls to go."

Sadie nodded and stepped behind the counter. "Daniel just put out a fresh batch." She removed two of the largest rolls and placed them in a bag. "Would you like *kaffe* to go along with them?"

Eli looked to Faith, who nodded. "*Jah*, two for the road."

While Sadie filled their order, Eli glanced out the window at the burgeoning new day. The street in front of the bakery was illuminated by headlights. Someone coming to enjoy a warm breakfast, perhaps. The knot in Eli's stomach had him on edge.

He grabbed Faith's arm and pulled her along beside him until they reached the kitchen and were away from the view of the windows.

Sadie's husband, Daniel, appeared surprised by their sudden arrival in his kitchen.

Eli did his best to explain. "Someone bad is looking for Faith. We have to stay out of sight here, please."

"Who is after you?" Daniel asked, his expression growing troubled.

"An *Englischer* from New York. He's trying to kill me," Faith told him. "He's driving a dark-colored truck."

The shock on Daniel's face was clear, but he did not hesitate. "I've seen this truck around the community. He stopped in here and was asking questions about you, but I had no idea what he was talking about," he told Faith.

Sadie came into the room. "What is going on?"

After Eli explained, Sadie's eyes widened. She glanced back to the dining area. "I saw him pass by, as well. I thought it curious because he's an *Englischer* and he's been hanging around the community."

Vincent had been combing the community for them two days. "He's up to no good," Eli said. "Did you see which way he went?"

Sadie nodded. "*Jah*, he is heading back toward your family's property."

The news was unsettling. Was Vincent going back to Aaron's home? Eli was grateful his *bruder* had thought ahead and taken the family to *Mamm*'s house, but what would happen when Vincent realized the family was gone? By now, he'd know Eli's *mamm* lived close by.

"Stay here," Daniel told them. "I will check for his truck."

The three waited in the kitchen while Daniel stepped outside. He was only gone a few minutes before he returned.

"There's no sign of him. He must have kept going."

"*Denki*, Daniel. We should be on our way before he returns." Eli hesitated. "I hate to ask this of you, but I'm worried about Sarah's animals and mine. We had to leave them behind. Could you please stop by our places to make sure they are cared for? And my mare was set loose by the creek. I'd appreciate it if you'd confirm she made it home."

Daniel nodded. "*Jah*, I'll take care of it."

"*Denki*. Please be careful." Eli paid for the sweets, then he and Faith headed out the back entrance.

Once they were safely ensconced in the buggy again, Eli directed the mare back onto the road.

Faith handed him a coffee and cinnamon roll. He accepted it, but his appetite for the sweet was gone. All he could think about was his family's safety.

His thoughts returned to the conversation they'd overheard the night before. Vincent was involved with a dangerous person. He stood to lose much if the information Faith had on him went public. And there was no doubt Vincent knew this. He was all out of time to contain the problem before the thug from New York did it for him. Ghost wouldn't want to leave any witnesses behind, which meant Vincent was in serious danger of losing his life.

They reached Eli's family's furniture shop, where some of the pieces Aaron and Fletcher made were sold. As they started past it toward the community phone shanty, Eli's heart sank. Vincent's truck was parked behind the building out of sight. Somehow, the man must have circled back around without them seeing it.

"Oh, no." Faith spotted the vehicle at the same time he did.

Eli's mind raced with decisions. Turning back wasn't an option at this point. It would call more attention. "Quick. Get in the back and out of sight," he told her while he kept his attention on the truck.

So far, Vincent hadn't looked up. He appeared to be studying something in his hand.

Faith clambered over the bench seat to the two seats in the back that faced each other.

Once she was in place, he felt somewhat better prepared. Eli clamped the hat down as low as it could get it and still see where he was going. With his heart pounding, he passed by the parked truck. Vincent glanced up at that moment and looked straight at him.

Eli prayed he hadn't left a lasting impression on the dirty cop. Because if he had, Vincent wouldn't waste time coming after them.

Chapter Twelve

Faith crouched out of sight and tried to keep from panicking. This was a different buggy than they'd used before. Vincent would have no way of knowing it was them unless he got a good look at Eli.

"We're past him," Eli murmured while keeping a close watch behind them.

"Did he recognize you?" Faith asked from her crouched position.

"I'm not sure. He looked right at me. But I can't be certain."

Faith peeked out the back window and watched the truck slowly ease from the road. Was Vincent simply tired of sitting still and had decided to search someplace else or…

"He's pulling onto the road," she said, and Eli whirled around in his seat. There was no doubt. Vincent was coming their way.

Eli picked up the mare's speed, but the truck continued to gain on them until he was within a few feet of the buggy. The noise of the powerful engine spooked the mare, who slung around her head and side-stepped down the road.

While Eli tried to calm the horse, Vincent plowed into the back of the buggy, sending it lurching forward. The mare whinnied and reared up on her hind legs.

Vincent revved up behind them again and prepared for another attack.

"If he hits us again, the buggy will splinter apart," Eli said in a tight voice. "Come up here and take the reins. Keep the mare as steady as you can."

Faith quickly scrambled over the seat. Eli handed her the controls and grabbed the shotgun. Faith's heart threatened to explode in her chest as she gripped them tightly and kept her attention on the mare who wanted to flee the danger behind them. While she struggled to hold on to the animal, Eli leaned out of the buggy and fired.

Faith glanced over her shoulder in time to see the truck veer off the road and come to a jarring stop in the foot-deep ditch that was covered in snow.

"We have to get off this road before he comes after us again," Eli said in a strained tone. And she had no doubt Vincent would.

In front of them, the Lake Koocanusa bridge came into view. Crossing the bridge was far too dangerous. If Vincent caught up with them there, he'd push them over the side, and no one would ever be the wiser.

"There's an old logging trail off to the right. It's rarely used anymore, but we don't have a choice." Eli leaned forward and watched for the road.

Faith kept a careful eye on Vincent. Dark smoke shot

from the tailpipes as he got the truck running again. He didn't waste time getting back on the road.

"He's coming," Faith warned.

"There's the trail. It's pretty overgrown, so I'm hoping he won't be able to fit the truck inside." Eli coaxed the mare onto what could barely be called a trail. The path was just wide enough for the buggy to fit through. Trees that hadn't been pruned in years scraped along the sides.

The horse was still on edge from what happened and continued to sling her head around in a fretful motion.

A tree limb grated along the side of the buggy, probably taking paint along with it.

"After what's happened, I don't think it's wise to use the phone. Vincent will probably be expecting that move. We need to get the buggy and ourselves out of sight as quickly as possible because he knows what we're driving, and he'll be looking for us."

While she understood they couldn't afford to stay in plain sight, the thought of retreating stung of failure.

Eli kept the mare at a fast clip despite the cramped conditions.

She looked behind them and could no longer see the road. "I sure hope he doesn't try to follow us."

Eli held her gaze. "He's determined."

His words didn't settle the nerves in the pit of her stomach.

Eli entwined their fingers. "I don't believe he can fit that big truck through the opening, but he definitely saw which way we went, and he'll be looking for another way to cut us off. He'll expect us to return to Aaron's place. If he goes there, he'll find it empty."

But he'd keep looking for them. Vincent would check every place where they'd been until he found them.

"We need to find a safe place to hide until he has moved from the area." But it had been years since she'd last visited the community. She was all turned around.

"There's an old logging camp close by. It's pretty much been reclaimed by the woods. I don't see how Vincent could find us there."

They were safe for now, but how long would it last?

It had been years since Eli visited the logging camp. As boys, he and his *bruders* used to explore every square inch of the woods around the community. Once they were older, they'd hunted for food near here.

He stopped the buggy, and they both got out. The damage from the tree branches was great. There were deep grooves on both sides.

"It can be fixed," Eli assured her, but she shook her head and turned away.

He clasped her arms and turned her to face him, spotting the tears in her eyes. "It can be fixed, and this isn't your fault."

"I set this in motion," she murmured in a shaky voice. "All of it."

Eli gathered her in his arms. "I wish I could erase him from your life so you wouldn't have to go through any of this, but I can't. So, I will do the next best thing and be by your side until Vincent is in jail."

Holding her close, it scared him how much he felt she belonged there.

She pulled away and smiled up at him. Tears dampened her cheeks, and he brushed his thumb across them. More than anything he wanted to kiss her. Hold her close. Wish away the danger coming after them. But he couldn't and he needed to stay focused.

He let her go and stepped away. "Let's keep going," he said. "If I remember correctly, the camp should be right through there."

Thick overgrowth would make it impossible to get the buggy through. "Let's see if we can reach the camp first, then we'll find another way to bring in the buggy." He glanced at the mare with doubts. "I don't like leaving her here alone for long, especially when she's so spooked."

Eli thought about his mare that Vincent had deliberately let loose. Had the animal made it home safely? Once he was able, he'd return and make sure the horse was there.

He did his best to calm the worried animal while Faith watched the path.

Once the mare had been quieted, he tied the reins to a tree.

Eli read every single one of Faith's misgivings. "We'll be fine. Stay close to me, *oke*?" He stepped into the thicket with her behind him.

"How do you know about this logging camp?" she asked. "Did you work here before?"

He smiled to himself at her assumption. "*Nay*. It was shut down long before I was old enough to work as a logger. My *bruders* and I used to explore the area."

Working their way through the thick brush was challenging. Perspiration formed on his brow despite the cool weather.

"You and your brothers always did fun things together. I loved it when you let me tag along."

Eli remembered the sweet little girl who wanted to be part of everything they did. "And it almost got you into trouble a couple of times."

One incident in particular came to mind. It was one of those times when she'd followed Eli and his *bruders* into the woods. "Like the time you decided to pick some wild blueberries." Eli had noticed her wandering off and followed. "That black bear wasn't happy with you trying to poach his food."

"Oh, I remember that day." Faith started laughing. "I thought you were mad at me."

"Not mad, only worried," he corrected. "You always were a curious child, and your *grossdaddi* encouraged your adventurous spirit."

The woods in front of them began to thin. "This is it." They'd reached the camp, and no sign of Vincent met them.

Eli stepped into the clearing and glanced around. The woods were slowly reclaiming most of the buildings. Rusted equipment was sinking into the earth.

On the opposite side of the camp, a trail appeared usable. Though he had no doubt the place hadn't been operational in years, someone from the community visited frequent enough to leave a trail. Eli hoped Vincent wouldn't stumble onto it.

"We can bring the mare in through there." He pointed to the spot. Together they fought their way back to the buggy and eased it forward until Eli picked up the trail leading into the camp.

Once they were back in camp, Eli led the mare behind the one building that appeared to still be useable. He tied the animal to a nearby tree and out of the wind before he returned with the bucket of oats he'd brought for the trip. She'd need water, but he'd search for that once she'd finished her meal.

"Shall we see if we can get out of the cold for a bit?" He glanced up at the clear sky. The sun was shining, yet the temperature was closing in on freezing. Life in the mountains.

Faith tugged her jacket tighter and agreed. "That's a good idea. It's cold out."

He went over to the front of the building and twisted the knob. While it moved, the door didn't. The frame was swollen shut by years of snow and rain.

Putting his full weight into it, Eli tried again. It gave a little. Two more tries and they were inside.

The place was set up to be barracks for those working in the camp. It was basic and typical of most logging camps—a couple of chairs, several cots spread around the room and a potbellied stove in the center to warm the entire space.

Though a fire would take away the chill, it was too risky. Vincent might spot the smoke.

"At least it's warmer than outside in the wind," he said and looked at the exhaustion that clung to Faith's face.

"This must be a primitive way to live." She glanced around the dust-covered space.

"It is." He recalled his time in the logging camp near Libby. "It's a place to eat and sleep. Nothing more."

She peered out one of the grimy windows. "How long do you think we should wait here before we can leave?"

Eli had no idea what Vincent could be thinking. "I'm not sure. A while. I'm hoping he'll think we worked our way out of the woods and returned to my house."

"Which means we can't go back there or to my grandmother's place."

He agreed. "It will be too dangerous. The same goes for Aaron's place, but we'll need my *bruder*'s help. Using the phone near the community businesses is too risky with Vincent hanging around. He may be watching the phone shanty now, expecting us to reach out for help. I'll ask Fletcher to head to the sheriff's station in Eagle's Nest and tell him what's been happening. So far, Vincent hasn't seen his face. Hopefully, the sheriff will be able to come to us."

It wasn't much of a plan, but it was the best he could think of on short notice and he felt better having it. For now, they just had to stay out of sight.

Faith came over to where he stood and cupped his cheek with a tender look on her face. "You've never doubted my innocence, which couldn't have been easy."

His protective instincts resurfaced as he stared into her beautiful eyes. He deeply cared for her. She'd always been important to him, even as a child, but he wasn't worthy of her. He'd let down Miriam. He wouldn't do that to Faith.

Eli stepped back and turned away, his heart heavy. He had nothing to offer her but trouble. And she had enough of that on her own.

Chapter Thirteen

It was frightening how quickly life changed. A year ago, hers appeared perfect on the surface. A handsome husband. A great career that she loved. And then...

The foundation holding her world together crumbled and she realized everything had been a lie. There was nothing perfect about her life.

Her attention came back to Eli. Childhood memories returned. Her hand in his as they walked the path to her house. If she closed her eyes, she could almost feel the rough calloused on his hand from hard work. The ready smile that was always close whenever she said something funny or if he decided to tease her. It was as if he'd been imprinted on her heart for years, waiting for this time. Their time?

Something must have showed on her face because Eli came over to where she stood.

"Is something wrong?" He'd misunderstood the sudden heat in her cheeks. The quick pulse that she was sure he'd heard.

Faith cleared her throat. "No, I was just remembering how you used to tease me when we were little."

His lips lifted into a smile. "That's because you were easy to tease. You took everything so seriously."

Her eyes widened. This unburdened side of him mesmerized her. "Of course, I was." She pretended to be offended but her smile gave it away. This was the Eli she'd grown up knowing. Before the cares of the world weighted him down, much as they had her. If only they both could go back to that simple time.

"I loved everything about this life back then. My grandfather was my hero. He taught me so many things and we'd have these wonderful adventures together."

"Oh, I remember. Like the time your *grossdaddi* told you lost treasure was hidden in the woods and you both went in search of it." A glint of mischief hinted in Eli's eyes.

"Are you saying buried treasure isn't really in the woods?" Faith held a straight face as long as she could before she burst out laughing. "I'm only kidding. I know he was only pretending for me and I loved him for it."

Eli chuckled along with her. "He was. I miss your *grossdaddi* and mine. Those two were so much fun together. They grew up here. Never thought about leaving West Kootenai. They loved the land. Their families. The Plain way of life that focused on *Gott* and family above all else."

She swallowed several times. "It's a special way of life most people never fully understand."

He didn't respond, but his dark eyes watched her in a way that made her yearn for the impossible.

"I really miss this life," she said with a catch in her voice. "I wish…"

His eyes held hers captive. "What do you wish?"

She shook her head. "That I'd never left West Kootenai. I wish my father hadn't dragged us away from everyone we loved. And I wish that I'd never met Blake St. Clair." Her voice died into a sob and he tugged her close.

Crying was a weakness she couldn't afford, yet the regrets she had brought tears to the surface. Coming on the heels of a year of grief, discovering the truth about Blake's crimes had destroyed any good memories she had of her marriage.

"Things happen for a purpose. Even the bad things." A touch of regret hung in his voice and she pulled a little away.

He'd been through so much himself. Losing his wife and child in such a violent way had to have been horrific. Then being accused of causing their deaths.

She brushed her palm across his cheek. "I'm so sorry. I know how much you loved Miriam."

He looked into her eyes and clasped her hand. "I did. I thought I'd died with her and the *kinna*."

A love like that didn't come along but once in a lifetime. She thought she'd had it with Blake.

"But *Gott* had different plans for me. He wanted me to go on." He shook his head. "So, I do. I get up each day and I work hard and try to understand His purpose."

Tears filled her eyes. She hated to admit it but she was jealous of the relationship Eli had shared with Miriam.

He spotted the tears and brushed a calloused thumb

across them, a look of wonder on his face. "Why are you crying?"

How did she put into words the depth of sorrow in her heart? "I always thought Blake and I had a fairy-tale marriage. That nothing could pull us apart, but to be honest with you, for a few years before his death, we'd been drifting apart. We rarely spent time together. He worked long hours and when he wasn't working, he barricaded himself in his office for hours at a time. He kept so many things secret from me."

As she looked into his handsome face, something inside her stilled. She waited for him. He leaned down and touched his lips to hers. The gentleness was her undoing. A dying sob escaped, and she kissed him back, her hands framing his face. She'd forgotten how much she once cared for Eli. Looked up to him. Had a crush on him. At one time wanted to grow up and marry him.

The kiss ended so abruptly that it took a second for her catch up. Eli was inches away, but he wasn't looking at her, but the window. His head cocked to one side.

"Did you hear that?" he asked.

The tender moment between them evaporated when she did. Someone was tromping through the underbrush and heading straight for the camp.

Eli quickly covered the space to the grimy window hidden beneath dust-covered tattered curtains. He edged them apart while Faith peered over his shoulder.

Vincent emerged on the opposite side of the camp. Eli let the curtain drop and went over to the front door and clicked the lock. It would amount to little if Vincent tried to get inside but gave Eli a sense of slightly more control.

"We can't stay here," Faith told him. "He'll search every building in the camp."

And they couldn't leave by the way they'd come. Which left the back door.

"Keep an eye on him and I'll see if I can open the door without making too much noise. If he starts this way, let me know." Eli tried the doorknob. It proved as difficult to open as the front.

"He's checking on the opposite side of the camp, but most of those quarters are falling apart. It won't be long before he tries this one."

Eli freed the door. "Hurry, Faith." He grabbed her hand and started outside. "We'll have to get to the buggy and hope we can get a head start before he hears us." Vincent would be armed and ready to shoot them on sight.

The mare saw them approaching and dipped back her ears. Eli reached her side and did his best to soothe the animal before she made a sound.

"Get inside and stay out of sight," he whispered. "I'll lead the mare through the woods until we're away from the camp. With me close, I hope she'll remain quiet."

"Be careful," she whispered, her eyes frozen wide and fearful.

He waited until she was safe before he grabbed the mare's bridle and started walking toward the treed area behind the barracks. Though he did his best to be quiet, it was impossible to move a buggy and mare soundlessly over frozen ground.

Once they reached the last building in the camp, Eli eased down the buggy's side and peered around. Vincent stood in the middle of the camp looking in their direction.

Eli ran back to the buggy and climbed inside. "He heard us," he told Faith. The mare bolted toward the trail opening someone had carved from the woods, as if sensing danger. Eli gripped the leather straps tight in a desperate attempt to contain the spooked animal but finally loosened his hold and let the mare charge toward freedom.

A glance behind them proved Vincent wasn't giving up even on foot. "Stay down," Eli warned when he spotted the weapon in Vincent's hand. Seconds later, the back of the buggy was riddled with bullets. Eli did his best to remain out of sight and still see what he was doing.

The mare ran harder, her mane fanning upward in the wind she created. Froth flew from her mouth.

"Where did he leave his truck?" Faith asked the question Eli hadn't had time to consider.

"He must have left it out on the road and walked in." The overgrowth thinned as the road appeared in front of them. Eli pulled hard on the reins to get the horse to slow to a fast trot.

On the side near the woods, Vincent had left his truck. An idea occurred that might buy them time enough to escape. Eli brought out the shotgun. "Come up here. I'm going to try something," he told her as she scrambled to the seat beside him.

He gave her the reins and opened the door. "I'm going to shoot out his tires."

While Faith kept the animal under control, Eli leaned out and fired at one of the front tires. It blew on impact. He reloaded and shot the second one out.

That should keep Vincent from following. He closed the door and set the shotgun at his feet.

Faith handed him back the reins and glanced over her shoulder. "He's almost to the road."

Eli whipped around in time to see Vincent emerge from the woods and empty his weapon in their direction. Several shots damaged the back of the buggy before the vehicle was no longer in range. For the moment, they were safe.

A thankful prayer slipped through his head. "That was scary."

"Yes, it was." She held out her hands. "I'm shaking all over. How long before he finds another way to come after us?"

Eli looked her in the eye. "He managed to get a car before. He'll find a way to get another vehicle."

"This just keeps getting worse," she said and rubbed her temples. "What are we going to do?"

"We go to *Mamm*'s house and Fletcher can fetch the sheriff right away." Eli hoped he sounded more confident than he felt.

A pronounced sigh slipped from her lips. "I have a feeling it's only a matter of time before the person Vincent spoke to last night arrives here."

If that happened the community would be caught in the middle of an all-out war between two dangerous men, and he and Faith would be completely outnumbered. The sheriff had to be warned about the upcoming battle. Because anyone who got in their way would be fair game. Including the Eagle's Nest Sheriff's department. Including Eli and Faith.

Chapter Fourteen

An exhaustion that went beyond physical burrowed down deep. Just when Faith thought it couldn't get any worse, it did.

She'd brought shame to her family and harm to everyone around her. Now an all-out invasion was coming to this peaceful community. All because of her selfishness.

As the buggy continued down the road, Eli slowed the horse to a trot and directed her onto a smaller dirt road. He was doing his best to keep them out of harm's way. Faith was grateful he was thinking for them both because she couldn't sling a single coherent thought together.

Time stretched out filled with its own fears. Her mind continued replaying the terrible things that had happened since she'd arrived in West Kootenai.

"Do you remember that one time our families went down to the creek for a picnic?" Eli said.

She twisted toward him and tried to recall the time he spoke of. "I don't... Oh wait, I do," she said, and started laughing. It had been a warm summer day for Montana. Both families had gotten into the routine of sharing a picnic several times during the warm months. They'd go to Silver Creek, two wagons filled to the brim with their members and food.

"That day was perfect," she said, but he gave her strange look.

"What day are you remembering?" He cocked his head toward her with a grin on his face.

Her eyes widened, but then she recalled and shook her head.

The women in the families had prepared their best dishes. Eli and his brothers had put together two picnic tables to make room for everyone to be seated.

Grandmother Sarah had purchased two exceptionally large watermelons as a treat because they were not always available so far north.

When no one was looking, the Shetler brothers snuck away with one of the melons. They'd planned to split it among themselves. Unsurprisingly, Mason was the ringleader of the caper.

Only the boys' grandfather had spotted them and gone to investigate. At the time, he hadn't realized Faith had followed him.

The boys had the knife ready and were just about to start cutting when Levi confronted them. Mason tossed the melon to Aaron, who passed it to Fletcher and on along to Hunter. Hunter got nervous and he meant to chuck it to Eli, but instead it landed at Levi's feet. The melon burst into pieces. Juice went flying all over Levi, and Eli started laughing and couldn't stop.

Faith had been so sure everyone involved would get in serious trouble.

Levi Shetler had glanced from the broken melon to the boys and burst out laughing himself. Then, he reached down and tossed pieces of the watermelon at each of the boys. Soon, an all-out food fight began, and Faith was right in the middle of it. By the end, everyone was covered in sticky watermelon juice, including Faith. They'd waded out into the creek and washed off as best they could.

"I remember Grandmother Sarah's expression when we all showed up at the table soaking wet." It had been a huge joke for weeks following.

"I was so sure *Grossdaddi* was going to kill us all," Eli said with a chuckle.

She grinned at him. Eli was trying to distract her from the troubles they faced and for that she was grateful. "I thought so too. But he was always an easygoing man. And he loved you boys so much."

Eli nodded. "*Jah*, he did. He taught me about logging and about life. He sent me a letter after Miriam and I moved to Libby. *Grossdaddi* always tried to talk me into returning. He said it would all work out with Mason in time, but it didn't." His jaw flexed and he looked over at her. "I guess we both have parts of our past we wish we could change."

"I guess we do."

Looking back at the time, the little girl she'd been couldn't have imagined that way of life ending, but it did. By summer's end, her family had packed up and called an Amish taxi to take them to Billings. From there, they'd taken a bus far away to strange places she never imagined. Big cities with different ways of life. And she'd hated it.

A thousand times over she'd wished she'd returned to West Kootenai when she was old enough. Come home where she belonged and had those precious years with her *grossdaddi*.

She couldn't change the past, but she could do everything in her power to make sure she never left the community or her grandmother again.

No matter what the future held for her and Eli, if they survived Vincent's rampage, she was home. Finally, back where she belonged.

Eli kept away from the shops this time as a precaution. Glimpses of them peeked through the trees. The path they were on ran parallel to the main road. Though he'd incapacitated Vincent's truck, Eli couldn't let down his guard. These past few days had left them with no time to catch their breaths in between Vincent's attacks. He was worn out to the bone. He couldn't imagine how tired Faith must be.

She leaned against the side of the buggy as if she didn't have the strength to sit upright.

Something near the front of the bakery caught his attention and he halted the mare.

"What's wrong?" Faith turned to see what he was looking at.

Through the trees, he confirmed three dark SUVs crawled along the main road as if they were looking for something…or someone.

"I've never seen those vehicles before," Eli whispered almost to himself.

Faith opened the door and started toward the buildings. Eli hopped out and hurried after her.

"What are you doing?" he asked when he caught up.

"I want to get a closer look. It could be Ghost and his men." Her full attention was on the SUVs as they continued along.

Eli grabbed her arm. "Hang on, I'm coming with you."

Together they eased along the side of the bakery until they were close enough to see the vehicles as they passed.

"Do you recognize any of the people inside?" Eli asked once the last vehicle passed.

She shook her head, a frustrated expression on her face. "I don't, but three dark SUVs in an Amish community at one time is suspicious." She faced him. "I think those men are from New York." The weight of the world seemed to settle on her shoulders. "Are we too late?"

He tried to keep from showing his concerns. "I hope not. Let's get out of here." He reached for her hand and they ran back to the buggy.

"They're here to kill me," she said once they were moving again. She turned terrified eyes to him, and Eli's jaw tightened. He would do everything in his power to keep that from happening.

"They will deal with Vincent first."

She nodded. "We just have to keep them from finding us until the sheriff can help."

He worried that Vincent might stumble upon his *mamm*'s home once he got the truck going again.

Though it was some distance from Aaron's, a determined person like Vincent would leave no house untouched. "It won't be wise for us to stay at my mother's house for long. We'll be putting Sarah and my family in jeopardy by being there. Unfortunately, Vincent knows about my place and your *grossmammi*'s. And he's been to Aaron's."

"Then where can we go? He's found us everywhere we've tried to hide."

There was only one place he could think of that would provide some amount of safety. "Miriam's *grossdaddi* had a farm that has been sitting vacant for many years. It's isolated. Toward the end of this life, he lived outside of the community. We can go there. It won't be the most pleasant place to stay, but no one should look for us there."

He fought not to show her the turmoil churning his insides. They still had a long way to go before they reached *Mamm*'s house. Now there were more dangers lurking. Men far worse than Vincent would think nothing of taking them out.

Eli hated putting his *bruder* in the line of fire, but he and Faith couldn't do this alone. He'd caused his family so much trouble in the past. Would they regret having him back?

The road they were on petered out and Eli turned back toward the main one. With sweat beading on his forehead, he headed toward his *mamm*'s home while fearing Vincent would already be there. He prayed his family and Sarah were *oke*.

Though they'd only be on the road for a short time,

the exposure unsettled him. The trees had been taken down along this stretch of the road. There were a couple of vacant shops. At one time, the community had a blacksmith shop down this way, but the owner had moved away a few years ago and no one had claimed the shop since.

As Eli drew close to the former shop, he glanced over his shoulder in time to see a vehicle top the hill behind them.

Faith noticed him looking and turned. Her attention jerked toward him. "Eli, that's them."

He had to get off the road as quickly as possible. The blacksmith's shop was the only option. The mare balked for a second under his command, confused by the sudden change of direction. She stumbled on the gravel road before regaining her footing.

"Get in the back and get out of sight," Eli urged while he guided the buggy toward the shop.

Eli stopped out front. A single SUV headed their way. Where were the others?

He turned in his seat. "Can you make it to the shop?"

Faith peeked out the back window. "I think so."

"Then hurry. It won't take the driver long to reach us. I don't know if he saw us come this way, but he might be suspicious about our sudden turn if he did. Find a place to hide and wait for me."

She opened the back door and jumped out. He watched her slip inside the building.

The SUV reached the shop. Eli hoped with all his heart that it would pass on by.

He kept his attention averted but snuck glances as

the vehicle passed him. Eli blew out a huge sigh before he noticed the brake lights.

His heart stuttered as the SUV backed up. It stopped and pulled into the drive.

Please, Gott, protect us both. The prayer sped through his mind. Eli got out once the SUV stopped beside the buggy.

He waited beside the mare while the driver of the SUV exited followed by two more men.

All three were armed.

"Can I help you?" He tried to keep his tone even despite the warbling fighting in his throat. If these men had any idea of his connection to Vincent and Faith, they'd kill him in a heartbeat and take her out next. He couldn't do anything to tip them off.

"Is this your shop?" the driver asked. His accent was slightly more pronounced than Faith's.

Eli scrambled to come up with a believable response. These men would have no way of knowing the blacksmith shop was closed.

"*Jah*, it is." Eli kept his attention on the driver. The two other men walked around the buggy then started for the shop.

"I'm not open for business," Eli called out when they started to go inside.

Both men turned toward him. Their hard expressions sent a chill crawling up Eli's spine. Their attention went to the driver who motioned them back.

"That's okay, buddy, we're not looking to have our SUV fitted with horseshoes." One of the men cracked the smart remark as he passed by Eli. The second laughed along with his buddy until they got a good look at the driver. Their expressions turned sheepish.

"Sorry, boss."

Eli just wanted them out of here so he could get Faith to a safe place.

"How can I help you?" Eli asked the man in charge. The driver stuck out in the simple surroundings in his dress suit and white shirt. His dark hair was swept back from his forehead. And Eli was sure the shoes he wore cost a small fortune. The two men with him were equally attired.

"I'm looking for this man." He pulled out his phone and brought up a picture and turned it toward Eli. Not to Eli's surprise, a photo of Vincent returned his stoic expression. "Have you seen him?"

Eli shoved his hands into his pockets to keep these armed men from seeing his jitters.

"I do not think so. Why do you believe he is here? He appears to be an *Englischer*."

The man's brows rose, and his jaw hardened as if he wondered if Eli was making fun of him.

"I mean he is not Amish," Eli corrected.

"Oh, well, that doesn't matter. We have information that he's here somewhere." He stared down Eli.

Eli swallowed a couple of times. "Why are you looking for this person?"

The man's expression hardened. "That's none of your business."

Eli remained silent and the man finally added, "He works for me and I need to get in touch with him."

A lie, but Eli wasn't about to challenge it. He wanted to get rid of these men as quickly as possible.

"As I said, I do not know him." That much was true enough. He didn't really know Vincent and he didn't want to.

He pinned Eli with piercing dark eyes. "You wouldn't be lying, would you?"

Eli's heart slammed in his chest, but he kept silent.

The man's face broke into a smile. "I'm just kidding you." He brushed his finger over the phone and turned it back to Eli once more. "What about her? Have you seen her?"

Eli stared at a photo of Faith with a man he was certain was her husband.

He kept his attention on the photo as he answered. "She is not familiar either."

The man stared Eli down for a long moment before he motioned to the men to get in the SUV. He opened the driver's door and swung back to Eli. "Well, if you do see him, you'd better warn him, his boss is looking for him, and he knows why. And if you run across this woman, tell her she'd better keep moving because we're coming for her next."

The man's merciless gaze bored into Eli. He hopped inside the SUV and drove away, sending mud and slush flying in his wake.

Eli moved closer to the road while trying to stay hidden by trees. From where he stood, he saw the vehicle ease out onto the road and head back toward the shops. The driver stopped in front of the bakery. All three men got out and went inside.

While Eli was confident the young couple would not give them up to these thugs, the sooner the men left, the better.

He hurried back to the blacksmith's shop and opened the door. Faith popped up from behind a stack of firewood.

"Are they gone?" He nodded and she hurried toward him. "I was certain they'd come inside."

Eli had been, as well. "They are in the bakery now. I'm not sure how convincing I was. We should go."

Before she left the shop, he stopped her. "They had a photo of Vincent and one of you. We can't take the chance of them spotting you if they come back this way. It's best if you are out of sight until we are a safe distance away."

She nodded and he helped her up into the back of the buggy. Eli shut the door, climbed inside and started toward his *mamm*'s home.

It felt as if they were being threatened on all sides. Eli had thought Vincent was one of the most dangerous people he'd ever met, but after his run-in with the man he believed was the drug dealer, he realized he hadn't even begun to understand the true meaning of danger.

Chapter Fifteen

"I don't think we were followed. It should be safe to come up here," Eli said. Even though only a small space separated them, Faith felt safer being close to him.

"These men are dangerous," she said with a relieved sigh. "They think nothing of killing people who threaten them. They won't stop until I'm dead and I'm so afraid." She faced him. "Eli, I can't let them hurt you, or my grandmother, or your family because they think you may be a threat to them, as well."

Eli squeezed her shoulder, a gentle look on his face. "Then you must do everything you can to stop them before that happens." He brushed his hand across her cheek, and she closed her eyes. Amid this nightmare, she was falling in love, and all she could think about was the danger facing them.

He spoke her name, his warm breath fanning across her face. She swallowed and opened her eyes and looked at him.

"We will get through this. *Gott* brought you back to

West Kootenai for a reason. He won't let those men or Vincent have victory over you. You must believe that."

She smiled sadly. "And He brought you back, as well. He has a plan for your life too."

"I pray you are right," he said and faced forward. She could almost feel him distancing himself from her and she knew why.

"What happened to Miriam wasn't your fault, Eli. You can't blame yourself forever. Miriam wouldn't have wanted that."

A bitter laugh ripped from deep inside him. "*Nay*, she would not." His answer wasn't affirming in any way despite his agreement. "But how can I not hold myself responsible. She asked me not to go back to the logging camp. She was troubled by something that happened. I should have listened. Instead, I thought about the money I could make for us."

Her heart went out to him. "Oh, Eli, you were trying to take care of your family. She understood that."

He didn't say anything.

"Was there ever another suspect?"

"Not in the eyes of the police, but there was someone. A few days before the fire, Miriam mentioned something in passing. She said an *Englischer* had come by looking for work. She let him clean out the barn and help with feeding the animals for some wages. Miriam mentioned he'd returned again and made her feel uncomfortable. I told her I would speak with him the following week, only…"

Miriam had died.

"Did you tell the police about this man?"

He nodded. "I did. But I didn't have the man's name or a description, so they believed I'd made him up to take suspicion off myself."

Eli was doing everything he could for her, yet he'd carried this burden of guilt for years. "If we can ask around your old community perhaps, we can find someone else who saw this man. There has to be a way."

He faced her with a bitter smile on his face. "I tried asking around, but everyone in the community had their minds made up about my guilt. They were not willing to help me."

"Oh, Eli." She reached for his hand. They might not have been willing to help, but she was going to do everything in her power to find out who killed Miriam. If she survived Vincent and the thugs he worked for, she wouldn't stop until she had answers, because if anyone deserved a second chance at happiness, it was Eli.

He glanced down at their joined hands but made no move to pull away—and she was happy about it. No matter the mountains standing between them, the doubts that kept her from trusting she could ever give her heart fully to someone else, those were problems for another day. Right now, she just wanted to sit beside this strong and courageous man and simply enjoy the feel of her hand in his.

The beauty of the mountains in the distance and the woods that surrounded the community tugged her back to a simpler time when she couldn't imagine life outside this community.

Through the years she'd told herself this wasn't her life anymore, yet everything inside her urged her to return. How different her life might have been if she'd come back sooner. There would have been more time with her precious *grossdaddi*. She could have been there for Grandmother Sarah after his passing. Married an Amish man and settled down with a family of her own. Never met Vincent.

Mamm's homestead came into view and Eli expelled a relieved sigh. Every mile they'd traveled he'd expected those dangerous men or Vincent to appear and take them out.

He kept replaying his conversation with the man he was convinced was the drug dealer. The same one who bribed New York City detectives to keep him out of jail. The person responsible for setting this terrible thing happening to Faith in motion. Dealing with such darkness was something he wasn't accustomed to and he felt ill-equipped to protect Faith from men determined to keep their crimes secret.

Letting go of his feelings of inadequacy was hard but he couldn't let them stand in the way of keeping Faith safe.

Eli stopped the buggy on top of the hill. *Mamm*'s homestead spread out below them. Almost there, yet he couldn't dismiss the feeling that something bad was coming. He scanned the countryside. Nothing appeared out of place.

He turned to Faith because he didn't trust his judgment. "Do you see anyone?"

She shielded her eyes against the morning sun and carefully surveyed the property. "No. Nothing. What troubles you?"

He couldn't explain it. "I'm not sure." Eli pulled in a breath and clicked his tongue. The mare started forward. "Vincent knows we're in this buggy." He spoke his thoughts aloud. "It will be too risky for Fletcher to use it to fetch the sheriff, which means we'll have to stay off the roads as best we can."

Faith kept her attention in front of them. "I don't understand how Blake could let someone like Vincent lead him into a life of crime he couldn't get out of. He obviously regretted what he'd done. Tried to make things right in the end. But the man I married wasn't a criminal." Her hands clenched in her lap. "Or maybe that's what he wanted me to believe. Maybe I never really knew who Blake was. All this time, I've blamed Vincent for making him into a criminal, but what if he was that way before?"

"I'm sure he loved you," Eli said, but he didn't really know much about their relationship. Faith had indicated she and Blake had been married for many years. How had Blake kept his true self hidden from her for so long? "Money can be a strong motivator." He thought about his own brush with greed. "It makes you do things you wouldn't normally do."

When she didn't answer, he looked her way. Faith's full attention was on something below.

"What is it?" He followed her line of sight. A familiar truck slowly eased along the road that ran near *Mamm*'s house. "Is that…"

"It is. It's Vincent's truck."

"How did he find us so soon?" Eli turned around the buggy and headed back into the woods while praying

Vincent hadn't spotted the movement. "And how did he get those tires fixed so quickly?"

Faith continued to watch the truck's progress. "Vincent is a police officer. He probably knows who you are and where every member of your family lives." She pulled in a breath. "Blake mentioned how Vincent was paranoid about being followed. At the time, I didn't think anything of it, but now it makes sense. With everything he'd been up to, he must have had enemies everywhere." She shook her head, unable to imagine living such a life. "Blake said his brother was always heavily armed and carried tons of extra supplies wherever he went. I thought he was exaggerating, but maybe Vincent had a couple of spare tires with him."

Eli tried to recall the contents of the back of the truck where he'd found the bat. He hadn't seen extra tires, but some trucks kept them underneath the beds.

Once he had the buggy out of sight, he and Faith got out and went over to the edge of the road. The truck turned onto *Mamm*'s drive. His concern for his family escalated.

Vincent reached the house. From their vantage point, the door wasn't visible. Seconds ticked by before voices carried their way. Eli cocked his head and listened. He couldn't make out what was said but he did recognize the man speaking to Vincent. His *bruder* Fletcher.

After what sounded like a heated argument, Vincent stormed back to the truck and climbed inside. He sped down the drive and turned onto the road. Straight toward their hiding place.

Faith's posture became rigid. "He's coming toward us."

If Vincent noticed their tracks going into the woods, he'd realize someone had been there recently.

"Let's go back to the buggy." He and Faith hurried through the woods while the adrenaline spiking through his body warned they had to keep moving to live. The truck noise grew louder. Eli turned to listen. Through the trees, his worst fear came to life. Vincent had seen their tracks.

Chapter Sixteen

"Run!" Eli yelled and grabbed her hand. They raced toward their closing window of freedom while Faith struggled to keep fighting against the insurmountable odds facing them. She and Eli had survived some of the worst situations of their lives, yet they were nowhere close to being finished.

Gott, please, help us. We can't keep going like this.

Eli didn't waste time once they were inside the buggy. "Go, mare!" Eli slapped the reins hard and the horse jolted forward, heading back the way they'd come.

"Hey, stop!" Vincent yelled behind them. "You're not getting away this time."

There was just enough time to duck before bullets shattered the back window, flew through space and lodged in the buggy near where they were crouching. As the barrage of gunfire continued, the mare, spurred on by the danger, raced through the woods.

The shooting ended, and an eerie silence replaced it.

Faith looked behind them in time to see Vincent pulling the truck into the woods. "He's coming after us!"

Their only hope was to stay in the trees and hope Vincent wouldn't be able to get the truck through.

So far, he didn't appear to have a problem. He headed straight for them.

Her stomach clenched and she watched in horror as the massive truck bounced over a downed tree without stopping.

"He won't be able to follow us through there." Eli turned hard to the right.

Eli kept the buggy moving while carefully picking his way around the trees.

She closed her eyes and prayed with all her heart for *Gott*'s protection over them.

She jerked around in her seat when a loud grinding noise sounded. Vincent had wedged the truck between two trees that appeared to be even with the doors and blocked his exit. He gunned the engine to free the truck, but it wasn't budging.

"He's stuck." She turned back to Eli, her skin tingling from shock. "Thank You, God."

Eli glanced back at Vincent who continued to spin tires, digging the vehicle into a deep rut. "He's not going anywhere for a while." He eased the buggy from the trees.

"We need my *bruders*. Without their help, we won't be able to get word to the sheriff about what's happening here, and Vincent or those other men will catch up with us. I think I can circle around behind *Mamm*'s property and come in from the back without using the road." The strain on his face confirmed they were running out of options. The longer they were out like this the more likely someone would find them.

"Do it," she said. "It's our only chance."

They traveled in silence for a while. The noise of Vincent's overworked engine faded the farther away they moved. The woods in front of them thinned into pastureland.

"We'll make better time using the pasture," Eli said when she couldn't hide her concern. "It sounds like he's still stuck. Let's hope it stays that way."

Faith's heart felt as if it were permanently installed in her throat. Her attention ping-ponged from what lay ahead to the woods they'd cleared. She expected to see Vincent emerge at any time.

Eli slowed down the mare once they reached the end of the pasture and started up an incline to the treed space separating his *mamm*'s property.

Faith's muscles tensed. Her thoughts fled in opposing directions. She couldn't get those men out of her head. "I wonder if Vincent knows they're here in West Kootenai. If he does, he'll realize his days are numbered unless he can prove himself to his boss. He's out of options." Nothing in her life, not even being a cop's wife, had prepared her for this. She couldn't imagine such evil and she never wanted to be exposed to it again.

No matter what the future held for her and Eli—whether there was a chance for them or if they were too damaged to heal—she was done with the *Englisch* ways. She'd strayed from her Plain roots, but she wanted to find her way back. Wanted to make up for all the things she should have done.

* * *

His brain swam in a fog of exhaustion. His shoulder ached. Thinking clearly was nearly impossible but he had to keep fighting. For Faith. For his family.

"Where are we?" the woman who made him want to try harder asked, and he glanced her way. She was barely hanging on, as well. He indicated the path in front of them. "These woods back up to *Mamm*'s property. We're almost there."

She managed a nod without speaking. He wished more than ever that he could take this all away for her sake. Erase it from her memory. But he couldn't.

When he looked at Faith, he saw the future that might have been. And the one he so desperately wanted, if only he was deserving of someone like her. He'd had love once and he'd messed it up terribly.

Eli gave himself a mental shake. The future was in *Gott*'s hands and he would trust Him and lean on His understanding instead of his own. Like he should have with Miriam. Until *Gott* chose to answer his prayers, Eli would do everything possible to help Faith be free of the danger following her.

The family barn appeared through the trees and his shoulders sagged with relief. Eli gave thanks to *Gott* under his breath.

"Whoa, mare." He stopped the buggy in front of the barn, the sight a welcomed one.

"Let's get it inside and out of sight. If Vincent sees it, he'll know we're connected to the house and the people here. He may try to harm my family and Sarah to force them to talk."

Eli hopped down and struggled with the door against a blustery wind that had picked up. His *bruders* must have heard the noise because Aaron and Fletcher hurried out to greet him.

"That man was here not long ago," Aaron told him. "I recognized him from the window and had Fletcher answer the door. He ranted about looking for you and Faith. He appears to be coming unglued."

Eli thought about the drug dealer Vincent worked for. With that kind of threat coming after him, Vincent was no doubt desperate to find them before this Ghost.

Once the buggy was safely inside, they left the barn. Eli told his family what happened.

"Fletcher, this is Sarah's granddaughter, Faith. You remember her from when we were *kinner*."

Fletcher nodded her way. "*Jah*, I do. I'm happy to see you again, but sorry it has to be under these circumstances." He glanced around the farm. "We should go inside. I do not trust that man not to return." They followed him to the house.

"We need your help, Fletcher. Can you use the back road and go to Eagle's Nest to bring the sheriff here?" Eli told them about what happened as the *bruders* reached the porch. "With Vincent roaming around along with those other men, I think it's too risky to use the phone shanty."

"I will be happy to help," Fletcher assured them. "I will saddle the horse and start out right away."

Eli hesitated. He didn't believe it would be safe for him and Faith to remain here for long and he told Fletcher this. "I've been thinking and the best place I can come up with for us to hide out is Miriam's *gross-daddi*'s house outside the community. No one's lived there in a long spell. I don't think those men or Vincent will look for us there."

Fletcher nodded. "A *gut* idea. I will fetch the sheriff and bring him there."

It was a small measure of relief knowing Fletcher would have help coming. *"Denki, bruder."*

They left Fletcher to saddle the horse and walked inside where the family had gathered.

Everyone turned as they entered.

"I've been so worried." Sarah hurried to her grand-daughter's side and hugged her close.

"I know, and I'm so sorry." Faith held on to her grandmother while Eli explained what they'd gone through.

Eli explained about the men from in the SUVs. "Fletcher is heading to Eagle's Nest for the sheriff. It's best if Faith and I don't stay here for long."

Details about his plan followed.

"It could take a while for Fletcher to reach the sheriff," Aaron reminded him. "Take some supplies with you."

Eli tried to pull his muddled thoughts together and agreed.

"Martha and I prepared a casserole for the midday meal," Sarah told them. "I will pack some for you to have a meal once you arrive." Together with his *mamm*, the women disappeared into the kitchen.

While the women gathered food, Aaron found a couple of flashlights along with an extra lantern and matches.

"Take *Daed*'s rifle just in case." Aaron handed Eli the weapon their *daed* had taught all the boys to shoot with.

"*Jah*. I don't know how much *gut* my shotgun will do against so many. It will be good to have extra firepower." Eli handed Aaron back his shotgun. "Just in case," he added when Aaron would have protested.

His mother brought extra blankets to keep them warm. They would come in handy since Eli didn't know if the house was even in usable condition.

"*Denki, Mamm.*" Eli kissed his mother's cheek before looking to Faith. "We should go."

The family helped pack the supplies away in the buggy.

While Eli kept careful watch on the nearby road, Faith hugged her grandmother close for a long moment before she released her and got into the buggy.

Eli started to follow when Aaron stopped him. "Be careful, *bruder*. These people are far beyond anything you and I are accustomed to dealing with. Get to the house and stay out of sight. Fletcher will bring the sheriff as quickly as possible."

With Aaron's warning still ringing in his head, Eli switched horses and guided the animal toward the back of the property again.

He glanced at the woman who was settled in beside him. Faith hadn't said a word since she'd said goodbye to her grandmother. Her shoulders slumped. The guilt she carried with her was as heavy a burden as the gathering storm clouds.

He understood about the blame. He'd let it control his life. Had replayed every scenario of what-ifs in his head and they all led to him to sinking deeper into a sea of self-pity and guilt that threatened to take him under. But he didn't want to keep living that way. He wanted more. A chance to clear his name and let go of the guilt once and for all. Yet the only thing standing between him and that freedom was everything.

"I just want this to be over," Faith murmured, her tone exhausted. "I want Vincent and those other men out of my life for good."

Eli wished for the same thing. "They will be. Soon. Once the sheriff and his people know what's happening, they will take care of this. We just have to stay alive for a little while longer."

Her eyes shone with hope. "Thank you for trying so hard for me, Eli. You didn't ask for any of this when you found me at Silver Creek."

Though he couldn't explain it, what happened that night at the creek was a blessing. It had jarred him from his simple existence. Made him realize he still had breath in his body. A life to live. Happiness to find. *Gott*'s purpose to fulfill.

"I'm grateful for what happened because it brought us back together," he said. "I thought about you a lot over the years." Her expression softened. She seemed moved by his admission.

"I thought about you, as well." A whimsical smile touched her lips. "Back then, this community was my whole world. I loved everything about it."

"You can still have this life. It's possible for you to return to the Amish faith. You were but a child when you left. With time and the bishop's blessing, it's possible."

Sadness entered her eyes. "But my family moved away." The look on her face scared him.

Eli stopped the buggy abruptly. "You had no choice but to go with them, but this is your home. You are Amish." He leaned in closer. "You are Amish," he insisted.

A simple breath separated them. "I wish that were true."

"It is. It can be if you accept it." He touched his lips to hers. No matter what the future held, he cared for her and he wanted so much for them to have a chance.

She kissed him back for a moment, then pulled away. Tears hovered in her eyes.

"What is it?"

She shook her head. Each moment that passed without her saying a word had him wondering what ugliness waited to jump out and grab him by the throat.

"You know my father forced us to leave the community?"

She had his full attention and his thoughts scattered. "I do. He and your *grossdaddi* argued. Your *daed* didn't want to be a farmer."

Her eyes turned dark and tumultuous. There was more coming. "They did argue. Toward the end it was all the time. Dad hated everything about being Amish. He finally talked my mother into leaving. I remember when they told me. I was devastated. Mom promised once we were on our own things would be different, but they weren't really." Faith tilted her head as if she were looking back in time. "No matter where we were, or what he did for a living, my father wasn't happy and it took its toll on my parents' marriage."

She pulled in an unsteady breath. "When I met Blake, I told myself things would be different between us. Even though we hadn't known each other all that long before we married, as long as we loved each other everything would be okay." A tiny smile lifted the corner of her lips. "I thought we had the perfect life."

She rubbed her hands over her arms. "And for a while, it was perfect. I loved everything about our life together." She stopped for a breath. "And then things began to change."

Eli tried to understand what her failed marriage to Blake had to do with her returning to her Amish faith, but he couldn't put the pieces together.

She waited for him to say something. When he wasn't able to bring words out, she continued. "Blake worked long hours. We rarely saw each other, and when we did, Blake didn't really talk much. I thought he wanted to spare me the horrific things he witnessed on the job." She shrugged. "I told you that I had no idea what Blake was doing, but that's not entirely true. I suspected something was wrong and I should have pressed him for answers, but I didn't. Maybe I was afraid of what he might say."

"You can't take on Blake's guilt, Faith," Eli said, and wanted her to agree. "He chose to commit those crimes, not you. And what happened between yourself and Blake doesn't mean you should shut yourself off from finding love again."

"Doesn't it? I should have seen the type of person Blake really was, but I didn't." She held his gaze. "Maybe some people are better off alone. I can't go through that again. I can't."

Eli felt as if someone had slugged him hard. "You cannot shut yourself off from finding happiness because of one mistake in judgment. Everyone makes them. Perhaps Blake wasn't the man *Gott* intended for you? You can't give up on life and happiness simply because of what happened."

More than anything, he wanted to make her see how important she'd become to him. "You are a *gut* person. With a lot to offer…someone." He'd almost said *me*. Almost given away the secrets of his heart. "And you are the first person who believed in my innocence since my family and Sarah."

Her face crumpled and she looked away. "I won't remarry. My grandmother needs me, and I will be there for her like I should have through all these years. It's for the best this way."

It felt as if the ground had disappeared beneath his feet and he was free-falling.

From her rigid profile, he believed her mind was made up. So where did that leave them?

The answer was simple. Nowhere.

Eli kept his eyes on the road ahead while his thoughts spiraled into despair. He'd let himself have hope and it had vanished before his eyes.

From here on out, he'd do what he could to help Faith gain her freedom from Vincent and those thugs, and then he would do what he had for two years. Put one foot in front of the other and not allow himself the luxury of hope ever again.

Chapter Seventeen

Her heart was breaking into a million pieces. She cared about Eli. He was a good man who deserved happiness. Would that ever be possible with her? Could she trust herself enough to love again?

Eli hadn't looked at her since she'd told him about her fears. His body language remained tense. She'd hurt him, yet every time she thought about the future, instead of seeing the possibilities of a world free of the danger chasing her, she saw a life controlled by the past. Eli deserved so much more.

The deteriorating sunny day matched her heart's gloominess.

"The weather is changing quickly," Eli said, finally breaking the silence between them. The wind continued to gust, and clouds gathered into one big mountain of a cloud. "It's unpredictable at this time of the year."

She shivered. Almost as if the weather had become a forewarning of things to come.

"Miriam used to tell me stories about her *grossdaddi*.

How he changed after his *fraa* passed away. She told me Peter withdrew into himself. Whenever the family visited, it was always strained. He bought a house outside of the Amish community and let the home he and his *fraa* had shared for so long just go to waste."

"It sounds like he really loved his wife. He must have missed her a lot if he left the home they shared."

He finally smiled. "He did. I always thought it sad until I went through the same thing."

At one time, her reaction to Blake's death had been the same. She'd wondered how she would get through the pain. So much changed when she realized she had no idea who Blake really was.

What would have happened if Blake hadn't died? Would her life have continued the same way as always? With the hindsight of twenty-twenty vision, she realized the truth. She and Blake were not meant to be. If she hadn't rushed into marriage, would she have figured that out for herself?

A clap of thunder had her shrinking away. The dark clouds released their rain. Faith was grateful for the security of the enclosed buggy despite its battered state.

Eli glanced up at the sky. "We are still some ways from the house." Lightning flashed across the sky as the rain fell harder. Whipping in through the shattered back window, it soaked everything. "Let's find a spot to get out of the weather until the storm passes. There's the covered bridge over Jacob's River. It's just down from here."

Faith remembered the bridge from when she was a child. It was on a less-traveled road and had been in bad shape when she was young. She couldn't imagine what it must look like today. But if it afforded them some relief from the cold rain pouring into the battered buggy, it would be a welcomed relief.

Eli eased onto the road leading to Jacob's River.

As soon as they were out in the open, goose bumps sped up her arms. She was just being paranoid and with good reason. Still, it was hard not to be anxious when there were armed men searching for her and Eli.

Jacob's Bridge appeared in front of them through the driving rain. Even from where they were, Faith could tell it was in bad condition.

"It's been out of use for years," Eli told her when he spotted her concern. "Several years back, the county rerouted the road after building a newer bridge over the water. This bridge rarely is used anymore." He pulled the buggy onto the bridge and toward the end of the covering. Sheets of rain would make it hard to be seen should someone happen their way.

"We should be dry enough here," he said with a shrug. "Want to stretch your legs while we wait for the storm to pass?"

She did. Faith stepped down beside him.

The sad old bridge reminded her of how things changed. Nothing stayed the same. The one thing that could be counted on.

"It's a shame," she said and glanced around with a touch of sadness. "I remember how much fun it was as a little girl to travel across this bridge."

Eli looked her way and smiled. "We'd come here to fish and swim in the river. *Daed* taught all us boys how right here."

"*Grossdaddi* did me, as well." She remembered coming to the river with him often. Sometimes with her father. She smiled at the precious memories. The times when her father was happy and fun to be around.

Though rain churned up the river, there were spots under the protection of the bridge that Faith could see through the crystal-clear water. Rocks of various colors dotted the riverbed. Fish swam through the water unaware they were being watched.

"It's beautiful here," she said. Despite the rain, a peaceful feeling permeated the area.

Eli shifted toward her. "It is." Something else was on the tip of his tongue, but the words were interrupted by the noise of squealing tires.

He and Faith whirled toward the sound. Several vehicles had stopped along the new road.

She and Eli ducked out of sight. Four vehicles—one of them was Vincent's. Though their hiding spot was secluded, if the people looked closely, the buggy might be spotted despite the rain. Faith prayed the mare would hold her peace.

While she watched, doors opened and several men emerged from SUVs. Faith edged closer to Eli. Their weapons were still in the buggy.

"What are you doing here?" Vincent's raised voice carried over the noise of the rain. The uncertainty in his tone captured Faith's full attention.

"I told you I'd give you five hours to handle the problem. You didn't. So, I will."

"I'm handling it, Ghost." Vincent almost appeared subdued. "You shouldn't be here. It's too risky."

Ghost. Hearing the name sent chills down her spine. She recognized it from the video Blake recorded. Her husband and Vincent had spoken to a man they called Ghost. This was the man she'd heard on the video. The dangerous drug dealer her husband and Vincent worked for.

Ghost's laughter drifted their way. It was a disturbing sound. "Too risky? You and your brother almost destroyed my business. I trusted you and your police minions to ensure I was insulated from the spotlight, but you've brought more upon me. Leaving this for you to handle is too risky." The man moved to within a few inches of Vincent. "Tell me why I shouldn't kill you right now and take care of the woman myself."

"Because I know where she's hiding."

Faith's troubled gaze tangled with Eli's. He shook his head as if to say that Vincent was lying. She sure hoped he was right.

"Where is she then?" Ghost asked with doubt in his tone.

Vincent hesitated. "Well, I don't know exactly where she is, but I'm closing in on her location. It's only a matter of time." He was trying to buy himself time.

"You have two hours to bring her to me. If you don't fulfill your promise this time, I'll find you, Vincent. And what you did to your brother and your wife will be nothing compared to the pain I'm going to inflict on you."

Vincent struggled to get out his words. "I'll handle it."

Ghost motioned to his men who headed back to their

respective vehicles. But he wasn't ready to let go of Vincent just yet.

He jabbed his finger into Vincent's chest. "Know this. We are looking for her too. If we find her before you, then I don't need you alive. You remember I have plenty of other cops on my payroll. You helped recruit them."

With those chilling words, Ghost turned on his heel and headed back to the SUV. While Vincent stared after him in shock, the men swerved onto the road and barely missed Vincent's truck.

Faith reached for Eli's hand. Neither said a word as they watched Vincent relax. He gulped in several breaths and looked around the deserted space while rain continued to drench his clothing.

Faith ducked lower with Eli when Vincent appeared to stare in their direction.

Eli motioned toward the buggy. "Stay down low. We need to get back to the buggy to reach our weapons. Without them we are defenseless."

She swallowed before nodding. They eased toward the buggy as fast as possible in a crouched position.

They'd almost reached the back of the vehicle when the mare whinnied loudly.

Faith froze. Eli turned. His gaze slipped past her shoulder to something beyond, eyes wide and troubled.

She whirled in time to see Vincent running their way.

"Go, Eli, get to the buggy. Get away from here," she urged. But she knew he wouldn't leave her behind.

Vincent fired a shot and Faith ducked.

"Got you," Vincent murmured as he quickly closed

the space between them with a smug smile on his face. He'd won in his mind, but she wasn't about to let him kill her without fighting him every step of the way.

Vincent reached her and yanked Faith to her feet. "You've caused me enough trouble." He jerked her close. "It's time to end this once and for all."

Vincent aimed the weapon at Eli. "I'll take care of him first so that you can watch him die." A gleeful expression simmered in his eyes. "I can't say that I'm going to miss you much, Faith. You always were sticking your nose where it didn't belong." He shook her roughly. "Well, look what you did to her and yourself."

Vincent held Faith in a death grip while he pointed the gun at Eli and pulled back the trigger. One of the things Blake had taught her right after they married was if someone ever tried to accost her, she was to kick and scream—do whatever was necessary—but never let the kidnapper get her into his vehicle.

Faith slammed her foot hard against Vincent's. Taken by surprise, he yelped but she didn't let up. The second blow connected with this shin. Before Vincent could react, she shoved him and he stumbled backward.

Eli sprang into motion and rammed into Vincent with full force. They stumbled along the uneven bridge. Vincent quickly lost his footing and fell to the ground.

Faith grabbed his weapon before Vincent could use it. She and Eli ran for the buggy.

Vincent sprang to his feet and started after them. They'd never make it to the buggy before he reached them.

Faith turned, planted her feet and shot the way Blake

had taught her. The bullet struck Vincent's side. He screamed again and clamped his hand down on the spot.

Eli opened the buggy door. Both dove inside. Seconds later, the buggy was charging down the rough road with Vincent trying to catch them. When the buggy pulled out of Vincent's reach, he ran for the truck.

"Does the new road intersect with this one at any place?" Faith asked while watching the truck pull onto the road.

Eli shook his head. "No, unless he can find a way to cross over the guardrail that separates the two roads. If he does, the buggy will be no match for him. Hold on—I'm getting off this road."

Faith grabbed the bottom on the seat as the buggy raced down the road for a stretch.

The trees separating the two roads thinned. Vincent had spotted them and rolled down the passenger window. The glint of the gun barrel scared the daylights out of her. "He has another gun. Get down."

Eli doubled over just in time. A round of bullets flew through the space where they'd been sitting.

When the shooting stopped, Faith peered over the door. Vincent kept them in his sights while still watching the road ahead.

Eli sat up and whipped the reins to keep the mare moving.

The two roads were separated now by only a few trees and the guardrail.

"The old Beller place is coming up on the right. Past it, there is pastureland and then we are no longer in the community. Miriam's *grossdaddi*'s place is not too far from there."

Faith kept a tight grip on the seat while Vincent appeared to look for a place to cross over.

"There's the Bellers' drive." Eli slowed the buggy and the horse turned into the overgrown opening.

The mare galloped along, fleeing from her own nightmare, while outcomes chased through Faith's mind. None of them welcomed.

Their path emptied onto the homestead that hadn't been used in years. The barn had collapsed in upon itself and the house wasn't in much better condition. Both passed by in a blur as the animal charged forward.

The pastureland Eli spoke of appeared in front of them. Every chance she could, Faith watched through the shattered opening in the back door. No sign of Vincent appeared yet, but she had no doubt he would circle around and come after them. They couldn't afford to slow down.

The mare tromped across the pasture, kicking up mud as she ran hard.

"There's the road." Eli pointed to a small county road. The horse struggled onto the pavement. Eli slowed their speed a bit and blew out a shaky breath, the strain on his face conveyed the turmoil they'd escaped. "I don't see Vincent or any of those other men. Thankfully, we don't have far to travel before we reach the house. Which is *gut* because it is getting dark and the rain isn't letting up."

Being caught out here in the dark wouldn't be a welcome scenario.

"When was the last time you were here?" Faith asked.

Eli waited to answer until he'd turned onto a narrow passage. "Not since I've been back in West Kootenai."

In what kind of state would they find the place once they reached the house?

With darkness closing in and the continued rainfall, cold air seeped into the buggy. Eli and Faith were soaking wet and shivering.

"We are almost there," he said as she huddled against the brisk temperature.

The drive leading to the house did little to ease her fears. It had been years since anyone had been down it.

A large shape loomed out of the darkness. Eli brought the buggy to a halt and grabbed one of the flashlights as they got down.

He shone the light across the front of the house that appeared dark and foreboding. "Maybe it will be better on the inside."

They stepped up on the porch and muscled open the door.

Through the flashlight's beam, thick dust covered everything. Their entrance had released a cloud of it into the air. Faith coughed and covered her nose and mouth. Though it had been years since anyone had darkened the doors, at least the place hadn't been vandalized and the roof was still intact. It would keep out the turbulent weather.

"I'll carry in the supplies then get the mare out of the weather."

"I'm coming with you," she answered too quickly. The last thing she wanted was to be left alone.

Eli clasped her hand. They returned outdoors and carried in their meager supplies. Once the chore was done, he led the mare over to the barn that hadn't fared as well as the house.

It took them both pulling together to get the warped doors freed. Eli walked the mare inside. With Faith's help, they unharnessed her.

The animal hadn't eaten in many hours. Aaron had packed a bag of oats. While Eli went to the well for water, Faith dumped some of the oats into the trough and soothed the tired animal.

Once the animal was taken care of, she and Eli returned to the house.

Eli glanced longingly at the fireplace that dominated the living space. "It's too risky to start a fire."

Faith wrapped her blanket over his shoulders and grabbed a second one for herself. "That's okay." All she could think about was how much longer they had to wait before the sheriff arrived. Because her heart was ticking off every second as if it might be her last.

Eli kept close watch out the front windows and tried not to let his fears get the better of him, but it was hard. If something had happened, and Fletcher hadn't been able to reach the sheriff, they could be in serious danger.

Faith came over and handed him a plate of the casserole his *mamm* and Sarah prepared.

He smiled despite the worry in his heart. *"Denki."* He dove into the dish with relish. The simple chicken casserole, even though it was cold, had never tasted so *gut* before.

"There's water." She turned to go but he reached for her hand and held her there. Eli saw all the questions on her face.

"Just stay."

Those simple words held so much more meaning than for the moment. She nodded and took a bite from her plate.

"Do you think the sheriff is close?" she asked with her full attention and all her hope on him.

Much time had passed. His *bruder* would be careful not to take any of the more traveled roads. If all had gone well, Fletcher and the sheriff should be on their way here now. If…

"I do. It's only a matter of time now." Yet the knot in his stomach wouldn't ease. Vincent faced losing his life. It wasn't just about ending up in jail. The stakes were high.

"I hope it's soon. Eli, I'm so scared." She stared at him with troubled eyes and he reached for her hand. He loved her. There was no denying it. He wanted a future with her. Wanted her to stay and make that possible.

Eli set down their plates and tugged her closer. She went into his arms and wrapped hers around his waist.

She smelled like the outdoors he loved. A promise he wanted. Whether that promise would become a reality depended on them surviving Vincent…and her doubts.

She stared up at him and he wanted to believe that what he saw in her eyes was returned love. Was almost certain of it. He lowered his head to kiss her, but a noise outside pulled his attention away.

He let her go and opened the curtains a fraction. "Someone's coming. It must be the sheriff."

But the fear wouldn't ease.

A vehicle idled somewhere down the path. Why had they stopped before reaching the house? He couldn't think of a single scenario involving the sheriff that added up to this.

The only true explanation was...

The thought barely took life before the back door was pushed open and Vincent's menacing frame filled the door.

"He must have followed us. Seen our tracks. Run, Faith!" Eli just got the words out as Vincent lunged for him.

Before Eli could react, Vincent's hand snaked around his throat. Where was Faith?

Please keep her safe!

Eli clawed at the hands around his neck to no avail. Vincent's angry face blurred before his eyes. He was losing consciousness.

No! The word flew through his head as he fought with all his strength to be free. The world around him swam. His eyes rolled back in his head. His heart broke.

He'd let her down. She'd counted on him and he'd let her down.

Chapter Eighteen

Faith ran as fast as she could across the dark space behind the house. A noise inside grabbed her attention. A loud thud. Something hit the floor hard.

Eli! No, please, no. He needed her. She couldn't think of herself over him.

Faith turned back to the house. A figure emerged from the open back door.

Vincent spotted her and leaped off the porch. She fled across the yard, running blindly, her arms pumping at her sides while rain drenched her to the core.

Each breath burned in her chest. She could hear him gaining, but she didn't dare look behind. If she could reach the trees, she had a chance of hiding from him.

Just a few more feet. But Vincent was too fast. He grabbed a handful of her hair and yanked. Faith stumbled to the ground.

He knotted his hand in her hair and hauled her up beside him. "Did you really think you could outsmart me?" The fury on his face was terrifying. "You have nothing.

I have Blake's note. The hard copies. And the drive," he said with a triumphant look.

She struggled to keep from falling apart in front of him.

A smile spread over his face. "Now all I have to do is get rid of you. I already took care of him."

Her legs buckled beneath her. The thud. Eli. She loved him. Despite everything that happened with Blake, she'd fallen in love with Eli and she wanted to spend the rest of her life here in West Kootenai with him.

And now she was too late.

Tears filled her eyes. She couldn't give up. Had to keep fighting until the sheriff arrived. "You can kill me, but it won't matter. I told you, there's another file out there."

Vincent's gaze bored into her. "There is no other file." He shoved her to the ground. "You've caused me so much trouble, just like that worthless husband of yours."

She had to keep him talking until help arrived. "You killed your brother. Your own flesh and blood."

The accusation had no effect on Vincent. "You think I cared about Blake. He made a vow to me that he broke. I brought him in on what I did for my New York friends. I vouched for him. We had a sweet setup. Sure, we broke a few laws, hurt some bad people, but we were paid well for what we did. Blake could have anything he wanted."

He shook his head with disgust on his face. "And then he grew a conscience. Said he couldn't live with what we were doing any longer. He told me he was going to turn himself in. Advised me I should do the same. It would go easier on me if I did." Vincent looked at her with disbelief. "I told him, he would kill us both, but he didn't care. It was all about him again. Blake wanted out so everything had to end."

Vincent looked at her without seeing her. "Cheryl had her suspicions through the years, but she never said anything. I knew how to keep her in line until you called her that day," he seethed. "There was something different about her when she confronted me with what was on those pages. It was as if I'd lost control. I knew she had to die." He finally focused on Faith. "Just like you. I have to make things right with him. I'm not dying for that worthless husband of yours. And I'm certainly not dying for you."

Eli's eyes shot open. He coughed and sputtered as he struggled for air. Pulled in a dozen breaths. Faith. She was in danger.

He stumbled to his feet. The house was empty. She was gone.

Fear spiraled through him. He searched for his weapon, but it was gone. Vincent must have taken it. Eli ran out the open door.

The rain plastered his hair against his head. He had no idea where Vincent had taken her. Eli forced himself to stop and listen.

Off to the left, someone was yelling. Vincent!

He ran toward the sound. As the man's voice grew louder, Eli stopped when he reached the edge of the woods. Peering through the deluge, he spotted them. Vincent stood over Faith, the gun inches away.

Eli charged Vincent. The man heard him coming a tick before Eli slammed into his frame.

Despite being injured and losing blood, Vincent fought with the strength of someone who had everything to lose. As they scuffled, Vincent put the handgun into position and fired. The bullet sliced across the same arm that Vincent had shot before. Eli grabbed the injured limb while Vincent prepared to shoot him again.

He couldn't let this man win. He had too much to lose. Eli grabbed for the gun. The shot ripped through the air close to his ear, temporarily taking away his hearing.

But Eli didn't give up. He fought with a strength he didn't know he possessed. With everything he could muster, he slugged Vincent. The blow landed. Vincent's head shot sideways, then his eyes slammed shut and he crumpled to the ground.

Relief and spent adrenaline weakened Eli's knees, and he dropped to them.

Faith rushed to Eli's side. "Are you okay? He shot you."

"It is not so bad." Eli played down the pain in his arm. She helped him to his feet. He had to find a way to restrain Vincent until the sheriff arrived. Eli didn't want him getting away again. It was time for Vincent to pay for the terrible things he'd done. A set of handcuffs was attached to the man's belt. Eli removed them and with Faith's help, they dragged Vincent to a nearby tree. Eli secured Vincent's hands around the trunk with the cuffs.

Eli found the key to the cuffs in Vincent's pocket and searched for any other weapons. Inside one pocket he found something far more important—the drive Faith had been searching for.

All he could think about was he'd almost lost her. Eli gathered her into his arms. Facing death made him realize how much he cared for her. How much he loved her. She'd brought him back to life when he didn't believe it possible. Would she trust him enough for him to prove he'd be at her side no matter what the future brought?

"*Komm*, let's get out of the weather." With his arm around her waist, they headed back to the house.

As they neared the structure, strobing lights approached the abandoned farm. Fletcher had brought help and plenty of it.

The sheriff had arrived along with several of his men and EMTs.

Sheriff Collins and Eli's *bruders* approached where he and Faith waited.

"There's a man restrained to a tree through there." Eli pointed toward where they'd left Vincent.

The sheriff motioned to two of his men who went after Vincent.

"Looks like you have a couple of nasty injuries." The sheriff nodded toward Eli's arm. "Let the EMTs have a look at it before I get your statement."

Faith waited beside the sheriff while Eli was treated for his wounds.

With everything that happened, he'd almost forgotten the drive. He pulled it out and handed it to the sheriff. "Everything you need to convict Vincent St. Clair should be on this, but you should know there are some men from New York out there looking for Faith as well."

"You found it," Faith said in surprise and Eli nodded.

"I did. Vincent had it tucked in his pocket."

The sheriff tipped back his hat. "Not anymore they're not. We picked up half a dozen men earlier. I ran their names. Most have outstanding warrants in New York. One of them, Isaac Hamilton, goes by the street name of Ghost. There have been more than a dozen murders associated with him. No one's been able to make any of them stick." The sheriff examined the drive. "It appears salvageable."

"There's a video on it showing Vincent and my late husband along with one of the men you have in custody," Faith told the sheriff. "Ghost. They are discussing a drug deal." Faith managed a brief smile as she finished. The days of being on the run had taken their toll on her.

Sheriff Collins held up the drive. "It sounds as if it will help. Along with both of your testimonies, we should have enough to get these men off the streets. Maybe we can convince one of them to turn on the others and we can convict the rest of the dirty cops."

Faith looked to Eli for support before she gathered a breath and told the sheriff about Cheryl's death.

Once she'd finished, Sheriff Collins shook his head. "I have no knowledge of you being wanted for her murder, but I'll check with New York. I think once St. Clair sees the evidence against him, he'll back off on the claim you killed his wife. It will be better for him if he cooperates and helps us put away the man he's been working for."

The sheriff's gaze shifted to where his men brought out Vincent. "Excuse me," he said and headed that way.

Once it was the two of them, Eli looked into Faith's eyes. It was as if the weight of the world had been freed from her shoulders and he was so happy for her. He loved her and wanted to be there for her through all of life's ups and downs. But would his love be enough to convince her not to live in fear any longer? He wanted to take that chance.

He clasped her hand and drew her closer. Wanted to clearly see her face when he told her how he felt about her.

"I love you, Faith, and I want to spend the rest of my life with you." He stopped just for a second to collect his thoughts. He wanted to say this right. "I never thought it would be possible to feel this way again, but you've made it possible. You make me feel alive again."

Tears filled her eyes, yet she remained silent.

"I know you've been through a lot and you said you would never remarry, but I'm asking you to trust me not to be like Blake. Trust me to be at your side no matter what goes wrong. Trust me to be the man you need me to be. I love you, Faith, and it doesn't matter to me what the future holds as long as I have you."

He waited. Uncertain of what she would say until she smiled. And all his fears evaporated.

He brought her into his arms and kissed her with all the love overflowing inside his heart.

"I love you too, Eli. And I want to spend the rest of my life with you here in West Kootenai."

"No matter what?" he asked because he had to be sure he wouldn't lose her again.

She smiled with all her heart. "No matter what."

He kissed her again and marveled at the love that had come from so much heartache. He held her tightly and realized, no matter what the future held, as long as they had *Gott* and each other, they'd weather every storm that came their way.

Epilogue

One year later...

The sound of a vehicle approaching caught Faith's attention and she hurried to the front window.

She had never imagined her life could be so happy until she married Eli. Being his *fraa* had made her realize what she had with Blake had been an illusion. This love—this life they had built here in West Kootenai—was real.

A sheriff's patrol slowly eased down the path toward the house. Faith wiped her hands on her apron and stepped out to meet the man who had become her and Eli's *gut* friend.

Sheriff Collins and many of his people had attended Faith and Eli's wedding six months ago.

After arresting Vincent and Ghost and his men, Sheriff Collins had kept them apprised of what was happening. She and Eli had given their statements and were prepared to testify once the trial began, but Vincent had worked out a deal where he would serve out his sentence in a prison away from Ghost and his people. In exchange for the deal, Vincent provided information that would put the other criminals away for a very long time. He'd rolled on his former boss and his fellow cops. She and Eli would not have to appear at the trial. For that she was relieved. If she never saw Vincent again, it would be too soon.

Faith realized the approaching vehicle belonged to Sheriff Collins.

Eli must have heard the noise, as well. He came from the barn to join her on the porch. Her husband wrapped his arm around her waist and tugged her close as Sheriff Collins got out and waved before heading their way.

"Good to see you both," he said in his usual friendly way. "I came because I have news for you, Eli."

Eli's gaze shot to her. "What kind of news?" She could feel her *mann*'s tension growing. Eli had been living under the cloud of his past far too long and she so wanted to free him.

Sheriff Collins was smiling, so Faith was certain it was not bad news. "I just got off the phone from the chief of police in Libby." He stopped and watched them both before adding, "They found the person who killed Miriam."

Though Faith had prayed for this moment for a long time, she still couldn't believe it was happening.

"Would you like to come inside for some *kaffe*?" she asked, and the sheriff agreed.

She poured three cups, placed one in front of the sheriff and waited.

"The man who killed Miriam is named Henry Langston, a local Libby man." The sheriff looked to Eli for recognition.

Eli shook his head. "I don't know the name."

Sheriff Collins nodded. "I'm not surprised. He kept to himself a lot. But apparently, he was going through some hard times and was doing odd jobs around the community. He'd asked Miriam if she could use some help. Langston said she let him do a few chores around the place. Apparently, he became infatuated with her." The sheriff waited for Eli to say something, but he stared at the sheriff, unable to speak.

"Anyway, Langston broke into another house and killed the owner. He tried to set a fire to cover up the crime, but the homeowner had an alarm system so the Libby police caught him before he was able to cover up his crimes. The similarities between this murder and Miriam's death were enough to make the chief question the man further. He eventually confessed to killing Miriam."

Faith watched Eli. What the sheriff said matched what he'd told her before.

"On the night of the fire, he went to the house and told her he loved her. She tried to shut the door on him, but he forced his way in. When she ran, he choked her unconscious and then set the fire to cover the crime."

Faith grabbed Eli's hand and squeezed it. Her husband stared at the table, swallowing several times.

"I can't believe it. Miriam never mentioned his name. A man whose name I didn't know took her life."

"I know you feel guilty about not being there to save her," Sheriff Collins said. "But you can't hold on to that guilt, Eli. You have too many blessings to keep it in your life." He looked to Faith and smiled. The sheriff finished his coffee and rose. "I should be on my way. I just wanted to let you know, you are clear of any suspicion. Live your life in the now and in the future, Eli. Don't look back."

They followed the sheriff out onto the porch and waved as he headed to his cruiser.

Once he'd gone, Faith put her arm around her husband's waist. "I'm sorry that Miriam had to die like that, but this proves it wasn't your fault."

Eli stared into her eyes. "It's still hard. I feel I let her down by being obsessed by making money, but Miriam wouldn't want me to hold on to the past. And the sheriff is right. I am truly blessed because I have you."

And so was she.

Eli leaned down and kissed her tenderly and she placed her hands on his face, keeping him there.

"I love you," she said with all her heart. "More than anything, I love you, and I'm so glad I found you."

As he looked into her eyes, he slowly smiled. "And I love you, too, my beautiful *fraa*. You have made me happier than I ever thought possible, and I look forward to every moment of my life together with you."

A happiness Faith never thought possible again filled her heart. This was where she'd belonged all her life. The place she'd been searching for even when she didn't realize it. This was home. And she'd never leave it, or Eli, again.

* * * * *

SEEKING AMISH SHELTER

Alison Stone

To my wonderful family,
including my adult children, who all came home to
keep me company while I wrote this book during the
spring of 2020. It was like old times, minus car pool.
Love you guys, always and forever.

Casting all your care upon him; for he careth for you.
—*1 Peter* 5:7

Chapter One

The transit bus door whooshed open and dumped Bridget Miller off four stops short of home. The hum of traffic and pedestrians newly released from their downtown office jobs had become a familiar pulse these past five years that had generally energized her. Made her excited for the vast opportunity that lay ahead, especially on a Friday afternoon.

But lately, the vibe—so different from the farm she had grown up on—had a higher frequency, making her edgy and cautious. Ready to snap. And rightfully so, considering her life of school-eat-work-sleep-repeat had been upended when she stumbled upon something—possibly illegal—that made her feel uneasy at the health-care clinic where she worked while attending nursing school.

Today had been her last day of work before her scheduled vacation prior to starting her last year of nursing school ten days from now. She had saved enough money to get her through the final push. The only thing left was to report what she had witnessed.

Bridget plucked at her T-shirt, which was sticking to her on this hot August afternoon. The crowd of unfamiliar faces swirled and blended into one giant blob of humanity. Her throat went dry. *Calm down.* She drew in a deep breath through her nose and immediately wished she hadn't. A putrid smell assaulted her. She'd never be able to identify all the city smells and, quite frankly, she wasn't sure she wanted to.

She yanked open the door to a coffee shop, one unfamiliar to her. That had been intentional. She found a table for four near the back and took a seat facing the door. Her rule-following nature made her feel conspicuous taking up a table without buying a coffee. A sip of caffeine would snap her already jittery nerves. And she wasn't exactly hungry. She dug her smartphone out of her backpack and swiped a finger across the screen to check the time. She had arrived on schedule. The others were late. Ashley Meadows, her coworker, had insisted they arrive separately so they wouldn't draw attention. Besides, her friend had taken the day off, which was strange because she hadn't mentioned it. The office manager had assured her that Ashley had texted in her vacation request this morning.

Bridget's constant companions, self-doubt and indecision, twined in her stomach. Maybe she should go. But before she had a chance to bail, a man in jeans and a T-shirt strode into the coffee shop on a gust of wind that nearly took the door off its hinges, if the man hadn't had quick enough reflexes to grab the handle and yank it shut.

His intense gaze scanned the dining area, not settling

on anything or anyone in particular. He was handsome in the "my T-shirt fits snugly over my firm pecs and my five o'clock shadow darkens my square jaw" sort of way. He was the kind of guy Ashley would have called dibs on, as if the two college-aged women had control over such matters. Well, maybe Ashley did. Bridget chose to focus on more serious things, like school and work.

Bridget's hand twitched. Should she wave him over? No, he seemed too casual to be with the DEA. Then again, what did she know about law enforcement? About any of this? If it hadn't been for Ashley, who'd set up this meeting, Bridget would never have had occasion to meet with an agent from the Drug Enforcement Administration. *Ugh.* The nausea clawing at her throat made her wish she could rewind the clock and say no to this ridiculous plan.

Her conscience would never allow her to ignore what she suspected Dr. Seth Ryan, the clinic director, was doing at the clinic.

The man she was watching made directly for the counter and placed an order. It seemed he wasn't the agent she had been waiting for. Her shoulders sagged at the momentary reprieve, and she returned her attention toward the front door again.

Come on, Ashley. Where are you?

Once Ashley got here, Bridget wouldn't be forced to figure out what to say to the agent on her own. She checked her phone. The throbbing pang of uncertainty roared in her ears. *Be in this world, not of this world.* God had wanted her to be in the healing profession— she knew that with every fiber of her being. Had He wanted her to get involved with this? A health-care fraud investigation? Despite learning about fraud in her college classes, she had never thought she'd be part of something like this. Wasn't that exactly why they discussed these topics in class? So that they'd be knowledgeable?

Bridget twisted her fingers in her lap. Reading about it in a textbook was one thing—meeting with a DEA agent was entirely another. She had never met someone in law enforcement in person. Her childhood had taught her to stay separate. God's law above man's law. Yet God wouldn't want her to look the other way on this.

What if she was wrong?

What if innocent people were hurt by her accusations?

Biting her lip, she stared at the blank phone screen. *Still* no message from Ashley. She couldn't possibly have gotten cold feet. Or had she? Something about how all these events had unfolded had bothered Bridget from the beginning. When Bridget confided in Ashley, she was the one who'd initially suggested Bridget look the other way when it seemed Dr. Ryan had ordered a prescription for a controlled substance for a patient who had died the previous month from complications due to diabetes. After all, the middle-aged doctor had been good to his employees. He was beloved by his patients. He had run the clinic for longer than Bridget had been alive. He certainly wasn't getting rich from running an inner-city clinic.

That was the first thing that niggled at the back of Bridget's brain.

Her instinct was to go to the doctor—who had forgotten to log out of the computer—and tell him he had
made a mistake, but she feared he might wonder why
she was using his computer. She had slipped into his
open-door office when the computer that the nurses
shared had locked up. Then curiosity made her return
a few times to see if it was a one-off.

It wasn't.

When Bridget could no longer ignore her concerns,
Ashley had warned her that the physician might not
take kindly to the accusation, but she'd ultimately suggested they contact Agent Zachary Bryant, a childhood
acquaintance, hoping he could look into it. According
to Ashley, audits of controlled substances were standard practice, and this way no one would have to know
they'd made a report.

It all seemed logical. Easy. Ashley had called Agent
Bryant a few weeks ago, and because of work-related
obligations, today was the first time he could meet. A
heaviness weighed on Bridget's chest, making her claus-
trophobic in the crowded café.

Where is Ashley?

"Bridget Miller?" A deep voice made her jump. The
handsome man she had watched wrestle the door into
submission was staring down at her, holding two cof-
fees in his hands.

"Yes?" she responded hesitantly.

He slipped into the seat across from hers, and a ghost
of a smile touched his lips. "Special Agent Zach Bryant." He kept his voice hushed. "I thought you might
like some coffee." He slid one of the cups across the

table and tipped his head toward a counter along the wall. "Cream and sugar are on the stand."

Bridget placed her hand on the plastic lid and dragged the cup closer. "This is fine." She was too polite to tell him otherwise. "Thank you."

The DEA agent peeled off the lid of his coffee and dumped in three sugars and stirred the drink with a wooden stick. He took a sip and studied the room with sharp brown eyes. "Where's Ashley?"

"I don't know." The plastic lid made a satisfying sound under Bridget's fidgety fingers. "I'm hoping she's just late. She hasn't responded to my texts since last night."

He seemed to regard her thoughtfully over the rim of his cup while he took another long sip. "Should we start without her?"

"Um, yeah, I guess." She hated how timid she sounded. She had worked hard over the years to shed the submissive nature that had been bred in her since childhood. She squirmed in her seat before catching herself, squaring her shoulders and giving the agent a confident, "Yes, let's start." Reflexively, her gaze drifted to the door.

"Ashley told me you have concerns at your place of employment?" The agent shot a furtive glance over his shoulder toward the door, then around the café. Nearby patrons seemed too engrossed in their own business to be paying much attention to theirs.

"Yes." Bridget's heart felt like it was going to beat out of her chest as she recounted how she'd first discovered prescriptions for deceased patients.

"How long ago was that?"

"Um…" Bridget swallowed hard. "Two months ago."

"And you're reporting it now?" The agent's stern glare sent a sheen of sweat coursing across her skin.

She bit back another "um" and forced herself to return his steady gaze. "To be fair, you've been hard to reach. Ashley insisted we wait to talk to you."

The agent seemed to settle back in his seat. "Tell me what you know."

"About two months ago, I borrowed my boss's computer. I saw a prescription for a deceased patient that caught my eye." She pressed her lips together and considered how to frame this. "I hesitated to report this immediately because I was afraid it could have been a misunderstanding, and Dr.—" she stopped herself short since they were speaking in public "—and if I accused the doctor and I was wrong, I could cause him a lot of problems." And, as selfish as it sounded, she didn't want to lose her job over a false accusation.

"But you're convinced now?" The hint of doubt in his question made her stomach bottom out.

Bridget's gaze moved over his shoulder toward the door. "How much did Ashley tell you? Does she think I'm wrong?" The slow sting of betrayal worked its way up her spine. Had Ashley purposely left her to respond to this agent's inquiry on her own? Was Ashley leaving her to take the fall in case she was totally wrong about the doctor's activities?

No, no, Ashley had been a loyal friend.

And Bridget wasn't wrong.

"I don't want to get into specifics in a public venue.

Ashley told me about your concerns after you used your employer's computer. Tell me your thought process on this."

"People make honest mistakes. I really wanted to believe that was the case. The doctor works hard. He seems tired." Bridget rubbed the bridge of her nose, and her eyes burned. The agent sat silently, apparently waiting for her to continue. "However, a patient of mine—an older woman—told me last month that her son overdosed on drugs that are readily prescribed by physicians. I know sometimes these same drugs are prescribed fraudulently because there's a lot of money to be made." Bridget pushed the coffee toward the center of the table. The thought of it made her stomach flip. "I couldn't look the other way. If the doctor at the clinic is involved with anything unethical, he needs to be stopped."

The agent seemed to consider this for a moment. "Unfortunately, there's a lot of this going on. Do you know if the doctor has had any money trouble?"

"I don't know."

"Okay." The agent took the last sip of his coffee and stuffed the wrappers from the sugar packets inside the cup.

Bridget looked around at the unfamiliar faces and kept her voice low. "I understand the DEA audits clinics for compliance. That perhaps I wouldn't have to get involved."

The agent seemed to regard her a moment. Then he pulled out his cell phone and tapped out something with his thumbs.

The reality of what Bridget was doing hit her. Dots

danced in the periphery of her vision. "The doctor seems like such a good-hearted person. He helps low-income patients. He's waived their co-pays. Recently, he's been caring for the homeless." She knew how naive she sounded. People weren't always what they seemed.

How did I get involved in this mess?

The agent looked up from his cell phone. "Have you noticed any other unusual activity?"

"After my patient told me about her son's overdose, I did some searching on the internet about how—" she threaded her fingers, then twisted her hands "—about how people get drugs." She shook her head, realizing she probably sounded ridiculous. She plowed forward anyway. "We seem to have a lot of repeat patients, and we do have a pharmacy on site." Shrugging, she felt her face growing red. "I could be seeing what I want to see. Since I didn't want to do anything unethical in case I was wrong, I confided in Ashley, and she told me she knew someone who investigated these types of things." *Stop rambling.* She checked her phone again. Still no Ashley. "Will you look into it?" Hope made her voice squeak.

"I'll take the information to my office and see when we last audited the location. The DEA is very stringent on the requirements to make sure there are no violations of the Controlled Substances Act." The agent stood and picked up his cup. He obviously had better things to do. "I'm currently on…" He seemed to be about to say something, but then changed his mind. "I'm on vacation now. I just came off a rough case. I'll hand off your complaint."

"Hand it off?" The band around her chest that had

been easing grew tighter. She'd have to explain herself again?

The agent lifted a shoulder as if to say, *Whatcha gonna do?* He ran a hand over his short brown hair. "Does anyone other than you and Ashley Meadows know about this?"

"No one." Bridget pushed to her feet, and her chair bumped into the half wall behind her.

"Keep it that way." His solemn note made her shudder. He handed her his business card. "I'll inform my supervisor. She'll be in touch."

"Okay." Bridget would be lying if she didn't admit to herself that she was upset that Ashley's handsome friend was passing the case off.

"If there is fraudulent activity, the perpetrators aren't going to be happy to be shut down. There are a lot of violent people involved in drug trafficking."

"Drug trafficking. That's not..."

The agent lifted his eyebrow. "Just because a person has an MD after his name doesn't mean he's any less guilty of trafficking drugs than the gangs and cartels."

"Can I drop you off somewhere?" They stepped outside the coffee shop, and Zach turned to Bridget The late-afternoon sun cut across his line of vision, and he slowed to slide his sunglasses on. He had a bad feeling about this young woman's report, and he was rarely wrong. Bridget was obviously a bright woman who would recognize inconsistencies in prescriptions, but he feared her naivety would make her a prime target. He let out a long breath. And Ashley Meadows being a no-show nagged at him. He had confirmed their appointment yesterday afternoon after having the worst day in his career.

"No, thanks. I don't live far." She smiled up at him, a weary look on her face he had seen on a number of innocent bystanders who had gotten wrapped up in something they never in a million years thought they would. "I could use the fresh air." She flicked her hand in a wave and started toward the intersection.

Zach scanned the faces of the pedestrians filling the sidewalks. *Where are you, Ashley?* His former neighbor had claimed she had changed, but her absence today brought back a lot of hard feelings. When Ashley had called him about her coworker's concerns, she had painted Bridget as a wide-eyed nursing student who had grown up out in the country. He had gotten the distinct impression Ashley had wanted to control how and where Bridget made a report, and to perhaps convince her that her concerns were invalid. Or maybe Zach was being too hard on Ashley. He still hadn't forgiven her for the role she had played in his sister's death.

Don't go there. You've got enough going on without delving into old hurts.

Zach did another quick check of his phone to see if Ashley had called. *Nope.* It seemed Bridget, walking away with her head dipped, was doing the same thing. Debating if and where he should grab some dinner before going home, Zach hesitated and watched the commuters surge forward at the intersection. The crosswalk beacon flashed red numbers: thirteen…twelve…

eleven… If he hustled to the corner, he could make it. He slid his phone into his pocket and broke into a jog.

A car revved its engine, drawing Zach's attention. A bright blue muscle car with tinted windows flexed its impatience. He rolled his eyes, then checked the signal. Five…four… He stepped off the curb. He'd make it across easily.

"Excuse me, sir." A gentle tap on his arm made him stop and look down. An elderly woman who came up to his elbow tugged on an unmoving two-wheeled metal pull cart. "The wheel is stuck. Can you help me?"

"Of course." He grabbed the side of the cart and lifted it up and out of the narrow grate slit. "There you go."

"Thank you," the woman said, then she squinted at the traffic light. "Sorry, I made you miss the light." A black SUV whizzed past, confirming that they had indeed missed their chance to cross.

"No problem." Zach guided the woman back up onto the curb, then pressed the button to cross. The next surge of pedestrians crowded in around them. On the other side of the road, Bridget waited to cross the next street. Based on the tilt of her head, she appeared to still be distracted by her phone. Zach noted the muscle car idling in the far-right lane, its engine revving. *How obnoxious.* The side windows were tinted, making it impossible to see the offender. Probably some twentysomething trying to impress with a car and its payment that forced him to live in his parents' basement.

Across the way, pedestrians stepped off the curb to cross, and Bridget trailed behind. Just then the idling car shot forward, its tires squealing as it made a sharp right turn directly into the crosswalk.

A woman screamed.

Cars screeched to a stop.

Horns blared.

Zach's heart lurched. He ran into the street, slapping his open palm on the hood of the closest car to get the driver's attention. Thankfully the car had slowed to a crawl due to the commotion. With a job as an undercover agent, he knew one of these days, things weren't going to go his way. Until then, he'd keep taking chances.

Was that what he had done with his CI? Taken too many chances? Now the poor kid who'd been giving him key information on some drug dealers higher up in the chain was dead. No redemption for that kid.

A horn blared, and Zach reflexively held out his palm and then jabbed his index finger in the general direction of the impatient driver. By the time he reached the crosswalk, a crowd had gathered, making it impossible to see what had happened. He scanned each face. *Where's Bridget?* The roar of the muscle car grew distant, weaving around cars and disappearing down the street.

"Excuse me, excuse me..." Zach pushed his way through the gawkers. When he reached the center of the crowd, he found a young man crouching down next to a seated Bridget. Her pink face indicated she was either in pain or embarrassed, possibly both. Thankfully, she was conscious. Talking. Relief washed over him. He touched the man's arm. "We're good here. Thank you." The man stood, nodded and walked away.

Bridget's eyes brightened with recognition. "I had the right of way in the crosswalk."

He took her elbow. "Are you okay to stand? Let's get you out of the street."

"Yes. Thanks." He helped her to her feet. Bridget shuddered, as if shaking away the cobwebs. "I know better. I should pay more attention." She lifted her hand, still clutching her smartphone. The other palm had bits of gravel embedded in it. The crowd had begun to disperse. Apparently, a walking and talking victim didn't have the rubbernecker appeal of a chalk outline on the pavement. In his rush to check on Bridget, Zach had made a tactical error. Any witnesses to the near miss had been swallowed up in the crowd.

He guided Bridget to the corner restaurant's outdoor dining area that spilled out over the sidewalk. "Sit." A waiter came by and set down a glass of water without saying anything. "Are you okay?" Zach asked.

Bridget pulled up her skirt and examined a scrape on her knee. She studied her red palm before looking up sheepishly. "I think I'll live." She silently picked the pieces of gravel out of her palm, then gently rubbed her hands together.

"Did you see the car? The person behind the wheel?"

A tiny line furrowed her brow. "No. I heard the loud car, turned my head and barely had time to jump out of the way. I lost my balance and fell."

"The car didn't hit you?" Zach asked, doing a quick top-to-bottom assessment of Bridget.

"No. I'm fine. Really."

"Do you know anyone with a bright blue muscle car? Maybe someone who hangs around the clinic?"

Her brow furrowed. "I don't even know what a muscle car is." She shook her head. "I don't know anyone with a bright blue car, either way." Her eyes grew wide. "You think that was on purpose?" She scooted to the edge of the seat, making like she was about to stand. "I need to go."

"Wait. Have a drink of water."

Bridget took a sip, then set the glass down. "I'm fine. I want to go home." Worry clouded her pretty brown eyes.

Rubbing the back of his neck, Zach considered how the car had idled on the side of the road before gunning it around the corner. It felt too coincidental. "Are you sure no one besides Ashley knows that you were going to meet with me today? Perhaps someone overheard you two talking at work?"

Bridget lifted her hand to her throat. She'd be clutching pearls if she were wearing them. All the color drained from her face. She lifted the glass to her lips, and a splash of water landed on her lap. "No one knows. We were careful." The spark of defiance in her eyes lacked conviction.

"Someone could have tracked your computer usage."

"I was careful." Bridget slid the glass away from her, and the water sloshed over the sides. She stood, wobbled and grabbed the back of the chair. "No one knows except Ashley."

Despite her assurances, he wouldn't leave her safety to chance, even if he was officially on leave. A forced vacation, really. "I'll drive you home." Zach scanned the crowd again, grumbling to himself that he hadn't had a clear view of the license plate.

She pinned him with her gaze. "I'm perfectly fine to walk."

"Humor me."

Bridget tilted her head, and a long strand of silky brown hair fell into her eyes. She absentmindedly dragged it out of her face with her pinkie. Her nails were short and unpainted. "Fine, if it will make you feel better."

He hiked an eyebrow and stifled the grin that was forming on his lips. "It will make me feel better. I'm parked in a nearby lot. You okay to walk?"

"I *said* I could walk." A spark of indignation flashed in her eyes. She gathered her long brown hair over one shoulder and raked her fingers through it. A nervous tic. The faint freckles on Bridget's nose grew more pronounced on her peaked face.

Zach suspected the hard edge to her tone was more from fear than annoyance. Like her, he wanted to believe that some cocky driver had taken a corner too fast with complete disregard for the pedestrians in the crosswalk. His gut told him otherwise. This near miss felt more like a warning.

First Ashley's a no-show. Now this. His gut was rarely wrong.

Chapter Two

Zach hesitated for a moment with his hand on the gear-shift of his pickup truck before he pulled out of the downtown lot. "We need to find Ashley."

"Now? Do you think she's in trouble?" Bridget searched his face, his concern mirrored in her eyes.

"I'd feel better if I talked to her."

Bridget tucked a strand of hair behind her ear. "My sister's in town and staying at my place. She'll wonder where I am if I don't get home by a certain time, Agent Bryant."

"Call me Zach. You okay if I call you Bridget?"

"Yes, sure." She smoothed out the fabric of her skirt over her thighs. This young woman dressed more conservatively than most women her age. He found it charming.

"I feel like maybe we got off on the wrong foot in the café."

Bridget shrugged.

"I can come off gruff. I'm used to dealing with…" he tipped his head "…all sorts of people who you probably wouldn't want to bring home to your parents." He gave her an apologetic smile, and she rewarded him with one in return. One of her eye teeth was slightly crooked. Again, charming. He shook his head to dismiss the distracting thoughts. Maybe he really did need this leave. He *was* getting soft. Losing his edge.

"And I'm sorry I snapped when you offered me a ride home." She balled up her hands in her lap, then straightened her fingers to check out her scuffed palm. "This is so far out of my comfort zone. Dr. Ryan is such a nice guy." She gently brushed her fingers across her palm. "I can't imagine why he'd get involved with something like this." Her lips thinned into a grimace. "Do you think he paid someone to hurt me?"

"My office will look into it."

Bridget leaned back on the headrest and turned to face him. "Your office? I know you said you were on vacation, but can't you look into it?" Her soft voice washed over him. He wanted nothing more than to say yes, but it wasn't his call. He had been told in no uncertain terms that he had to take some time off. He had a strong feeling that he was at a pivotal time in his career, and this leave wasn't a request.

"I recently came off a rough case." He cleared his throat, picking his words carefully. "I was asked to take leave."

"I don't understand what that means."

"I guess you could call it standard protocol when things don't go exactly right on a case." He wasn't about to tell her someone died because of his recklessness.

Bridget rolled her head to look out the passenger

window. "I'm sorry, I assumed…" She looked back in his direction. "I shouldn't have done that. Obviously, you met me as a favor to Ashley." He wondered how much Ashley had told him about their history. About her friendship with his sister. "Now what? You give me the name of someone else in your office?"

"Well, let's hold off on that. What I'd like to do first is check on Ashley. Can we do that real quick? Then I'll get you home." He ran a hand roughly over his jaw. He hadn't been clean-shaven in months, and he was still getting used to the stubble. "Maybe call your sister. Give her a heads-up that you're going to be late."

"I can't call her. I don't have her number." Her monotone made it hard to determine if she was being sarcastic.

Zach made a noise with his lips and pulled out of the city parking lot. "You know where Ashley lives?"

"I don't know her address." Her eyes brightened. "But I can show you. I've been to her house." She shifted in her seat. "Turn right here." Bridget tugged on the strap of her seat belt. "Ashley never told me how she knew you," she said. "Oh, wait, turn here."

"Ashley was a friend of my sister's when they were in high school." That's all Bridget needed to know. His little sister's bright blue eyes flashed in his mind's eye. He hadn't seen her beautiful face in over seven years. He had been stationed in the Middle East when he got the call that she was dead.

"Did they have a falling-out? Oh, wait—" Bridget pointed toward the street on the left. "Turn at the stop sign."

Zach turned, happy to avoid the question. "Is her house on this street?"

"Yes. There." Bridget pointed to a neat double on the right. It had two entrances.

Zach pulled his truck up alongside the curb. It didn't appear that anyone had followed them. Four years as a DEA agent did that to a person.

They climbed out of the truck and approached her apartment. "Her unit's on the left." Bridget checked her phone again.

"Still no word?"

"No." Bridget looked up at him with worried eyes. "This is so unlike her. She's one of those people who responds to texts. Always."

Zach knocked on the front door. Deep inside somewhere, a dog barked. "She have a dog?"

"The neighbor does." She pointed to the window next door. A lace curtain danced in time with the frantic jumping of what Zach's mother used to call a yippy dog. Everything annoyed his mother.

"I'm going to walk around the outside. See if anything looks out of place."

Bridget crossed her arms and cupped her elbows. For a fraction of a beat, Zach wondered what her story was. All he knew about her was what he'd gotten from Ashley—Bridget was a nursing student working as a nurse's aide at the clinic. She had a look of innocence about her that made him wonder if she'd get beaten down by the demanding nature of nursing. The job had eaten his weak-willed mother alive and had destroyed their family.

He scrubbed a hand across the back of his neck and turned his attention to a car approaching. Easier to throw himself into work than deal with his own demons. A vehicle that had traveled the salted streets of more than a decade of winters pulled into the driveway.

A female driver on the plus side of sixty took her sweet time and finally emerged with a bundle of Target bags in both hands. "Can I help you?" she asked, curiosity more than wariness rounding her eyes.

"Do you live here?" He pointed to the unit next to Ashley's.

"Yes. Who wants to know?" She transferred one of the plastic bags to free up a hand.

Zach dug out his credentials and flashed them at her. Most people didn't check them out; this woman proved the exception and squinted, drawing closer to check out his ID. "DEA? What's going on?" Her pale eyebrows rose above the thick frames of her glasses.

"I'm looking for your neighbor Ashley Meadows. When was the last time you saw her?"

The woman's Target high went poof, and her features grew pinched. "Did something happen to her?" She pointed to her excited dog at the window. "Barney was barking at something last night around midnight."

Next to him Bridget sucked in a breath.

"Did you happen to look outside when your dog was barking last night?" Zach asked, wondering if he'd catch a break.

"Only caught a pair of headlights pulling away." She adjusted the plastic bags again. "Not sure if that's what had my Barney all wound up or not. Listen, I need to put these bags down. I'm sorry I don't have more information for you." The woman awkwardly fished for something in her purse while juggling the bags. If Zach hadn't been so anxious to locate Ashley, he would have offered to carry her bags in for her.

"Are you her landlord?" Zach asked. Maybe she'd have keys to the apartment.

"No, someone else owns the house. We both rent." The woman frowned. "I *really* need to get these things inside."

Zach tipped his head. "Please, go. Sorry to keep you. Thanks for your time."

"Never a dull moment," the older woman muttered as she stepped up on the stoop and unlocked her front door.

Zach scanned the street. "Does Ashley have a car?"

"Yes." Bridget frowned and looked around. "I don't see it."

"Well, let me take a walk around the property." Zach brushed his hand on Bridget's elbow. "Maybe you should wait in the truck."

"I'd rather stick with you, if that's okay."

"Sure." Zach's pulse roared in his ears, his naturally honed radar on alert. Something was definitely off here. "Do me a favor and stick close."

They circled the garage and crossed the back lawn, a few weeks past due for a cut, unlike the tidy front yard. He stepped up on the concrete back patio, and Bridget followed. Each unit had a single door leading to the patio. A few dirty white plastic chairs were arranged in a circle. Perhaps Ashley had had some friends over.

The vertical slats of the blinds covering the neighbor's back doors moved, revealing a more subdued Barney. Perhaps with his master safely inside, he was more intrigued by the strangers than concerned.

"What are you looking for?" Bridget asked, rolling up on the balls of her feet.

"I want to make sure nothing's out of order."

Bridget crossed her arms again and trembled.

Zach reached for the handle on the back door, twisted it and muttered when it popped open. He pivoted and locked gazes with Bridget. "Stay here." He reached for his gun strapped to his ankle under his jeans. With one hand, he pushed the door open wide, and with the other, he aimed his gun into the heavily shadowed apartment of Ashley Meadows.

As she stood in Ashley's backyard, Bridget's legs wobbled, and the blue sky and green trees went monochromatic. She dragged one of the white plastic chairs closer to the dirty siding and sat down. Her stomach threatened to revolt, and she was grateful she hadn't drunk that coffee Zach bought her at the café. She closed her eyes and tried to calm herself.

God, please let Ashley be okay.

A lifetime of her father's, the bishop's, the entire Amish community's warnings about staying separate from the evils of the outside world rang in her ears. Fortunately for her, she wouldn't have to see them gloat, because she wasn't welcome in her hometown of Hickory Lane. Either way, it wasn't in their nature to gloat. The goal had been to strike fear in the hearts of the youth so that they'd never leave. However, Bridget's passion had overridden their caution, and look at her now. Bouncing her legs with nervous energy while a DEA agent searched her friend's apartment.

Oh, why did I stick my nose into someone else's business? I should have done my job and gone to school. Today was my last day at that clinic anyway... Please, please let Ashley be okay.

Bridget tucked the folds of her skirt under her thighs, then pulled out the fabric and smoothed it. Her stress had exceeded the heart-racing, mind-scrambling, nausea-inducing levels she'd experienced the night before she jumped the fence and left Hickory Lane.

Look how that turned out.

Self-doubt had a way of ramping up her worst fears.

Bridget stood and shook out her tingling hands. A moment later, Zach appeared in the doorway. He had holstered his gun and concealed it under his pant leg. "Ashley's not here."

"No?" Her squeaky voice could barely be heard above her thrumming pulse. Was that good or bad?

The intensity in his eyes suggested the latter. She stepped inside without taking his offered hand. He closed the door behind them, trapping them with the stale scent of day-old garbage and something Bridget couldn't quite identify.

"I need you to tell me if you notice anything missing."

Bridget scanned the room, taking in the little details of Ashley's life: a sweatshirt tossed aside, a pair of shoes kicked off, dirty dishes on the counter. "I don't know."

Zach walked toward the back hallway. "How about in her bedroom?"

Bridget slowed. "Her bedroom? Aren't we invading her privacy?"

"We need to find Ashley." When Bridget didn't immediately respond, Zach added, "She'll understand."

Zach palmed the door to open it all the way. Ashley's bed was unmade, and one sneaker was upturned on the hardwood floor. Perhaps the other one had been kicked under the bed. Zach gestured to the closet with his chin. "There's not a lot of clothes." He pulled open a couple of drawers in the only dresser. "Not much in here, either."

The whooshing in Bridget's head grew louder. "Do you think she took off somewhere?"

He tilted his head as if considering. Why would Ashley have taken off when they had plans to meet the DEA agent? Bridget walked out of the bedroom and went into the bathroom. She didn't know what she was looking for—maybe proof that her coworker had left on her own. Bridget had made up for lost time after growing up without a TV—she'd watched her fill since moving to Buffalo. Didn't bad guys stuff clothes into a suitcase to make it look like their victim left?

Bridget tugged on the edge of the bathroom mirror. Zach lingered in her peripheral vision. It opened with a click, revealing a medicine cabinet. She picked up a prescription bottle. "Allergy meds." She put them back in the cabinet.

Zach leaned on the bathroom door frame. "How well do you know Ashley?"

"I met her my sophomore year in an advanced biology class. She recommended me when there was an opening at the clinic. We've worked together for about two years." Bridget knew a nonanswer when she heard it. How well did she really know Ashley? "She wouldn't just up and go. I know that." Wouldn't her Amish neighbors have said the same thing about her? How many hearts had she broken when she ran away in the middle of the night?

Bridget brushed past Zach on her way to the family room. Everything seemed mostly where it should be. "Ashley wasn't really neat, so it's hard to know if anything is out of place." She twirled a long strand of her hair around her finger, then let it drop. She was about to ask Zach for his take when a black object poking out from under the couch caught her attention. She bent down and scooped it up. She palmed the weight of the cell phone, and the screen lit up revealing all the missed texts, mostly from Bridget.

Where are you?
You're late.
Is everything okay?

Bridget's hand began to tremble. Everything was definitely not okay. Behind the text bubbles, her eye was drawn to the wallpaper image: a selfie of Ashley and Bridget sticking their tongues out with Dr. Seth Ryan in the background throwing double peace signs.

A crack that had splintered across the screen distorted the image.

Bridget handed the phone to Zach, fighting back her growing panic. "Ashley would never have gone anywhere without her phone."

Chapter Three

"Come on—we have to go." Zach pocketed Ashley's cell phone and took Bridget by the elbow, ushering her toward the back door leading to the patio, where they had come in.

Bridget swung out of his grasp and glared at him. Disbelief and fear flashed on her pretty face. "Where is Ashley? We have to find her."

"We'll talk in my truck." He had to get Bridget to safety. *Now.* Ashley Meadows's apartment wasn't the place.

"We're going to leave?" Bridget held out her palms, indicating Ashley's apartment. "Maybe there's a—" she seemed to be searching for the right word "—clue or something here. Aren't you trained in this sort of thing?"

"I do have a plan." Zach needed to get her moving without panicking her. "Once we're in my truck, I'm going to reach out to a contact in the Buffalo Police Department. He'll come back here, make sure it's secure and interview the neighbors. Okay? Let's go."

This time Bridget hustled around the side of the house with Zach keeping her close, hyperaware of his surroundings. Nothing seemed out of place in this tranquil neighborhood. The tires on his truck squealed when they pulled away from the curb. He made the promised call to his buddy, Freddy Mack, of the Buffalo PD. His time at the DEA had him working closely with officers of various law enforcement agencies, including Freddy. When he ended the call, Bridget whispered, "Please take me home now."

"Is there someplace else you could stay until we locate Ashley?"

She shrugged. "No. My sister is visiting. I have to go back to my apartment."

"Listen…" He made a quick decision to zip onto the expressway without signaling. He kept checking his rearview mirror. No other car seemed to be following him. Perhaps he was being paranoid.

Bridget leaned forward and slowly lifted her thumb. "I live back—"

"I need to make sure no one is following us before I take you home." He checked all his mirrors again. Nothing suspicious. If Bridget wanted to go home against his advice, she had to know what she was potentially up against. "I'll drop you off and go back to Ashley's apartment to investigate myself, if that's what you want. However, we don't know what we're dealing with. Maybe you almost getting run down and Ashley disappearing are both major coincidences and have nothing to do with your meeting with a DEA agent." She had to realize the potential danger she was in. "You're welcome to get on with your life and hope for the best if that's what you want." Never in good conscience would he actually let her do this.

"Of course I want to get on with my life." Her tone was harsher than he'd expected. "I reported what I saw at the clinic because it was the right thing to do." Bridget released a long sigh and looked up. "I should never have gotten involved with this." Some of the fight seemed to be draining out of her.

"You did the right thing. We both know that." Zach had no idea what they were dealing with. "I can't make you do anything. What you do next is up to you." He glanced at his smartwatch. No messages. "We both know Ashley didn't leave that apartment because she wanted to, and I think you're a smart woman."

"You don't know me."

"No, I don't. I do hope you'll take my advice and find someplace else to stay until we know Ashley's safe and her disappearance has nothing to do with your meeting with a DEA agent and the suspicious activities at the clinic."

"Even if Dr. Ryan was improperly prescribing prescription drugs, he wouldn't hurt Ashley." Her tone had a faraway quality. "He has two children. The oldest is in college."

"Do you think people who commit crimes don't have families?" His eye twitched. He blamed the caffeine. Ashley wasn't kidding when she'd mentioned Bridget was naive. However, he had to give her kudos for coming forward. Now he had to nudge her not to lose her nerve.

Before someone made the decision for her.

Zach pulled into the busy parking lot of a super-store. He put the truck into Park and met Bridget's gaze squarely. "I've been a DEA agent for four years. I mostly work undercover." He pressed his lips together and shook his head, trying to shut out the gruesome images he'd seen on the job. "Please let me take you and your sister somewhere safe for the night. We can reevaluate the situation in the morning once we locate Ashley. Please."

Bridget ran her thumb over her bruised palm, seeming to be working something out for herself. "I don't want my sister to know what's going on." She looked up at him with wide brown eyes.

"I'm willing to go at this any way you want." He raised an eyebrow, waiting for her to continue.

Bridget threaded and unthreaded her fingers. "My sister, Liddie, is supposed to go home tomorrow. I wish she had already left." She seemed to be thinking out loud. "I can't have her reporting this back to my family."

"Do you have a friend you both could stay with? Someone not associated with the clinic?" He didn't want the bad guys to find their safe house.

Bridget shook her head. "I'm busy with school and work. I don't socialize much."

"Anyone from school?"

"Not really. Ashley's my closest friend." The knuckles of her clutched hands grew white. "Do you really think we won't be safe at the apartment?"

"Something went down at Ashley's place, and she's missing. I don't want to sit back and wait for you to go missing, too."

A shudder seemed to rack Bridget's small frame. Her silky hair fell forward and hid her face. After a moment, she lifted her head and stared at him. He didn't know her well enough to read her mostly blank expression. "I can probably spring for a cheap motel for the night for me and my sister. I'll frame it as a girls' getaway." She twisted her lips, as if the lie pained her. "And you're a friend from work who kindly offered to give me a ride since I don't own a car and all that." She blinked slowly, perhaps surprised at how quickly she had come up with a cover story. "She can't know what's going on or that could put her in jeopardy, right?" The lilt of her voice suggested she was looking for his approval.

"You're making the right decision." He put the truck in Drive again. "Now tell me, where do you live?"

"Can't you wait in the truck?" Bridget turned to stop Zach from following her across the parking lot to her second-story apartment.

"I'm sticking close."

"Hmm…" Bridget mentally rehearsed the cover story for her sister. Lying wasn't part of her nature. This was about protecting Liddie. About protecting both of them. Having Zach hanging over her shoulder wouldn't help.

If this horrible day *had* to happen, Bridget wished it could have waited twenty-four hours. Her sister would have been home in Hickory Lane and none the wiser. The last thing she needed was for Liddie to tell her parents how royally her big sister had screwed up in the big, bad outside world. This fiasco would only prove her conservative Amish parents' point—it was better to remain separate.

A hot flush washed over her as she reached the stairwell.

I've done far scarier things in my life. I can handle this.

Oh, man… How much longer could she give herself this pep talk? She picked up her pace, her hand skimming the railing and her full skirt tangling between her legs. "Liddie!" she called when she opened the apartment door. She strode through the small apartment to the spare bedroom, where her sister's things were neatly piled in the corner. She must have started packing.

"That's strange." She met Zach back in the living room. "She's not here." Her mind flashed back to Ashley's empty apartment, and a surge of panic rolled through her. Then a bright yellow Post-it glowing on the kitchen counter caught her eye. Bridget read the note and sent up a silent prayer of thanks. "Ah, she's down by the pool."

"Text her. Tell her to come up," Zach said.

"You're forgetting I don't have her number." Bridget bristled at his authoritative tone. "She owns one of those cheap disposable ones." Liddie picked it up when she arrived, claiming she wanted to chat with her other friends who had either smuggled a phone into their Amish homes or were also currently on *Rumspringa*. Funny thing, Bridget never broke the rules when she was living at home. She bided her time and broke the ultimate rule.

"The pool is in the courtyard. It'll take me two seconds to get her."

"I'm coming with you," Zach said, and Bridget didn't bother to argue.

They left the apartment, and Bridget locked the door behind them.

A familiar laugh caught her attention when she reached the thick green hedge surrounding the pool. Her sister. Bridget let out a relieved breath that she hadn't realized she'd been holding. She paused, partially hidden by the thick screen of bushes, and held up her hand to Zach. "Hold up," she whispered. She wanted to see who her sister was talking to. Despite having left Hickory Lane five years ago, she automatically felt protective of her younger sibling.

Liddie was sitting on a lounge chair wearing the only pair of jeans Bridget owned and one of her college T-shirts, her legs crossed under her. She looked like every other *Englisch* twenty-one-year-old. She was twirling her hair and flirting shamelessly with a young man, probably about her age, who wore a baseball cap pulled down low over his forehead, shadowing his eyes. This kid wouldn't know what hit him when her sister disappeared as suddenly as she had appeared. Bridget's stomach flipped. Her sister had better not tell him she was Amish. Former Amish. That was a secret Bridget kept from everyone. It was easier to say that she was from farm country. That usually stopped people in their tracks. People weren't curious about farmers. Long ago, she had grown tired of being the object of curiosity of tourists who flooded her small hometown to see the Amish, as if they were some sort of reenactors there for their entertainment. She didn't want to bring that kind of scrutiny upon herself unnecessarily.

"We have to go." The urgency in Zach's voice, whispered close behind her, made goose bumps race across her arms. She still couldn't wrap her head around the idea that she was in danger. *What did you expect, silly girl?*

"Stay here." Bridget touched the back of his hand and was surprised by how smooth it felt. Her eyes lifted to his, and something stretched between them. Inwardly she shook her head. *There's nothing there. He's just doing his job.* "Please, stay here."

"Hurry, please." Zach gave her a subtle nod.

"Hey, Liddie." Bridget spun around and pushed down the latch on the security gate and entered the pool area, plastering on her best "nothing going on here" smile.

"There you are." Liddie leaned forward. "You're late." Her sister untucked her legs and planted each bare foot on either side of the lounge chair and wiggled her toes. She must have painted her toes pink when Bridget was at work. "This is my friend Jimmy. We've hung out at the pool a few times when you're at work."

"Hi, Jimmy," Bridget said politely, aware of Zach lurking behind the hedge where he couldn't be seen. Ordinarily, she'd feel protective of her sister hanging around some random guy, but today she was feeling protective for completely different reasons.

"Hello." Jimmy pulled his cap down lower.

"Sit down, join us," Liddie said. "Jimmy got here a few minutes ago when I was trying to get a shot of that cute chipmunk we saw the other day. Remember how cute it was?"

"I'm afraid I made dinner plans for us and don't have time to sit down," Bridget said, pointing with her thumb in no particular direction. "Excuse us?"

"Yeah, no prob." Jimmy crossed his tattooed arms over his chest and settled in, apparently content to soak up the last of the evening sun.

"We have dinner plans?" Still sitting, Liddie held up her hand to shield the sun from her eyes. "Wait, what happened to you?" Leave it to her little sister to recognize immediately when something was wrong. Bridget must have made a face, because Liddie added, "Your hair is messed up and…" Liddie scooted to the edge of the lounger, and it tipped precariously under her weight. Surprise flashed across her face, then she giggled and adjusted her position. The back legs of the lounger clattered against the cement. Liddie pivoted and scooted off and stood. "Are you okay?"

Bridget played with her skirt, grateful its length hid the scrape on her leg.

Liddie pulled up the fabric of Bridget's skirt, revealing the angry red mark. "What happened here?"

Heat pulsed off Bridget's entire body. "I'm fine. I stumbled when I was crossing the street. I wasn't paying attention. It was stupid."

Liddie frowned and flipped her hair over her shoulder. She had become an expert hair flipper during the short time that she had been here, considering she had to wear her hair neatly tucked under a *kapp* in Hickory Lane. "You're the least clumsy person I know."

Bridget shrugged. "I'm fine. Let's go in." She made eye contact with Zach, who peeked out from behind the shrub. He jerked his head impatiently toward the apartment.

"So, dinner, huh? Where are we going?" Her little sister's enthusiasm was contagious.

"Hey," Jimmy called, "did you want me to send you that photo?"

"Oh, yeah." Liddie giggled. She jogged over to Jimmy. They chatted for a few moments while Bridget waited impatiently. She could feel Zach's eyes boring into the side of her face. When Liddie came back, she said, "He got a cool photo of that chipmunk." She waved her hand. "Anyway...you sure you're okay?"

Bridget smiled tightly. "I've had better days." She cleared her throat. "I thought maybe we could have a girls' night before you go home. Let's go upstairs and talk about it." She pushed on the gate and held it open. Zach stood on the other side of the hedge, drawing the women up short.

Liddie was about to walk around him when Bridget said, "And this is *my* friend Zach."

"Oh..." Liddie seemed to shake her head to clear her confusion. "You have friends?" *Leave it to Liddie.*

"Ha-ha." Bridget forced a smile. "I'm full of surprises."

"Apparently." Liddie rolled up on the balls of her sneakers. *Bridget's* sneakers. "Nice to meet you, Zach."

"This is my sister, Liddie."

"Nice to meet you." Zach greeted her sister, his gaze constantly sweeping the courtyard. Another chill raced down her spine. Did he think someone had followed them here?

"Are you cold?" Liddie asked with disbelief. "You'd think that long skirt would keep you warm." Her sister had playfully harassed her about her business wear, claiming it was one short step away from the Amish dresses they wore growing up. Bridget would be the first to admit she didn't have much business savvy. She thought a long skirt and conservative top were safe choices. She saved her most casual clothing for home. Or for Liddie to borrow.

Bridget rolled her eyes. "Let's go upstairs. I want to tell you about our plans. Zach said he'd drive us."

"Oh, cool." Her sister's eyes screamed, *Nice going, sis.*

Bridget jogged up the stairs, suddenly very eager to get inside.

"What's the rush?" Then, perhaps sensing the vibe, Liddie asked, "What's going on? There's something you're not telling me."

Zach brought up the rear and ushered them inside. "We should probably get moving."

Bridget clenched and unclenched her hands, suddenly unable to think straight. She cleared her throat, and a warm flush spread across her cheeks. "Zach's going to drive us to a hotel. We can order takeout, watch TV and veg before you have to go home tomorrow. Won't that be fun?"

Liddie narrowed her eyes, studying her. "I smell a fish. What's really going on?"

Bridget caught Zach's attention. He didn't offer any help. "I thought it would be fun to stay in a hotel," she quickly added.

"You act like I've never stayed in a hotel."

Bridget bit her lower lip, afraid she wouldn't be able to convince her sister to leave without telling her the truth. For some reason Bridget was especially determined that Zach not find out that she had grown up Amish. *Why does it matter, really?* Perhaps because she had spent the past five years doing her best to keep her past in the past. To break out and live a new life.

"Remember the time *Mem* and *Dat* took us to Niagara Falls?" Liddie asked, still not making any effort to gather her things.

"Yes, of course. We can order room service and movies. Then you can catch the bus home tomorrow." Bridget opened the closet by the door and grabbed her sister's jacket. Bridget was hoping she could shuffle her sister out of Buffalo tomorrow morning, none the wiser of what was going on in her life.

Liddie took the spring jacket from her sister and draped it over the back of the couch. "What's the rush? Oh, I suppose your friend has plans. Zach, are you in a hurry, too? Do you have a date?" Liddie was not a wallflower. Once she got herself into trouble with their father because she refused to apologize for beaning the schoolyard bully with an apple from her lunch. She claimed he deserved the whack and not an apology. Man, Bridget had missed her younger sister. Well, mostly. She'd have to get her back for this.

Bridget's face was on fire. "Stop harassing my friend. Let's go. I'm hungry." Well, she should be hungry. She hadn't eaten since breakfast. The knot in her stomach made it impossible to eat.

"Room service, huh?" Liddie asked, a flash of excitement in her eyes.

"Burgers, maybe?" Bridget was really going to miss her sister. She had no idea if she'd ever see her again—well, for more than a brief visit. She still couldn't believe their parents had allowed her to come for a visit. Even though Liddie enthusiastically answered all of Bridget's questions about their family and life back in Hickory Lane, her sister had never once tried to convince Bridget to come home.

"Let's go so we can take advantage of the time we have left," Bridget said, the band easing around her lungs as her sister finally started picking up her personal items strewn around the living room.

"I'll pack an overnight bag." Bridget locked eyes with Zach, who nodded slightly.

"How did you and my sister meet?" Liddie picked up the book that she had been reading from the table next to the couch.

"He's a friend from work. Now hurry up," Bridget called from the hallway.

A loud crash sounded on the other side of her closed bedroom door. Her heart exploded, and her pulse roared in her ears. Panicked, she spun around. Zach was on her, apparently in full DEA agent mode. He firmly shoved her behind him. With the palm of one hand on the door, he turned the handle with the other. Thick smoke poured out, and he slammed the door shut. "We've got to get out of here. Now!"

Chapter Four

"Go! Go! Go!" Zach checked the landing outside Bridget's second-story apartment and hustled the two women out the door.

Liddie turned to grab something, and Bridget pulled at her arm. "We've got to go!"

He scanned the area outside the landing again, his eyes stinging from the black smoke. Whoever had set the apartment on fire couldn't be far. He pounded on each door as he passed and yelled, "Fire!" He didn't slow to see if anyone came out. He couldn't leave Bridget exposed.

Bridget and her sister got ahead of him when they reached the parking lot. He aimed the key fob at his truck and hollered, "Get in! Get in!"

Bridget spun around, and Zach followed her gaze above the roofline. Black smoke pumped out from her apartment on the far side of the building. She blinked, seemingly snapping out of it, and ordered Liddie to get into the truck. As naturally protective of Bridget as he was—it was his job, after all—she was equally protective of her sister, perhaps more so.

Bridget climbed into the passenger side after helping Liddie get into the back seat. Once Zach was behind the wheel, he called 9-1-1 on his smartphone, which was connected by Bluetooth to his vehicle. "There's a fire at…" He tipped his chin toward Bridget and asked, "Address?" On cue, Bridget hollered her address, holding firmly to the grip bar as he pulled out of the parking lot, made a sharp left and raced down the road, all while constantly checking his rearview mirror.

"I have the occupants of the apartment with me. I'm taking them to safety." Zach gave Dispatch his name and badge number to confirm he was a DEA agent. "Make sure the building is empty. I had to get my witness to safety."

Once Dispatch assured him that Fire Rescue was on the way, he ended the call. "Now do you have any doubts you're the target?" He hated his sharp tone, but he was not going to let this poor, naive woman be a sitting duck because she didn't want to believe her decision to speak up had put her in harm's way. He checked his rearview mirror again. The road was quiet. Liddie sat wide-eyed and silent. He made a quick right, then another left, keeping his foot pressed on the pedal.

Zach cut a sharp gaze over to his passenger. All the color had drained out of her face. A dark smudge marred one cheek. He didn't want to think about what would have happened if she had been in her bedroom when whatever it was that set the room on fire came crashing through the window. He should have taken her directly to his office, made a full report. He should not have let her go back to her apartment.

"Are you okay?" Zach eased off the gas. They were safe. For now.

"What am I going to do?" High-pitched alarm made her voice squeak.

Her sister leaned forward in the back seat. "What in the world is going on? I'm going to guess Zach here isn't a friend from work." Despite the seriousness of the situation, a hint of excitement laced her tone.

Bridget shook her head tightly and seemed to be at a loss for words.

"I'm a law enforcement agent. Your sister reported—"

"Stop." Bridget finally spoke up. "Liddie doesn't need to know everything."

"Um, Liddie's right here."

Bridget shifted in her seat to look at her sister. "You can't tell *Mem* and *Dat*." Zach had a hard time placing her accent.

"I think they'll wonder why I've returned home with none of my things." In the rearview mirror, he watched her pluck at her T-shirt. "I don't have my plain clothes."

Plain clothes?

"We can stop to pick some up before you go home." Bridget lifted her chin in determination. "You have to go home in the morning."

"Where's home?" Zach asked.

Bridget lifted her hand in a silencing gesture. Liddie ignored her. "Hickory Lane."

"Where's that?"

Bridget sagged into her seat and tugged on her seat

belt. "Hickory Lane is about an hour from here. It has a large Amish community."

"Amish?" Zach nearly sputtered out the word before he had a chance to consider his audience. He cleared his throat. "Did you grow up Amish?"

Bridget ignored his question. "Liddie is going home first thing in the morning. It will draw more attention if we were to drop her off tonight."

"I can't go home without making sure you're okay. And you're definitely not okay. Someone set your apartment on fire," Liddie said. "I may not be worldly, but I'm not stupid."

"I never said you were stupid." Bridget's tone softened. "I can't deal with all of this. *Please.*"

"Tell me what's going on," Liddie pleaded. "What did you report?"

"Take us to the hotel." Bridget tilted her chin, as if that settled everything.

"Fine, we'll go to a hotel, but I'm not going home until you tell me what's going on." In the rearview mirror, Zach watched Liddie cross her arms tightly over her chest.

"I'll figure it out. My classes start the week after next." Bridget shrugged. "Maybe I can get temporary housing through the university."

Zach was done holding this tongue. "I need to make sure you're someplace safe until we figure out who's targeting you."

"Isn't that obvious?" Bridget shook her head. "Someone knows I was meeting with you." She fidgeted with the seat belt. "Shouldn't someone go find Dr. Ryan?"

"The doctor you work with?" Liddie asked, obviously confused.

"All that will have to be investigated," Zach said. "Until then, you need to be tucked away someplace safe."

"Bridget, you have to come home. *Please*," Liddie begged. "You'll be safe there."

"I'm not going home." Bridget shot her sister an unmistakable "stop talking" glare.

"*Dat* and *Mem* will be happy to see you. They will, I promise." Liddie was nothing if not persistent.

"The only way they'll be happy is if I return for good." Bridget shook her head. "That's not happening. I told you I have school next week. It's too far to commute."

Zach felt like he was intruding on a conversation he shouldn't have been privy to.

"Humor me," Zach said. "Do your friends in Buffalo know where home is?" Ashley had mentioned something about Bridget growing up on a farm somewhere.

Bridget's face grew pink. "No one knows where I grew up, and I'd like to keep it that way."

"Is there a reason why you couldn't go there for the week, at least?" Zach suggested.

"Okay, here's the deal. I grew up Amish. My sister here is on *Rumspringa*. She's going home tomorrow. *Alone.* I never told anyone about my background because it lends itself to questions." She must have read something on his face, because she pointed at him. "Like that." She shook her head; frustration slanted the corners of her mouth. "It was a huge sacrifice to leave my family, and returning to Hickory Lane to stay with them is not an option. And if they learn that some evil *Englischers* are trying to…" she seemed to change course midsentence "…hurt me, they'll never let the rest of my siblings out of their sight forever." She dipped her head and scratched her forehead. "There's no winning here."

Before Zach had a chance to question her more, his cell phone chimed. "It's my contact in the Buffalo Police Department. I need to take this." He pressed Accept on the controls on the steering wheel. "Hey, Freddy, before you give me any updates on Ashley, I need to let you know you're on speakerphone. I have a friend of hers in my vehicle."

"Sorry, no updates. Still canvassing the neighborhood," Freddy said, his tone direct. "We put out an alert for her car. Wanted to keep you in the loop." The officer cleared his throat. "We'll keep looking."

"You should know that someone set Ashley Meadows's coworker's apartment on Spring Street on fire," Zach said.

"Heard the call go out on that one. Looks like someone tossed a Molotov cocktail through the window. Everyone okay there?" Freddy asked.

"Yeah, I'm taking the occupants to a hotel." Zach tapped on his steering wheel. "Let me know if you hear anything else?"

"Of course. Seems you're right in the middle of some serious stuff."

"Afraid so." Zach slowed at the red light and took notice of his surroundings. Nothing suspicious. "My office will be involved in the investigation, for sure, but we could use the BPD's eyes and ears." He hoped his supervisor agreed with him, since he was technically on leave after the Kevin Pearson incident. An incident he'd never be able to forget. Or forgive himself for.

"Sure thing," Freddy said. "Be careful."

Zach ended the call and his phone immediately rang. It was his supervisor, Assistant Special Agent in Charge Colleen McCarthy. She wasn't going to be happy.

"Agent McCarthy," Zach said into the phone by way of greeting.

"I hear you're not exactly taking it easy." The ASAC had sent him on leave.

"Just have a few things to take care of for a friend." Zach smiled tightly at Bridget as she fidgeted with her hands in her lap.

Colleen's deep sigh filled the interior of the vehicle over the Bluetooth speakers. "How important is this?"

"Life and death."

Silence stretched across the line before his boss finally said, "Agent Bryant, you're technically on leave and what you do on leave is your business. But if this blows back on the department, you'll live to regret it."

"Thanks." He understood her need to cover her backside.

"You won't be thanking me if you don't get cleared to come back to work."

"That won't happen," Zach said curtly. He was about to state all the reasons he didn't need this leave in the first place, but he had already lost that argument.

"Don't let it. Take care of your personal business and lay low. Got it?"

"Got it," he said as he turned on his directional for the hotel.

Zach ended the call just as they pulled up under the porte cochère of the hotel. "Looks like I'm cleared to help you."

"Didn't exactly sound like that to me," Bridget said in an even tone, turning to study the two-story, non-descript hotel.

"You don't know my boss like I do." He smiled. "Let's get you both inside. Then I'm going to go see what the good doctor has to say."

The next morning Bridget woke from a fitful sleep. Her nerves were humming in time with the loud AC unit on the wall of the dank hotel room. Her life had been turned upside down yesterday. Reporting her concerns to law enforcement had been worse than she could have possibly imagined. After much discussion with Zach last night, Bridget had decided she had no choice but to go back to Hickory Lane.

Bridget had no home and limited funds, which meant limited options. She prayed they'd be able to find who-ever set her apartment on fire. Then, maybe she could find housing on campus and start her classes in a little over a week, as planned. The ache in her stomach told her it wouldn't be that easy.

Zach had warned her. Depending on how deep Dr. Ryan had gotten involved with his alleged prescription fraud, the drug-dealing networks were complex and had long tentacles. How was she supposed to know what she was getting into? *Ugh*...

She closed her eyes briefly and sent up another prayer for Ashley. When she was done, she rolled over and plumped up her pillow and settled her head back down, not quite ready to start the day. Would she ever be ready? Across the narrow space separating the double beds, Bridget found her sister watching her.

"Guder mariye." Good morning. Liddie had her hands tucked under the pillow, and her eyes shone bright in the soft light spilling in around the heavy curtains that hadn't been pulled all the way shut. For her little sister, yesterday's tragedy meant her big sister was coming home. It was a bright side to an otherwise awful day. For Bridget, it was more awfulness. It wasn't that she didn't love her family. She loved them dearly, but following her dreams meant severing ties completely with her loved ones. Going back would only tear open those wounds. Wounds she had worked hard to heal over the course of five years.

Would she have it in her to leave a second time?

"I'm not so sure it's a good morning," Bridget muttered.

The mascara Liddie had been experimenting with yesterday was smeared under her eyes. She pushed up on one elbow, and her long, loose hair fanned out over the pillow. "Maybe this is a sign." Bridget had told Liddie about the discrepancies in the prescriptions. That perhaps Dr. Ryan had been part of a pill mill. She had come across that term during her internet search. About how she finally summoned the nerve to report the well-loved doctor after she learned about a patient's son who had overdosed on this very same class of drugs.

Bridget grunted and sat up. "A sign?" The AC unit clicked off, and the room grew still. "A sign that I'm supposed to return to Hickory Lane for good?" The comforter slipped down, exposing Bridget's bare arm, and she shuddered. "Do you think this is God punishing me for leaving?" All the thoughts swirling around her brain came spilling out, directed angrily at her sister, her poor, sweet sister who had no idea how hard Bridget had worked to get this far. On her own.

Liddie smiled sadly. "We've missed you. That's all. I've been praying that Ashley is found safe. And I'm worried about you. Don't be mad at me."

Bridget's shoulders sagged. "I never meant for any of this to happen." She swung her legs around and climbed out of bed. "*Dat* isn't going to want me in the house unless I submit to God and the Amish ways in front of the community. You know that."

"Maybe once your friend explains the situation, he'll understand," Liddie said, sitting up and raking her fingers through her tangled hair.

"The DEA agent is not my friend. I met him yesterday." Bridget picked up an elastic from the bedside table and pulled her hair back into a high ponytail.

Liddie's lips flattened. "Really? Yesterday? I got a different vibe. He was all protective of you." She waggled her eyebrows. "I think he likes you."

"Oh, silly girl. That's his job." Bridget secretly took pleasure in her sister's observation. "He has no interest in me other than keeping me alive." A worldly man like him would never look twice at a simple girl like her.

"We'll see," Liddie said, laughing.

"Stop. Ashley knew Zach from her childhood. Since he works for the Drug Enforcement Administration, she suggested we meet with him." She waved her hand in dismissal.

"And still no word from Ashley?" Liddie asked, growing somber.

Bridget grabbed her cell phone from the desk. "No messages." With her free hand, she flung open the room-darkening shades in an effort to dispel the gathering sense of doom surrounding the whereabouts of her friend.

"Zach will find her," Liddie said, offering her encouragement.

Bridget sat down on the edge of the bed. "When we get home, please let me tell *Mem* and *Dat*." This was her way of grasping onto the last bit of control.

"What should I say?" Liddie asked. "I can't stand there like a dummy."

"I'm not asking you to do that. Maybe leave out the bit about my apartment?" Bridget's posture sagged. She turned, rested her chin on her shoulder and locked eyes with her sister. "That won't work, will it?"

"Might be hard to explain why I don't have any of my things."

"The truth is best," Bridget said, resigned.

Liddie flung the covers off her legs and crawled over to kneel on the bed next to Bridget. "Once you're home, it'll be like old times."

"That's what I'm afraid of." Bridget patted her sister's hand.

"Elijah and Caleb will be so happy to see you. We've all missed you."

Dread and longing twisted in Bridget's stomach. "They must have grown so much." Elijah was only eleven and Caleb seven when she left. She had resisted asking Liddie too many questions about her brothers prior to now, knowing that it would make her more homesick. However, today, she'd get to see them. "Elijah must be running wild himself nowadays. He's sixteen."

"He's a good kid." Liddie vibrated with excitement, making the mattress bounce. "They'll be so happy to see you."

"What happens when I leave again?"

"Maybe you'll change your mind." Liddie sounded so hopeful that it made Bridget more bummed.

"You have to get that idea out of your head. I have a good life here. I am going to graduate with my nursing degree next spring."

Liddie squeezed Bridget's hand. "You're coming back with me to Hickory Lane today. That's what counts."

Bridget jerked her head back, not quite sure what to say. She couldn't blame her sister for not feeling the same sense of apprehension. She didn't know Ashley. Her whole life hadn't been turned upside down. Before she had a chance to formulate a response, Liddie gave her sister a quick peck on the cheek, then bolted off the mattress toward the bathroom.

"Beat ya," Liddie said before closing the door. The shower curtain hooks scraped across the metal pole and the faucet knobs screeched a fraction of a second before the old water pipes hummed to life.

Bridget released a strangled laugh. Leave it to Liddie. Bridget flopped back on her bed and tried to quiet her mind. She was going home. To Hickory Lane.

Chapter Five

Bridget's family home was an easy drive west on the Thruway and another thirty minutes on back country roads south of Fredonia, New York. Zach had never explored this part of Western New York and had never heard of the small town of Hickory Lane. In the back seat, Liddie kept up her friendly banter until Bridget's silence made it evident that she wasn't in the mood for small talk.

Their first stop was a store in the center of the small town of Hickory Lane. The women needed new clothes. Zach waited in the truck. When the sisters reemerged, he had to blink twice. Bridget was almost unrecognizable in her bonnet, gray dress and black boots.

Bringing her here for safekeeping had been a brilliant idea.

"All set?" Zach asked when they both climbed back into the truck.

"Yes," Bridget said tersely. "Go straight and I'll let you know when you need to turn."

"Will do." Zach pulled away from the curb.

"What is your plan once you drop us off?" Bridget asked. "How long before I can head back to Buffalo?"

"I don't have any answers."

"I thought you made some phone calls last night." Bridget tapped her fingers nervously on the door.

"I did. The doctor's wife claims he left on a golf outing yesterday after work and isn't expected home for a few days." Mrs. Ryan had been fuzzy on the details of her husband's sudden trip, either purposely or unintentionally. Zach didn't want to believe she knew what— if anything—her husband was up to. "An agent in my office is actively tracking him down."

"And once your coworker finds him?"

"You realize it's not that simple." Zach slowed behind an Amish buggy. "Like I mentioned yesterday, it's unlikely that he acted alone." He sensed she kept asking the same question in hopes of getting a different answer.

"Bridget can stay in Hickory Lane as long as she needs to," Liddie said optimistically from the back seat.

Bridget groaned. "If I stay, you'll let me know the minute I can come back to Buffalo? Classes start a week from Monday."

"Of course." He rested his arm on the ledge of the open window and followed Bridget's directions. Fields of corn swayed in the light breeze. The last time he had been out in the country, it had been to raid a meth lab in a double-wide. Drugs had no socioeconomic boundaries.

"There," Liddie said from the back seat. "The house is the first one on the right."

A well-maintained wood structure sat between a field of corn and trees. A dirt driveway ran back toward a red barn. Flower beds interrupted the luxurious green lawn. Apparently, the Amish took pride in their homes, or at least the Miller family did.

"Pull over on the side of the road. My father won't appreciate having your truck on his property," Bridget said, her voice soft. "We can get out here."

"I'm not going to drop you off and leave," Zach said. "I need to make sure you're settled."

Bridget anxiously played with the folds in her long skirt. He followed her gaze out the front windshield. Someone dressed exactly like Bridget and Liddie was in the side yard pinning laundry to a clothesline. A row of matching pants and shirts flapped in the breeze on a parallel line.

"I'll be safe here. No one knows about my Amish roots. I made sure of that." A flash of defiance sparked in her brown eyes. "There's no need for you to stay. You can reach me on my phone when you've taken care of everything." She lifted up her smartphone, and the sunlight glinted off the screen, momentarily blinding him.

"Do you have a place to charge that?" he asked, feeling the full weight of Liddie's uncharacteristic silence in the back seat.

"I'll figure it out." Bridget slipped it into the brown bag holding the clothes she had changed out of.

Zach smiled at Liddie over his shoulder. "Would you mind giving us a minute?"

"*Yah*, of course. It was nice to meet you," Liddie said,

her voice softer than it had been earlier. Perhaps the change in clothing had altered her personality somehow.

Zach smiled. "You too. Take care."

"Wait for me at the bottom of the driveway. I don't want to greet our parents alone," Bridget said, the panic evident on her face.

The woman hanging clothes had now lifted her hand to shield her eyes to get a better look at the vehicle. He didn't have long before they'd have company. "I don't think you understand how much danger you're in."

Bridget's eyes sparked with anger. "I don't?" She practically spat out the words. "Do you think I'd up-root my life, put on this dress and return home because I'm in the mood for new scenery? I *know* what's going on, and I need you to fix it. That's why Ashley said we should call you. She said you could discreetly find out what was going on. That everything would be okay." Tears filled her eyes, and the words that she had ob-viously been holding back filled the small space be-tween them.

"I'm sorry everything went south." Of course, Ash-ley would think he could make everything okay. Grow-ing up as neighbors in the University District of Buffalo, Ashley and his sister had been inseparable since they met in kindergarten. A million times over his little sister had come to him for help and he took care of things—a flat bike tire, an empty belly, the bully on the play-ground. Until he deployed and left his little sister to figure things out on her own. She hadn't been able to get a handle on her drug problem alone. He'd never forgive himself for leaving her with their mother, who couldn't take care of herself, much less her daughter.

Zach shook away the memories crowding in on him. He may not have been there for Leann, but he was here now. If he knew one thing well, it was his job. His job. He didn't exactly have that, right now, did he?

Through the rear window, Liddie could be seen pacing, her arms crossed tightly over the bib of her dress. "Please don't be upset. We only met yesterday, and I know you have no reason to trust me." He cleared his throat. "But you need to trust me. I have a lot of resources at my disposal." The only people he ever trusted were people he worked with. "Dr. Ryan is only part of the problem. Once he's in custody, there will most likely be others."

"That only sounds a little bit reassuring." Bridget rubbed her neck, then dropped her hand. "I didn't mean to be rude." Pink blossomed across the fair skin of her cheeks. "This is very stressful."

"I understand. No need to apologize."

"Okay," she announced, seeming to have come to a decision. "I need to go. My mother won't linger by the wash line forever." Two rows of laundry flapped in the wind. Her mother had gone back to pinning identical brown shirts to the remaining line, shooting curious glances over her shoulder. "If my parents agree to let me stay, will you go? Your presence won't be welcomed." She laughed, a woeful sound. "I won't exactly be welcomed, either, but at least I'm dressed the part."

"Is there a hotel nearby?"

"You're kidding me. You plan to stay in town?" She

held out her palm. "I've never told anyone I'm Amish. How would they track me down here?"

"I'm not going to take the chance."

Shaking her head, Bridget pushed open the door, climbed out and slammed the door. She walked up the driveway with her sister, and her new black boots kicked up a cloud of dust. From the back they could be twins.

Zach had handled all sorts of situations in his line of work: the dealer who tried to jackrabbit on him only to be hung up on the top of a barbed-wire fence, the time a woman threw her baby at him when they raided her apartment and the shootout at the pharmacy when the zing of a bullet whistled past his ear.

He suspected Miss Bridget Miller was going to prove to be equally challenging, in her own stubborn way.

Bridget and Liddie's *mem* watched them approach, hands fisted and full of clothespins. A riot of emotions—shame, nostalgia, overwhelming love—heated Bridget's face, and she found herself fidgeting with the strings of her bonnet. She'd never thought she'd be back in Hickory Lane, not dressed in plain clothes. What would she tell her family?

This is such a bad idea.

Stepping back onto her family's farm had been like returning to her childhood. Nothing had changed since she left five years ago. Nothing had changed in a hundred years, for that matter.

The crisp scent of cornstalks, the fresh country air, the earthy fragrance—all felt like home.

Bridget stopped abruptly and grabbed her sister's

arm, panic setting her skin on fire. "I can't do this." It would be too hard to leave again.

Liddie smiled and patted her hand reassuringly. "*Yah*, you can. I'm here. And *Mem* is waiting. She'll be *so* happy to see you. You can't turn around now. You'll break her heart."

Memories from Bridget's childhood rolled over her, some happy, some not. The most tumultuous time was the year, months, weeks and days leading up to her secret departure. She had been fraught with indecision. One of the hardest parts about leaving the Amish was not being able to say goodbye to her family. That's not how it worked. When a person left, they left. No goodbye. No *I'll see you when you're in town*. None of that. Otherwise they would have talked her into staying. *Guilted* her into staying.

"Okay," Bridget finally whispered. A conscious effort to relax did nothing to ease the knot tightening between her shoulder blades. Next to a clean blue dress billowing in the breeze, her mother tossed the clothespins in the basket and slowly lifted her work-worn hands to her mouth. Tears glistened in her eyes. Bridget's heart softened. *"Mem."* The single word came out on a squeak.

"Wilkum." Welcome. Her mother held out her hands. Bridget fought the urge to run into her mother's arms and accept the warm homecoming, not wanting to give the older woman false hope. Her mother's heart had been broken. She couldn't do that to her all over again. It wouldn't be fair. *"Wie bischt?"* How are you?

"Ich bin gut." I am well. An automatic reply from her

childhood in a language she hadn't used since she left. A rush of adrenaline made her grow dizzy. She took a step backward. "This was a mistake," Bridget whispered so only Liddie could hear. Behind her, the sunlight reflected on the windshield of Zach's truck. She couldn't see him, but she felt his gaze. She was trapped between her past and an uncertain future.

"You're home." Her mother's soft voice washed over her. So familiar. Soothing. The woman who had cleaned her scrapes, wiped away her tears, first made her love the idea of taking care of others.

"*Mem*, Bridget needs a place to stay," Liddie said. "I told her she should come home." Her sister plowed forward, needing to explain, not giving *Mem* a chance to say no, and trying to keep Bridget from fleeing to the getaway vehicle sitting a hundred-yard dash away. Even if their gentle mother welcomed her home, their father wouldn't be quite so quick to forgive. Not unless Bridget asked for forgiveness. Returned to the Amish ways and followed the rules of the *Ordnung*. Another wave of emotion made Bridget's stomach flip.

As if on cue, a deep voice bellowed from behind her. "What's going on?" *Dat*. "Why is she here? This is unacceptable."

Bridget fisted her hands, bracing herself as she turned around. Her father's dark gaze, glaring out from under his straw hat, pinned her. A look so familiar, she still saw it in her dreams—nightmares. A thousand emotions rained down on her, taking her back to her tumultuous teenage years when she still believed she had no choice but to accept the Amish ways and give up her dreams of becoming a nurse. Tears threatened, and she clenched her teeth. She would not cry in front of her family. She couldn't give them any ammunition to suggest she was sorry. That she was wrong.

Was she?

Was her current mess of a life a reflection of all the bad choices she had made? Was God punishing her?

She felt her sweet *mem*'s gaze on her. How she loved that woman. Then she locked gazes with her sister. "I can't do this." She grabbed the fabric of her long skirt and ran toward the truck, forcing back the threatening tears. As she approached the truck, she tore off her *kapp*. She reached for the passenger handle and yanked the door open. She couldn't read the expression on Zach's face, dark like her father's, and something else…

"I'm not staying." Bridget climbed in, reached behind her and yanked the seat belt forward and clicked it in place.

"You have to." His tone was even, ominous.

"I can't. Go." She leaned forward and tapped on the dash, like she used to slap the hindquarters of Honey, the family's American Saddlebred. When he didn't move, she added, "Please." Her mind whirled. "Take me back to Buffalo. I'll reach out to the university. Maybe they can find a spot in the dorms for me. They might be open already. Right?" When he still didn't move, she shifted in her seat, her brow furrowed. "What are you waiting for?" She didn't bother to hide her frustration.

"You have to stay." He held out his smartphone. "A call came in."

Zach reached for her hand, and she pulled it away. If

he couldn't comfort her, he couldn't give her bad news, right? As she clutched her hand to her chest, dread spread across her skin, making her feel like she had downed three cups of coffee on an empty stomach. Finally, she was able to force out a single word: "Ashley?"

"Yes." His warm brown eyes radiated his hurt. "They found Ashley near the bike path."

Bridget's brow twitched. "She liked to run there." Her phone had been smashed in the apartment. "I told her it wasn't safe." This had nothing to do with running alone. "Is she…?" She pressed her fist to her mouth in a feeble attempt to stop the overwhelming emotion welling up inside her.

No, no, no. Ashley's fine. She's fine.

Zach reached for her wrist and pulled her fist away from her mouth. He tilted his head. A sad smile slanted his lips. Every movement, every moment, marked time.

This moment.

An eternity.

Before and after.

Her shoulders sagged, and she slumped into the seat.

"Bridget…" Zach slid his hand up from her wrist to her hand and squeezed it. She slowly lifted her face to meet his consoling gaze. Her heartbeat raced in her chest. "I'm so sorry. Ashley's dead."

Bridget's hands sought the release of the too-tight seat belt. "This had nothing to do with the clinic. Did it?" *Did it?* This was a horrible, unrelated tragedy. Ashley had been jogging alone on a bike path. That's what it was. Her death was unrelated to the apartment fire, to the near miss in the crosswalk. It had to be.

"My business card was crammed down her throat."

Bridget bent over and covered her face with her hands. "This is all my fault."

She felt Zach's warm hand on her arm. "This is not your fault," he whispered. "Please stay here, for your safety."

She pulled her hands away from her face and swiped at a tear. "I can't. I'm not welcomed."

"Your parents must understand." He tipped his head to look out the passenger window. Cornfields waved in the wind.

She shook her head. "*You* don't understand." She sniffed. *Hold it together.*

"I have to keep you safe until they find the parties responsible." His phone dinged, and he quickly checked it. If the text had anything to do with her or Ashley or Dr. Ryan, he didn't say.

Every fiber of her body vibrated with the nightmare she found herself in. "My father won't let me stay. Perhaps if you can convince him?" Bridget knew she was taking the coward's way out. She also knew that her father could never be swayed from his convictions, especially by an outsider.

Chapter Six

Zach followed Bridget, a step behind, as she readjusted the bonnet on her head after ripping it off in frustration moments ago. She frantically tucked fine strands of hair under the white material, as if donning armor to approach her father. Her upswept hair exposed her delicate neck. She carefully navigated the rutted driveway. There was much he wanted to ask her about growing up in an Amish community, but it would have to wait. He was about to get a crash course in what it would take to convince a stern Amish father to allow his prodigal daughter to return—albeit temporarily. Zach'd appeal to the man's sense of paternal love. That should be universal. His daughter's life was in danger.

Unfortunately, not all parents were created equal. His own mother came to mind, and he quickly dismissed the thought. This case was challenging his finely honed skills of compartmentalization.

"He's never going to go for this," Bridget muttered when they reached the steps to the front porch. "I was foolish to come back. Or maybe I was foolish to report what I saw at the clinic."

Before Zach had a chance to reassure her, a man he suspected was her father opened the front door and stepped out onto the porch. He crossed his arms over his chest and arranged his face in a stern expression. Bridget came by her conclusions that this was going to be a hard sell honestly. Her mother joined them. Her body language softened, but the subtle tip of her head suggested she'd defer to her husband.

"You came back," her father said without much emotion.

"*Yah.* This is…" Bridget seemed to be debating how to introduce Zach. Since she had hoped to keep him away from her parents, they had never discussed this. Perhaps they'd respond to the bold truth.

"Sir, ma'am—" He offered his hand, and when neither made an effort to accept it, he dropped it. "I'm Agent Zach Bryant."

"This is my mother, Mae, and my father, Amos," Bridget said.

"Your daughter—"

"What did you do?" Her father glared at her.

"Sir, your daughter has been very brave."

"Too brave, if you ask me." Amos shifted his crossed arms under his long beard.

Next to Zach, Bridget drew in a shaky breath. Her mother gently touched her husband's arm. Her father tipped his straw hat slightly, suggesting Zach should go on.

"Bridget needs a place to stay," Zach said, "for a short time."

"We're not a hotel." Amos's lips twitched. "What's going on, and is there a reason my daughter's not speaking for herself?" He adjusted his stance and slipped his thumbs under his suspenders. He was definitely a man who ruled his home. Zach supposed there was nothing wrong with having a strong male role model, as long as he was a benevolent leader.

"Dat." Bridget spoke up. "A friend of mine was killed, and I'm afraid the same people are going to hurt me." Her voice held a confidence that surprised Zach.

"Oh dear." Her mother pressed a hand to her chest. *"Umkumme...?"* *Killed*, she muttered.

"You have brought this on yourself by going into the outside world. You didn't believe me when I told you about the evil in the *Englisch* world." Her father shook his head in disgust.

Zach bit back his strong impulse to defend Bridget and gave her room to do it herself. He couldn't believe her father was willing to make a judgment without knowing the details.

"Can I stay or not?" Bridget spit out. "I promise I won't be here long."

A muscle ticked in her father's jaw. He obviously wasn't used to his daughter speaking to him like this.

"Please." Bridget softened her tone, seemingly resigned that she'd have to mend fences if she wanted to stay in Hickory Lane. "I'm tired and I'm scared."

Her father's posture relaxed, seemingly receptive to

his daughter's apology. "Why was your friend killed and why are they after you?"

Zach gently touched Bridget's hand. "It would be better if we didn't discuss that."

"You're asking to stay in my home," her father said, his voice even.

"*Yah, Dat.* I never told anyone I was Amish. No one would ever find me here." Bridget smiled tightly. "I would never knowingly put my family in danger."

His nostrils flared, and it seemed to take considerable restraint for him not to speak his mind.

"Amos, we can find it in our hearts to let our daughter come home," her mother said, a pleading quality to her voice.

Amos tipped his head slightly and turned on his heel and strode down the porch steps toward the barn. Her mother turned to them. "You are welcome to come home, Bridget."

"What about *Dat*?" Across the yard, Amos yanked open the barn door and then disappeared inside.

"In his own way, he has agreed. Don't push him," her mother warned. "Your friend cannot stay here, though. That would get the neighbors talking." Her warm gaze met Zach's. "The Amish like to stay separate. That includes from those in law enforcement."

He nodded. "I understand." Truth be told, he understood nothing about the Amish. "I'll check in at the hotel in town."

"Why do you need to stay in town? No one knows I'm here," Bridget said. "Why can't you go back to Buffalo and let me know when it's safe to return home?"

"You are home," her mother whispered, and for the first time Zach could see how Bridget's coming here was going to take an emotional toll on her entire family.

How did he explain that he couldn't leave her unprotected? He refused to make another mistake that cost an innocent person their life, never mind that he was supposed to be on leave from the DEA. For now, that made it easier because he could do whatever he thought necessary without clearing it with his supervisor. "I'll stay close for now. Maybe that will change," he said to appease her.

Bridget seemed to regard him with a sense of apprehension.

"I'll be right in town. Minutes away." Then he turned to her mother. "Nice to meet you, Mrs. Miller," Zach said before descending the porch steps. He decided against giving Bridget last-minute instructions to keep a low profile. She was a smart woman, and he didn't want to cause more concern for her sweet mother, who seemed to be basking in the glow of her long-lost daughter's return. Zach's goal was to keep Bridget safe, not meddle in family dynamics that were far more complicated than his pay grade, especially because he was technically off duty.

Bridget stood on the porch of her childhood home and watched Zach pull away in his truck. A wave of unease pressed into her heart. It was hard to imagine that twenty-four hours ago she was taking blood pressure and weights of patients before they saw the doctor, trying to act like everything was okay. Had Dr.

Ryan suspected anything? Not possible. He had been his usual friendly self.

A soft breeze blew a stray strand of hair across her face. With the hook of her finger, she tugged it away and turned to take in the farm. Her mother and sister had disappeared into the house. Inside the barn across the way, her father was probably taking his aggression out on his chores. She imagined her brothers were in the barn doing their chores, too, otherwise they would have come to greet her.

Bridget lowered herself onto the top step and smoothed her skirt. Her brothers. They had been little guys when she left. Soon they'd be about to embark on their own adventures. Bending forward, she hugged her thighs. She had really missed her family. She had kept homesickness at bay by not letting herself think about what she was missing. Now that she was back here, she could no longer deny her sense of loss.

When she had left under the cloak of darkness all those years ago, she feared the only time she'd ever return would be to help bury her parents. She was grateful to have this time with her parents while still on this side of heaven. Sadly, her return wouldn't lead to some grand reconciliation, not unless she got down on bended knee, then received baptism and married.

There would be no happily-ever-after for her here among the Amish.

Bridget closed her eyes and inhaled. Sweet grass. A hint of manure. Dried cornstalks. *Familiar.* She blinked away the threatening tears. She couldn't put this home-coming—however temporary—off any longer. She rose to her feet and crossed the porch to the screen door, the same one she had carefully closed so her parents wouldn't hear her leave in the middle of the night.

She stepped inside, this time not caring if the door clacked in its frame behind her. She followed the smell of her mother's fresh-baked bread. "Hi, *Mem*." Her mother was stirring something on the stove.

Her mother set the wooden spoon on the ceramic rest and turned around. A small smile that spoke volumes curved her lips. "You're just in time to help with preparations for tomorrow."

Bridget scrunched up her nose, momentarily confused. "You're hosting Sunday service tomorrow?" What unfortunate timing.

"*Yah*, and many hands make light work."

Renewed dread pooled in her gut. She'd have to face the entire community. Maybe she could hide in her bedroom.

"Could you help your sister cut the celery?" her mother asked.

"Um…sure." Bridget locked gazes with Liddie who seemed to be enjoying herself.

Her mother wiped her hands on her apron. "The celery has already been rinsed."

Bridget grabbed a knife and another cutting board and began chopping. The activity, here with her mother and sister, brought her back to a life she'd thought she had abandoned forever. Liddie playfully nudged her with her elbow, and Bridget rolled her eyes.

A moment later there was a commotion at the side door leading into the mudroom adjacent to the kitchen.

Two young men she barely recognized stood there watching her with wide eyes. "*Dat* said you were home. I had to see for myself," Elijah said, his voice cracking. He was no longer a little boy.

The youngest brother was more reserved. Caleb had been so much younger when Bridget left Hickory Lane.

"It's really me." Bridget set the knife down. "My, how you boys have grown." She gestured with her chin toward Elijah. "The girls must be swarming around you at Sunday singings."

"The only thing that's swarming around him are the flies," Caleb deadpanned, scrunching up his nose.

"Now, that's not nice," their mother scolded. "Now go clean up for lunch. Your sister will make you sandwiches."

Without missing a beat, Bridget made her brothers sandwiches and set them on plates on the table. The boys disappeared and returned after washing their hands. They slipped into their chairs and scarfed down their food. When she was growing up here, they were never allowed to eat until their father had sat down at the head of the table. She wondered what else had changed since she left.

She went back to help her mom make food preparations for tomorrow. A rustling sounded at the back door, and Bridget found herself tightening her grip around the knife. She set it down and waited for the inevitability of the confrontation with her dad.

Suddenly she felt sixteen again the morning after she had missed her Sunday-night curfew. Moses Lapp, a boy who liked her, had refused to take her home, instead insisting they hang out with a few other young couples. Bridget didn't feel comfortable among her Amish peers. They were pairing up with the intention of settling down. Her good friend Katy came to mind. Bridget had no doubt she was married and wondered how many kids she had by now.

She released a slow breath. She wasn't that same girl.

Her father sat down at his place at the table without saying a word. The air hung thick with tension.

"Bridget, your father would like a sandwich," her mother said.

"She should not be serving me food." Her father pushed back from the table and stilled, his arms crossed over his suspenders like a petulant child.

Her mother held out her hand, encouraging him to relax. "I'll get it. I'm sorry. I got distracted with everything going on," Mae said apologetically.

"We don't need any more distractions around here," her father said, placing his hands flat on the table, not looking in Bridget's direction. "We have a lot of preparation to do for tomorrow. We need a little less horseplay from Elijah and Caleb, or we could have had the barn swept out already. And don't forget Levi should be here with the benches after lunch."

"We'll get it all done," her mother said reassuringly. "We always do." Each family in the district took turns hosting Sunday service every other week. Due to the size of the district, each family only had to host it once every year—or at least, that's how it had always been.

"Too many distractions," her father muttered again.

A knot twisted in Bridget's heart. Since she had secreted away, she had only imagined the stress she had created by leaving. She had imagined that her family had been going on with their lives just as before, but without her. Seeing them now made her sadder. Leaving had affected everyone. Why had she been so selfish? Because she wanted to become a nurse.

Bridget found herself mute in the presence of her father. She had always been afraid of him. He ruled with an iron fist. She dried her hands on her apron, then stepped out on the back porch, leaving only the screen door between them. The community would gather tomorrow at her childhood home, and she would be forced to stay separate. It would only cause problems for her parents if they didn't make an example of her.

Maybe she'd get to hide out in her bedroom after all.

"Here's your lunch." Bridget could hear her mother's soothing voice through the screen door. Forever the peacemaker.

"Mae, she will remain separate. She cannot dine with us. She cannot worship with us. We cannot condone her actions," her father instructed her mother. "Until she repents and goes down on bended knee in front of the bishop, she must be under the *Bann*."

Anger began to replace the emptiness in Bridget's heart. Her father couldn't even use her name. She grabbed the handle on the screen door and yanked it open. The door bounced off the wood siding, then swung back and slammed shut in its frame. She stormed into the kitchen. "*Dat*, I have no plans to stay longer than I have to."

Her father's dark eyes flared wide, obviously surprised by her outburst. She had never confronted him. Until now. "Perhaps you should leave now, then. Since you're too ashamed to tell anyone that you come from an Amish home."

"Why would I tell anyone? They'd only think I was a freak." Bridget's pulse roared in her ears. Bile tickled the back of her throat. Exploding at her father would serve no purpose other than to release the anger and fear she had been bottling up since Zach told her Ashley was dead.

Liddie spun around from where she worked at the counter. Her face was blotchy, and she seemed on the verge of tears. "You have to let her stay."

"Apparently, I don't have much control over what she does. She has ears but doesn't listen." Her father narrowed his gaze at her. "*She*—" her father emphasized the word, making Bridget wonder if he'd ever use her name "—made her decision when she crept out of here in the middle of the night. She didn't have the decency to say goodbye to your mother."

"Bridget's in danger," Liddie said, alarm in her voice.

"It's okay, Liddie." Bridget willed her sister to stop talking.

"She has nowhere else to go. Someone smashed the window in her apartment, and it went up in flames. If Bridget had been in her bedroom, she might have been really hurt. Agent Bryant already told you her coworker was murdered."

"Murdered," Caleb said, his tone a mix between being horrified and intrigued.

"Liddie," Bridget warned her sister again, "please."

Their father held up his hand. "We should have never allowed you to go to Buffalo, Liddie. It only exposed you to the evils of the outside world. It was a mistake. And now you have brought your drama here."

A groundswell of anger and disbelief pressed on Bridget's lungs. Hearing how easily her father dismissed recent events was too much.

"*Dat*, I had no intention of sharing the details of my life in Buffalo." She lifted her chin and met her father's dark eyes. *Why can't you love me for who I am?* "I'll get out of your way."

"No!" Liddie yelled. She clasped her hands together and pressed them to her chest. "No one is listening. We have to make sure Bridget is safe. She can't leave."

Mem repeatedly dried her hands on the dish towel. Their father took a bite of his sandwich, then swallowed. He dabbed at his lips. A crumb settled in his unkempt beard. The silence filled the room with heavy expectation. "*She* will eat separate from us. *She* will have chores. If and only if she is ready to ask for forgiveness and be baptized, she can fully join this family. We will not discuss the outside world."

Apparently, Bridget had been invited to stay. On *Dat*'s terms. On Amish terms.

She wouldn't be staying for a minute longer than she had to.

Chapter Seven

Later that night, Zach found himself driving along the country roads and staring up at the spectacular display of stars visible in the dark night sky. He had been unable to sleep due to the commotion of a few teenagers who had congregated on bicycles in the motel parking lot. Their laughter and loud voices traveled through the thin walls. He could have easily sent them on their way, but his objective was to be low-key, not announce his presence by annoying a handful of bored locals who weren't really bothering anyone except him.

Zach navigated the roads to the Miller farm. He parked on the side of the road. Back at the motel, he had searched "Amish" on the internet. After scrolling past several hits on reality shows—which he took a leap and assumed weren't actually "reality"—he clicked on a few sites that discussed the basic tenets of the Amish. Prior to his dive down the rabbit hole, he hadn't known much about the Amish other than the fact that they didn't drive cars or use electricity. Their lifestyle was fascinating. From his cursory search, he now had a sense of why Bridget was reluctant to return. The Amish didn't take kindly to those who left and often shunned those who did, unless they asked for forgiveness.

Zach pushed open the truck's door, and the sound of crickets filled the night air, louder than he had ever heard. The blackness swallowed him. The weight of his gun on his hip was reassuring. It took a moment for his eyes to adjust. He looked up and immediately spotted the Little Dipper, sadly the only constellation he could name. It reminded him of the time his parents had taken him and his sister to the beach when they were kids. He had never experienced the night sky without light pollution before. Back when life was still innocent. Back when he and his sister were best buddies and their biggest concern was keeping sand out of their eyes and reapplying sunscreen.

Back before his mother had back surgery and started taking prescription drugs. Back before his father bailed because he was unable or unwilling to manage a family spiraling out of control.

Zach's thoughts came fast and frantic, like cracks in thinning ice, promising to plunge him into icy-cold water, drowning him. A break from work was the worst thing for him. He needed to keep busy to outrun his thoughts. To make meaning of all the tragedy he had experienced.

He tilted his head from side to side to ease the kinks in his neck. He scanned the Miller farm while he strolled toward the house. He strained his ears for anything out of the ordinary. He chuckled to himself.

What was out of the ordinary on an Amish farm? There were no vehicles parked anywhere nearby, so unless the bad guys discovered her location and stomped through the woods or across the fields, Bridget should be safe.

Zach made a sweep of the grounds. Other than the house and barn, there was one other outbuilding. Bridget had mentioned that her grandfather lived there. The stillness was so complete, the kind that could only be achieved in the country on a property where they didn't use electricity. There wasn't even the hum of a generator competing with the sounds of nature. He'd go back to his motel room and wait for morning.

There was nothing for him to do here.

Any leads would be in Buffalo. Zach had made a few calls, and a coworker in the DEA office was doing some digging. Standing on the sidelines made him itchy. His supervisor claimed that what he did on his leave was his business, but he doubted she'd go for this. He hoped she wouldn't extend his leave if he pushed his involvement here too far. Or maybe she'd realize making him take a break was pointless. It wouldn't change what happened. He was good at his job. He thrived on his undercover work. He had a knack for getting on the inside, gaining the trust of strangers who didn't generally trust people. The key was to cut off the head of an organization and not focus solely on easy arrests, like the street-level dealers. Dealers were easily replaceable. The traffickers higher up the chain of command needed to be the focal point.

And here he was on the far, far sidelines, sidestepping horse manure on an Amish farm. He laughed to himself at the absurdity of it, then suddenly froze when the distinct scent of sweet tobacco reached him. He tilted his head, and this time he heard shoes shuffling on gravel. He sank back closer to one of the buildings and watched a dark figure emerge from around the side of the structure. The person moved slowly, taking deliberate steps. Before Zach had a chance to say anything, a raspy voice said, "Are you the man who brought my granddaughter home?"

Zach stepped away from the building. Under the stars, light glistened in the elderly gentleman's eyes. His hair was mussed, and a straggly beard extended down his chest. "Yes, I'm Special Agent Zach Bryant with the DEA."

"DEA?" the elderly man asked.

"Drug Enforcement Administration."

The man harrumphed. "I don't know anything about that. All I know is that you made my daughter Mae happy by bringing Bridget home."

"I wish it could have been under better circumstances."

"*Yah*, well, I suppose if things had been better, she wouldn't have come home."

"I didn't expect to run into anyone in the middle of the night. Is everything okay?" Zach looked around, not able see much in the heavy shadows. He kept his phone and its flashlight app in his pocket, because he didn't want to be rude.

"I guess I could ask you the same. Is everything okay?" The elderly man ran his hand down his beard in slow, deliberate sweeps.

"Yes, everything seems to be quiet tonight."

"That's why we live here." He seemed to regard his surroundings. "Nice and quiet. Separate from the outside world."

"I can see the appeal," Zach said. "Some local kids decided to throw an impromptu party in the parking lot of the motel. Made it a little hard to sleep."

"Hmm." The elderly man seemed to consider that. "Well, I'm old. Don't sleep much anyway. I enjoy getting out at night." He looked up at the stars. "Soon the evenings will grow chilly." He turned his attention on Zach. "If you think it's quiet now, come out here when the ground's covered with snow. *Friedlich*."

Zach narrowed his gaze and after a beat, the other man said, *"Peaceful."*

Zach had taken two years of German in high school and he had learned in his internet search that Pennsylvania Dutch was a derivation of German, not that he was going to respond in kind.

"I'll have to take your word on that. I'm not much for the cold," Zach said, for lack of anything else to say. It seemed people of all walks loved to talk weather.

The elderly man tipped his head again. *"Mei enkelin* is in danger? My granddaughter was never content here."

Zach ran a hand over the itchy stubble on his jaw, deciding to be straight with this man, if not overly generous with the specifics. "Yes, she was witness to something at work, and she was very brave to come forward. Now it seems she made some people unhappy."

"Unhappy?" Bridget's grandfather planted his cane

and took another step. "*Unhappy* seems to be an understatement. Her friend was found dead. And you work for the DEA. Do I understand correctly?"

Zach's lips twitched at the elderly man's candor. "You didn't misunderstand, sir, I'm sorry to say."

The elderly man lifted his cane a fraction. "My name's Jeremiah. Might as well get used to calling me that if you're going to be hanging around."

"My name's Zach."

"Nice to meet you, Zach. I trust you'll keep Bridget safe."

"I'll do my best, sir." Zach wasn't sure how long he was going to be hanging around. Bridget should be safe here where no one would think to look for her.

"Jeremiah," Bridget's grandfather repeated.

"Yes, s— Jeremiah. I understand you live on the property. In this separate house?"

"*Yah*, right here. It's nice that the Amish take care of their old folk."

"I imagine it is." When the silence stretched out a beat too long, Zach said, "Well, I better head back to the motel for some shut-eye." He turned toward the road.

"You'll need rest for tomorrow. Lots of work to be done." Jeremiah took a few limping steps toward the small structure from which he had emerged, then he paused. "I have an extra cot. Stay here."

Zach lifted his head. "I'm fine at the motel."

Jeremiah shrugged. "No youths rabble-rousing around here. Grab some shut-eye. We could use a few more strong hands to make sure the benches are arranged in the barn."

"The benches?"

"*Yah*, they need to be set up in the barn. The entire community will arrive early for the nine o'clock worship service."

The aroma of coffee woke Zach from a sound sleep. He rolled over on the narrow cot, and a metal bar that had been jabbing into his back now pressed into his hip. Despite the thin mattress, he had fallen asleep almost as soon as Jeremiah pointed to the folded-up cot at the far wall of an oversize pantry. All he had to do was pop it open and make it up. With the window open a crack, he fell asleep to the sound of nature and not teenage boys goofing off.

Grunting, he pushed to a seated position and wiped the sleep out of his eyes. The first hint of dawn had softened the darkness outside the small window. He reached over and checked the time on his smartphone. *Ugh*, it was early. He strained to listen, surprised he couldn't hear a rooster crowing. Instead, he heard the shuffling around of Jeremiah outside the pantry where they had set up Zach's cot, his host's idea of privacy.

Zach slipped on his pants and T-shirt and ran a hand over his hair. He could zip back to the motel, shower and get back in time to help with whatever chores Jeremiah had lined up for him. He didn't mind staying busy. He'd also have to talk to Bridget about the long-term plan. Yesterday had been about getting Bridget to safety. Today was making sure she didn't run back to Buffalo too soon.

He stuffed his feet into his shoes and stepped out

into the kitchen with his laces still untied. Jeremiah sat at the small kitchen table drinking coffee and reading a newspaper.

"Guder mariye."

Half of Zach's mouth curved into a smile. "Um... good morning." He really should have paid more attention in German class.

"How did you sleep?" the elderly gentleman asked before taking another sip from his mug. "There's a pot of coffee on the stove. *Schnell! Schnell!*" The old man frowned. "Hurry. We have a lot to do."

"I'm going to run back to the motel and clean up. I'll grab coffee later."

Jeremiah set down his mug. "No time for that. Last-minute chores still need to be done. You need to change." He lifted his cane that leaned against the table and pointed. "I set some clothes on the bench there."

Zach followed the man's cane to a neat pile of men's clothing. *Amish clothes.* "I have fresh clothes at the motel. It won't take me long."

Jeremiah lifted a bushy gray eyebrow. "No need. Get dressed, move your truck into the *Englisch* neighbor's driveway about a half mile down the road. We have a good relationship with our neighbors. Then get back here to help with the preparations. If you plan on protecting my granddaughter, you need to fit in."

Zach scooped up the clothes and held them to his chest, suddenly feeling compelled to follow the orders of his host.

"The clothes should fit. I used to be a little taller before my back issues." Jeremiah smoothed his hand over the newspaper spread in front of him. "If they need any tailoring, I'm sure Bridget can handle that for you."

Zach smothered the smile pulling at his lips. He didn't know Bridget well, but he suspected asking her to tailor his clothes wasn't going to ingratiate him to her.

"I'll get dressed." Zach had spent a large portion of his young career with the DEA working undercover to get some of the most dangerous criminals, pretending to be someone he wasn't to get information he needed. He'd have to regard this as more of the same. Sort of.

He closed the door in the pantry and picked up the pair of trousers with a hook and eye closure. No zipper. Interesting. He held them to his waist. They might fit. He tossed off his T-shirt and put on the dark blue shirt.

"I have a pair of suspenders out here for you."

Zach dragged his thumb around the waistband of his pants. "I think I might need that." He smoothed his hands down his shirt, wishing he had a full-length mirror. Less than forty-eight hours ago, he had had an appointment to meet Bridget and Ashley for a tip related to potential health-care fraud, and now he was on an Amish farm about to see if he looked good in plain clothing.

A rapping sounded at the door. "You best get moving. Your truck parked out front is going to raise a lot of questions."

"I'm on it." Zach yanked open the door. "I'll move it right now."

Jeremiah extended his hand with a pair of suspenders.

Zach took them and fastened them to his pants. He

rolled back on his heels and patted his midsection. "How do I look?" He supposed his black sneakers would pass.

Jeremiah raised a bushy eyebrow and nodded. "It'll do. It'll have to."

Zach hooked his thumbs under his suspenders then let them snap. "Ouch."

Jeremiah shook his head with a hint of amusement. "You can admire yourself later." He reached over and snagged a straw hat off a hook. "You'll need this, too."

Zach stuffed it on his head and hustled out the door and down the dirt driveway. The country air smelled sweet. Fresh.

He had officially entered another world.

Bridget rose before the rest of her family and mixed some instant coffee with hot water from the stove, since she was too lazy to mess with the French press. She missed the coffee maker at home, a rare splurge for her. Grabbing the mug of black coffee, she slipped outside and settled into one of the rockers on the back porch. She missed the stillness of the country, but she hadn't missed how conflicted she had been while growing up here. She had always known there was more in the world but feared that going after more would condemn her spiritually.

Settling back into the rocker, she took another sip of coffee. Maybe during her short stay she could make peace—however fragile—with her family. Escaping during the middle of the night had made her departure more painful.

With her bare foot, she rocked slowly. It was such a soothing motion. As a kid, she used to sit here with a book until her *dat* scolded her and told her to get back to her chores. The memory made her smile. *Englisch* parents would take pride in their children reading instead of being hunched over smartphones or tablets. She had watched them, fascinated, in the waiting room of the clinic, almost oblivious to anything going on around them.

The clinic.

Dr. Ryan.

Ashley. Poor, poor Ashley.

Icy dread pooled in her stomach. Had Ashley's parents been notified? Did her siblings know? Bridget had worked long days with Ashley, yet she didn't know a ton about her family life. Now she never would. Tears pricked the backs of her eyes.

What have I done? If I had never told her about what I saw...

Maybe she'd check her cell phone for any news later. It was tucked away in her bedroom wardrobe, and digging it out would wake Liddie.

Drawing in the rich aroma of the coffee, she kept up the rocking motion, trying to root herself in the moment. *Let go and let God.* It wasn't exactly a Bible verse, but she had clung to the mantra after she heard it in the home of the woman who took her in when she first left Hickory Lane. She stared out over the land that hadn't changed, other than through the seasons, since she had left. The familiarity of that was soothing. The first streaks of pink and purple stretched across the sky. She smiled to herself. When was the last time she sat and studied the sky? She had been so busy with work and school.

Soon, her brothers would be up, feeding the animals and mucking out the stalls. Bridget hadn't missed that one bit.

Out of the corner of her eye, she noticed something moving out in the field. She turned her attention toward it, fully expecting a deer. Or maybe the neighbor's cow had broken through the fence again. She squinted and tucked in her chin. It was a person.

Panic sliced through the early morning tranquility. She slid forward on the rocker, and the chair dipped low. Her feet melded to the wooden planks. Her heart raced, and her fight-or-flight response kicked in. She planted her hand on the edge of the chair and stood, her knees wobbly under her.

Had *they* found her?

She spun around, her long skirt swooshing around her ankles, and reached for the door handle, fearing that she had brought danger to her family's doorstep. The latch caught. She glanced over her shoulder and nearly collapsed against the back door with utter and complete relief.

"You scared me," Bridget said, wiping her sweaty palms on the folds of her dress. "What are you doing?" She stepped off the porch, the damp earth cool on her toes, and gave DEA Special Agent Zach Bryant a once-over. "How? Why? Who gave you those clothes?" The first hint of amusement sparked in Bridget's chest, a welcomed reprieve from the sadness and uncertainty that had kept her tossing and turning last night.

"You want the long or the short version?" Zach tugged on his suspenders and smiled. She wasn't sure if it was the relief that she was safe or the early morning lighting that made him seem vulnerable. Human. Less law enforcement–like. Maybe it was because the plain clothing had softened his hard edges.

"Want coffee? I've got time for the long version." She turned to go in.

"No, wait. Sit." Zach stepped up onto the porch and held out his hand to one of the rockers. She sat, and Zach sat next to her. "I had to move my truck. Your grandfather told me to park it at the neighbor's. Walking across the field seemed like the quickest route back."

"Yeah, to giving me a heart attack."

"Sorry, I didn't realize you'd see me." He kept his tone hushed, almost reverent.

"Why are you here already?" She furrowed her brow. "And dressed in those clothes? What did I miss? Did something happen?" Her tendency to pepper someone with questions when she was nervous was in full force.

"Nothing new to report, so no worries there." He slid back in the rocker and ran his strong hands up and down the smooth arms of the chair. "I couldn't sleep, so I drove over last night to make sure the farm was secure, and I ran into your grandfather."

Bridget smiled. "No further explanation needed." Her grandfather exuded quiet authority. *Mem* claimed he was a force to be reckoned with when he was a younger man, but he had allowed the next generation to take up the mantle after his wife died and he settled into the *dawdy haus*.

Zach seemed to study her for a moment. "Should I

be worried about your grandfather?" He offered her a bemused smile.

"No, of all my family, I always felt like he was the one who understood me. I mean, I could never confide in him regarding my plans to leave. I didn't want to do that to him. He sensed I wanted more, though." She set her empty coffee mug down on the porch floor and leaned back in the chair and resumed rocking. "I felt his quiet support."

"Do you miss living here?"

"I've missed my family. Living here is a world away. A completely different culture. I could never be a nurse here."

"I don't mean to pry with all my questions. The Amish way of life is fascinating."

"A lot of people feel the same way. That's why there are so many tourists." She was unable to hide the disdain in her voice. Most tourists were respectful, but she had had enough bad run-ins to make her weary.

"I was thinking of Ashley this morning," Bridget said, needing to change the subject. "Did someone let her family know?"

"Yes, her family was notified." There was a faraway quality to his voice.

"Her poor family." She let out a shaky breath. "This is all my fault." She stilled and shifted in her seat to face Zach.

He surprised her by reaching out and covering her hand on the arm of the chair. "This is *not* your fault. You hear me?"

A lump in her throat kept her from doing more than

nodding. She pulled her hand out from under his. "How long do you think I'll have to stay here?"

Zach ran a hand over his scratchy jaw, debating. She had gotten good at reading people; she had spent a life-time reading her father's moods and then used that skill to read her patients.

"I don't know. My office has people on it. I'm think-ing I could expedite the process if I returned to Buf-falo." She sensed he wasn't telling her something.

Bridget's heart sank. She wasn't sure why. It wasn't like she didn't feel safe here. Not without him. This was ridiculous. She had just met him. Maybe it was because he represented security. Or a link to her new life. If he left, would that somehow leave her unanchored back in a life that she never wanted?

Apparently sensing her concern, he said, "We have to locate Dr. Ryan. He needs to answer our questions. Then we'll know exactly what we're dealing with."

"What about the clinic?" She had been so worried about her situation, she had neglected to consider the community that relied on the clinic. "Many people have nowhere else to go." What had she done? A groundswell of self-doubt threatened to overwhelm her.

"My office is searching the clinic today. Depend-ing on what they find, the clinic could be shut down indefinitely. In past cases like this, the clinic eventu-ally reopens under a new director." He made a smack-ing sound with his lips. "I won't lie—it may take time."

"You mentioned you were on leave from your job," she said, leaving her comment open-ended, hoping he'd explain.

"Let me worry about that."

"Okay."

"You did the right thing," he said, realizing Ashley's death weighted heavily on her.

"Ashley wouldn't think so."

"Ashley had a mind of her own. You didn't coerce her into doing anything."

"I'm not so sure." Bridget bit her lower lip.

"I am. She was best friends with my sister, Leann." There was a strange quality to his voice. "Ashley had a strong personality. No way you talked her into anything she already wasn't on board with."

"Your sister must be devastated."

"My sister's dead."

"Oh, I'm sorry." Tingles raced across her scalp.

"It was a long time ago." He spoke softly and stared straight ahead over the field. "She overdosed. Ashley was with her."

A band of sympathy squeezed all the air from her lungs. "I'm truly sorry. I had no idea." Why hadn't Ashley shared that piece of information? No doubt, it had been too painful for everyone.

Zach tapped his index finger on the arm of the rocker. "Leann's tragic death shaped the course of my life." He seemed lost in thought, yet eager to tell his sister's story. "I was serving overseas at the time. I hadn't realized how bad her drug use had gotten."

Had Ashley been involved with drugs, too? Bridget didn't want to ask. Tarnishing her friend's memory seemed disrespectful in light of her death.

The weight of guilt slumped his shoulders. No reassurances from her would lift the burden. She understood guilt. She was wallowing in the deep end of it right now. "Is that why you're a DEA agent?"

His face transformed into something painfully handsome when he smiled sadly at her. "Yes. Sometimes I wonder why. It feels futile. The drug problem in this country is enormous. In the case of your clinic, it'll most likely be shut down once they uncover the problem, a few arrests will be made, but the traffickers will find another health-care provider looking to make some quick cash. Money they're willing to risk their lives for."

Hearing him talk like this wasn't very reassuring. "You're doing what you can."

"It never seems like enough. We need to find a way to end this horrible epidemic before more people die."

Despite his determination, they both knew more people would die.

Chapter Eight

Bridget watched in awe as Zach joined right in with preparations for Sunday service. She helped with last-minute food prep, and if her participation wasn't warranted due to the *Bann*, no one said anything. She suspected her father would remind her of her place before the first guest arrived. Appearances were everything.

Bridget set the loaf of bread on the table and turned to wipe the crumbs from the counter. From the window over the sink, she watched the guests climb out of their buggies and greet her mother. Her brothers were charged with unhitching the horses and taking them to the fenced-in field. While the female guests would stop into the house with their covered dishes, the men would gather outside until they were called in for the service.

As the first group of women approached the house, a wave of unease warmed Bridget's skin. She plucked at her white cape covering her dress. She had forgotten how warm it could get with fabric down to her ankles in this heat. Her mother gestured to the house with a bright smile. The Amish neighbors turned their gazes toward the house—toward her?—with wide eyes and polite smiles. Bridget ducked away from the window. Perhaps her mother was eager to let everyone know that her daughter was home. Perhaps the circumstances didn't matter. She *was* home. Her mother had hope. The impulse to run upstairs and hide was strong. But Bridget didn't want to embarrass her mother by disappearing upstairs.

A thudding sound snapped Bridget's attention toward the stairs. Liddie appeared flushed, excited, as if she were hiding a secret.

"Where have you been? I thought you'd be down here helping already," Bridget said, regretting her harsh tone that had nothing to do with Liddie's absence.

Her little sister smiled. "I was helping earlier…" she lowered her voice to a whisper "…I had to make a call."

"You didn't get rid of your phone?" Bridget was careful to keep her voice low.

Liddie shrugged, a mischievous smile splitting her face. "Don't tell."

"I wouldn't dare." Bridget checked out the window. The women were still chatting. "Who were you talking to?"

"I'll tell you later." Liddie tucked a wayward strand of hair under her bonnet. Her attention also shifted toward the window. "Do you think I could go back to Buffalo with you?"

"What? Why?"

Liddie adjusted her cape over her dress. "No, don't

worry. I'm not going to leave Hickory Lane. I'd like to visit again. That's all." Her tone held a forced casualness.

"Why?" Bridget studied her sister's face. Liddie wouldn't meet her eyes, a tell that her sister wasn't being completely honest.

"I made a friend."

"The person you were talking to on the phone."

Liddie hitched a shoulder and her eyes shone brightly.

Bridget narrowed her eyes slightly. Her questions would have to wait for another time. "*Mem* and *Dat* would never allow it. Besides, I have no idea where I'm going to be living." She shook her head tightly, too stressed to deal with her sister's request. "No. It's not going to happen."

Liddie rolled her eyes. "I could always do what you did and leave in the middle of the night."

Bridget felt like she had been sucker punched. "You said you weren't going to leave Hickory Lane." The excited chatter of the women grew closer to the screen door. "Can we talk about this later?"

"Sure," Liddie said, making a final adjustment to her bonnet. "Zach looks handsome in plain clothes." Her sister's eyes flashed mischievously. "Do you suppose he's hiding his gun somewhere under there?"

"Hush," Bridget said, shoving a pitcher of water at her sister. "Put this on the table. The older folk should stay hydrated." Memories of sitting in a sweltering barn or airless home on a backless bench floated to mind. If staying separate meant she couldn't go to service today, she'd take it.

"Listen to the nurse," Liddie teased, apparently in

an especially good mood. Then she waved her hand in dismissal. "It's not like we haven't seen someone pass out at a service before."

"I'm trying to prevent that."

Before Liddie had a chance to argue, their mother came bustling in with a few women. Each placed a covered dish on the table to stay safe from bugs until after the service, when everything would be carried outside for the communal meal.

Bridget found herself averting her gaze while she tidied up from the preparations.

"Hello, Bridget."

She looked up to find Mrs. Yoder standing in front of her, a strained smile on her face. "You've come home?" Her somber tone reflected her obvious skepticism.

Bridget felt her mother's gaze on her. They hadn't discussed what she should tell the neighbors, perhaps assuming Bridget would stay safely tucked away. Obviously, they hadn't thought this through.

"We're happy to have her home," Bridget's mother answered for her. "She's been a big help in getting everything ready today."

"Oh…" Mrs. Yoder seemed at a loss for words.

"How is Katy?" Bridget quickly asked about Mrs. Yoder's oldest daughter, who had been one of Bridget's best friends growing up. Through Liddie, Bridget learned that the bishop had come down especially hard on Katy after Bridget jumped the fence. Some people suspected she knew. That Katy had helped her friend leave. Of course, none of that was true. Bridget had left without telling a soul.

Mrs. Yoder straightened her back and smiled. "My Katy is happily married and keeping a wonderful home." She got a faraway look in her eyes. "She has two little ones." No doubt, Mrs. Yoder was relieved her daughter hadn't been tainted by her childhood friend who had broken the rules of the *Ordnung*.

"I'm happy for her. Please tell her I said hello." Then in a burst of nostalgia, she added, "I've missed her."

Mrs. Yoder's lip twitched, and she seemed to be holding something back.

"If you'll excuse me, I have a few more things to do before the service." Bridget tipped her head and brushed past the women. She whispered to her mother, "I should probably go upstairs. *Dat* wouldn't want me to cause a spectacle." Any more than she already had.

Her mother's open expression suggested she wanted to invite her daughter to partake in the day's service and meal, but she wouldn't go against her husband's wishes.

That wasn't the Amish way.

"It's okay, *Mem*," Bridget reassured her mother. "I found one of my old books in the wardrobe in a box." It had broken Bridget's heart to think of her mother tucking away a few of her daughter's things after she had run away. They were all harmless items, tokens from an innocent childhood. However, the likelihood of her father disposing of her possessions made her mother's efforts to hold on to them even more precious.

Zach hung back and watched the Amish women proceed into the barn, which had been converted into a place of worship, followed by the men, in some sort of prearranged order. Then a few stragglers, including teenagers, picked up the rear. Bridget's grandfather Jeremiah had encouraged Zach to join them, assuring him that visitors were welcome. However, Zach hadn't been inside a church building since he was a young boy, and he wasn't going to start now, even if it was a barn. Besides, he felt more comfortable as an observer of all the comers and goers. So far, they all seemed to be Amish people. No threat to Bridget. Since they were all dressed the same, she truly blended in.

He had scanned the faces of the women, wondering if Bridget would join her community. But she was a no-show. After a deep melodic singing began, he walked toward the house. Jeremiah had warned him that the service could last three hours. He entered the empty house and called out to her and heard a rustling upstairs. A few moments later, she came downstairs.

"Oh, it's you." Her shoulders visibly sagged. She tore off her bonnet and adjusted a bobby pin in her hair then put the bonnet back on. "Is something wrong?"

"Skipping the service?" He leaned against one of the support beams in the center of the room.

"My father forbade it." Despite the severity of the claim, there was a light quality to her voice.

"I'd think they'd be happy that you're home. That they'd want you to go to the service with them."

Bridget held on to the pine handrail and lowered herself to a seated position on one of the bottom stairs. Her bare feet with pink toes stuck out from her long dress. "My *dat* has to make everyone think he's mad at me. I may never know how he really feels. He's the head of this family, and they look up to him to determine how to act. However, the rules aren't up to him. The Amish believe in the ultimate form of tough love. If they shun me and keep me 'separate'—" she lifted her fingers in air quotes for the last word "—the hope is that I'll see the error of my ways and ask for forgiveness. My *dat* can't appear to be accepting of my transgressions. It would set a bad example for my siblings."

"Ah," Zach said. "I guess I should have asked you more questions about your living situation before I brought you here." However, being strict wasn't the worst crime. Being neglectful and absent were far worse. Many of the young men he came across in gangs had been largely ignored by their families.

"I knew what I was in for when I agreed to come home."

"It's a shame." Her father's punitive nature seemed overly harsh, especially toward a young woman who was making a good life for herself. Perhaps they didn't realize the real trouble people could get into. How would her parents have reacted to a daughter like Leann, someone addicted to drugs? He supposed everyone had to follow their own path and make their own mistakes, including shunning a perfectly decent person.

Bridget sagged and rested her head on the edge of the railing post. She played with the strings on her bonnet. "It's what they know. They want to guilt me into returning."

Zach plucked at his suspenders. "It's hot in here. Would you like to talk a walk? Get some fresh air?"

Bridget pulled herself up to standing. "I'd love it."

She spun around and took the stairs two at a time. "Let me put on my boots," she called over her shoulder. "I'll meet you out back."

Bridget had made herself presentable—by Amish standards—before heading outside. She figured they had a solid three hours before the service in the barn ended. As she and Zach crossed the field, she lifted her face toward the sun and bit back the automatic tendency to fill the silence with talk about the weather. After all the excitement of the past couple days, she wanted to try to just be. Enjoy the moment. Enjoy this glorious late-summer Sunday morning.

Zach walked by her side, allowing her to lead the way. She followed a familiar path that wound for a few hundred yards into the trees, around a man-made lake, then to the far side of the barn. Then they could cut across the field to the house. Zach could leave and she'd retreat to her bedroom and pray that someone thought to bring her some food.

They reached the tree line, and the dappled sunlight created dancing shadows. An earthy smell reached her nose and took her right back. It was surreal. The Miller kids had spent hours playing by the lake between their chores. When her little brothers weren't around, she and Liddie used to talk about the husbands they'd have, their homes and children. Liddie never had any reason to believe that it wouldn't come to fruition. Bridget had believed it, too, at first, because leaving seemed like too big of a leap. Until staying became more of one.

"I thought I'd spend my entire life here," Bridget said, no longer wanting to be alone with her thoughts.

"What made you decide to leave? I'm starting to see how hard that must have been." Zach slowed and squinted against the sun streaming through the trees.

"You should have grabbed a hat."

Half his mouth quirked up, making him more handsome. "I'm more of a baseball hat kinda guy. The straw hat was making my head itch." The power of suggestion made him scratch his head.

"The hat might have been too small." She resisted a strange urge to run her fingers along the subtle red line marking his forehead where the hat had sat. Lacing her fingers, she added, "I'm pretty impressed the clothes fit, though."

She reached up and plucked a yellowish-green leaf off the maple tree. In a couple months, they'd be vibrant red. She twirled the stem between her fingers, her mind traveling back to the time when the idea that her vocation might be outside this patch of dirt.

"I can't get used to not having pockets." Zach ran his thumbs under his suspenders. "I had to leave my wallet in the glove box."

Bridget laughed. Despite the tough-guy vibe she had initially gotten from him at the coffee shop, she was sensing something else. A soft heart somewhere deep down, one he seemed to be fighting hard to protect.

Maybe she should share with him why she had left. It might make him realize how important it was that she get back to Buffalo for the start of classes in a week.

She had to complete her nursing degree. "When I was around fourteen, my *mem* was expecting another baby."

Zach stopped and turned to face her, obviously sensing she was about to share something important with him.

She smiled up at him, hoping to stop the heat crawling up her neck. "My *dat* was away at an auction overnight," she continued, her pulse thrumming in her ears. Zach's expression remained neutral. "She wasn't due to have the baby for another two months. She went into labor early. I had to help her deliver the baby."

"That's incredible. At fourteen?"

"*Yah*, well, I didn't know what to do. My mother was feverish. The baby was so tiny. I sent Liddie down the road to call an ambulance. I left Liddie with the younger kids and went with my mom to the hospital." Bridget dropped the leaf and watched it float to the ground, landing on a dry patch of dirt. She started walking again and Zach held back a branch so she could pass.

"They saved my *mem*." She sniffed. "My brother didn't make it." She worked her lower lip. "I overheard one of the doctors at the hospital say the baby would have had a fighting chance if my mother had delivered in the hospital. Those words really stuck with me. It was the first time I had been in a hospital. I was fascinated with the men and women who devoted their lives to saving others." Bridget shrugged as if it were no big deal, but it was a very big deal, enough to make her leave everything she knew in Hickory Lane. "I wanted to be able to do that for someone."

"You couldn't do that here?" Zach asked.

"Not in the same way. Sure, we have midwives who help with births, but I wanted to be a nurse. I wanted to make sure my patients had every chance. The most advanced medical care." She cleared her throat. "Unlike my brother."

Bridget took another few steps, then looked up at him. For some reason, she suddenly felt the need to defend the Amish. "Don't get me wrong. We—or the Amish—do use hospitals when we have to. However, if I stayed here, I would have never been allowed to study to become a nurse. To have a career. I owe the life of my mother to those nurses who took care of her. And maybe if my brother had been born in a hospital…

"I felt so helpless. That day changed my life." Across the field, rows of buggies lined up. The horses had been set loose in the fenced-in field. "I had to leave everything I knew in order to become a nurse. It's been a long road. I had a lot of education to make up. We only go up to the eighth grade here."

"Why? Don't the Amish value education?"

"Education is something that could take a person away from the community." She shrugged. "You don't need more than an eighth-grade education to run a farm."

"Are all Amish farmers?"

"Not all of them. As land gets more precious, some of the men have had to find other jobs in factories or with building crews." She grabbed her skirt and stepped over a branch in the path.

"You're a very impressive woman." The admiration in Zach's voice made her blush.

"I don't know about that. Women you know have all sorts of impressive careers." Bridget's face blazed hotter. She wasn't sure why she said that.

"I've never met anyone like you." His deep voice washed over her, and she was glad she was a few steps ahead, where he couldn't see her face.

She found herself picking up her pace as they walked around the short side of the pond and reached the clearing. Seeing the barn and all the buggies gave her the courage to finally ask, "Do you think we could retrieve some of my things from my apartment?"

Zach caught up with her. "We can run to the store and pick up whatever you need. You can't go back to the apartment. It's not safe. And, to be honest, a lot of your stuff was probably destroyed in the fire."

She stopped and tapped the toe of her boot on the hard earth. Hard-fought confidence straightened her spine. "But there's a chance some of the things were saved, right? Because I'm not talking about things I could easily replace at a store. I'd like to pick up my laptop and a few books."

One of his eyebrows drew down. "I could have an agent go to the apartment…"

"I'd like to go myself. See the damage and gather a few things. I was thinking last night, two of my classes next semester are online. This way if I'm a few days late starting the classes, I'll still be up-to-date with two of them. It'll make it easier to catch up."

"Someone could be watching the apartment."

She held her hand out to him, indicating his clothing. "You've proved to me you're good at undercover."

"More than you realize," he muttered.

"Well, we can sneak in. I can wear a baseball cap pulled low. Something. Somehow. Please?" Her voice grew high-pitched. "I can dress like a boy. Come on… There has to be a way."

Across the field, a young Amish woman emerged from the barn holding a toddler. Something about her frantic, jerky movements sent cold dread straight to Bridget's heart.

"Something's wrong." Without waiting a beat longer, Bridget raced across the field, frustrated that the fabric of her long dress tangled around her legs, slowed her down. She reached the woman, and another shock surged through her system.

"Katy!" Bridget's childhood friend was panic-stricken, jostling a toddler in her arms. The child's eyes were wide and her face was red. She was cramming her fist down her throat. Without waiting for permission, Bridget tugged the toddler from her mother's arms. "Did she have something in her mouth?"

"She had a handful of grapes. She was fussing. I thought the grapes would help her settle down." The Amish woman clasped her hands together and pressed them to her lips.

With tunnel-like focus, Bridget set the toddler on her feet and knelt down behind her. She gently leaned her forward, supporting her with one arm, and gave a solid back blow with the other. It didn't work. "Come on, little one." She tried again and again. On the third blow, the little girl threw up and then let out the most terrified cry. The child's arms swung up, reaching for her mother.

Bridget sat back on her heels and sagged with relief. *Thank You, God.* Zach placed his hand lightly on her shoulder. For the briefest of moments, she had forgotten he was there.

The commotion drew a few of the elders out of the barn. Bridget's heart stuttered when she recognized the bishop, silently taking in the situation.

Katy wept openly. She clung to her little girl and she held out her hand toward Bridget. "You saved my baby. *Denki, denki, denki.*"

The bishop met Bridget's gaze. If he was grateful or impressed, he didn't show it.

Mrs. Yoder ran out of the barn holding a smaller child. "What happened?"

"The baby was choking." Katy cupped her toddler's face and drew her to her chest and rocked back and forth, the relief evident on her pretty face.

"Oh…" Mrs. Yoder patted her granddaughter's head. She seemed to take note of the bishop. "Everything's okay. Please go back in. I'll tend to my daughter and granddaughter."

"Take the child to the house to get some water," the bishop said and turned with the others and went back to the barn.

"Come on," Bridget said. "I'll take you inside."

The toddler lifted her head and smiled through her tears. Bridget gently wiped a tear away from the little girl's cheek. "What's your name, honey?"

"Gracie." Katy smiled.

"Well, let's go get Gracie something to drink." Bridget

met Zach's gaze. He nodded, and a small smile played on her lips.

Being proud wasn't a familiar trait of the Amish, and it wasn't one Bridget was used to. Right now, she was grateful she had been in the right place at the right time.

As they walked toward the house beside her childhood best friend, Zach leaned in and whispered, "You did great."

Bridget tipped her head. "If it wasn't me, it would have been someone else."

"Don't downplay what you did. That young mother left the barn because she didn't want her child to disrupt the service. Who knows what would have happened if you hadn't been here?" He gently placed his hand on the small of her back, directing her toward the house.

She shifted to say something to Zach, but then she saw her father lurking near the door of the barn like a storm cloud blowing in on the horizon.

Bridget settled Katy with Gracie in her lap on a rocker on the back porch and got them a drink of water. Mrs. Yoder stayed inside with the baby. Zach had disappeared. Bridget wondered why he hadn't said goodbye. She shoved aside the hint of disappointment and crouched down in front of her friend. She reached out to touch the toddler's bonnet string. "She's beautiful." She smiled up at her friend. "She has your eyes."

Katy pressed her cheek to her daughter's. "She has her father's feet." Her friend giggled, reminding Bridget of their childhood days.

"Did you marry Levi Shetler?"

Katy's cheeks turned pink. "*Yah*. You know Moses Lapp came back."

"He came back? From where?" Bridget fidgeted with Gracie's shoelace, then stood up and leaned back on the railing. Moses had been courting Bridget at the time she left Hickory Lane. He was a popular boy, and she'd assumed he'd move on to the next girl without missing a beat. After all, that was five years ago.

"Shortly after you left, he left, too. I thought you knew." She lowered her voice. "I guess you wouldn't."

"Where'd he go?" Curiosity got the best of her.

"There's a few rumors." Katy smiled with a flash of mischief in her eyes, then grew subdued. "I shouldn't repeat gossip." She wrapped her arms around Gracie, who was drifting off to sleep. "Liddie never mentioned him?" Bridget wrote off the odd lilt to her voice as the strain between two friends who hadn't seen each other in a long time.

"No, she never mentioned him," Bridget said. Moses had hung with the wilder crowd in Hickory Lane, but that was all relative. Everyone figured Bridget would have a calming presence after he started taking her home after the Sunday singings. "Is he married?" Bridget asked when the awkward silence had taken on a life of its own.

"*Neh*. I heard—"

"Are you going to come in and help or what?" Liddie appeared suddenly on the other side of the screen door. She had slipped out of the service to help with the final preparations for the meal.

Bridget ran her palms down her cape. "I'm coming." She smiled at her friend. "Sorry, I have to go."

Katy reached out and touched Bridget's wrist. "Are you happy?"

Bridget frowned. "It's been a little stressful lately. I'm not sure how much you know." The Amish way of communication was old-fashioned but no less effective. When Katy didn't say anything, Bridget added, "I am happy."

"That's great." The positive sentiment sounded forced.

"Are you happy?" Even though Katy had been the first to ask, Bridget was genuinely curious. Katy was living the life that Bridget had given up. She was twenty-five. Married. And a mother. Other than her age, Bridget no longer had anything in common with her friend.

"I am happy." Katy hugged her daughter tight. "I can't thank you enough for helping Gracie."

Bridget squeezed the little girl's foot. "I'm glad I was there."

"Me too," Katy said. She straightened her daughter's dress over her socked foot. "I did hear the rumors about you. Does this mean you might be coming home?" The hope in her friend's voice broke her heart.

"Classes start next week. I'm going to be a nurse in nine months."

Katy paused a moment, as if reflecting, then said, "You're going to make a wonderful nurse, but I've missed you."

"I've missed you, too."

"I need help in here," Liddie called again, this time from deeper in the kitchen.

"One more thing…" Katy pressed her daughter's head to her chest and covered her ear. "Why didn't you tell me you were leaving?"

"I didn't want to get you into trouble. I had to do it on my own." Bridget straightened. "You understand."

Katy kissed the top of her daughter's bonnet. "I do. I wished we could have talked about it."

"Bridget!" Liddie called again, this time with an edge of impatience.

Across the lawn, a sea of black clothes spilled out of the barn. The service was over. "You couldn't have talked me out of it."

Her friend looked up at her with wide eyes, as if Bridget had uncovered her darkest worry. That she hadn't recognized that her friend was unhappy and hadn't done something to make her want to stay. Bridget touched Katy's shoulder. "I need to go before Liddie short-sheets my bed."

Katy laughed. "Go. And promise me you'll come by before you leave next time."

"I will." Bridget slipped inside the door. Liddie was nowhere to be seen.

"Everyone okay?" Zach appeared in the kitchen doorway.

"Yes." Especially now that Bridget realized Zach was still here. She peeled the foil off a dish. The sweet smell of red peppers and olive oil made her stomach growl.

"Need help?" Zach asked.

"I thought you wanted to blend in."

He furrowed his brow, clearly not understanding.

"You can't blend in if you hang out in the kitchen."

She lifted one skeptical eyebrow. Was this his idea of working undercover? "Go outside and find my grandfather. He'll be happy to share a meal with you."

"I will." Zach stepped closer and lowered his voice. "I made a few phone calls. We can get you back inside your apartment to grab a few things. Looks like the fire department did a good job."

Bridget spun around and, in her excitement, she stumbled forward and planted her hands on his chest. He placed his hands on her hips to steady her, then quickly dropped them to his side.

The sound of someone clearing his throat drew their attention. Her father stood in the doorway. "I will not tolerate your being disrespectful under my roof."

Bridget's face burned from embarrassment. "I wasn't... I didn't..." She bowed her head and turned around and fussed with the cling wrap covering a plate of chocolate chip cookies. "I should probably set out the food."

"No disrespect meant, sir," Zach said. "I was headed outside. Is there anything I could do for you?"

Her father seemed taken aback, an expression Bridget rarely saw on his face. He seemed to be debating, then finally he said, "The young men are carrying the benches out of the barn and rearranging them into tables on the lawn. Perhaps they could use a hand."

"Of course," Zach said, then to Bridget, "I'll be outside if you need me."

Before Bridget had a chance to form the right words, her father had slipped back out the door. A moment later her mother breezed in. "Everyone's saying you saved baby Gracie. Is that something you learned in school?" Her mother's voice sounded reverent.

"I didn't mean to draw attention to myself. I was taking a walk when Katy came outside. Her baby was choking."

Her mother surprised her by smiling. "*Gott* put you where you were needed."

Bridget nodded, unable to speak as emotion clogged her throat. She wanted nothing more than to be back on her mother's good side. Her father's, too. But that would never happen if she wanted to become a nurse. And she'd never be able to become a nurse if she stayed in Hickory Lane.

Chapter Nine

Early Monday morning, Bridget and Zach headed into Buffalo. Bridget had hardly slept last night wondering if her *dat* would try to stop her at the door, if her things at the apartment had been damaged beyond repair, if she was naively putting herself and Zach in danger. If…if… if… Her worries nagged at her until the first signs of dawn dragged her out of bed. She stuffed her *Englisch* clothes into a cloth tote and almost made it out of her childhood bedroom before Liddie sat up and begged to tag along. Definitely not. Then Bridget said goodbye to her *mem* in the kitchen, promising she'd be back later today, and slipped out while her father was in the barn. She'd deal with his anger later.

From the passenger seat of Zach's truck, Bridget stared at the stately buildings of the University at Buffalo's Main Street campus on the way to the DEA office downtown. Apparently, Zach's supervisor wanted a statement in person before they swung by her apartment. Bridget pressed a hand to her midsection and gulped air, hoping her nerve-induced nausea would pass. She focused hard on the college campus outside her window, imagining it buzzing with students, and she prayed by this time next week she would be one of them. It had been a long, hard road to get here, and she could *not* give up now.

Once the campus was out of view, Bridget shifted in her seat to face Zach. "Thanks for taking the long way downtown."

"Yeah, sure, no problem. I enjoy taking Main Street downtown every so often. I love this city." She would have heard the smile in his voice even if she hadn't been looking at him.

The tension of yesterday began to fall away. Her father had barely spoken two words after his initial admonishment for daring to be seen, forget that she'd helped sweet little Gracie. His body language spoke volumes. He was brimming with agitation that he wasn't able to control his older daughter. Yet she loved the man. He was her father. He was also a product of the community in which he lived, and he truly believed he was doing the best thing for his daughter and his family in the eyes of God.

Did he really think his tough love would bring her back for good? Would he ever accept that God was bigger than their small Amish community? That she could serve Him and be a nurse?

She rubbed her forehead, trying to stop the constant barrage of concerns that threatened to give her a headache.

"You okay?" Zach cut her a quick glance. The warm concern in his eyes softened the edges of her worries.

"I'm fine." She fidgeted with the zipper on her hoodie. The morning chill signaling the approaching end of summer would burn off soon. They had stopped at a rest area outside Hickory Lane so she could put on *Englisch* clothes. She wished changing her mind-set was as easy as switching her plain black boots for her favorite sneakers.

"You know, I didn't intentionally spring this trip to the DEA offices on you. It wasn't a bait and switch." He laughed, a mirthless sound. "My supervisor called me late last night. They want to get an official statement from you, and since we were already planning a trip into town, I set it up. Things are moving fast. We'll head to your apartment right after. I promise." Zach slowed at the red light.

"I know," Bridget said quietly. "I trust you." She did, even after only knowing him a few days.

A little while later, Zach pulled into a parking spot near a building with beautiful architectural detail. Bridget often found herself staring at the buildings in downtown Buffalo. The massive structures were unlike anything she knew growing up. They hustled toward the door and took the elevator up to his office and into a large conference room with floor-to-ceiling windows overlooking the city. She took in the view. Beautiful.

A few moments later, a smartly dressed woman came into the room with a laptop tucked under her arm. She smiled, more businesslike than friendly and she offered her hand. "Hello, I'm Assistant Special Agent in Charge Colleen McCarthy." She slipped in front of a chair and pushed it back with her knee, set her laptop down on the large conference table and sat down. She held out her palm to Bridget. "Have a seat. We appreciate your cooperation. This shouldn't take too long."

Zach closed the conference room door after Bridget asked to be excused following an intense interrogation. He turned and faced his supervisor with his hands on his hips. "Did you need to be that hard on her? She's not involved. She's the one who reported the activity."

His supervisor, ASAC McCarthy, snapped closed her laptop and swiveled in her seat to face him. "First of all, you are supposed to be on leave. We talked about this."

Zach pulled out a chair and sat down. He rolled it toward his boss and rested his forearms on his thighs. "I can't leave this woman high and dry. She trusts me."

"Listen—" Colleen leaned back, resting one elbow on the table next to her "—you delivered her to safety at her family's Amish farm." One brow dipped down at the word *Amish*. "She's good. Now you need to take a break. I can't risk losing one of my best agents."

"She's in danger. Her coworker was murdered." He straightened and crossed his arms over his chest. "Any word on that investigation?"

Colleen hesitated for a moment. "Ashley Meadows was attacked on the running trail near the university."

"Cause of death?"

"Strangulation." She paused a beat, then said, "We're going to get this guy. I promise."

Zach scratched the back of his head. He should have done more sooner. He cleared his throat. "What about the Kevin Pearson investigation?" Kevin was his confidential informant who had been shot last week. Zach worked day in and day out in a stressful job, but the past few weeks had been the worst of his career.

"Nothing yet." Colleen relaxed her posture and leaned forward. "You have to let it go. You'll be cleared."

Zach shook his head, deep in thought. Had he put too much pressure on the kid? Kevin had claimed he was getting clean and only hung around the bar because he felt like he had a purpose helping Zach take down his suppliers. That was the goal: get the little fish on the hook to reel in the big ones. Didn't always work out.

"I should have pulled the plug," Zach said, turning to stare out over the Buffalo skyline. He had regretted not getting the kid out, but that hadn't been his decision, nor had it been his job. His job was to use the little guy to get the big guy. Otherwise, the Kevins of the world could just be replaced. He scrubbed a hand across his face. It still didn't make it any easier.

"Don't do this to yourself," Colleen said. "You've got to take a break. Get your head straight. Put that incident behind you. I'm confident you'll be cleared of wrongdoing, and I can't have you coming back to work second-guessing yourself." Half her mouth quirked up. "I need my take-charge agent back here once you're cleared. You have to take Bridget back to Hickory Lane and get out of there. That's an order."

Colleen must have read something in his expression, because she narrowed her eyes and leaned closer. "I've never known you to let a case get personal."

"Kevin was just a kid. Maybe I pushed him too hard."

"I wasn't talking about your CI."

"You're talking about Bridget? It's not personal." He returned her unflinching gaze, proving he meant it. No one had ever accused him of not knowing how to play a role. Going deep undercover. Pretending.

"Are you sure?" Colleen tilted her head and paused before standing.

Zach studied the industrial-gray carpet. *How do I really feel?*

He had been stuffing down the feelings that had sparked the moment he first noticed Bridget sitting alone in the coffee shop. Ashley had sent him a photo. But he hadn't expected to feel something. Her gentle nature was soothing to his battered soul. Most of the people he dealt with through work had a pent-up energy that kept him on high alert. Something about her threatened his carefully guarded heart.

Or maybe he really was simply run-down and vulnerable.

Colleen picked up her laptop from the conference table and tucked it under her arm. "You look beat."

Zach's smile sneaked up on him. "The haggard look is usually an asset." Working undercover had been his primary gig the past four years. None of his druggie associates ever accused him of looking tired, probably because most of them saw the world through heavily lidded eyes.

"You don't need to babysit Bridget."

Babysit.

Zach ran the back of his fist across his mouth. "She's pretty skittish. I'd hate to scare her off."

Colleen shifted her laptop to her other arm. "She gave her official statement. I'm not sure how much more we need. We've been through this before. Far too often. Once the forensic analysts go through the records at the clinic, they'll determine if they can issue an immediate suspension order. The good doctor—even when they find him—won't have the ability to prescribe controlled substances. You know how this works."

He did. "Any updates?" Hovering around the periphery of an investigation wasn't familiar to him.

"Frank—" another agent in the office "—put a call in to the Philadelphia police department. The good doctor apparently doesn't believe in cash. Lucky for us. He used his credit card at a hotel. So, unless he realizes his mistake and bolts, we should have him in custody any moment now."

"Why didn't you tell me this the minute I got here?" Zach asked.

"Because you're on leave." Colleen pressed her lips together and opened her eyes wide. "You're one of my best agents. I need you back here whole once you're cleared."

Bridget needed him, too. "I think I should stick close to Bridget. Her friend was killed. Bridget was nearly run down. Her house was firebombed." Zach ticked the items off on his fingers.

"Who's going to find her in Hickory Lane?" She shifted her weight and gave him the "how many times do we have to go through this?" stare.

"Don't we owe her something?" Zach bit out. "She came forward with her report."

His supervisor's expression was inscrutable. She didn't get to where she was by being soft.

"Bridget deserves more respect than to be told to sit tight while we figure this out. She's a college student. She wants to start classes next week."

"Her safety is top priority. She's going to have to be patient. But there's no reason you have to stay in Hickory Lane, too. It's a perfect safe house."

When he didn't answer, Colleen tipped her head. "Do you have any reason to believe she's not safe in Hickory Lane?"

"No." The single word came out clipped.

"Then there's your answer. No need to take it personally, Zach." Colleen tapped his forearm with a soft fist bump before opening the conference room door. Bridget was standing on the other side. Based on her flushed face, he didn't need to ask if she overheard their conversation.

"Ready to go?" Zach stepped into the corridor, walls lined with photographs of long-retired agents.

"Sure." She ran a hand over her ponytail in what he now recognized as a nervous gesture.

"We'll keep you updated on the investigation," his supervisor said, holding her laptop to her chest. "Thank you for coming in."

"I had to," Bridget said. "What they're doing is wrong."

When they reached the bottom of the stairwell, Bridget turned to him. "What now?"

"Let's run by your apartment and get your things."

"Do you really think it's okay?" She dropped her hand from playing with her hair.

"You're not getting cold feet on me now, are you?" He tried to make light of the situation.

"No, no," Bridget said, not sounding very convincing.

Maybe once Bridget had her laptop and textbooks, she wouldn't mind being left alone in Hickory Lane.

Chapter Ten

About a block from Bridget's apartment, Zach pulled his truck over. He reached into the back seat and grabbed a Buffalo Bills baseball cap and offered it to her. "Do you think you can stuff your hair into this?"

She began twisting her ponytail into a high bun. "Can't be harder than fitting it under a bonnet, right?"

"Yeah," Zach said distractedly. He craned his neck to check his surroundings, it seemed. "Got it?" His attention landed on Bridget stuffing the last bit of hair up into the baseball cap. His steely gaze made a chill run up her spine.

"I'm all set." She pulled the bill of the hat low on her forehead.

"Maybe I should run up to your apartment and leave you in the truck."

Disappointment edged out her apprehension. "Please, I want to go in. I need to search for a few things, if that's okay with you."

His eyes stared, unseeing. His shoulders sagged

a fraction, and she knew he'd relented. "We have to hurry." The seriousness of his tone set her teeth on edge. Did he really think someone was waiting for her?

Bridget gave him a quick nod. With that, Zach drove to a parking lot across the street from her apartment complex, and they got out and walked the long way around to her unit. They both wore ball caps, looking like they were ready to go to the team's home opener, not that she'd know from experience.

They strode through the courtyard. Her eye was drawn to the emergency-closure boards nailed to the frame of her bedroom window. In the middle of the day, the area was deserted. Most of her neighbors were at work, making it easier for her and Zach to sneak in and out unnoticed. Bridget jogged up the stairs, and Zach followed close behind. With key in hand, Bridget approached her apartment door. Her mind flashed back to the first time she had gotten the keys to her very own place. Her very first tangible evidence of freedom.

Poof. Gone.

The key slipped in her sweaty fingers.

You can do this.

The key slid into the lock, and she heard the solid click of the dead bolt retracting. She pushed open the door, and the dank air hung thick with smoke and dampness. It was a far cry from the scent of the lavender air freshener she loved.

Zach entered the room behind her. "Get what you need. I'll wait here. And hurry."

A lump of emotion made it impossible to speak. Bridget walked through the untouched family room to her bedroom. She opened the door and slid her hand along the wall, reaching for the light switch and flicked it back and forth. Nothing. The only source of light was from the hallway since boards covered the windows, leaving the room cast in heavy shadows and making it seem smaller. The cloying scent didn't help.

"The electricity has probably been shut off because of the fire," Zach called from the living room. "Do you have your phone on you? Use the flashlight app."

Bridget directed the beam around the bedroom. Gingerly she fingered her pink comforter, now charred and damp from the fire and subsequent firefighting efforts. Suddenly she felt very tired. Exhausted. Had all the challenges she had faced to get here been for nothing? Tonight, she'd be back in her bed in Hickory Lane with no real timeline for returning to Buffalo.

"Did you find what you needed?" Zach hollered from the other room. "We should get going."

Zach's impatience made her nervous. She scanned the beam of light around the room. She peeled back the closet doors and found her backpack. It seemed to be mostly untouched by the flames, and the nylon had protected it from the water. She hoisted it onto her shoulder. She grabbed a couple textbooks from the top shelf of the closet. Then she found her notebook and favorite pens in her desk drawer. The pages of the notebook were a little wavy from the dampness. She shook her head to try to dispel the constant unease that made her skin buzz. She had her laptop and books. She'd be able to keep up with two online classes.

She backed out and scanned the room one last time,

the light from her smartphone touching on the life she had made here for the past couple years after she moved off campus. The life that clearly no longer existed. Even if—no when—she returned permanently, this wouldn't be her home. She'd never be able to live here again without reliving the explosive crash and fire.

She turned off the flashlight and balanced the phone on the textbooks in her arms. She pulled her bedroom door closed out of habit.

"Got everything?" Zach opened the outside door a fraction.

"Almost." Bridget ducked into the kitchen to grab her migraine meds. Just then, a commotion sounded in the next room. She poked her head out of the kitchen to find Dr. Ryan pointing a gun at Zach and forcing him back into her apartment. Her heart dropped.

Instinctively, she backed up while clutching her things. Zach lifted his hands and seemed to be trying to tell her something with his keen gaze.

Her boss pushed the door closed with his foot. "Why did you have to do this?"

Bridget's gaze moved from Dr. Ryan to Zach and back. Zach shook his head slightly. Taking his cue, she stayed quiet.

"Dr. Ryan, it's over," Zach said.

The physician scoffed. "For who? I'm the one holding the gun."

"Killing isn't in your nature. You're a healer."

Her boss seemed to blanch.

Zach held out his palm. "Hand me your weapon. This ends here."

The physician seemed to consider this for a moment before shaking his head. He glared at Bridget. She had never seen him this angry. He always had a wonderful bedside manner, and only once had she heard him get upset with one of his employees. The nighttime janitor had accidentally left the alley door unlocked. Anything could have been stolen. Yet the doctor himself had been the biggest threat to the clinic.

"It should never have gone this far," the physician said ruefully. "Why didn't you mind your own business?" Dr. Ryan scrubbed a hand over his face and shuddered. "You and Ashley should have minded your own business."

"Ashley…" The single word slipped out of Bridget's lips. Her mouth felt dry. "You killed Ashley."

"Bridget…" Zach warned.

Something flashed in the doctor's eyes. "I didn't mean… She wouldn't listen."

"You don't want this to go any further," Zach said, his voice calm yet authoritative.

Bridget's boss turned, and in one swift motion, Zach disarmed him and had the man's face pressed against the wall.

Bridget slid down the wall to the floor, sagging with relief and finally letting the tears fall.

"You okay?" Zach asked, pressing his knee into Seth Ryan's back and yanking his arm up in the most uncomfortable position.

Bridget nodded and set her things on the floor next to her. She swiped at a tear running down her cheek.

"Any chance you have a zip tie in that kitchen of yours?"

"Yeah." Bridget got to her feet and ran to the kitchen. He could hear her opening and closing drawers until she returned with a black zip tie. "This?"

"Perfect." He took the plastic zip tie and wrapped it around the doctor's wrists and cranked it tight. The doctor grunted. The fasteners should hold, because the doctor didn't have much fight left in him. Zach grabbed the doctor's arm and dragged him a few feet, letting him sit with his back against the wall. "Who's down in Philly?" The DEA had tracked his credit card to a hotel down there.

Seth's eyes narrowed, and he shook his head. It seemed the doctor wasn't going to talk. Instead, he bowed his head and sobbed, loudly and with little dignity.

Zach joined Bridget, who was sitting on the edge of the couch shaking. She looked up at him, and he reached out and took her hand.

"Is it over?"

He wanted more than anything to say yes, but he knew that wasn't true. In his experience, each of these guys was just a cog in the wheel. "Hang tight. I'm going to call this in."

She exhaled a long, shaky breath. "Okay."

It didn't take long for a Buffalo police officer to come pick up Seth Ryan, then Zach turned to Bridget. "Let me get you home."

"Home?" she asked when they were alone again. She straightened the footstool that had been jostled in the skirmish.

"Not here. You need to go back to Hickory Lane until we finish our investigation. It shouldn't be long." He wasn't sure if the last bit was a white lie or not. Either way, he needed to reassure her.

"Are you going to drop me off and leave? I overheard you talking to your supervisor."

The protest died on his lips. Bridget shrugged, seeming so frail and thin. "I get it." She sniffed. "With Dr. Ryan in custody, the case should be over soon, right? Besides, you have better things to do than babysit me."

Inwardly he winced at her choice of words. The same ones his supervisor had used in the office. They lacked respect. "Come on." He held out his hand, and she accepted it, coming to her feet. How could he explain to her that these cases were never cut-and-dried? "We don't know who else is in involved, but this is a huge start. Huge. Okay?"

"Okay…"

"I want you to go back to Hickory Lane for a few more days, at least."

"Alone, right?" Her dejected tone suggested she already knew the answer.

"I'll make sure you get settled."

Bridget hoisted her backpack on her shoulder and picked up the items she had set on the floor. "Let's go."

Shortly after they got into the truck, his cell phone rang. His mother's name flashed on the caller ID on his dash. He hit Ignore. A moment later, it rang again.

"Go ahead and answer it," Bridget said.

His thumb hovered over Ignore before curiosity got the best of him. "Hello." He hadn't taken a call from his mother in over two years. The last time she'd been slurring her words and berated him. He hadn't stayed on the phone long enough to find out why she had been all bent out of shape.

"Zachary, it's your mother." Her voice cracked over the line, filling the inside of the cab. She sounded tired but clear. Sober. He tightened his grip on the steering wheel.

"How can I help you?" Realizing how formal he sounded, he was acutely aware of Bridget's presence.

Her mother sniffed. "I heard about Ashley. Poor, sweet girl…" She went quiet before finding her voice again. "I saw her not that long ago. I gave her your business card. Did she call you?"

Zach rested his elbow on the door and rubbed his forehead. "She called me." He cleared his throat. "Did you read about her death in the paper?"

"You know I don't get the newspaper."

Actually, he didn't know. He had moved out of his mother's house when he was eighteen for college. From there, he'd enlisted. He'd avoided his childhood at all costs, including his baby sister.

"Ashley's parents told me. They said she was murdered." His mother emphasized the word *murdered* as if it were offensive solely to her. "Her poor mother. I did what I could to comfort her, you know, one mother to another who lost a child. Only another mother could understand that."

Growing anger bubbled in his gut. His mother loved the martyr card. What she failed to acknowledge was that she'd been too strung out to recognize the same symptoms in her own daughter. He gritted his teeth to avoid saying something he'd later regret. "Is there anything else? I have work to do."

"Always work…"

He checked the traffic before turning right. "Well, there's a lot of drugs out there." He couldn't help the dig.

"If you took the time to visit me, you'd know I've changed," his mother said, her voice growing soft.

Not soon enough. Bridget stared out the passenger window. "I have to go. Please express my condolences to the Meadows family."

"Goodbye, Zachary." His mother's tone was resigned. "It's obvious that you don't have time for me."

Zach ended the call. Silence hung thick and heavy in the air.

Bridget shifted in her seat. "You're estranged from your family, too."

He hitched a shoulder. "My mother always chose drugs over us."

"Now you're doing the same." Bridget sounded faraway.

"I'm on the right side of the law." A hard edge sharpened his words. Zach turned on his directional and took the on-ramp to the Thruway.

"How do you suppose Dr. Ryan found us so quickly?" Bridget's abrupt change in conversation caught Zach off guard. He checked the rearview mirror. He had been careful to take a circuitous route before he got on the Thruway, and he planned to get off an exit or two after the one to Hickory Lane and then double back. He couldn't be too careful.

"They'll look into that. My guess, someone close by was watching the apartment." He cleared his throat. "That's why I was reluctant to take you there." He sensed Bridget was about to apologize, so he held up his hand. "In the end, going back there was a great way to flush him out. Ideally, I would have had an agent go in with me, not a civilian. Thankfully it all worked out. Now we have him in custody."

"Why do you think he did it?" Bridget asked. "I thought he was a good man."

"I'm sure we'll find out now that he's in custody."

Bridget let out a long breath. "How long will it take before I can come back to Buffalo for good?"

"Analysts are going through the records and the videos of people coming and going from the clinic. The Buffalo Police Department is investigating Ashley's death. With more than one crime scene, the pieces will come together. Quickly." Zach reached out to pat her on the knee, then thought better of it. "And now they have the doctor in custody. It shouldn't be long."

The protective shield he had built around his heart was crumbling. His heart ached for Bridget. The pain on her face made it evident that his confident reassurances meant little to her.

His mind flashed to the good doctor sobbing in the apartment. The compassion that he might have felt for a life ruined was replaced by hot anger at the lives destroyed in greed's wake.

Chapter Eleven

Bridget's twelve-year-old brother, Caleb, came charging across the field backlit by bold streaks of orange and purple in a glorious evening sky. If Bridget were to list the things she missed about Hickory Lane, the sunset would be near the top, somewhere after her family and the gentle quiet. She *really* missed the quiet.

Her little brother pulled up short, apparently embarrassed by his enthusiasm. "You came back," he said with an air of disbelief.

Bridget's heart broke for her sweet little brother. He had been only seven when she left Hickory Lane to become a nurse. They had been especially close. She'd read to him, helped him sound out words, determined to make him a strong reader. Her parents shrugged off his struggles. It was her own quiet rebellion. Little did her family know that soon she'd be committing the ultimate rebellion by leaving.

Bridget planted her hand on Caleb's shoulder, not wanting to embarrass him by a full-on hug. The Amish weren't much for displays of emotion. "I'm back." She left out the words *for now.* She had no stomach for conflict or making others feel bad. That's probably why she had initially been reluctant to report her suspicions about the clinic. Even now, thinking about Dr. Ryan being led out by the police made her heart break for his family. How had a man gone so wrong?

Bridget made a show of swatting at a mosquito. "Let's get moving before I get eaten alive." The three of them continued to traipse across the field. Bridget had her backpack hoisted up on her shoulder. It must have made an odd sight with her plain clothes. Zach hadn't bothered to change because he was leaving. This definitive announcement was like a sucker punch to the gut.

Seemingly satisfied that his sister hadn't left him for good, Caleb ran ahead to the house. He picked up a volleyball on the way and tossed it up in the air and caught it. When Bridget reached the house, she turned to Zach. There was so much she wanted to say—Would she see him again? Would he let her know when it was safe to come home? Was he going to reach out to his mom?—but all she could muster was, "Thank you for taking me to my apartment to get my things."

"And we smoked out the good doctor." A smile tilted the corners of his mouth. She was going to miss that handsome face.

"Kinda like he initially smoked me out?" She pressed her lips together. "I still can't believe he was involved with all this. He was such a good man." Bridget held her crossed arms close.

"People make bad choices." He tilted his head to

look into her eyes. "You made the right one. Don't ever doubt that."

Bridget nodded, slowly. Still not entirely convinced. "I'm going to miss the entire semester, aren't I?" Pinpricks of anxiety reached every corner of her scalp. Despite having her laptop and her books, if she couldn't return to campus, she'd inevitably fall behind. She blinked rapidly, then consciously tried to slow down her thoughts, her breath. This was only meant to be temporary.

Zach placed his hand on hers, stilling her fluttering motions. "I won't leave you here longer than necessary. I'll call when it's safe. I'll send someone to get you."

Disappointment crushed her heart. *He'll send someone?* Of course he'd send someone. She had no right to expect it to be him. He worked in a big office with lots of people. Forcing a smile to hide the hurt, she settled on a simple "Thank you."

Zach leaned closer; a soft smile played on his lips. He smelled of aloe and mint. Her face grew flushed, and he pulled his head back a fraction. "Would you mind if I kissed you?"

Her mind went blank. All she could do was give her head a slight nod in the affirmative.

He reached out and cupped her cheek, his hand both strong and gentle. He leaned in again, and this time she closed her eyes. His warm lips brushed ever so softly across hers. Tingles of awareness rushed through her body. Slowly, she opened her eyes. He had a sad smile on his face.

"I'm going to miss you."

"Yeah."

"Maybe if circumstances had been different…" He searched her face.

"Yeah." *Say something more.*

"You're going to make a great nurse. Don't ever give up on that dream."

"I won't." Her heart beat wildly, drowning out her soft voice.

"Well…" Zach took a step backward. "I'm going to grab something I left at your grandfather's. Then I'm driving home. I'll be in touch."

"Okay, sure." She waved, feeling self-conscious. "'Night," she said, more enthusiastically than she felt. Afraid her emotions were going to get the best of her, Bridget slipped into the house and went right upstairs.

She was surprised to find Liddie fumbling with something in the closet. She seemed startled when Bridget called her name. Her younger sister spun around. "Did anyone ever tell you not to sneak up on someone?" She laughed nervously. Then her shoulders slowly slid down from her ears. "You're home."

"I am." Bridget plopped her backpack on the bed, tempted to gush about what had just happened. A bigger part of her wanted to keep it to herself. A cherished memory.

"How'd it go?"

"Fine." She wasn't ready to tell her sister everything. Talk of the doctor's arrest would obliterate the warm and fuzzies she was still enjoying from her last interaction with Zach. "I had to make an official report before we went to my apartment." She sounded normal, right?

No sign that a handsome man had sent her pulse into overdrive with the most innocent of kisses. She rubbed the back of her neck and smiled to herself.

"Glad you had a good trip, even without me," Liddie said, sounding like a petulant child.

"It was a quick visit." Bridget unzipped her backpack and pulled out her computer.

"Wait." Liddie narrowed her gaze. "Why do you have that funny smile?"

Bridget quickly schooled her expression and shrugged. She patted her laptop, eager to change the subject. "I need this for school. I should probably tuck it away so *Dat* doesn't get mad?"

Liddie held up a finger and spun around and opened the wardrobe. She unfolded the top layer of a blanket on the bottom shelf. "Tuck it in here." Liddie unfolded another blanket, revealing her cell phone.

Bridget met her sister's excited gaze with concern. "How long are you going to keep this phone?"

Liddie smirked. "I don't think you should be telling me what I can or cannot do."

"You're right." Bridget couldn't be a hypocrite. Hopefully, Liddie would find her way through *Rumspringa* and emerge on the other side, the adult she was meant to be. Funny, Bridget was still struggling with finding her place.

Did it include Zach? No, not possible. His life was undercover work. Her sole focus was school and beyond that, a career in nursing.

Bridget placed her laptop on the blanket in Liddie's arms. Her sister folded the material over the top and then tucked the package in the bottom of their wardrobe. "I suppose we'll have to find another hiding place once it gets cold and we need the blanket." She shrugged. "Works for now."

How long did her sister think she was staying? A hint of nostalgia burned the back of her nose. Bridget was already missing these days. Missing this day in particular. She cleared her throat and decided for however many days she had left in Hickory Lane, she'd try to stay present.

Liddie flopped down on her bed and crossed her legs at the ankles, and twirled her bare feet. They were black on the bottom. "Did you figure out how you are going to charge your laptop?"

Bridget laughed. "I'm hoping I'll be back in Buffalo before classes start, but if I'm not, I'll have to go into town and use the Wi-Fi and electricity at the coffee shop."

"Wait till the tourists get a photo of you in your bonnet on your laptop." Liddie stared at her with an amused expression. She shook her head, as if dismissing the idea. "Grandfather has a generator. I'm sure he'd let you charge your laptop."

"Good to know. Thanks." Bridget sat down on the opposite twin bed, the one she had slept in as a child. The one where she'd lain wide-awake planning her uncertain future and then secretly crying with self-doubt and indecision.

"One day at a time." Bridget threw out the cliché to hide her frustration that she hadn't had time to think any of this through. Maybe she should chase down Zach and beg him to take her back to Buffalo, because the unknown certainty she faced in Buffalo seemed less scary than the familiar side-eye and cool glares she'd face here.

Is that the only reason you want to chase Zach down?

She laughed quietly to herself. So much for staying in the moment.

Zach took a moment to take in the sunset. He couldn't remember the last time he had slowed down to do something so basic. He also couldn't remember the last time a woman had gotten under his skin like Bridget had. Considering his upbringing and life experiences, he had kept his heart guarded.

And he never crossed the line when it came to work and his personal life.

You're officially on leave, remember? No lines crossed.

He filled his lungs, then slowly exhaled. Sounded like an excuse to him.

The kiss had been innocent, but perhaps he had been selfish. Maybe a little curious, too. Bridget had enough on her mind without him playing with her emotions. Yet he couldn't help himself. She looked so pretty, the sun catching the gold specks in her hair, the sunset casting her in the perfect light.

He took a step backward and rubbed the back of his head. Yeah, he probably should have resisted the impulse to kiss Bridget. His life didn't leave room for women like her. Someone who'd eventually want a husband and kids. A normal life. His life, his work, were anything but normal. He shook away the thought, realizing the simple kiss, after knowing Bridget for exactly four days, had sent his mind spinning.

Yeah, he definitely needed that leave. He was losing his focus.

Zach squared his shoulders, and after a quick knock on the door of Bridget's grandfather's house, he slipped inside. He found Jeremiah sitting at the table, chewing on the mouthpiece of his pipe, studying something in front of him.

"I suggest you get a good night's sleep." Jeremiah rested his pipe in a tray and turned to look at him expectantly. "We have a lot of work in the morning."

"I think there's been a misunderstanding," Zach said, pausing on the way to the small room off the kitchen where he had slept last night. He wanted to make sure he didn't leave anything behind.

"Oh?" Jeremiah's pale, bushy eyebrow drew down.

"I'm afraid I'm headed back to Buffalo tonight." In that moment, Zach felt sad to be going. For the short time he had been here, he had enjoyed the elderly man's company. By all accounts, he was a faithful follower of the ways of the Amish, but it seemed that age had softened him and allowed him to be more open to the possibilities of the world beyond this small farm.

"And you're taking Bridget?" He folded the small paper and tucked it under a black leather-bound book. Without waiting for an answer, he added, "We'll be sad to see her go." He pushed back from the table, and the smooth, carved pine legs on the chair screeched on the hardwood floor.

"Bridget is staying," Zach said, wanting to deliver some good news to this kindly old man.

"For how long?"

"I don't know." Mentally Zach sifted through all the information, but before he could say more, Jeremiah held up a shaky hand, gnarled from years of hard labor. "We still have to—"

"I don't want to know."

Zach laughed, imagining the list of chores Jeremiah had in mind. "I appreciate your hospitality, thank you."

Jeremiah seemed to consider this. He adjusted his glasses on his face. "Ah, yeah, I suppose I shouldn't have looked a gift horse in the mouth."

"Well…" Zach started to say goodbye when the elderly man grabbed his cane resting against the table and slowly walked toward him.

"I don't need to know what's going on in the outside world, but I can see what's going on right outside my home." He gestured to the view from the window over the small kitchen table.

Zach reflected on his tender interaction with Bridget moments ago. Perhaps her grandfather had been watching them, misinterpreting it. *Is he?* He opened his mouth to explain, then snapped it shut. There was nothing to explain.

Jeremiah dragged his hand through his beard in a contemplative manner. "You got family?"

Zach shrugged, a nonanswer, then realized Bridget's grandfather would never accept that. "My mom lives in Buffalo. I don't see much of her."

Jeremiah tilted his head. "Why is that?"

"Long story."

"I've got plenty of time." Jeremiah pinned Zach with a steady gaze. "Family is important. That's something the Amish got right." He raised his hand, palm up. "I have this cozy little house right on the property. My family takes care of me."

"Can't say my family is the same. We're what people might call dysfunctional." Zach hadn't planned to get into any details with this chatty old man.

"I can tell you're hurt. The hurt doesn't go away if you keep feeding it."

Zach tossed another brick on the wall he had built around his heart. "You don't know my mother."

"Forgiveness is not only for those who are receiving it." Jeremiah motioned to nothing in particular with his chin. "You need to let go of the hurt."

"I'll take that under advisement." Zach carefully chose his words. He didn't want to offend Bridget's grandfather. His mother didn't deserve forgiveness. People who made choices like she had would never change.

"Before you go, I could use some help." Jeremiah shuffled over to him. "We're expecting heavy rain in a few days, and I need to clean out the gutters."

Zach tilted his head and smiled. "You want me to clean your gutters? I was going to hit the road tonight."

"Can you make time for an old man? I was thinking we'd get started first thing in the morning." Jeremiah waved his hand and made his final plea, "They're not going to clean themselves."

Zach bit back a sigh and agreed.

* * *

The next morning, a commotion sounded outside her childhood home. Bridget sprang out of bed. She planted her hands on the sill and strained to listen.

"Go on now." Bridget's grandfather was talking to someone outside her line of sight.

Bridget spun back around. Liddie's bed had already been made. A pang of guilt jolted her. If she planned on staying—for the week, at least—she should help with chores. Make an effort. Stop treating her parents' home like a bed-and-breakfast.

Bridget hurriedly washed her face and got ready for the day, making sure her hair was neatly tucked under her bonnet. She paused when she caught her reflection in the mirror and stared at her *kapp* and makeup-free face. How was it possible to look so much like the young woman who had escaped in the middle of the night at age twenty, but to feel like a completely different person inside? Wasn't she a different person?

A wave of certainty stiffened Bridget's spine. She could play the role for a few days. Whatever it took to remain safe. She went downstairs. Her mother was sitting at the kitchen table doing some mending. "Hello, sleepyhead."

Bridget drew up short. "What time is it?"

"I'll be getting lunch ready soon."

"Oh… I had no idea." Bridget must have been exhausted. "If you don't mind, I'm going to take a walk. I'll come back in time to help you with lunch."

"Of course," her mother said. She gave her daughter an expression that Bridget couldn't quite read.

"Thirty minutes okay?"

"Perfect."

Bridget nodded and stepped outside. A soft late-morning breeze kicked up the hem of her dress. She stepped off the porch and went in search of her grandfather. She found him around the side of his house giving instructions to a man on a ladder. A man who looked most definitely like Special Agent Zach Bryant dressed in plain clothing with a straw hat perched on his head. She blinked a few times, feeling a smile pull on her lips. He was the most handsome "Amish" man she had ever seen.

Shielding her eyes with her hand, she looked up at Zach at the top of the ladder. "I thought you were going to leave?"

Zach cut his eyes toward her grandfather. "Me too." A handsome smile lit his face. "Your grandfather is persuasive." He reached into the gutter with a gloved hand and pulled out a stack of leaves and threatened to drop them on Bridget's head.

She took a giant leap back and laughed. "You wouldn't."

"Then you better stay out of my way. I've got work to do here."

The sweet country air filled Bridget's lungs. One of her brothers ran toward the *dawdy haus* with the wheelbarrow, and the other one had a rake. In their plain clothing and straw hats, one brother was hard to distinguish from the other. Caleb and Elijah were both growing into strong young men. Bridget hated the idea of not being a part of their lives once she left again. She quickly shoved the idea away and focused on this very moment. *Be present.*

Her grandfather was in his element, giving directions to those under his charge. Liddie appeared after a while and then disappeared, promising to return with sandwiches. She waved Bridget off when she offered to come in and help. The only element that created a whiff of tension was when their father crossed the yard on the way from the barn to the house. His silent disdain was palpable.

Shortly after Zach finished clearing the gutters and her brothers pushed the wheelbarrow into the line of trees and dumped the leaves, her sister emerged with sandwiches and sliced apples. She spread out a large tablecloth over the picnic table. Liddie encouraged Bridget to join her family for the meal despite the *Bann.* "No one out here is going to mind. Please sit," Liddie whispered. "Besides, Zach's not exactly on the path to Amish baptism." Liddie laughed at her own joke, and their grandfather shook his head, light dancing in his eyes.

"My friend Zach was good enough to dress the part," Jeremiah said. "I figured it might appease your father." Her grandfather added the last little bit in a tone that suggested there was no appeasing her father.

Bridget found her gaze drifting toward the house. She suspected her father was watching them. She could sense his disapproving gaze. She shook off the foreboding feeling. She owed her father respect, but she was an adult and had to make her own decisions. She refused to give up her calling for him.

Bridget took a seat next to Zach. She closed her eyes briefly, then opened them, half expecting that the family that surrounded her—and this handsome man who had come suddenly into her life—would be gone.

They weren't. They were right here. With her. Under the warm summer sun.

Bridget took a bite of her sandwich and savored it. All of it.

Because soon, this would all be gone.

Chapter Twelve

Bridget ran her thumb over the flat surface of a perfect skimming rock while Zach took a phone call on their after-lunch stroll. She walked a little bit ahead to give him privacy. She palmed the rock, gauging its weight. Being out here brought back carefree memories from her childhood when she and her siblings had finished their chores and then escaped to the pond. She tossed up the rock and caught it in the same hand, then zinged it across the pond.

One. Two. Three. Four. She counted the skips before the rock sank to the water's depths.

An exceptionally good skipping rock combined with the right flick of the wrist had her looking around to share her excitement. She found Zach watching her, a smile softening the hard plains of his face. "Nice." Zach flashed her a thumbs up, then checked the phone again. He had graciously agreed to go for a walk with her when she knew his plans to return to Buffalo had already been derailed multiple times. And based on the phone calls, he probably couldn't delay his return much longer.

The knot of dread in her stomach had loosened a fraction, replaced by something she was afraid to identify. She hadn't felt this kind of spark since Moses Lapp had courted her. No, not even then. Moses had been more persistent in pursuing her than she had been in being pursued. She had accepted the rides and his attention because Bridget thought maybe if she found the right partner, she'd finally settle in and do what was expected of her. Be the nice Amish girl.

Obviously, it hadn't taken.

"You're pretty good at that," Zach said, stuffing his cell phone into the back pocket of his jeans.

"I've had a lot of practice." She forced a nonchalance into her tone. She gestured toward the phone with her chin. "Sounded important." She'd never get used to how cell phones had the potential to interrupt any of life's moments. Part of her didn't want Zach to tell her what the call was about so they could continue their outing and shut out the world for a little bit longer.

Bridget bent down and picked up another rock, then dropped it. She rubbed her hands together to get rid of the grit.

"I have some bad news," Zach finally said. She closed her eyes briefly, wanted to stop this conversation, stop it from happening here where she had so many happy memories.

Bridget crossed her arms tightly over her chest to brace herself. *Please, dear Lord*, she prayed, not knowing what she was pleading for.

"Dr. Ryan's dead."

Bridget's arms fell, and she rocked back on the heels of her boots. The news set every inch of her skin on fire. "Dr. Ryan? He was in jail."

Zach took a step closer to her. He seemed hesitant before lifting his hand and gently cupping her elbow. "Someone got to him."

A wave of nausea rolled over her. "Someone got to him?" she repeated, trying to figure out how that had happened. Her pulse chugged in her ears, making her feel disoriented. "How is that possible in jail?"

"I wish I could say it's impossible. It's not. People can be paid off." Zach scrubbed a hand across his face.

"His poor family." Tears burned the backs of her eyes. "His poor wife." She shook her head slowly, feeling sick. "His sons."

"The doctor didn't deserve to die. No one does. Not like that."

Bridget lifted her eyes to study his. "I started all of this…" A warm breeze fluttered her dress and made her shudder.

"You didn't start this." He pulled her close and wrapped his arms around her. "This is not your fault."

She stepped back, out of his embrace, suddenly in a panic. "I shouldn't have come here. I've put my family in danger." *You knew that all along. You never think. You're selfish.* The voice of self-doubt mocked her. "I can't stay here anymore."

Zach caught her hand and stopped her frantic movements. "You are safe here. You have not put your family in danger. You've done everything right. You came forward when you suspected Dr. Ryan. You did the right thing," he repeated. "These drugs are killing people."

The intensity of his last statement made her blood run cold. She locked gazes with his probing brown eyes. "Your sister's death has given your life purpose."

He never took his eyes off her. "I can't go back in time and bring my sister back. But I can save other people from suffering the same fate." He dragged a hand through his hair. He bent and picked up a rock, dropped it, then found another. He flung it, and the stone sank fast and deep.

His vulnerability drew her closer. "My father warned me—warned all of us about the dangers of the outside world. I never wanted to listen."

"Do you really think nothing bad can go on here?"

"Not like in Buffalo." Bridget slipped her arm around his back and placed her head on his strong shoulder. What if they had met under different circumstances? What if he didn't live his life undercover?

Zach kissed the top of her head. "I never should have left my sister. Leann got involved with the wrong people, and my mother was helpless to stop it." His solid chest rose and fell on a heavy sigh. "For all I know, my mom was the one who brought the drug dealers into my sister's life. I should have stayed and gotten the both of us out of there."

Bridget looked up at him, his face only inches from hers. She resisted the urge to reach up and run the tips of her fingers across the stubble of his unshaven jaw. He looked good. He always looked good, but she preferred him clean-shaven. Maybe because all the men in her life growing up had beards. A clean-shaven man represented the outside world to her. "Maybe you should go see her."

"No point." Zach smiled sadly. "I can't forgive her. She'll never change."

Bridget shifted her gaze to the pond, not quite ready to step away from Zach. Tiny diamonds of sunlight danced on the pond's small ripples in the soft breeze. "Forgiveness isn't only about the other person. It's about finding peace in your heart. If you forgive your mom for what you suspect are her shortcomings—"

"Suspect?" He interrupted, the single word sharp and accusatory. He stepped away from her. "I know what my mother was like."

"Okay," Bridget said softly, "okay. If you can forgive your mother for not being the mother she needed to be, it doesn't mean you accept what she did or didn't do. It means you've forgiven her shortfalls and can move forward in your own life without the burden."

"Your grandfather was talking about forgiveness, too," Zach grumbled. "Well, that might not work in the real world."

"This is no less the real world than life in Buffalo. My family and my ancestors chose to live this way. Separate from the world. And considering everything that's going on in the outside world, it's not necessarily a bad choice." The weight of her message had her lowering herself onto a large rock and stretching her legs out in front of her. "This whole situation with Dr. Ryan and the drugs is never going to go away for me, is it?" She adjusted her long skirt over her legs and studied her boots. "I'm never going to be safe if I go back to Buffalo."

His concerned look said more than any words could.

"Maybe this is a giant sign." Bridget held up her palms to the sky.

"A sign that, what, you're supposed to move back to Hickory Lane?" Zach took a step back and held out his arms. She had definitely hit a sore spot.

Bridget dropped her hands into her lap. "Yes. It's like God wanted to show me how truly dangerous the outside world was. That I should have never left the Amish. It was selfish of me to only consider my own wants." All the thoughts that had been swirling around her head came pouring out.

Zach drew closer and crouched down next to Bridget, clasping his hands between his knees. "I'm not the best person to be talking about God and what He wants. I'm not willing to consider this forgiveness angle you're trying to sell—" he laughed, a mirthless sound "—but I believe those who choose to go into nursing are hardly the selfish sort."

Bridget lifted her gaze to meet his. "It's hard to feel like I'm doing the right thing when my entire world is imploding." She dragged her pinched fingers down the length of the string on her bonnet. "Maybe my life would be less complicated if I stayed here." Was she just looking for someone to tell her what to do?

He gently tapped the back of her hand with his clasped hands. "Do you really believe that? Would you be happy?"

Bridget pressed her lips tighter. "Life is not about

happiness. It's about being selfless. About caring for others."

"You've described nursing," Zach said, his voice gravelly, like the small pebbles sliding under the heels of her boot.

"I've missed my family." Sitting here by the pond, she could almost see her younger brothers horsing around, skimming rocks. Proclaiming themselves to be the winner. A hollowness expanded in her chest. "Until I walked into the coffee shop and met you, I hadn't taken more than a minute to look up from my books. Now that that's all been stripped from me, I realize I have nothing else."

"You have me." The openness on his face suggested he was baring his soul.

It was Bridget's turn to smile sadly. "I don't have you." Her pulse beat wildly, making her own words sound faraway in her ears. She flinched, as if the notion was ridiculous. "Besides," she quickly backtracked, "you'll soon go on to another case. Your life is undercover. Pretending to be someone else."

Zach jerked back, almost losing his balance in his crouched position. He straightened and looked out toward the water, then he looked back at her. "Is that what you think I've been doing? Pretending?"

Bridget lowered her head, heat stinging her cheeks. "We've known each other for less than a week. None of this can be real."

Zach and Bridget walked back to the farm in silence. Her stinging words gave him pause. Were his feelings a product of everything they both had been through? Her carefully crafted world had suddenly spun out of control, and his all-or-nothing undercover assignments had sent him on a path of self-destruction a long time ago. He hadn't been real with himself—with anyone— for a very long time. It took practice to suppress who you really were to pretend to be someone else when you were undercover. No one said he wasn't good at his job.

Probably too good.

Had he reached for Bridget because he was drowning? Needed a lifeline? Wanted to know what it would be like to be a part of someone's life? Someone who was so genuine. So real. But how was that fair to her?

"I thought maybe you fell in," Bridget's grandfather joked when they got back.

"No, I was enjoying the pond. I've missed this place." There was a wistful quality to her voice that made Zach wonder if she were truly considering staying.

"I got seven skips the other day," Caleb joined in enthusiastically. He and his grandfather were the only two still sitting by the picnic table.

"You must have taken lessons from your sister," Zach said.

Bridget's eyes widened a fraction, recognizing his compliment was meant to break the dark mood surrounding them ever since their heart-to-heart discussion.

"No way," Caleb replied, oblivious to the exchange between Zach and Bridget. "I taught her everything she knows."

"He did." Bridget gently patted her brother's cheek, seemingly lost in thought.

"Well," Zach said, "I better hit the road before Jeremiah assigns me any more chores." He turned to the elderly man. "Thanks for putting me up."

"I appreciated your help today," Jeremiah said, running a hand down his beard. "It's been a few years since I've been able to climb a ladder."

"No problem," Zach said. He enjoyed the simplicity of the tasks and a job completed without any complications.

"I better see if Liddie needs any help in the kitchen," Bridget suddenly blurted out. Splotches of pink blossomed on her cheeks. "If I'm going to be staying here, I need to pull my weight." She clapped her hands together and bowed her head slightly. "Thanks for everything. I trust you'll keep me apprised of…" she seemed to be searching for the right word "…everything."

"Sure." Zach hated how awkward everything suddenly felt. Before he had a chance to smooth things over, she spun around and jogged toward the house.

"Why don't you go help your sister, Caleb?" Jeremiah suggested.

"In the kitchen?" He seemed horrified.

"Or I could find more gutters for you." Jeremiah gave his grandson a pointed stare.

"All right…" The boy's shoulders sagged, and he ran after his sister.

"I'm going to change and then head out." Zach slipped into the *dawdy haus* and a few minutes later returned to find Jeremiah waiting for him.

"It wonders me why you're so quick to leave," Jeremiah said.

"There's been a development."

"Oh." The older gentleman seemed to consider this for a moment. "I hope this means my granddaughter will be safe."

"I'll make sure she's safe, sir."

"Seems like a hard thing to do if you're in Buffalo and she's in Hickory Lane."

The screen door slammed, and Caleb ran outside, followed by Elijah. The older brother grabbed a volleyball and lobbed it over the net set up on the far side of the property.

"She's safe here," Zach said.

Jeremiah made a noncommittal sound. "Bridget's a lot like me. Not sure she knows it. I don't talk much about my youth. She's got a restless spirit." He stared off into the middle distance, considering something, then he snapped his attention back to Zach. "She's a good kid, and she needs to follow her own path."

"Yes, I've come to see that in the short time that I've known her." Zach swatted at a mosquito that landed on the back of his hand.

Jeremiah waved a weathered hand. "When this situation is under control, you need to convince Bridget to go back to school. Become a nurse."

Zach glanced back at the house, then at Jeremiah. "That's not my job." He wasn't sure she'd appreciate his interference anyway, especially if she didn't believe it was genuine. Had he truly lost sight of himself with all the years of being undercover?

"Did your job require that you clean out my gutters?"

Zach laughed. Nothing got past Jeremiah Smucker. The screen door creaked open again, and Bridget appeared, drying her hands on her apron. She lingered a moment, then slipped back inside.

Jeremiah limped toward his little house. "Come in for some tea."

Zach hated to refuse the kindly old man. "Don't mind if I do."

The two men settled in at the small kitchen table. Jeremiah was the first to speak. "When I was a little younger than Bridget, I left Hickory Lane. Made it all the way to Wyoming. Worked on a ranch for two years. It was beautiful country. Mountains. Landscape like I've never seen."

"Why'd you come back?"

"Word got to me that my father died, and my mother wasn't well enough to take care of the farm. Since I was the oldest, my siblings were looking to me to help." He patted his thigh. "I had saved up a tidy sum working on the ranch. I came back and saved the farm, as they say. Started courting my Sarah…" He held out his hand in a sweeping gesture. "And here we are."

Through the window, the men watched the young Miller boys by the volleyball court. Caleb spent more time chasing the ball than lobbing it over the net. Elijah shifted his weight from foot to foot in frustration or boredom, maybe a little of both.

"I'm happy I came back. This is where I was meant to be."

"I don't understand." Zach took a sip of his tea, then

set his mug back down. "You're happy here. Why are you asking me to convince Bridget to leave?"

"Bridget is meant to be a nurse. She won't be content here."

Zach nodded. "Okay... I'll do what I can once it's safe for her to come home." He didn't know what else to say. "Does Bridget know about your adventures?"

"Neh." Jeremiah palmed his pipe. "It's something best not discussed. I need to lead by example. You understand."

Zach nodded.

Seemingly satisfied, Jeremiah scooted away from the table and returned with two pieces of pie. "Figured you'd like something sweet."

Zach picked up his fork. "Looks great." The two men ate and chatted like old friends. After a while, Zach asked, "Do you ever wonder about the life not lived?" Zach often wondered that himself. How different would things be for him, his sister, his mother. Drugs had infiltrated the lives of all those he loved and changed them irrevocably. His poor, sweet sister had died of an overdose, and he spent a life pretending he was someone he wasn't to catch drug dealers.

"There's no sense in doing that at my age. I've had a good life. *Gott* had a plan. He's blessed me with a wonderful family. I wouldn't change a thing." He smooshed a few crumbs that had fallen on the table with his finger, then dropped them on his plate. "I might have to deny this if you share what I'm about to say with the bishop. The Amish are a good people. A godly people. But I know in my heart that there are good, *Gott*-fearing people out there." He lifted his hand, indicating the general "out there." He smiled slowly. A wariness lingered in his eyes. "I love Bridget. I'd love her to stay in Hickory Lane, but I feel *Gott* has called her to be a nurse so she can help people." He looked at Zach expectantly. "Did she tell you how she decided she wanted to be a nurse?"

"Yes."

"Well, then you know how important it is." He nodded his head slowly. "If it's within your power, make sure Bridget doesn't give up on that dream."

"Not sure I have that kind of power."

"I've seen you with her."

Zach wanted to protest, but this man didn't miss much.

"You care about her," Jeremiah added.

"I do," Zach admitted. "She's an incredible woman." He frowned. "I'm afraid our careers are going to take us in completely different directions."

"They don't have to." Jeremiah's matter-of-fact tone gave Zach pause.

Zach slowly pushed back from the table, feeling uncomfortable at the turn of the conversation. "It's getting late."

"You're good company."

"So are you." Zach smiled. He genuinely liked Bridget's grandfather. He'd miss him when this was all over.

"But you're not very smart."

Zach laughed. "I'm afraid to ask."

Jeremiah reached for his cane propped up near the table. He made no effort to stand. "There's an old Amish saying, 'A man is never old until his regrets outnumber his dreams.'"

I must be very, very old. Zach kept the thought to himself. No sense spoiling a great day.

Chapter Thirteen

When Bridget first wandered outside on the porch, she hadn't realized Zach was still there. When she saw him chatting with her grandfather, she found herself doing an about-face and slipped back inside. The mention of her name made her pause at the screen door. She hadn't meant to eavesdrop. Her grandfather didn't exactly have what she heard some of her fellow nursing students call an indoor voice.

"When this situation is under control, you need to convince Bridget to go back to school. Become a nurse." A wave of heat washed over her. Her grandfather's request baffled her. Zach had no authority over her. Why would he ask that of him? Didn't her grandfather want her to be baptized and stay in Hickory Lane?

Later, while Bridget was reading on the back porch, she was surprised to see Zach just then leaving the *dawdy haus*. Bridget tossed her book aside and strode across the yard to meet the DEA agent who had come into her life only recently and turned everything upside down. Or, more fairly, her life had been turned upside down not coincidentally at the same time she met him.

"Hi." His brown eyes seemed to warm at her presence.

"Hi. You're all set?" Bridget asked, suddenly feeling foolish because they had already said their goodbyes.

Zach patted his bag. "Yes, all set." His eyes twitched a fraction. "You want to walk over to my truck with me?"

Bridget glanced over her shoulder at her parents' house, feeling like she needed permission, even though that was ridiculous. "Sure. You and my grandfather had a long visit."

"He's a nice man."

"He is."

They crossed the field in silence; flecks of mud splashed up on her boots. The words she really needed to say clung to the back of her throat, making each second feel precious. Finally, when they stepped onto the neighbor's gravel driveway, where Zach's truck was parked, she turned to face him. "I feel like I put my foot in my mouth by the pond. I'm sorry. I shouldn't have said what I said. I had no right." Now that she'd found the words, they spilled out. "Thank you for everything you've done."

"It's my job." He popped open the tailgate and tossed his duffel bag under the tonneau cover. He must have sensed her mood, because he turned and said, "We're going to figure this out. You're going to be able to come back to Buffalo and finish school."

There it is.

Bridget glanced down at her boots, then up at him. "I heard part of your conversation with my grandfather. Your voices carried across the yard and through the screen door." Her face flushed hot again. "It's not your job to make sure I pursue my dream. I don't want that weight on you. I made my own choices when… well, from the time I first sat down at Dr. Ryan's computer. I could have looked the other way. My job was nearing its end. I could have gone back to school quietly. It would have been so much easier," she muttered. Her stomach knotted at the reality of it all. "I made my own choices, and I'll work through the consequences."

Zach reached out and brushed a strand of hair away from her face. Her skin singed under his touch. "I'm not going to abandon you. I'm going to put whoever's involved in this in jail and make sure you're free to do whatever you want in life." A small smile flashed on his lips. He seemed to hesitate a moment, then took a step back.

Bridget took a step forward. She planted her hand on his chest and leaned up on her tiptoes. They locked eyes for the briefest of moments before she leaned in and kissed him. He wrapped both his arms around her and pulled her close. She grew more confident from his strength.

Reluctantly, she broke off the kiss. "I wanted to let you know that I didn't think you were pretending. I'm not pretending, either. I really like you, but we both know life is pulling us in different directions." She reached behind her and removed his arm and stepped out of his embrace.

"Hey," he said, his voice husky. "I am going to do everything in my power to make sure you get back to school. Become a nurse."

Bridget looked up at him and squinted against the late-afternoon sun, its beams diffused through the nearby trees. "I'm not your responsibility." *Like your sister wasn't.*

"I care about you…" Zach took a step closer and cupped her cheek. This time she didn't back away. She took a step closer, and he kissed her gently on the lips. She rested her head on his solid chest. If only they had met under different circumstances. He pressed her close to him. A door opening sounded close by. The neighbors.

Bridget stepped back, a twinge of embarrassment snaking its way through the momentary feelings of warmth, connection.

"Let me drive you home," he said.

Bridget shook her head. "It's only across the field." She smiled. "I'm safe here."

Bridget watched him climb into his truck, then she turned to stroll across the field, wondering if she'd ever feel as safe as she had in his arms.

The entire drive back to Buffalo, Zach couldn't get the thought of Bridget's soft lips out of his mind. His last memory of her was her long dress blowing in the wind and her shielding her eyes from the sun before she turned to cut across the field to go home. He had no business getting involved with someone who was part of his investigation. *Technically, you're on leave.*

That argument didn't squash his concern that she was Amish. They could never be together. No, she wasn't Amish. She was hiding among the Amish.

He rubbed the back of his neck, wishing he could clear his head. Figure this out.

The kiss had been innocent. Yet he had never crossed the line while working on a case. Hadn't he? *Well, never romantically.* Bridget was straddling two worlds; he could read the indecision in her eyes. And his work was his world. One undercover case after another. He had created a life where having a family was next to impossible. He laughed to himself. The two of them made a pair, both trying to figure out where they fit in the world.

Zach had spent most of his life pretending he was someone he wasn't: a dealer, a junkie in need of a fix, the lookout. A guy could get lost in all the pretending. Bridget hadn't been wrong in suggesting he was good at it.

He wasn't pretending with her.

The green-and-white Thruway signs announcing the first few Buffalo exits came into view. He scrubbed his hand across his face when he saw the familiar sign announcing the exit to his childhood neighborhood. He lived in Buffalo, but he rarely drove the same streets he used to travel on his first ten-speed bike.

As if the truck had a mind of its own, Zach found himself merging off the highway. It was getting late, so he decided he'd drive by his mother's house. He wouldn't stop.

Maybe.

He passed the ice cream stand—a long line snaked in front of a single order window—the same one that he and his little sister used to ride their bikes to and buy cones from with the money he made cutting grass. He shoved aside the thought and almost turned back before he decided to push through, despite the feelings of nostalgia.

Zach slowed as he drove down his tree-lined childhood street. Each tree and house were so familiar he could tell which trees had died or been cut back since his days of playing hide-and-seek in the neighborhood. All the shades on the windows on the Meadows's house were drawn. Maybe they were all at Ashley's wake?

Too much death in his line of business.

His childhood home hunkered in the gathering shadows. He pulled over along the curb. With his bent arm resting on the open window frame, he sat in silence, trying to remember the kid he had once been. Despite the five-year age gap, he and his little sister had been close. Very close. In one of his psychology classes in college, he'd learned that kids of dysfunctional parents tended to lean on one another because that's all they had. He didn't need to take a three-credit college-level class to learn that. He lived it.

His attention drifted to the small detached garage. The shadow of the basketball net brought him back to their spirited games of H-O-R-S-E. Leann loved that game. He was about to write this off as a very bad idea when the distinct scent of cigarette smoke reached his nose. The sickening, sweet scent of his mother's brand. Then he saw it. The orange glow grew brighter.

"Aren't you going to say hello?" Her raspy voice floated across the yard.

Zach closed his eyes momentarily to gather himself. He unclicked his seat belt and climbed out. He crossed the yard. He hadn't been here since the day of Leann's funeral.

He walked up to the porch and stuffed his hands in his jean pockets. "Hi, Mom." The word sounded foreign on his lips.

"Zachary." She said his name reverently, then stiffened. "Are you in the neighborhood because of Ashley?" He felt his mother's watchful gaze from the shadows.

"This whole case got me thinking about home," he admitted.

The tip of her cigarette glowed orange again. She released a billow of smoke between thin lips. "Least something got you back here." A strangled laugh-cough took him right back to his youth.

Zach climbed the steps and remembered posing here in his tux before prom. He leaned back against the railing, facing his mom, his eyes adjusting to the dusk. "I've been busy."

His mother had aged. Life hadn't been kind to her. He had expected her to be itching for a fight. Man, she loved a good fight. He held his breath. Her face softened, and she ran the back of her cigarette hand across her cheek. "I don't blame you for not coming around." She cleared her throat. "How have you been?"

"I'm okay. Work's busy." His mom had laughed when he signed on with the DEA, suggesting the work was a bit on the nose. "Lots of drugs in the world."

"Was Ashley into drugs?" His mother looked out over the yard in a thousand-mile stare. "Is that how she ended up murdered?"

"No. By all accounts, Ashley was a good kid. Wrong place, wrong time."

"She came here looking for you. Maybe if I hadn't given her your card." His mother's voice cracked for the first time.

"Not your fault, Mom," Zach said, his heart softening toward the only family he had left.

A soft laugh escaped her lips. "I better have my hearing checked. I never could do anything right in your mind."

His mother had gotten lost in her struggle with addiction. So had her daughter. And if he was being honest, he had, too. He had become single-minded in his focus. So judgmental.

Unforgiving.

His brief time in Hickory Lane had had a profound impact on him.

"How have you been doing, Mom?"

"Still working at the garden center." She had lost her nursing license years ago. She stubbed out her cigarette on the ashtray next to her chair. "I've been sober three years now."

Three years!

"That's great." Zach leaned back and wrapped his hands around the railing. He hated how formal they sounded.

"Yeah, I'm proud of myself." She stood and approached him. She placed the palm of her hand on his cheek. "My baby boy."

Emotion welled up in his throat, making it impossible to speak. The familiar scent of her shampoo mingled with the tobacco still lingering in the air.

"Do you have anyone special?" She tilted her head, curiosity lighting her eyes. "Sure you do. Look at you."

"There's someone," he found himself saying. "But my job makes it hard."

His mother's lips pinched. "Don't put anything above a loved one. Not anything."

Zach made a noncommittal sound. *A loved one?* It seemed too early to put Bridget in that category.

She dropped her hand and inhaled deeply. "You are one of the few things I did right."

Zach forced an awkward smile. After a moment, he found his voice. "I know you did your best."

His mother tucked in her chin, then looked up at him. Tears shone in her eyes. "You and your sister deserved more. I wish I had been able to give it to you. To both of you." Her regret was palpable.

"You need to forgive yourself."

His mother dipped her head.

The next words he had to force through the emotion clogging his throat. "I forgive you. You're human. We all make mistakes."

His mother gripped the gold pendant hanging around her neck, and a single tear tracked own her cheek.

Zach tapped his palm on the railing. "Well, I better go."

His mother took a step back and swatted at what he suspected was a mosquito. "Yes, it's getting buggy out here." She gave him a sad smile. "I'm glad you stopped by, Zachary. Maybe you'll come back again soon. When you have more time."

"Yeah…" He descended the steps.

"Maybe you can bring your friend," she added hopefully.

"Maybe." He climbed into his truck and slammed the door. A myriad of emotions played at his heartstrings. Lightness. Relief. Hope. Maybe there was something to be said about this forgiveness stuff.

Chapter Fourteen

A crack of thunder startled Bridget awake. She pulled the quilt up to her ear, wishing she could drift back to sleep in her childhood bed. She had been up late many nights over the past two weeks. She and Zach had gotten into a routine of catching up late in the evening. She'd tuck her cell phone between her shoulder and ear and let his deep voice wash over her while she rocked slowly in one of the back porch chairs. It was her favorite time of day.

Fortunately, she found a way to charge her phone and laptop by using her grandfather's generator that conveniently had the right outlet. Bridget believed he secretly enjoyed helping her stay in touch with Zach despite his half-hearted reminders that she was breaking the rules. Seemed to take one rule breaker to facilitate another one.

During their conversations, she and Zach shared everything from the details about her quiet days on the farm to how he was keeping busy by completing long-neglected house projects. There weren't many updates on her case, but he finally opened up to her on why he was on leave from the DEA. He was struggling with his guilt over the death of a young confidential informant. He felt responsible. The CI had taken too many risks. Now his boss worried Zach was on the cusp of burnout and needed to walk away. Albeit temporarily. Which lead to discussions about his plans to return to work next week. Would he be allowed to go undercover? Would he still have time for their phone calls?

On her end, she wondered if she'd ever catch up on her nursing classes that weren't online. She hated to postpone graduation next spring.

And where, exactly, did they think this relationship was going?

Another crash, this time louder, made her bolt upright. She blinked a few times. Heavy rain blurred the view from her second-story bedroom window. Liddie's bed was empty. Farm chores didn't stop for bad weather.

A familiar guilt nudged her. She hadn't exactly been carrying her weight since she'd been back, mostly because she had really hoped that it was going to be a very temporary situation. Sure, she helped her *mem* with dinner and keeping the house, but she had left the farm chores to her siblings and her *dat*. He was the only one actively shunning her, which basically meant he didn't talk to her and she had to eat her dinner on the back porch. Other than that, she had been able to get reacquainted with her family.

Boy, she had missed them. The daily interaction. The laughter.

Deep down, she worried that the longer she stayed in Hickory Lane, the harder it would be to leave again. She tossed the quilt back and quickly got dressed. She scurried downstairs in bare feet and came up short when she found her parents huddled in the kitchen talking in hushed tones. Bridget's blood ran cold.

"What's wrong?" she asked, her voice cracking.

Her mother looked on the verge of tears, and her father stopped speaking. More secrets.

Moving closer, Bridget's heart thudded in her throat. "Is someone hurt?" Her frantic gaze went to the window, then back to her parents. "Are my brothers okay? Liddie? Please, what's wrong?"

Her mother took a step toward her, twisting a dishrag in her hands. "No one is hurt. Your brothers are in the barn doing their chores."

"Is Liddie with them?" Bridget rushed to the mudroom by the back door and stuffed her feet into one of her boots, the leather cold from the early morning draft swirling in under the back door.

Her father's gaze cut through her. "Liddie's not here." He sounded angry, not distraught, unlike her mother.

Bridget straightened from tying her boot. Icy dread pooled in her gut. "What do you mean?" She wanted to shake her stoic dad. Liddie hadn't mentioned anything about going anywhere. Actually, she'd seemed exceptionally cheery lately. Bridget had thought it was because her big sister had returned.

"It seems…" Her father's cautionary look of warning made her mother's voice trail off.

"You have to tell me," Bridget pleaded.

Her father turned his stony gaze on his oldest daughter. "We don't have to tell you anything. You made your choice to leave this family."

Bridget focused on unclenching her hands, trying to calm her growing frustration. "I know you're mad at me. Stay mad at me. But this isn't about me—it's about Liddie. Why are you upset and where is my sister?"

Her mother sank into one of the kitchen chairs. The oil in the pan on the stove was popping over the flame. Bridget turned off the gas stove and froze, realization slowly creeping in. Her mother was devastated, and her father was his usual stern self.

Rewind the clock five years. Bridget had crept out in the middle of the night and her sister must have woken up to Bridget's empty bed. Her parents must have huddled in the kitchen, debating what to do. A new wave of guilt slammed into her. Was this how it had been when Bridget disappeared in the middle of the night? Of course, it was. How truly selfish she had been.

What other choice did she have?

Her pulse ticked in her head. She squared her shoulders and asked, "Do either of you have any idea where Liddie might have gone?"

Her mother slowly shook her head. Her ivory skin grew paler. Bridget turned to her father. "*Dat*, any ideas?" She wasn't hopeful. Amish children didn't usually confide in their parents.

Bridget felt her palms sweat.

Why hadn't Liddie confided in her? What if Liddie didn't leave on her own? What if Bridget had brought evil to the peaceful farm? She grew dizzy with the thought.

Bridget toed off her boot and took the stairs two at a time, her long dress flapping around her legs. She tore open the door to the closet and dropped to her knees. She pulled out the folded blanket. Her phone hit the hardwood floor with a resounding *clack*.

She patted the entire blanket, then stretched into the closet and checked the far back corners. Nothing.

She sank back on her heels. A sick wave rolled over her.

Liddie's phone was gone.

Bridget scooped up her phone and checked for reception. Three bars. *Thank You, God*. With shaky fingers, she called Zach. He answered on the first ring.

Zach was lulled out of a fitful sleep by the subtle vibration of his cell phone. He had put it on silent before he collapsed into bed after talking to Bridget late into the night. He feared their budding relationship would complicate his going back to work next week. Well, not if he was stuck behind a desk.

He palmed the offending device and dragged it toward him. He cocked one eye open and looked at the display: Bridget. He pushed up onto an elbow and swiped his finger over the screen. "Hello."

"Zach, sorry to wake you." He could hear the panic in her voice.

"I was up," he said without thinking. "What's wrong?"

"Liddie's gone." Before he had a chance to ask her to clarify, she added, "She wasn't in her bed when I woke up. No one knows where she went. Her cell phone's missing. That must mean she went on her own. That she's not in danger." The last statement sounded more like a question, and he didn't have the answer.

"Did she say anything about leaving?" If she had, Bridget had never mentioned it in their marathon late-night phone calls.

"No." The single word came out in a rush. "I thought we had patched things up a bit and that she would have confided in me." She let out a mirthless laugh. "I never told her I was leaving years ago," she muttered. "I mean, I thought I was protecting her from getting into trouble with our parents or the elders." He could imagine her pained expression. "I'm worried she's doing this to get back at me."

"Don't go there." He pulled clean clothes out of his dresser drawers and headed toward the shower. "I'll help you find her. Any idea where she may have gone?"

"I could contact some of the people who helped me when I left." Her voice grew quiet, as if the phone had moved away from her mouth. "I'm not sure if they have the same phone numbers or if they're still doing that sort of thing."

"Make a few calls. Meanwhile…" He glanced at the digital clock. "I can be there in about an hour."

"Thank you. I'd feel better if we could drive around town and look for her. Maybe she slipped out with friends."

"Sit tight."

Bridget ripped off her bonnet and changed into street clothes. She didn't want to stand out like a sore thumb when Zach picked her up. Liddie may have run off like she had, but Bridget had to make sure.

She bounded back down the stairs and tipped her head to acknowledge her parents and a few of the neighbors gathered in the kitchen. *Already.*

Mrs. Yoder, the grandmother of the child she had saved from choking, sat next to Bridget's mother, no doubt having made the untouched tea sitting in front of them. Her friend's mother smiled softly at Bridget, perhaps forgiving her for any past wrongs.

The atmosphere was downright morose, as if someone had died. Well, for those who left the fold, it was a death of sorts.

Self-consciously Bridget touched her bun. "I'm going out to look for Liddie." An apology for her clothing died on her lips. She loved her parents. She respected their ways. But she wasn't going to keep apologizing for who she was.

Her mother sat at the table with clasped hands. A crease lined her father's forehead, registering his silent disapproval. Bridget ran out the back door and headed toward the barn, sidestepping huge puddles. Thankfully the rain had stopped. Bridget had expected to find her brothers doing their chores. Instead they were sitting on hay bales talking to another young Amish man who had his back to her. She stopped in the doorway at the sound of their voices.

Her brothers seemed unfazed by her *Englisch* clothes. "You heard?" Elijah asked.

"Yah." Bridget wiped her palms on the thighs of her jeans. "Do you know—"

The man twisted to face her. "Hello, Bridget."

She rocked back on her heels and crossed her arms tightly over her chest, suddenly feeling very exposed. "Moses." The boy who had courted her years ago. The boy she might have spent the rest of her life with if she hadn't made a very bold move. "What are you doing here?" Her words came out harsher than she had intended.

Moses gave her a familiar smug look and waited a beat before saying anything, as if he had information that he wasn't quite yet willing to share. Only after she had left him and Hickory Lane did she recognize his behavior for what it was: his way of exerting control. "Nice to see you, too," he finally said. He was still clean-shaven, which meant he hadn't yet married. He was getting a bit long in the tooth. The same could be said of her if she had never left. In the *Englisch* world, however, she was still a baby. Too young to consider marriage. Many of her nursing friends were enjoying dating around. And until Zach, she hadn't given a serious relationship much thought. Education had been her primary focus.

"Do you know where my sister is?" A slow, steady ticking ratcheted up in her head. *What is this really about?*

"Can't say that I do." Moses hopped to his feet and moved toward the barn door. He tipped his hat to Bridget on his way out.

"Wait," Bridget said.

Moses slowed but didn't turn around. She jogged to catch up to him, fury heating her face. "Why are you here?" She didn't believe that he suddenly appeared on her family farm the morning her sister disappeared.

Something flitted across his face. She would have missed it if she hadn't been watching him closely. His eyes widened, as if he were going to make a smart-aleck comment, but instead he said, "Your father came to my family's farm looking for me. He wanted to know if Liddie was with me."

"Why would my sister be with you?" The ticking grew louder.

A slow, smarmy smile tilted his lips. "Didn't she tell you? We've been going together. We weren't doing anything wrong."

So many emotions swirled and expanded in her chest, making it hard to draw a decent breath. "*Neh*, she didn't tell me." Which left her wondering what else her sister hadn't told her. "If you know my sister so well, then where did she go?"

The oily expression slid off his face. "Like I told your father, I don't know. She's been acting strange." He glared at her. "Apparently, you Miller sisters are a lot alike."

"Unless you have something to contribute, I think you should leave." Bridget glared back at him.

"Cool your engines. I was on my way out."

Bridget waited until Moses was gone before she turned to her brothers. "Why did Moses come here?"

Elijah shook his head. "He was trying to find out if we knew where Liddie was. He seemed really mad."

Bridget could only imagine how he had reacted five years ago when he discovered she had left Hickory Lane. Bridget reached out and touched Caleb's arm and asked gently, "Do you have any idea where Liddie is?"

He frowned. "Did she leave us, too?"

Bridget's heart broke. Caleb's face had thinned, lost the roundness of childhood. His eyes mirrored the seven-year-old little boy's that she had abandoned. The little boy she remembered had loved handing her a bouquet of dandelions he had gathered from the field. Tears burned the back of her nose. She swallowed hard. If she owed her preteen brother anything, she owed him the truth. "I don't know. I'll find out."

Elijah jerked his thumb at her jeans. "Are you leaving, too? Or are you dressed to search for our sister?" Hope softened the hard edges of his accusation.

"Right now, I'm looking for Liddie."

"Maybe your police friend can help?" Caleb's voice cracked.

"He's on his way." She tapped Caleb's soft cheek in a rare display of affection. "I love you guys. I won't go anywhere until we know Liddie's safe. I promise."

Chapter Fifteen

Bridget found her grandfather approaching the barn, his travel hampered by his unsteady footing on the rutted lane.

He pulled his pipe from his mouth. "Is Zach on his way?"

"Yah." Nervous energy made her shift her weight from foot to foot.

"Do you think Liddie would want us to look for her?" He took another long puff on his pipe, regarding her carefully.

"What if…" She couldn't shake the sinking feeling that had been haunting her all morning. "What if she's in danger? What if the people who killed Ashley and Dr. Ryan got Liddie? Maybe they knew where I was and she got in the way somehow."

Liddie took her phone. She probably left on purpose, right? Bridget reasoned to herself. Her gaze drifted to the road, praying that Zach would hurry up and get here.

"Maybe she went on an adventure. Like you," her grandfather said, his tone oddly calm.

Bridget felt a smile pulling at her mouth despite the worry eating away at her. "And like you."

Her grandfather lifted an eyebrow. "You've been talking to someone."

"A lot." She pulled out the pins holding her bun, allowing her hair to drop into a long ponytail. "He only told me about your adventures out west because he thought it would reassure me that I wasn't the only one in the family who had dreams outside Hickory Lane. He didn't mean to betray a confidence. I'm sure of it."

Her grandfather waved his hand. "You're an adult. It's important that you understand your parents and grandparents are people, too. We have lives and dreams outside of our roles in the family."

Bridget had a hard time thinking of her mother and father as anything more than her parents. Especially her father, who was a stickler for rules. She'd never know their true feelings, thoughts, especially if they deviated from the rules of the *Ordnung*. "And sometimes you have to admit there are limits to some relationships."

"I hope whatever you decide to do, you'll send me letters. Keep in touch. Promise?"

Bridget nodded. "Of course." She shoved the tips of her fingers into the back pockets of her jeans. "I'm not going anywhere right now other than to find out where Liddie went. I promise I won't leave without saying goodbye." She had made the same promise to her brother.

Her grandfather laughed. "Liddie's off having fun. I'm sure of it."

Bridget's phone buzzed in her back pocket. She pulled it out and saw a number she didn't recognize. It could be her sister's disposable phone. "Maybe it's Liddie." She quickly swiped her finger across the screen. "Hello."

"Hey, Bridget."

Her heart leaped. "Liddie!"

"Hey, big sis," Liddie said, her voice breaking up over a bad connection.

"Are you okay? Where are you? We're all worried." The rapid-fire questions allowed no room for answers. "Liddie?"

"I didn't mean to worry you." Wind whistled across the line, yet Bridget still detected a hint of sarcasm. Maybe humor. "Don't tell anyone I called, okay?"

Her grandfather studied her while she talked into the phone. "*Mem* and *Dat* are really worried."

"They'll be fine. It's not like I'm leaving for good."

"Okay, then, where are you?"

Liddie seemed to be muffling the mouthpiece. Was she with someone?

"Tell me where you are," Bridget said again, this time more insistent.

Her sister came back on the line. "Meet us in front of the neighbor's driveway in five minutes. We'll pick you up. And don't tell anyone. If you're not there, we won't stop."

"Liddie…" Bridget dragged out her sister's name, a desperate plea.

"I'm not kidding. You've been where I am. Do this for me." Her little sister. Bridget would do anything for her.

"Who are you—" The call ended abruptly before Bridget had a chance to ask her who she was with or to promise she wouldn't tell anyone. She pulled the phone away from her ear. "Grandpa, that was Liddie. She doesn't want *Mem* or *Dat* to know she called. She's coming to get me." She reached out and touched her grandfather's hand. "I'll bring her home, okay? I called Zach. He's on his way. Keep an eye out for him. Tell him I went to meet Liddie in the neighbor's driveway."

Her grandfather tipped his head; a smile slanted his mouth. "Go on."

"Thanks." Despite the guilt nudging her, she decided against running back inside. "Let *Mem* and *Dat* know that I'll be back after I find Liddie."

He nodded but didn't say anything.

Bridget strode across the field, the shortest distance to the neighbor's house. Phone in hand, she slid her finger across the screen, searching for Zach's contact information. She should probably let him know about the change of plans herself.

"Where are you going?" her father called from the back porch.

She froze, shocked that he was actually speaking to her. She swallowed hard and waved casually. "I'm headed into town. I'm going to see if I can find Liddie."

"You're going to make a mockery of us." Her father glared at her, his gaze running down the length of her *Englisch* clothes.

"I'm sorry, *Dat*. I have to go." Bridget bit back the instinct to reassure her parents that Liddie had called her, that she was okay, but she had promised Liddie.

Sort of. She smiled at her mother, who appeared on the porch behind her husband.

A whisper of a smile swept across her mother's face. "Are you leaving for *gut*?"

"Not right now, *Mem*. I'll be back." Bridget's heart broke for her mother. Why did Bridget's dream of becoming a nurse have to come at the expense of her mother's happiness?

"This isn't a bed-and-breakfast," her father called out after her. "You have broken the rules and now your sister thinks she can do the same." He wrapped his work-worn hands around the porch railing, and even from this distance, Bridget sensed his agitation in his fidgety movements.

Of course, her father blamed her.

Bridget's face grew hot.

Suddenly anxious that she'd miss meeting her sister, she started to jog across the mucky field, wet from the rains last night.

When she reached the bottom of the neighbor's driveway, the sun broke through the dark clouds. Adrenaline hummed through her veins. She turned her focus to the phone again and found Zach's contact information. She was about to call when the deep rumble of an engine vibrated through her. Afraid she didn't have time for a phone conversation before Liddie arrived, she shot Zach a quick text. False alarm. Meeting Liddie now. She's with friend.

Bubbles popped up as if Zach was typing. Bridget glanced up as the loud car roared into view. It was painted an unnatural shade of blue. Something niggled at the base of her brain, sending a cold chill up her spine. Instinctively, she snapped a quick photo of the back end of the car and sent it to Zach. She flicked the switch to silent mode and shoved the phone in her back pocket and tugged her T-shirt over it.

The tinted passenger window whirred down, and her sister's smiling face appeared. She had her hair pulled back in a long ponytail, and she was wearing one of Bridget's T-shirts.

"What are you doing?" Bridget hollered over the loud hum of the engine.

"Of all people, I thought you'd understand." Liddie gave her one of her big, infectious smiles.

Bridget tipped her head to catch a glimpse of the driver. He had on a baseball cap pulled down low. He balanced his wrist on the steering wheel and drummed his fingers to the deep bass of the music. She'd have to hold the questions she had for Liddie until they didn't have an audience.

Liddie tapped her palm on the door frame and craned her neck to look down the road toward the family farm. "Hurry. Get in. Come on—I don't want to be seen."

Bridget hesitated for a fraction of a moment before hopping into the back seat. She slid back and buckled her seat belt. She looked up and met the eyes of the driver in the rearview mirror. A knot tightened in her belly. His shifty gaze returned to the road.

"We need to talk, Liddie," Bridget said.

"I know." Her little sister seemed giddy. "We'll go somewhere. Maybe Jamestown?" She deferred to the driver. "Jamestown cool with you?"

"Sure, no prob," he muttered.

No prob.

That's when it hit her. He was the man who had been sitting by the pool with Liddie in her courtyard back in Buffalo.

"You remember Jimmy, right?" Liddie said cheerfully.

"From my apartment complex." Bridget fought to keep her tone even. "Hi."

Jimmy tipped his head in greeting, but something felt off. Way off.

And his bright blue car. Had it been the same one that nearly ran her over? The incident in the crosswalk had happened so fast that she hadn't remembered the car, but the sound...

She met his gaze in the rearview again, and the hard set of his eyes made her blood run cold. Bridget slipped out her phone and discreetly sent her location to Zach, then slid it under the seat.

Then she said a quick prayer, hoping she was just being paranoid.

Zach was relieved to get the texts from Bridget that Liddie was okay. He tried to keep his eyes on the road, but the phone kept dinging. He glanced down at her last text. It was a photo of a vehicle, its license plate clear. A band tightened around his chest, making it difficult to breath. A metallic blue muscle car. Similar to the one that had nearly run Bridget down in the crosswalk.

Then a strange thing happened. Bridget sent him a link to an app that updated her location in real time.

With voice commands, he called her back. "Answer, answer, answer," he muttered aloud to himself. He swerved out into the passing lane, then back into the right lane. When she didn't answer, he shot her a text via voice commands. Don't get in that car. Danger.

His gaze kept drifting to his phone in the cup holder. No response.

The app showed she was moving. He muttered to himself and pounded his fist against the dash. He was at least twenty minutes away. He pressed the accelerator and the mile markers ticked by, but not fast enough.

His phone rang. His ASAC. His heart sunk.

"Hey, boss."

"Hey," Colleen said, her voice crisp and the conversation to the point. "Where are you?"

"I'm on my way to Hickory Lane. I think we have a problem."

"What is it?"

"Bridget just sent me a photo of a car that might be the one that tried to run her down in the crosswalk in Buffalo after she first met with me. I need you to run a plate." His pulse thrummed in his ears. The rearview and side-view mirrors were clear. He changed lanes and passed the snail in front of him.

Come on, come on, come on...

"I can do that. You also need to know that we found video surveillance of a person known to have ties with a street gang entering Dr. Ryan's cell shortly before he was found unresponsive. The video of the attack appears to be missing."

"Why are we just finding this out now?"

"I'm of two minds. The doctor's death is one more case in a heavy caseload. Either it took the officials a while to get around to checking the feed, or someone was paid off to keep the video under wraps."

"Can you send me the video?" The sign ahead indicated his exit was five miles away.

"I'll send a screenshot of his face. It was captured at the jail and they found another image of this guy from the alley behind the clinic."

"Thanks." Then Zach rattled off the license plate from the photo Bridget had sent.

"I'll get back to you on that. One more thing. We've been following the phone records of the gang members. They indicate communication with someone in Hickory Lane. Any chance Bridget has been keeping up with friends back home?"

"I don't think Bridget has any gang friends."

"She's the sort who takes in stray dogs, right? Maybe a person who wormed his way into her life. Maybe she unknowingly compromised her location."

"Not Bridget."

Zach ended the call and pulled up Bridget's GPS location on his phone. She was moving away from Hickory Lane. He got off at the nearest exit and pulled over to study the map closer. He noted the location and entered it into his GPS.

His phone dinged. A grainy photo popped up on his screen. He stared at the image captured on the jail monitors and the security cameras at the clinic. He didn't recognize the man. In the photo from behind the clinic, a second man lurked in the upper right corner. Zach squinted and realization twisted in his gut: this guy was sitting by the pool talking to Bridget's sister right before the Molotov cocktail crashed through the apartment window.

Zach's tires squealed as he pulled away from the curb.

Bridget hadn't compromised her location—Liddie had.

Chapter Sixteen

Sweat pooled under Bridget's arms. Her eyes darted around the back seat. Panic clouded her thinking. Something felt very, very wrong about all this. She could pull the door handle and jump out of the car. Two things gave her pause: the trees whizzing by outside the window and her younger sister in the front seat. She couldn't leave her.

Bridget cleared her throat. "Liddie, we should go back. *Mem* and *Dat* are worried. We can go for a walk around the pond and talk like we used to."

"No, I don't want to go back yet. I want to hang out with Jimmy. You made us leave Buffalo before we got a chance to really get to know each other." Liddie sounded like a petulant child.

"You were going to go home the next day anyway. You didn't miss out on much." Bridget tried to keep her voice even, not let on that she was trying to get away from Jimmy. *Should* she be worried?

There were a lot of bright blue cars, right? Just because Jimmy was in the courtyard prior to the fire in her apartment didn't mean he caused it. Were they in danger or were her instincts off?

"Yeah, we're not going back to the farm." It was then he took off his baseball cap. Darkness flashed in the depths of his eyes. "And we're not going to Jamestown."

Goose bumps raced across her flesh.

"Where are we going?" Liddie asked, the first hint of apprehension replacing her excitement. Then she squared her shoulders.

"You'll see." Jimmy's tone sounded ominous.

"But I thought…" Liddie let her words trail off.

"Why don't you just take us back home? Our parents are worried." Bridget did her best to keep her voice calm, not wanting to set Jimmy off.

Jimmy laughed and shook his head.

"Take us back home, Jimmy. I changed my mind."

Bridget hated the way her sister was trying to cajole this man into doing the right thing, as if she had to be nice while he ignored her request. Bridget felt sick, fearing the situation was escalating quickly.

When Jimmy responded by pressing on the accelerator, Liddie started pleading in earnest, "Come on, Jimmy, stop. You're scaring me."

Jimmy lashed out, his fist connecting hard and firm with Liddie's cheek. "Shut up!"

Liddie yelped and skittered away, confined by the seat belt. She held her hands to her face.

Hot fury exploded in Bridget's head. "Leave her alone," she growled.

Jimmy laughed again. "You can shut up, too." He

pulled out into the passing lane and went around a slower-moving car. "You should have left well enough alone at the clinic," he muttered.

"Why are you doing this? It's over. Dr. Ryan's dead."

"You're joking right?" Disgust dripped from his tone. "You stuck your nose in where it didn't belong. Now you're going to be made an example of." He reached over and dragged his knuckles across Liddie's red check. "If you think of doing something stupid, I'll kill your stupid sister."

Liddie cowered in the passenger seat, making an awful whimpering sound.

What could Bridget do? She already ruled out leaping from the car. And if she tried to distract the punk, they'd go careening into a tree or another car. No, she couldn't risk killing them or some unsuspecting driver.

Bridget stretched her foot and pushed her cell phone deeper under his seat, praying that Zach had gotten her location and was tracking her right now. She was grateful that a coworker had shown her that app, among others, while they ate lunch and chatted.

Jimmy suddenly took a sharp turn and bumped off the road into a field. The jarring turn made Bridget slam her head against the back passenger window. A clattering sound came from under the seat and her phone slid into view, but she couldn't snatch it because she had to brace herself. The car came to an abrupt stop. Liddie groaned.

The second Jimmy put the car into Park, the locks automatically disengaged. Adrenaline propelled Bridget into action. She unclicked her seat belt, snagged her cell phone and pulled the door handle. The door sprang open. She jumped out. The tree line wasn't far. She could make it. Hide.

Get Liddie first.

The whoosh of her pulse roared in her ears.

Bridget's laser-like focus landed on Liddie still sitting in the front seat. Jimmy had her sister's cheeks squeezed between his strong fingers. Her face was contorted in pain. Fear. The glee in his eyes mocked Bridget. He jerked his chin in a cocky gesture as if to say, *Go ahead. Leave. I've got your sister.*

Dear Lord, help us. Help us.

She dug deep, to the depths of her faith, still not seeing how they'd get away from this man. She let out a long, slow breath, and a strange calm washed over her.

Through the windshield she locked gazes with Jimmy. Her shoulders sagged, and she realized they had reached a silent understanding.

Bridget walked over to Liddie's door and opened it, all sense of urgency lost. This wasn't going to be Bridget's escape, but if she complied, it might be Liddie's. Bridget reached in and unbuckled her sister's seat belt while her younger sister quietly sobbed. "It's okay. It's okay. Let's get you out of here."

Liddie looked up at her with a tearstained face. "I'm sorry. I thought he was a nice guy."

"It's okay." She pulled Liddie into a fierce embrace, feeling the time slip away. "I love you."

Liddie sobbed into Bridget's shoulder.

Over her sister's shoulder, Bridget tracked the man as he sauntered around the vehicle. He paused at the rear.

The click of the trunk release forced Bridget into action. She didn't have a deal with this man. He was ruthless.

"When I let you go," Bridget whispered in Liddie's ear, "run toward the trees. Run and don't stop. Don't turn around. No matter what."

Liddie stiffened, and Bridget sensed her sister's refusal before she had a chance to voice it. "Now!" Bridget shouted, shocking her sister into action. "Now!" She shoved Liddie toward the tree line, away from the menacing approach of this man.

Liddie tripped. She scrambled to her feet, found her footing and started to run, her forward momentum hampered by the weeds and hidden ruts.

Go, go, go.

Bridget's gaze dropped to Jimmy's hand. *A gun!* Her knees went to jelly. He lifted the weapon and pointed it at Liddie. A sinister smile tugged on half his mouth. "Should I go for he. head or heart?"

Bridget held up her hands, forcing him to focus on her. "It's me you want. Let her go. She's harmless."

He pivoted and aimed the gun at her. She spread out her fingers. "You don't have to do this."

Dear God, please protect me.

"You have no idea what you got yourself into, do you?" He tucked his gun into the back of his pants. His arm snaked out and snatched the phone out of her hand and threw it in the field. He grabbed the front of her T-shirt and twisted and pulled her close. His stale breath reeked of cigarette smoke.

"Please, please, please…" Tears clouded her vision, and panic made her stomach revolt.

Jimmy yanked Bridget forward. She struggled to gain purchase, but he was too strong. Too fast. The tops of her sneakers dragged across the muddy field. The lid of the trunk yawned open, his intent unmistakable.

"Please, please, please, don't do this."

Her hip slammed on the lip of the trunk as he forced her against it. She fought against his hand palming the back of her head. Her feet scrabbled in the mud, a desperate attempt to stop the inevitable.

"Stop struggling," he said, his voice oddly calm. "Ralphie told me not to mess up your face. He wants to make sure I got the right person this time." Had he killed Ashley by mistake? His fingers dug into her neck. The pain made it impossible to think clearly. He positioned her between his hip and the vehicle. He forced her arms behind her and cranked on a zip tie. Bridget's racing mind flashed to Zach doing the same when he arrested the doctor.

Ugh, that hurt.

"Please, don't." Heat swept over her. Knowing this was her last chance, Bridget twisted and flailed. She bent one leg and kneed Jimmy, catching him in the gut. He doubled over in pain. She scrambled forward and lost her balance with her arms fastened behind her back. She fell forward, landing heavily on her shoulder with an oomph.

In a fit of rage, Jimmy grabbed her arm and picked her up handily. He tossed her toward the trunk, and her midsection slammed on the lip. He forced her the rest of the way in. Her arms were awkwardly bound behind her. His face shook in rage as he hovered over her. He pulled back his fist. "You brought this on yourself."

Gritting his jaw, he punched her in the face like he had done to her sister. Her nose exploded in light and shocking pain unlike anything she had ever experienced. He muttered an expletive and slammed the trunk shut.

Bridget was shrouded in darkness.

All the fight had been beaten out of her.

The engine of Zach's truck purred as he gained on Bridget's location. *Come on, come on, come on.* The indicator on the GPS showing her location had stopped about ten minutes ago. He didn't know if this was good or bad. At the very least, it gave him a chance to catch up.

As he drove beyond Hickory Lane, the occasional farm gave way to fields and trees. "Where are you, Bridget?" he whispered. "Where are you?" The remote location made him pause.

He slowed and double-checked the screen on his cell phone. He had gone past the little blue dot. Zach threw the truck into Reverse, twisted in his seat and rested his forearm on the steering wheel to stare out the passenger window. Trees thick with foliage blocked his view. Still in Reverse, he swerved over to the side of the road and jammed the gear into Park. He jumped out of the truck, keenly aware of the absolute stillness and his gun in its holster.

Why was Bridget's location indicating this field?

An imagine of Kevin Pearson's vacant eyes staring

up at him from the empty parking lot flashed in his mind. Zach had had a bead on his location, too. What if he was too late? *Don't go there. Focus.*

With the intensity of an undercover agent going into a stash house, Zach scanned the area. Fresh muddy tire ruts cut into the overgrown vegetation. An image of Bridget sprawled in the field gutted him. He had missed signs that his confidential informant was in danger. He hadn't been there to save his sister. He had finally opened his heart to someone. Found a connection outside of work.

He would not let Bridget down. He could not…

A hint of a long-forgotten plea whispered across his brain. A prayer a Sunday school teacher had taught him back when his mother was sober enough to remember it was Sunday. He had admired Bridget's faith through all of this.

Have a little faith…

Zach slid out his gun. He stalked toward the rustling in the field. He paused. The sound stopped. "DEA. Show yourself."

Liddie's tearstained face peered around the base of a tree where she had been hiding. "I thought you were him," she said, bracing her hand on the bark and pulling herself to her feet.

"Are you alone?" Zach asked, constantly scanning the area.

"Yah." The single word came out on a squeak.

He tucked his gun back into its holster and rushed through the tall weeds toward Liddie, extending his hand to help steady her. "Where's Bridget?"

"He has her. He has her." Liddie's panicked gaze bounced around the overgrown field. One cheek had an angry red bruise.

"Are you okay?"

She nodded hesitantly.

"You're safe," Zach reassured her. If only he could say the same about Bridget. He plowed a hand through his hair. "Who has her? The guy from the pool back at Bridget's apartment?"

Liddie narrowed her gaze in confusion. "*Yah*, it was him. I thought Jimmy liked me." She looked up at him with terror in her eyes. Her lower lip quivered.

"He's involved with whatever's going on at the clinic. He was caught on surveillance."

Liddie swung her hand in the direction of the field. "He tossed her phone out there. We need to find it."

"Okay." Zach grabbed his phone. He called Bridget's number. Something caught his eye. He pushed the tall stalks aside with his foot until he reached the muddy tire tracks. His number displayed on a cracked screen.

He picked it up. "Got it."

Liddie held out her hands for the phone, her only connection to her missing sister.

"Let's get you in the truck."

Even though it was a warm summer day, Liddie wrapped her arms around her midsection and shivered. Clumps of partially dried mud clung to the knees of her pants.

"You're going to be okay," Zach reassured her. "We're going to find your sister." He closed the passenger-side door and jogged around to his side of the truck. His pulse whooshed in his ears, reminding him that every fleeting second was another that Bridget was in danger. He yanked open his door and climbed in. "Was he driving a metallic blue muscle car?" He thought about the last photo Bridget had sent him.

Liddie nodded. "It's really loud."

"Tell me what happened. Did Jimmy mention anyone else? A location?" She kept shaking her head. He pulled out onto the country road and kept his eyes peeled for a vehicle that met that description, any sign of Bridget. He feared the kid had a good ten-minute head start.

Liddie retold the story of how she had befriended Jimmy when she had hung around the pool whenever Bridget was at work. They kept in touch by text. When she tried to explain why she had done what she had done, he gently touched her hand. "I'm not judging you. What we have to focus on now is finding your sister."

"He shoved her in the trunk. She's going to die and it's all my fault." Liddie's growing hysteria was frazzling his nerves. He prided himself on his cool demeanor in a crisis, so his growing agitation was disconcerting. He found himself saying another prayer for Bridget's well-being.

"I'll find her." Driving around here aimlessly was wasting time. "I'm going to make a few phone calls." His supervisor had probably had time to run the plate from the photo. "Now that we have more information, we might be able to figure out where he's hiding."

Liddie sniffed back her tears.

"I'm taking you to the hospital." He tightened and loosened his grip on the steering wheel.

"*Neh*, I'm fine." She gingerly touched her cheek. "It's just bruised. Take me home."

"Are you sure?"

Liddie nodded. "You have to find Bridget."

"Okay, okay… Now tell me, did Jimmy mention any names? Anything?"

Liddie stiffened and sat upright. She tapped her leg, as if the memory needed a moment to shake free. "He was screaming at Bridget." Her voice cracked. "He mentioned a Ralphie." She nodded. "*Yah*, a Ralphie." She shrugged, appearing frail and tiny in the passenger seat. "I don't know if that will help."

"Every little bit helps." Zach pulled into her driveway. "Go on in. I'll find Bridget."

Liddie pressed her hands to her cheeks. "I've made a mess of everything. I led him right to her."

Her brothers emerged from the barn and started running toward his truck. "I have to go. Reassure your brothers."

"We need our sister back." Liddie paused at the open passenger door.

"Stay calm. Have your family gather in the house and lock the doors until I get word back to you."

"What am I supposed to say?" Liddie plucked at her T-shirt with a dirty hand.

"The truth." His nerves hummed. He needed to go. "Everything will be okay," he added calmly.

Liddie gave him a watery smile. "You're good for my sister. Maybe when this is all over, you can start courting."

Zach laughed; he couldn't help himself. "Courting, huh? Yeah, I'd like that." His job wouldn't make that easy.

The two brothers reached the truck. "Where were you?" Caleb asked. "Where's Bridget? She went looking for you. *Dat*'s really mad."

"Hold on." Liddie held up her hand to her brother's barrage of questions. "My phone is in Jimmy's car. How will you reach me?"

"I'll reach you," he promised. He started to back out the lane when Jeremiah emerged from his little house. Zach flicked his hand in a wave, and the two men nodded in silent understanding. He'd allow Liddie to give her grandfather an update, but he had to make some calls. See if he could get a hit on this Ralphie guy. Bridget's life depended on it.

Chapter Seventeen

Bridget didn't know what was worse: the blackness, the dank smell, the cramp in her side or her rioting thoughts crashing over her.

I don't want to die. I don't want to die. Please, God, don't let me die.

Sweat trickled down her forehead. Something dull and hard pressed into her hip. No amount of shifting relieved the pressure. It didn't help that her arms were bound behind her. A nagging ache radiated out from where her shoulder supported her weight. She blinked rapidly, unable to see. Panic threatened to overwhelm her. She had to focus, stay clearheaded. Images of all the things he might do to her crowded in on her.

Relax. Be calm.

Jimmy seemed to be driving forever. She didn't know if this was good or bad. She dreaded the moment he stopped. She feared he never would.

Help me. Help me. Help me.

The only peace that kept her from letting a scream

rip from her throat was that her sister had gotten away. She only hoped Zach had followed the GPS location of her phone and found her sister. The GPS tracker had been her last hope.

Tears burned the back of her eyes. The throbbing in her cheek had dulled. Growing up Amish, she had been warned countless times to avoid the evils of the outside world. In her naivety, she assumed not following the *Ordnung* would be her downfall, not being stuffed into someone's trunk.

Please help me, Lord. Please...

The car made a sharp turn, and Bridget rolled against the wall of the tight space. A pain ripped through her shoulder. Something damp squished in her fingers. The plastic cut into her wrists. The car bumped over something. The car stopped, then inched forward. The engine cut off. Her heart raced. The sound of something rattled overhead.

The car door opened. Slammed closed.

Breathless anticipation made her dizzy.

Footsteps. A key fob chirp. The click of the trunk release.

Bridget gulped in the fresh air that was tinged with a whiff of exhaust. Her relief was short-lived. Jimmy reached in and yanked her out of the trunk. She blinked against a bright yellow fluorescent light. They were in a garage. An *Englisch* garage with large red toolboxes, motorcycles and folded lawn chairs.

"Please let me go—I won't say anything," Bridget pleaded.

Jimmy laughed. "Too late, sister wife." He was having

a good time mocking her. "You should have kept your mouth shut to begin with."

Bridget wondered what he was going to do with her next, but the words got trapped in her throat. Maybe it was better if she didn't know. Nothing good could come from this.

Jimmy grabbed her by her ponytail and led her into the house. Every time she tripped over her feet, he ripped a few more hairs out of her aching scalp. Her heart raced, and her vision tunneled.

Jimmy shoved her down on the couch next to a thin young woman who seemed only vaguely concerned with her sudden arrival. The girl seemed to be watching them through a haze.

"Where's Ralphie?" Jimmy barked at the girl.

"Ralphie?" she said dreamily.

Apparently disgusted with the girl's drug-induced confusion, Jimmy picked up a rope and threw it at her. The girl grunted and swiped at it. "Stop it!"

"Tie her up. Now!" Jimmy's nostrils flared.

The girl smirked and tilted her head lazily toward Bridget. "Her hands are already tied up."

"Unless you want her running out of here, you better find a way to tie her to something."

The girl's face twisted in annoyance. "You do it."

Bridget frantically scanned the room. Jimmy blocked the door. And she'd never be able to lift the window without his violent reaction—or her hands. The back of her head was still throbbing from when he yanked her ponytail.

Don't give up so easily. Maybe there's an exit. Her

gaze drifted to the arched doorway leading to a small front foyer. Blooms of brown water stains covered the ceiling.

Jimmy must have read her mind, because he grabbed Bridget by the arm and tossed her from the couch to the ground. She bit back a yelp when her hip slammed into the hardwood floor and her shoulder into the radiator. Every inch of her body ached, but that paled in comparison to the rioting fear scrambling her thoughts and sending a million pinpricks tightening her tingling skin.

Jimmy snatched the rope from the couch where the young woman had flung it. Bridget struggled to roll over, sit up, but before she had a chance, he kicked her back down. Her breath whooshed out of her. He lunged toward her, grabbed her ankle and dragged her against the radiator under the window. He worked quickly and tied her to the radiator.

Jimmy yanked on the rope to make sure it was secure. The plastic of the zip tie cut into her wrists. She clenched her jaw. He leaned in close and gave her a smile that made her blood run cold. "You're going to be a good girl, right?"

Heat washed over Bridget's face and she nodded, not trusting her voice.

"Ralphie wants to see you himself." He patted her cheek with his open palm. "Wants to make sure I have the right girl this time." He tilted his head, as if reasoning with himself.

"You didn't mean to kill Ashley?" Bridget finally found her voice.

"Ralphie told me I made a big mess. Your death

might have been written off as wrong place, wrong time, but two suspicious deaths, especially when you worked together, wouldn't look so hot." He peeled his lips back from his teeth making a sucking noise. "I figured I did him a favor. I found the DEA business card in her apartment when I followed her home." Still crouched down next to her, he scratched his jaw. "I tried to make it look like she packed up and took off, but she was a fighter. Killed her, took her car and dumped her where I watched her jog." He dragged a rough finger down her cheek and she squirmed with nowhere to go. "Even found a way to call in a vacation day so no one would come looking for her right away." He was obviously pleased with himself.

Bridget took shallow breaths, trying to focus as the walls grew close. He had been stalking them. Over his shoulder, the girl seemed out of it.

"So…" He pushed to his feet. "I'm gonna see that you keep your mouth shut forever."

Jimmy grabbed a gun from the side table. Bridget bit back a yelp and he gave her an ugly smile. "Don't worry. Ralphie wants to chat a bit first. Then I get to hurt you."

"You don't have to do this," Bridget pleaded. "Please."

Jimmy shook his head and rolled his eyes. "Your boss should have considered the people he was getting involved with."

Bridget's pulse roared in her ears. "How did you meet Dr. Ryan? I don't understand how he got messed up in all this."

"Far as I know, the doctor had a son with a gambling problem. A very big problem with some very bad people.

Started off simply enough. Sell drugs. Make cash. Pay off the loans. Easy to get sucked in, though. Like gambling, I suppose. Not so easy to get out. Turns out, the world is filled with lots of bad people."

Bridget drew in a deep breath and blinked slowly. "Did you kill the doctor in jail?"

Jimmy narrowed his gaze and something sparked in his eyes. He enjoyed all of this. "You ask too many questions." He set the gun on the table next to the girl and said, "Shoot her if she moves, but don't kill her." He locked eyes with Bridget. "I'll be right back." His even tone belied the evil swirling in the dark pools of his eyes. A shiver raced up her spine. This man was broken.

Bridget tracked Jimmy until he slammed the front door and the dead bolt clicked. Her shoulders ached at the awkward angle her body was contorted in, bound to the radiator. She turned her attention to the girl on the couch, who was focusing on the gun. She petted it as if it were a kitty seeking attention. The drugged-out girl's detached manner made Bridget's entire body tremble. Something was seriously wrong with this girl. Bridget's insides twisted at the thought that this intoxicated person was her only hope.

Bridget forced a smile. "Please untie me. He's going to kill me." She didn't mince words. "Please."

The girl playfully fingered the gun, the smooth metal twirling easily on the wooden surface. "What did you do to tick off Ralphie?" she asked without lifting her eyes from the gun.

"I'm a nurse at a health-care clinic. I reported some

prescription discrepancies." Bridget decided to try the truth.

The girl's gaze finally landed on Bridget. "Why?"

"Because it was the right thing to do." Bridget tried to shift her shoulders, but nothing would relieve the pain.

"That was dumb." The girl laughed. She stopped playing with the gun and reached into the side table.

Bridget's stomach threatened to revolt. She closed her eyes and said a prayer.

She didn't know how much longer she could hold on to hope.

Zach, come find me.

Zach worked the phone while he raced toward Buffalo. His gut told him this guy was taking Bridget to his home territory. His phone buzzed. It was his ASAC.

"Ma'am," he said into the phone.

"Where are you?"

"Headed back to Buffalo."

"Okay, good. We tied the license plate from the photo Bridget sent you to James Demmer." The guy Zach recognized in the surveillance photos.

"Address?"

"Sent an agent there. His mother hasn't seen him in weeks. Zach…" She seemed to be weighing her words carefully. "He's affiliated with one of the most violent gangs in Buffalo."

A knot fisted in his gut. Not the kind of information he wanted confirmed. "We need a list of their stash houses." *Stay focused.*

"Zach, I think you should get back to the office. I have agents on this. We'll find Bridget."

"But—"

"You're too involved with this case. Come in. You can work it from behind the desk. I can hear the emotion in your voice."

Zach drummed his fingers on the steering wheel. "Colleen..."

"Listen, you've been fully cleared to come back to work next week. You don't want to do anything to mess that up."

"I've got to find her."

"I know, I know. We'll find her. You need to come in."

Zach was about to protest when his ASAC added, "I was going to wait to share the report with you next week. They finished the investigation into Kevin Pearson's death."

"Oh..." His heart thrummed like molasses through his veins.

"Turns out your confidential informant was working both sides. He was relaying information back to his bosses."

"He knew how dangerous that was," Zach said in disbelief. "I warned him."

"Pearson went against everything you had told him. His death, although unfortunate, is not your fault."

Zach scrubbed a hand across his face. "I should have had a better read on the kid. If I hadn't recruited him as an informant—"

"His brother told one of our agents that he mocked your advice." Zach could imagine his supervisor shaking her head. "Kevin was reckless. In light of this, you're cleared to go back into the field."

"Undercover? Great, great." The traffic in front of him slowed.

"You'll come in to the office. I've got Frank on this. As soon as we pull up any potential locations on James Demmer and this Ralphie character, we'll send in a team. I promise."

Silence stretched across the line. "You're too invested in this. Report to headquarters. You hear me?" Colleen asked.

"I hear you." He went to change lanes, and a car honked at him. "Traffic is getting heavy. I need to go."

Zach ended the call and counted to five, then called Special Agent Frank Levy.

"I figured I'd be hearing from you," Frank said by way of greeting.

"What do you have?" Zach didn't bother with the formalities.

"Lots of our agents are out in the field getting eyes on any of the known stash houses of the BFLO gang."

"Jimmy's part of the BFLO gang? You're sure?" Zach's scalp tightened. *Not good.* He had hoped his supervisor's intel had been wrong. They were an especially violent gang. He kept tapping the brake, riding the bumper of the car in front of him. *Get over, get over, get over...*

"Yeah. And we found a Ralphie, a Ralph Booth. He's got ties to two addresses in Buffalo. We've got eyes on both." Frank's phone cut out. "Hold up. One of the agents is calling in."

The car in front of Zach finally got over. He put the pedal all the way down and raced toward Buffalo. His job might be in jeopardy if he didn't follow the ASAC's orders.

His career wouldn't mean much if he couldn't save Bridget.

Frank came back on the line. "One of our agents spotted Jimmy coming out of a house on Lisbon Avenue." He rattled off the house number.

"Was he alone? Do they have eyes on him?"

"Yes and yes. Our guy's following him. No sign of Bridget Miller."

"Is she in the house?" Zach entered the address into his GPS.

"We don't know. A police officer is watching the house in an undercover car. He'll report any action on the house. We'll get a warrant."

"I'm headed there."

"Gotcha." If Frank knew Zach had orders to come straight to the office, he didn't say. Working in a tight-knit group had some perks. They each covered the other's backs.

Zach ended the call and floored it. The GPS said he'd arrive in twenty minutes.

As long as no one got in his way, he'd be there in fifteen.

Or less.

Chapter Eighteen

Bridget's shoulders ached from the awkward position with her arms tethered to the radiator. The girl on the couch was more interested in searching for split ends than listening to Bridget's reasons as to why she didn't deserve to be held captive.

Bridget prayed that Zach could track her down. *Somehow.*

"What's your name?" Bridget asked.

"Heather," she said almost automatically before glancing up, annoyed, as if Bridget had tricked her into something.

"Do you live here? Or is this Jimmy's house?" She needed a thread of hope that Zach could track her to this address.

The girl harrumphed. "Stop asking questions."

Bridget changed tactics. "My family is going to be worried about me."

The girl's head snapped up, and her slack features contorted in anger. Instinctively, Bridget yanked on the rope. It wouldn't budge. "My family are a bunch of jerks. They don't care about me."

A sharp cramp stabbed her between the shoulder blades. She sucked in a quick breath, then tried to relax her muscles. "Sometimes I think my family doesn't care about me, either." The words came out of her mouth before she had a chance to consider their effect.

The girl's brow furrowed. "You brought it on yourself when you decided to be a tattletale."

"I thought I was doing the right thing." Bridget would have shrugged if she thought it wouldn't hurt. "I'm a nursing student. I want to put this all behind me."

"Boo-hoo," Heather mocked her. Then she picked up a couch pillow and hugged it. "Jimmy said he had to make a trip to Hickory Lane." She got a faraway look in her eyes. "I went there once with my grandma. Bunch of Amish there."

"I'm Amish," Bridget offered, hoping to somehow make a connection with the girl. "I mean, I grew up Amish."

"Really?" The single word came out on a laugh of disbelief. "What are you, on that *Rumspringa*?"

"Well…" Bridget grimaced. "Any chance you could untie me? My arms are killing me."

"Yeah…nope." The girl reached over and grabbed a small kit from the table and popped it open. Bridget couldn't see what it was.

"So, you and your grandma visited Hickory Lane?" Bridget tried to draw the girl back into conversation.

"Yeah…" Heather blinked slowly a few times. "I

can't believe you guys don't have TVs. What do you do at night?" Her words were slurred.

"Read. Quilt." Bridget scooted back in a useless attempt to relieve the tension on her shoulders and arms.

The girl shook her head and twisted her lips. She reached into the kit propped open on the pillow and produced a syringe. Bridget's stomach twisted. For the briefest of moments, she thought Heather was going to inject her with something. Instead, the young woman grabbed a band and wrapped it around her own arm.

"Please don't do that," Bridget pleaded. "There's places you can get help." She studied the girl's face. She seemed to pause a moment before putting one end of the band into her mouth and pulling it tight with the other. The girl prepared the drug, filled the needle, then plunged it into her arm. Bridget's heart ached.

All of Heather's features slackened, her eyes closed and her head fell back on the couch. A single tear tracked down Bridget's face. Despair filled her heart despite her prayers.

Bridget wasn't sure how much time had passed. She had begun to doze when a gurgling noise jostled her awake. The girl was slumped to one side and choking on her own vomit. Bridget yanked on her tethered arms. Pain and panic sliced through her. This girl was going to die.

"Help! Help!" Bridget screamed.

A moment later a key sounded in the front door. Jimmy stormed in, his face twisted in anger. He stomped over to Bridget and pressed his damp palm over her mouth. Nicotine was deep in his pores. "Shut up, you idiot." He jammed her head against the radiator, and a new pain sliced through the back of her head. "Shut up!"

Bridget opened her eyes wide and gestured toward the couch behind him. She made an unintelligible sound against his grubby hand. Seeming to sense something else was going on, Jimmy dropped his hand and spun around. "Heather!"

Her eyes were closed. She convulsed and foamed at the mouth.

He tapped her face. "Wake up, wake up, wake up." His frantic tone was in sharp contrast to his evil persona. "Oh, you stupid girl." Jimmy spun around. "She's choking!" He straightened and clasped his hands behind his neck and paced. "This is bad. This is bad. Ralphie's gonna be mad."

Bridget stuffed down her anger. He was more concerned about himself than the poor girl on the couch. "Jimmy! Jimmy!" she said sharply. "Stop. Look at me."

The man stopped midstride and glared at her. "Shut up. I can't think."

"I can help her. You need to untie me."

Jimmy scrubbed a hand across his face. "Shut up."

"She's going to aspirate if you don't help her. If you don't want to untie me, you help her. I'll tell you what to do." The intermittent coughs and sputters from the young woman assured Bridget that she was still breathing. "Put her on the hard floor. Turn her on her side..."

When Jimmy made no effort to move, Bridget said more forcefully, "You have to act now!"

Jimmy took a step toward the girl, then pivoted back toward her. "You know what to do?"

"Yes."

Indecision played on his features, then gave way. Dropping to his knees, he yanked at the knots that had grown tighter with her struggle. He reached behind him and pulled a knife out of a sheath on his belt. He sawed the rope, then the zip tie. Bridget's numb arms fell heavily.

She pushed to her feet and nearly collapsed because her right foot was asleep. "Move her to the floor." She rubbed her wrists vigorously to get blood flowing again.

Jimmy did as he was told, suddenly more concerned about someone other than Bridget. And himself. He set the girl down on the hardwood floor. Bridget crawled over to her and turned her on her side. She hesitated for a fraction. In an ideal situation she'd wash her hands, but a little dirt was the least of this poor girl's concern. She swept out Heather's mouth to clear her airway.

"Is she breathing?" Jimmy asked, hovering over Bridget's shoulder.

A flash of his humanity shone in his eyes. How did people go so wrong?

Bridget checked on her patient. "Yes, she's breathing…you need to keep a close eye on her. Or take her to the hospital."

Jimmy's eyes darted toward the door, then back at her. "That's exactly what you'd want, isn't it?"

Bridget sat back on her heels. "I don't want any of this."

His mouth twitched. Before he could lash out at her, a pounding sounded on the front door. Jimmy cursed. He stomped toward the front door and pulled back the heavy curtain on one of the sidelights to peek out. He unbolted the door, and another man came in. The subtle bow of Jimmy's head made it clear who was in charge. The man took in the scene. "What's going on here?"

Jimmy seemed to take in the situation, too. Bits of vomit were tangled in the girl's long hair that was splayed across the hardwood floor. Her leg was bent at an awkward angle.

Jimmy didn't need to answer for the man to come to his own conclusions. "You need to get her out of here."

Bridget straightened her back. "This girl needs to go to the hospital."

A slow slant curved the man's lips, making a cold chill skitter up her spine. "Ah, Bridget… You should be more concerned about yourself."

Bridget scooted away until her back was pressed against the couch. The man approached her menacingly.

The doorbell rang, and the man's head snapped up and found Jimmy. "You expecting someone?" His jaw gritted and his fist came up. "So help me…" He reached for the gun.

"No, no," Jimmy said, obviously agitated. "Ralphie, you have to believe me. I didn't tell anyone where we were."

So, this is Ralphie.

Ralphie raised a skeptical eyebrow at Jimmy. He pulled back the curtain and waved his gun at them behind his back. "Keep your mouths shut." The man yanked open the door. "What?"

"I was looking for Jimmy. He told me I could stop by

for…" The man outside coughed. "Man, maybe I have the wrong house."

A concerned expression pinched Jimmy's features as he watched the front door. Just then the man who had knocked on the door exploded through the opening and shoved Ralphie against the wall. Ralphie's gun dropped with a clatter. Another officer swept in and grabbed Ralphie and rushed him out of the house. Jimmy snagged the gun and grabbed Bridget's ponytail—ugh, her ponytail—and pulled her head back before the remaining officer had a chance to get her to safety.

"Please," she pleaded. "Let me go!"

Another crash sounded from the back of the house. Jimmy turned 180, his eyes wide.

Jimmy lifted the gun to her temple. He pivoted and put her body between him and whoever was coming through the back door. He swung around to face the other officer near the front door.

Help me, Lord.

Zach burst into the tight quarters with his gun drawn. Bridget's relief was tempered by the forearm cutting off her airflow and the cool barrel of a gun pressed into her temple.

"Step away before I take off your head," Zach growled.

Jimmy tightened his hold around Bridget's neck. "No way."

Zach nodded to the other officer, who quietly backed out the front door. "It's just you and me. Let her go."

Had all her decisions—to turn her back on the *Ordnung*, to leave her family, to get an education against her father's wishes—led to this?

* * *

Zach trained his gun on the punk who held Bridget. Her eyes radiated her panic as she clawed at the arm around her neck. His pulse deafened him at the thought of Bridget being hurt. Or worse.

"Let her go," he commanded. He continued his slow and steady advance.

The kid's eyes flared wide and moved rapidly. "Stay back or I'm going to kill her."

"No one's gonna die today," Zach reasoned, holding one hand out and the other on his gun carefully trained on the kid's head. "If anything happens to either of these women, I think your boss, who's currently getting tucked into the back seat of a police cruiser, will be more than interested to hear how you cooperated in this investigation. How you led the DEA right to his doorstep."

Jimmy's head swiveled as if on a stick. "I did not. I did not."

Zach shrugged casually, cautiously ratcheting up the kid's paranoia.

"If you put that information out there, I'm as good as dead," the kid said, his expression anguished.

Zach made eye contact with Bridget. She struggled to loosen the grip around her neck. Her face had grown red. Zach nodded ever so slightly, indicating that she needed to trust him. She blinked slowly in acknowledgment.

"Let her go now or there's no negotiating." Zach inched closer.

"They'll get to me in prison. Ralphie's got people everywhere." The kid's complexion had grown a deathly white. *Like they got to the doctor.*

"Let her go and maybe I can arrange witness protection. Keep you safe."

The kid's gaze slid to Zach's. The slight arch of his brow suggested he might be considering it.

"Come on," Zach coaxed, taking another step closer. "This is your last chance. Come on." He held out his palm for the gun, and that was the final encouragement the kid needed. His shoulders sagged, and he handed over his gun. In Jimmy's last act of defiance, he pushed Bridget toward him. Zach caught her, careful to hold the guns away from her. "I got you. Are you okay?"

Bridget rubbed her throat and nodded.

Zach gently sat her down on the couch, nearly tripping over the young woman on the floor. Jimmy plowed through the kitchen chairs on the way toward the back of the house.

"Give me your phone. I have to call an ambulance. And you need to go catch him," Bridget said, her voice raspy.

He tucked a strand of Bridget's hair behind her ear, knowing there was an officer guarding the back door. "I'll be right back." He straightened and strolled toward the back of the house. In the overgrown yard, he found Jimmy facedown on the driveway. Zach's friend Officer Freddy Mack was taking him into custody.

"You looking for this guy?" Freddy stood and yanked up the kid by the handcuffs. His head lolled forward in complete defeat.

"Thanks for covering the back."

Freddy gave him a subtle nod. The law enforcement agencies had worked well together to combat the drug trade. "I'll take this guy in."

"Thanks." Zach turned toward the house. The green paint had bubbled and peeled. An ambulance sounded in the distance. "I'll meet you downtown." Zach rushed into the house, anxious to see Bridget, to convince himself that she really was okay. Already the self-recriminations were pinging in his brain. He never should have left her alone in Hickory Lane. She could have been killed.

Back in the house, he found Bridget kneeling on the floor next to the unconscious girl, checking her vitals. A few minutes later, the paramedics bumped their stretcher through the small entryway. Zach crouched down next to Bridget. "Come on," he whispered. "The paramedics are here. You've done everything you can. And I'm going to drive you to the ER myself. Tell me what hurts."

A faraway look glistened in her eyes. He placed his hand on her back and helped her stand. "Come on." He guided her toward the door. Her attention drifted back toward the girl. "Her name's Heather. That's all I know. She injected the drugs from that kit on the couch. Her pulse is thready. She was vomiting."

One of the paramedics nodded. "We'll take good care of her." He set his medical kit down next to the young woman and began working on her.

Zach led Bridget outside to his truck. She spun around to face him. "Liddie! Is she okay?"

"Yes, she's fine. She's home."

Her eyes turned watery with relief. "So, you got my texts?"

"Yes." He planted a kiss on the crown of her head, then pulled back to meet her gaze. "You're one smart woman."

A smile slanted her pretty pink lips.

He gave himself a mental shake. He had to make sure she was okay. "Come here." He opened the passenger door of his truck and had her sit down. He cupped her face with his hand, examining her tender cheek. The skin under one eye was bruised. "What did he do to you?" He found himself holding his breath, fearful of what had happened when he couldn't protect her.

Bridget told him how Liddie had been in contact with Jimmy, ultimately leading him to her. How he stuffed her into the trunk and drove her here. How he tied her to the radiator and only let her go to help the girl who had overdosed. Bridget struck him as both calm and relieved. She was one impressive woman.

"Let's get you to the hospital." Zach's gaze traveled the length of her. "I should have been there for you."

She blinked a few times, then smiled up at him. "You were." She reached out and grabbed a handful of his shirt and pulled him close. "You were." She stretched up and kissed him. The warmth of her lips, the smell of her skin, her solid presence soothed the adrenaline that had been coursing through his veins.

Thank You, Lord.

When had he ever said a prayer in gratitude? Inwardly he smiled. Bridget had influenced him in more ways than one.

* * *

The fresh breeze cooled Bridget's fiery cheeks as she swung her legs again into the vehicle. Her fingers brushed across her lips, surprised at her boldness. He smiled at her again. "We should get you to the hospital," he said, resting his strong hand on her knee.

"I'm fine. Really." She rubbed her raw wrists.

"I'd feel better if you were examined by a doctor."

Bridget smiled and reached up for the seat belt. Oh, she was going to be sore tomorrow.

Tomorrow. Did all this mean that tomorrow her life would go back to normal? Just like that? Doubt niggled at her.

Zach stepped back to close the door when he paused and said, "What's that look for?"

"I was thinking. Does this mean I can go back to my normal life?" Where would she stay? Would she be able to catch up with her classes? What about her family? She rubbed her forehead, holding back the myriad of questions. After all, they weren't Zach's problems. He was officially off the hook. The bad guys had been arrested, and she was still on this side of heaven.

"I don't see why not. We'll want to make sure there's no lingering players still running around..." he nodded as if convincing himself "...yeah, you can go back to your life."

"I'll have to find a place to live." Bridget lifted her hand. "I'll figure it out. I always have."

Something flashed in the depths of his eyes, and he opened his mouth, then snapped it shut. "You ready?"

"I'll need to get my stuff and say goodbye to my

family and friends in Hickory Lane, too." She couldn't slip away in the dead of night this time.

"Of course. I can take you back after you're checked out at the hospital. I'm sure one of the police officers can take your statement while we're there."

Bridget crossed her arms and shivered. The air had grown chilly. "I can't deal with my family tonight."

"Whatever you need."

"Maybe I could find a cheap motel?" She ran her pinkie over the tender skin under her eye.

"I have a better idea."

"Oh?" Her stomach pitched.

"My mother's house is a few blocks away. I don't think she'd mind putting you up."

Bridget frowned. "I thought you were estranged. I don't want to cause any problems."

"I stopped by her house." He seemed to be considering something. "I think she wouldn't mind." One shoulder tipped up slightly. "Can't hurt to ask."

"If you think she wouldn't mind." She rubbed her palms on her jeans.

He tilted his head. "Should we go?"

Before she had a chance to reply, their attention was drawn to the paramedics carrying out Heather on a stretcher. "Hold on." Bridget released the seat belt and scooted out of the truck, brushed by Zach and walked gingerly over to the back of the ambulance. Heather had on an oxygen mask, and her eyes were open. "Is she going to be okay?"

"Yeah. This time." The paramedic's resigned tone suggested he had seen it all. The girl would recover tonight, but what about the next time? Unfortunately, that's all the assurance he could give Bridget.

She met Heather's gaze for a brief moment before the doors slammed shut and the driver rushed past her. Bridget stared after the ambulance as it pulled out of the driveway without lights or sirens. Perhaps Heather was going to be okay. And maybe Bridget had played a small role in that.

"You ready?" Zach said, placing his hand on the small of her back.

Bridget took comfort in his touch as they made their way back to the truck. A small crowd had gathered on the sidewalk across the street, gawking at the excitement on Lisbon Avenue. People were fascinated by other people's misery. People's lives ruined because of their drug addiction. Tragedy narrowly avoided. Cautionary tales?

Any doubt that Bridget had made the wrong decision to report the illegal drug activity at the clinic that, in turn, had upended her life had disappeared the moment the ambulance doors had slammed shut. She could never sit idly by.

Bridget exhaled sharply. "Yeah, I'm ready."

Epilogue

Nine months later

Downstairs among all the other graduates at University at Buffalo's Alumni Arena, Bridget straightened her mortarboard and her shoulders. She'd made it. She had actually made it.

It had taken a few weeks to catch up on her fall classes, but her professors were supportive. Her living situation had worked out well, too. Zach's friend Freddy Mack and his wife, Jess, had allowed her to rent a room in their home. Since both of them were Buffalo police officers, Bridget felt safe. Now, nine months later, it seemed any repercussions from her involvement in the fraud investigation at the clinic had truly blown over. Both Jimmy and Ralphie would be spending the fore-seeable future in prison for their roles in the drug trade, Ashley's death and the near misses on Bridget's life. And sadly, Dr. Seth Ryan had lost his life over his part.

So many lives ruined.

Last Bridget heard, Heather had successfully finished rehab and Bridget prayed the young woman from the stash house stayed sober. Any of Bridget's efforts to reach out to the Ryan family had been met by silence. Hopefully, the doctor's son had given up gambling and could live with the horrible consequences of his actions.

Fortunately for the residents of one corner of the Buffalo community, the health-care clinic had reopened under a small group of physicians who rotated through. Bridget had felt great relief at that. Maybe she'd volunteer her time there—or at another clinic that served those most in need—once she got settled in her new nursing career. She still kept kicking around the idea of continuing her studies. Maybe become a nurse practitioner.

Excitement bubbled to the surface at all the possibilities.

A girl approached her. "Are these the *M*s?" The graduates were lined up alphabetically.

"Yes, I'm Miller."

"Oh, good. Milliken here." The girl tugged on her honors rope and stepped into line behind Bridget, who found herself scanning the line of graduates ahead of her. Her friend Ashley Meadows should have been somewhere in front of her... She shook away the thought. Poor Ashley.

The graduation coordinator clapped her hands above the din to get their attention. The soon-to-be alumni quieted down, and the graduates began the procession up the stairs to the auditorium.

* * *

Zach met the passenger van in the loop outside the arena. He had told Bridget he'd do his best to attend her graduation, cautioning her that he might get stuck at work. He had been busy in yet another undercover assignment, but he wouldn't miss this day for the world.

Over the past school year, he and Bridget had grown close, squeezing in dates between schoolwork and undercover assignments. They filled the time between with texts. They kept talk of the future to a minimum, fearing his undercover work would never allow for a normal life.

The past nine months had changed him in ways he never imagined. He had fallen hard for the beautiful woman from Hickory Lane, and he suspected—no, he prayed—the feeling was mutual.

The van driver slowed, and Zach waved. The man tipped his chin and pulled over beyond the blue crosswalk. The side door popped open, and Bridget's family climbed out: Liddie, Elijah, Caleb, Jeremiah, Mae and Amos. Bridget's father had been especially hard to convince to attend his daughter's graduation. Zach had a feeling her grandfather Jeremiah had had a hand in his presence.

Zach enjoyed watching Caleb and Elijah take in the campus with slack-jawed expressions under their felt hats.

"Well," Zach said, holding out his hand toward the arena, "the ceremony is about to start. We better go in."

Zach ushered them into the arena to curious glances.

When a recording of "Pomp and Circumstance" sounded over the speakers, the audience shifted their attention to the processing graduates, hoping to spot their loved ones.

Bridget's parents sat quietly while Caleb and Elijah pointed out things and discussed them between themselves. Liddie leaned over to Zach and asked if he thought she should go to college. Zach smiled, not daring to cause any waves. On the other side of him, Jeremiah whispered, "Thanks for inviting us."

"Thanks for convincing everyone to come."

Jeremiah nodded.

After Bridget walked across the stage and made it back to her seat—Zach was able to watch her from the nosebleeds—he texted her with a bunch of celebratory emojis. Then he typed, You did it! Congrats!

Three dots appeared on the screen. You're here! Then more bubbles. I can't believe you spotted me in this crowd.

He tapped away with his thumbs. How could I miss this? You were easy to spot. You're the most beautiful graduate here!

She responded with an "aw shucks" GIF.

He laughed and texted one more time: Meet me outside by the buffalo after the ceremony.

When the recessional music started, excitement coursed through Zach's veins. He patted his suit coat pocket and squared his shoulders.

The audience spilled out into the aisles. Bridget's father's face grew pinched under the shadow of his felt hat. "We can wait a minute until the crowd clears," Zach suggested.

Mae smiled her agreement and patted her husband's arm.

Caleb and Elijah looked like they wanted to hop out of their seats and go exploring. Zach couldn't blame them. Liddie seemed to be taking everything in. He had a hard time reading her. On the one hand, she seemed like the dutiful daughter, but on the other, she seemed to be ready to push the boundaries. Zach supposed that children growing into adults often pushed boundaries, no matter what the culture.

Last year, when he had taken Bridget home to collect her things, he sensed Amos's displeasure with both his daughters. Bridget for her plans to leave again and toward Liddie, perhaps for having kept in communication with Jimmy. Zach hoped they could work it out. He knew the strain of harboring resentment toward a love one.

The crowd began to thin a bit. "Let's head out. I told Bridget I'd meet her outside." He overheard Amos lean in and tell his wife that maybe they should have brought flowers for their daughter, and Mae reassured him that being here was gift enough.

Zach smiled. It seemed that Amos had made peace with at least one of his daughters.

When they reached the exit, the pavement was teeming with people. Zach searched their faces. When his gaze finally landed on Bridget, she was staring in his direction with wide eyes. Apparently, she had spotted her family quicker than he had found her. Perhaps their Amish clothing made them stand out.

She broke through the crowd and into his embrace. He whispered into her hair, "You did it! Congratulations!"

Bridget pulled back quickly and brushed a chaste kiss across his cheek. "Thank you. Thank you for all of this." She clutched her diploma to her chest and turned to her family. "I can't believe you came." Her smile spread from ear to ear. "This means so much more to me with you all here."

"You must get your intelligence from me," her grandfather joked, the first to break the awkward silence.

Her mother smiled proudly but didn't say anything, perhaps taking her cues from Amos, who stood stiffly among the sea of graduates and their families.

"Hey, I heard there was food involved," Liddie spoke up. "I'm starving."

"Of course," Zach said. "I'll call the driver." His gaze touched on each of Bridget's family members before landing on her. "We can all go back to my mother's home for a celebration."

A single tear leaked out of the corner of Bridget's eye as color infused her face. "Thank you," she mouthed. "Thank you so much."

The sun had lowered in the sky, and a late spring chill was in the air. Bridget sat across from her parents at the picnic table in Zach's childhood yard. She couldn't believe Zach and his mother had organized all this.

His mother, Annie, came out with a fresh pitcher of iced tea. "Does anyone need a top off?"

Her father lifted his hand and readied himself to stand. "Thank you for your hospitality. It's time we go. We have a long ride home."

A hint of disappointment swept through Bridget. "Thank you for coming. It meant a lot to me." Her father had been his usual quiet self, but he had been gracious, and she sensed he had made peace with her decision.

Bridget's father stood to leave and she got to her feet to join him. He hesitated, then said, "Don't forget where you came from."

Bridget touched her father's arm. "I won't."

He tipped his hat and strode around the side of the house to the van parked out front.

"'Bye, *Mem*." Bridget pulled her mother into a tight embrace. "Thanks so much for everything."

Her mother seemed to be holding back tears. "Remember what your father told you."

"I will. I will." Her voice cracked, and she caught Zach's warm gaze.

"Well, *denki*. I better catch up to your father. Come on," she said to the rest of her family.

Elijah muttered his goodbyes, and Caleb bowed his head and dived into his sister's side. Bridget bent down and kissed his head. "You boys be good."

Caleb looked up with tears in his eyes. "Will you come visit us?"

Bridget looked toward the side of the house where her parents had gone on their way to the van. She didn't want to lie because she didn't know if she'd be welcomed home on a regular basis.

She locked gazes with Zach, then leaned over and kissed the top of her brother's sweaty head again. "I'll always be here for you." And she meant that. Then she playfully patted his arm. "Better go get into the van. It's a long walk to Hickory Lane."

"You wouldn't make us walk," Caleb said with an air of disbelief.

Bridget playfully hip checked him and laughed. "Don't test me."

The two boys raced each other around the side of the house. Liddie picked up her paper plate of graduation cake and a plastic fork. "Not going anywhere without this."

"Enjoy." Bridget smiled. Zach pulled Bridget close in a side hug.

Liddie took a bite of cake and licked a bit of frosting from her lip. "You will come visit us, right?"

"I'll try." Bridget was more forthright with her sister. "Dad made an exception to come here, but I'm not sure if he'll leave the door open for me to come and go as I please. It wouldn't set a good example." She reached out and squeezed her sister's arm. "I'm here. I'll always be here. You have my phone number." Then she playfully wagged her finger at her sister. "Be *gut.*"

Liddie pointed at herself with the fork as if to say, *Who me?* Bridget had asked Liddie about Moses, the man who had courted Bridget years earlier and who had strangely shown up on the day Liddie decided to meet Jimmy. Liddie had dismissed Moses. She claimed he was a nuisance. Nothing more than that. Bridget chose to believe her sister.

"I hope you learned your lesson." Bridget's grandfather stepped outside onto the back porch.

Liddie rolled her eyes. "Listen to the biggest rebel of them all." Apparently, her grandfather's misadventures had become well-known among his granddaughters in light of recent events.

He ran a hand across his beard. "Do as I say, not as I do." He laughed, then tipped his head at Zach. "Take care of her."

"Yes, sir." Zach squeezed Bridget's shoulders. "Thanks for coming. Let me walk you to the van."

Her grandfather waved him off. "I'm perfectly capable of walking to the van. Come on, Liddie. Our chariot awaits."

"'Bye, Bridget. 'Bye, Zach." Liddie's eyes danced, and she took another bite of her cake and strolled away.

Bridget stepped away from Zach. "Well, I better help your mom clean up."

"No, no." Zach had taken off his suit coat and now he wore only his button-down with rolled-up sleeves. "I've got this. Sit. Relax." He directed her toward a chair on the patio. "The bugs shouldn't bother you here."

Bridget sat and reflected on the day. It was perfect. The sounds of Annie and her grown son talking easily over the running of water and clanking of dishes floated out to her. Their relationship was definitely on the mend.

She tipped her head back and settled into the chair. The scent from the citronella candle tickled her nose.

Now that she had her bachelor's degree, she couldn't shake the idea of continuing on to graduate school. She hadn't yet discussed it with Zach. He had insisted she focus on school and not let him distract her. Yet as the months and days passed, she had found she wanted her plans to intertwine with his.

Would that be possible with his job?

A short time later, Zach returned with two iced teas. "Hey there. How's my college graduate?" The pride in his voice warmed her heart.

She took a sip and set the glass on the small table between them. "I start my job at the hospital on Monday." She swallowed hard. "Will you be starting a new assignment soon?" There it was. The thing she had been avoiding all day. How much time could they spend together before he got lost in another undercover assignment?

Zach scooted to the edge of his patio chair and set his drink down next to hers. "Well…" A slow smile played on his lips.

Excitement with underpinnings of apprehension and, if she was being honest, a touch of fear danced across her skin. "What is it?"

"I've spent the past several years undercover." He scrubbed a hand over his hair. "It's been a tough life."

"I can imagine."

"I was offered an assignment at the DEA Training Academy in Quantico. I'm ready for a change."

"Quantico." A fluttering started in her belly. "Where's that? Virginia?" Was he leaving her, too?

"Yes." He seemed to be studying her face. "I was hoping you'd come with me."

Bridget jerked her head back. "I have a job here."

"There are jobs there." He pressed his lips together. "And I know you were considering grad school. There are some fantastic graduate programs in that area."

Had he seen the college brochures at her house?

"I… How?" She couldn't wrap her head around this. Before she had another second to process the details, Zach had slid out of his chair and knelt down on one knee in front of her. He pulled out a box from his suit coat slung over the back of his chair.

"Will you marry me, Bridget Miller?"

She pressed her hands to her cheeks and stared at the ring. "It's so sparkly."

"Is that a yes?" Zach gently pulled her hands away from her face and drew her up into his embrace.

"Yes!" She buried her face in his chest. "Yes."

He took her hand and slipped on the ring. She held it out. "It's beautiful."

He drew a thumb across her cheek. "You're beautiful."

She smiled tightly, and a whisper of sadness threatened to dim this moment. "I wish I could share this with my family."

"We can visit Hickory Lane whenever you want. I promise."

She reached up and gently kissed his lips. "I know you'd do anything for me."

"I want you to know I'll support whatever you decide to do. Grad school. Work. Both." They laughed in unison. "Or if you decide to stay home with our children, I'll support that."

"Children?" Her face grew warm. She hadn't thought that far down the road.

"Yes, children. If you want." His hand brushed across her back, pulling her close. "I'd love to have children with you." He kissed her gently on the lips. "We can figure all that out together."

Bridget planted her left hand on his solid chest and tucked her head under his chin.

"I love you," he whispered into her hair.

"I love you, too." She drew in a deep breath. His subtle aloe aftershave and clean-soap scent reminded her of all the times he had held her like this. Made her feel protected. Loved.

This was home.

He was home.

* * * * *

Get 4 FREE REWARDS!

We'll send you 2 FREE Books plus 2 FREE Mystery Gifts.

FREE
Value Over
$20

Both the **Love Inspired®** and **Love Inspired® Suspense** series feature compelling novels filled with inspirational romance, faith, forgiveness, and hope.

YES! Please send me 2 FREE novels from the Love Inspired or Love Inspired Suspense series and my 2 FREE gifts (gifts are worth about $10 retail). After receiving them, if I don't wish to receive any more books, I can return the shipping statement marked "cancel." If I don't cancel, I will receive 6 brand-new Love Inspired Larger-Print books or Love Inspired Suspense Larger-Print books every month and be billed just $6.24 each in the U.S. or $6.49 each in Canada. That is a savings of at least 17% off the cover price. It's quite a bargain! Shipping and handling is just 50¢ per book in the U.S. and $1.25 per book in Canada.* I understand that accepting the 2 free books and gifts places me under no obligation to buy anything. I can always return a shipment and cancel at any time by calling the number below. The free books and gifts are mine to keep no matter what I decide.

Choose one: ☐ **Love Inspired**
Larger-Print
(122/322 IDN GRDF)

☐ **Love Inspired Suspense**
Larger-Print
(107/307 IDN GRDF)

Name (please print)

Address   Apt. #

City   State/Province   Zip/Postal Code

Email: Please check this box ☐ if you would like to receive newsletters and promotional emails from Harlequin Enterprises ULC and its affiliates. You can unsubscribe anytime.

Mail to the Harlequin Reader Service:
IN U.S.A.: P.O. Box 1341, Buffalo, NY 14240-8531
IN CANADA: P.O. Box 603, Fort Erie, Ontario L2A 5X3

Want to try 2 free books from another series? Call 1-800-873-8635 or visit www.ReaderService.com.

*Terms and prices subject to change without notice. Prices do not include sales taxes, which will be charged (if applicable) based on your state or country of residence. Canadian residents will be charged applicable taxes. Offer not valid in Quebec. This offer is limited to one order per household. Books received may not be as shown. Not valid for current subscribers to the Love Inspired or Love Inspired Suspense series. All orders subject to approval. Credit or debit balances in a customer's account(s) may be offset by any other outstanding balance owed by or to the customer. Please allow 4 to 6 weeks for delivery. Offer available while quantities last.

Your Privacy—Your information is being collected by Harlequin Enterprises ULC, operating as Harlequin Reader Service. For a complete summary of the information we collect, how we use this information and to whom it is disclosed, please visit our privacy notice located at corporate.harlequin.com/privacy-notice. From time to time we may also exchange your personal information with reputable third parties. If you wish to opt out of this sharing of your personal information, please visit readerservice.com/consumerschoice or call 1-800-873-8635. **Notice to California Residents**—Under California law, you have specific rights to control and access your data. For more information on these rights and how to exercise them, visit corporate.harlequin.com/california-privacy.

LIRLIS22R2

HARLEQUIN
PLUS

Announcing a **BRAND-NEW** multimedia subscription service for romance fans like you!

Read, Watch and Play.

Experience the easiest way to get the romance content you crave.

Start your **FREE 7 DAY TRIAL** at
<u>www.harlequinplus.com/freetrial</u>.

LOVE INSPIRED

Stories to uplift and inspire

Fall in love with Love Inspired—
inspirational and uplifting stories of faith
and hope. Find strength and comfort in
the bonds of friendship and community.
Revel in the warmth of possibility and the
promise of new beginnings.

Sign up for the Love Inspired newsletter
at **LoveInspired.com** to be the first
to find out about upcoming titles,
special promotions and exclusive content.

CONNECT WITH US AT:

 Facebook.com/LoveInspiredBooks

Twitter.com/LoveInspiredBks